JACK'S KISS SPARKED AS SUDDENLY AND VIOLENTLY AS THE LIGHTNING OUTDOORS.

His heart began pounding. It was happening to her, too, because he could feel her melt against him and heard the soft, high whimper in her throat.

Suddenly a thundercloud clapped overhead. Faye jumped, jerking back from his embrace, her cheeks flushed and rosy.

"That shouldn't have happened," she said softly.

"You're fighting Mother Nature, Faye. You see, there's this phenomenon about electricity and magnetism." He leaned closer, catching the scent of roses in her hair. "Both of which are flowing between us at this very moment."

Faye closed her eyes, hit by the magnetism he'd just described.

"I'm talking about natural forces," he said in a husky voice by her ear.

"I think that you should direct your natural forces elsewhere, Dr. Graham."

Mary Alice Kruesi

Second
Star
To The
Right

AVON BOOKS ◆ NEW YORK

This book is dedicated to my children:
Claire, Margaretta and Zachary

and to the young at heart everywhere

AVON BOOKS, INC.
1350 Avenue of the Americas
New York, New York 10019

Copyright © 1999 by Mary Alice Kruesi
Inside cover author photo by Michael L. Abramson
Published by arrangement with the author
Library of Congress Catalog Card Number: 98-93889
ISBN: 0-380-79887-5
www.avonbooks.com/romance

First Avon Books Printing: April 1999

AVON TRADEMARK REG. U.S. PAT. OFF. AND IN OTHER COUNTRIES, MARCA REGISTRADA, HECHO EN U.S.A.

Printed in the U.S.A.

WCD   10   9   8   7   6   5   4   3   2   1

Acknowledgments

This book was close to my heart, and as such, it was a joy to write. However, I couldn't have created this fictional world without the help of several people.

I am especially grateful to Linda Kravitz for bringing me into the world of advertising. Without her expertise and support, my heroine's tea campaign and all the colorful characters involved would never have come to life.

I wish to thank Gabriel Lombardi, Ph.D. and Marco Fabbrichesi, Ph.D. for coming to my rescue with their wonderful ideas for my hero's world of theoretical physics and for confirming my belief that scientists are our true heroes today.

Heartfelt thanks to Julie Beard, Suzette Edelen, Martha Powers, James Cryns, Charlotte Tarr, Mary Blayney, Carol Peterson, Jasmine Cresswell and the Chicago North RWA. And especially to Markus. I hope you know how much I value your critiques and help. Thanks also to the River Forest Library staff for all their continued cheerful assistance with my research.

My lodestars for this book were my editors, Lucia Macro and Carrie Ferron, and my agent, Karen Solem.

Most of all, Ruth Cryns-Rutledge and Marguerite Abramson provided me with countless insights during the writing of this book that tapped into our childhood and memories. How can I thank you for a lifetime? (Oh, and Peter Pan loved me best.)

My love and thanks to all—your help was pure magic.

Prologue

JACK AWOKE WHEN the light crossed his eyes. It was a quick flash—brilliant and piercing. Then it was gone. He bolted upright in his bed, rubbing his eyes, the tinkling sound of chimes still ringing in his ears. The pewter-colored darkness was pierced by a pale yellow stream of light flowing in through the open window. An ordinary London streetlamp, he realized, as he blinked away the sleepy stupor. He surveyed the familiar pieces of furniture in the shadows: a three-drawer bureau spilling out socks, a hard-backed chair burdened with tossed clothes, a floor lamp with a tilted shade. All was quiet. All was undisturbed. He rubbed his neck, then the stubble along his jaw, waking slowly.

There it was again! A small ball of light, no bigger than his fist, burst from the closet and darted across the floor and walls in quick, erratic spurts before disappearing out the door. Now Jack was wide-awake, and his heart was pounding. The chase was on! Whipping back his covers, Jack leaped from his bed and hurried across the creaking floorboards to peer out the door and listen.

Down the hall, the ball of light waltzed in dizzy circles

across the walls, bouncing from the floor, then jumped around the corner into the kitchen.

He stealthily reached toward the umbrella stand, his fingers grazing over the umbrella to close instead over a large butterfly net. This time he was going to catch that ball of light, he vowed as he followed the bouncing light to the kitchen.

The large old kitchen with its gleaming Aga stove and delft blue tile was still and silent, cloaked in eerie moonlight. Brandishing his net, Jack scanned the floor, the walls, the counters. Not a single beam of light pierced the darkness. Nary a shadow.

"Okay—who's here?" he called out, his voice gruff.

Only a flapping of the curtains sounded in the evening breeze. Jack went to the slightly opened window and squinted against the glass, but all he could see was the clutter of an old garden gone to seed. The back door was closed, and, on checking it, he found it locked as well. Outside, a swell of wind rattled the garden gate, and from somewhere came a sharp clatter, like a tile tumbling from the roof to the ground. Grabbing a flashlight from the cabinet, he swung open the back door and followed the sound to the rear garden.

His beam slunk like a snake along the surrounding stone wall, weaving in and out of the cracks. He moved it along the crooked flagstone of the terrace that held as its centerpiece a small fountain graced with a bronze boy playing his pipes. A fine coating of dust from the decaying walls covered the boy like pale, aging skin, giving him a ghostly aura. When Jack's beam shone on the bronze boy's face he discovered, beneath the disguise of dust, a cocky smile and teasing, taunting eyes.

A shadow fluttered in the sky to his left. Jack swiveled

on his heel and flashed the light up to the rooftop. On the third floor there was a large French window with a small ledge bordered by a wrought-iron railing. Very feminine. Very unreachable, he decided, checking out the thirty-foot drop. There was no one there, and, as far as he could tell, there was no way to climb up. Not even scale down from the roof. No point in alarming Crazy Wendy, who lived upstairs. She was ninetysomething, and the poor old dear needed her sleep.

And so, apparently, did he. He dropped his arm and shook his head, chuckling at his imagination. There was nothing here at all. No intruder, no ball of light—just some grown man in his shorts with a dumb look on his face and a tilting butterfly net in his hand. Whatever woke him up was gone now. Crazy Wendy wasn't the only one seeing things fly around at night, he thought.

Flicking off the flashlight, Jack leaned against the cool stone outside his door, yawning. Feeling more relaxed, he tilted his head back and stared out at the stars he'd loved since he was a boy in Nebraska, lying in a cornfield, sipping a grape NeHi. He readily spotted the bright pulse of the North Star, the Big Dipper. Then his gaze wandered toward the Corona Borealis.

Not that he wouldn't have enjoyed finding a UFO or some such. He was forever scanning the skies for the unexplained, looking under rocks for the creepy-crawlies never before seen. Isn't that what he did all day? As a thirty-six-year-old physicist, Jack Graham was forever the curious boy delighting in the discovery.

But not tonight, he thought to himself, running his hand through his curly hair. He released a wry smile. Nope, tonight the mysterious light was most likely explained by a bit of spoiled beef. The Brits might think a sip of peppermint tea would do him good—they thought a pot of tea solved everything. Tonight, however, he could use a belt of scotch. Jack pushed himself from the wall and headed back indoors, leaving his trusty net beside the door.

Before closing up, he felt a soft breath of air by his ear that whistled a high, tingling hum. His heart skipped and he swung his head around to take one last, curious scan of the night sky.

Just in case he got lucky.

Chapter 1

A SPRING BREEZE fluttered the paper in Faye
O'Neill's hand as she stood at the curbside staring up at
an imposing London town house. On her left lay a pile
of bulging luggage. On her right, her two young children
slouched, road-weary and cranky. She checked the address, then squared her shoulders. Number 14 was a three-
story, narrow, redbrick Georgian house in a line of similar
buildings well situated on the lane. A neat and tidy building, old yet gracious, with a broad front stoop that held
cheery red potted geraniums. With its high-arched windows and broad granite stoop, it seemed that the building
was somehow smiling, perhaps even welcoming, her.
Faye smiled back and squeezed Maddie's and Tom's
shoulders encouragingly.

"There's something about it ... I think we'll be happy
here. What do you think?"

"It's old and dumpy," Maddie said, scrunching her
face in disapproval. "I liked our house in Chicago better."

Faye closed her eyes and stilled her tongue. Her eight-
year-old daughter had been oppositional the entire flight

across the Atlantic Ocean and wasn't letting up on shore. Faye saw Maddie push out her thin lips in a pout, saw the sharp line of her narrow, straight-backed shoulders, and recognized the defiance in the pale blue eyes behind shaggy blond bangs. Faye exhaled slowly, knowing in her heart that her daughter wasn't going to make this easy for her.

"It's not so bad," she replied with forced cheer, spotting the chipping paint on the window trim and the patches of rust on the black-iron fencing. The building did look a little tired. "Nothing that a little spit and polish couldn't fix. What do you think, Tom?"

Her six-year-old son buried his face in her skirt for a reply. Faye sighed wearily.

Standing near the door on the high front stoop was a distinguished-looking older woman who also bore a broad front stoop, but instead of a potted geranium she wore a huge, peach-colored silk hat. In one hand she pressed a large black clutch purse to her breast: in her other she held a clipboard. Nudging the children forward, Faye firmly placed a smile on her face.

"Mrs. Lloyd?" she called out.

"Helloo there," crooned the older woman, waving. She clumped down the flight of stairs and advanced on them, all broad smiles. "And you must be Mrs. O'Neill. How do you do?" she exclaimed, extending her hand with vigor.

"We're tired but well," Faye replied taking the hand. "We've only just arrived in London."

"And these are your darling children?" Mrs. Lloyd peered down over a short, bobbed nose, sizing the two up as to the potential damage they could render one apartment. She attempted to disguise her obvious dislike of children with high-pitched, sugar-coated words.

Maddie and Tom immediately tried to duck behind their mother, each clutching Faye's skirt. Faye offered a tentative smile while tugging at her waistband, wishing that just once her two children would shake someone's hand and smile rather than slink and mumble.

"Say 'hello,' children," Faye said through a strained smile. "Maddie?" An appeal to her eldest.

Faye didn't have to see them to know her little darlings were glaring back at the stocky old woman with the funny, tilting hat and pale, critical eyes. Children had a second sense about people that she'd learned to respect.

"They're shy," she muttered, catching herself from falling over as the two butted against her. "And it's been a long trip. I'm sure they'll feel better once we're in the apartment."

"You mean the flat," corrected Mrs. Lloyd with an arched brow. "You'll have to get accustomed to the Queen's English now."

Faye pressed her lips together. So, Mrs. Lloyd was one of those people who delighted in correcting others and always being in the right. "Yes, the flat," she replied softly, her toes curling in her leather pumps.

Mrs. Lloyd dug into her vacuum of a purse and emerged in triumph with a tagged set of keys. "Here we are," she exclaimed. "Shall we go in for a look-see? Your flat is on the first floor, and it is the nicest in the building, I believe. Careful with your luggage. It's a bit of a hike. Here in London, the first-floor flat is over the garden flat, don't you know."

She led the ragtag group half-carrying, half-dragging luggage out of the hot sun, up the flight of stairs into the welcome coolness of a small, dark, exquisitely paneled foyer. Faye dropped her bags, closed her eyes, and smelled lemon wax on the wood and the sweet perfume of flowers. Cotton lace hung at the hall window, and beneath it stood a small Hepplewhite table covered by a crisp white doily and a vase of lilacs. Faye smiled, relieved. She'd always found that the foyer set the tone, and this one was secure and spotless. When she spied three brass mailboxes by the door, she envisioned her own name over one soon.

Tom tugged at her skirt and furtively pointed to three small, polished brass bells hanging one over each mailbox.

"The bells are quaint," she said. Quaint, however, didn't mean safe. "But is there a buzzer system as well? Keyed to the lock? One can't be too careful."

"This is a small building, Mrs. O'Neill. There are only three flats." Mrs. Lloyd sniffed. "The bells do their job. Quite well."

Silly little noisemakers hardly do the job, Faye thought, scanning the door and windows for locks. "Is there a security system for the building?"

Mrs. Lloyd raised her brows and appeared to have tasted a sour lemon. "This is a reputable area. And crime in England is not as rampant as it is in your country," she added, her voice suddenly assuming a more aristocratic tone. "I've not seen the need."

"And if I want one for my flat?" Faye persevered.

"You're welcome to install a system for your flat, if you wish. It would be a personal expense, of course." Her nostrils flared and she turned sharply to open the door of the flat. "Here we are . . ."

Faye's anxiety fled the moment she entered the sunlit front room with its wide curved windows and fourteen foot, molded ceilings. The smile she felt from the outside of the building overflowed inside with a sense of joy and goodwill. Her heart skipped happily as she wandered through the airy, comfy rooms, grazing her fingertips along antique tables with scuffed legs and overstuffed chairs with deep depressions in the plump cushions. This was a lived-in house that thought of comfort before style. This house invited you in to tea. This house welcomed children.

She felt the irresistible tugs of sentimentality she always experienced when reading favorite novels by Jane Austen, or smelling hothouse roses or looking at the smiling faces of loved ones in faded photographs. The dark wood floors were covered with the muted colors of well-worn oriental rugs. Across the room, a gold-filigree clock chimed the quarter hour over an elaborately carved wood mantel. Faye's heart softened, thinking that this flat was a far cry from the square, unimaginative tract house in Illinois that she'd just left.

Rather, this flat looked exactly like she'd dared to dream it would, like any American would think a proper British middle-class house should look. She could show her children a different lifestyle here, she thought with hope. She prayed she could make them happy.

"It's perfect," said Faye.

Mrs. Lloyd smiled in satisfaction. "This house was my mother's," she explained, her voice softening. "These were her things. *Are*, rather. Mrs. Forrester lives upstairs still. This was a single-family home once upon a time, but like so many others in the neighborhood we converted it to what you Americans would call a triplex. Goodness, what . . . it must have been twenty-five . . . thirty years ago already. It was a grand place once upon a time, but now, well . . .'' A hint of irritation crossed her face as she followed the sound of someone jumping on the sofa.

"No child! Mustn't pounce on the sofa."

"Tom . . .'' Faye followed up. Tom scowled and hurried to her side and leaned against her thigh. "They're tired," she repeated through a tight smile.

"Of course," replied Jane Lloyd, her gaze shifting to Maddie, who was fingering a collection of porcelain animal figurines on a shelf. "Careful, dear! Those are quite fragile."

"Maddie . . .'' Faye called out.

Maddie returned the whimsical unicorn and moved on to the books overflowing from the shelf.

"As I was saying," continued Mrs. Lloyd. "This place was simply much too big for one elderly woman to live in alone. And, of course, the expense of upkeep and all. So I . . . *we* decided to convert the house to more manageable units. Mrs. Forrester is a widow, you see."

"You call your mother, 'Mrs.'?" asked Maddie, turning her head.

Mrs. Lloyd puffed up her chest. "It's considered polite, my dear," she replied, delivering a sidelong, assessing glance at Faye.

"Oh?" said Maddie, not the least bothered by the underlying criticism. "How come you don't live here with her if she's so old?"

"Me?" Mrs. Lloyd was taken aback. "Why," she sputtered, "I must live with Mr. Lloyd now. In our own house. It's not too terribly far away. I can hop over to check on Mother anytime. She has a visiting nurse, of course, but I manage all her affairs."

Faye was amused to listen to Mrs. Lloyd's flustered

rationalizations to an eight-year-old child. Guilt, she knew, could wield incredible power.

Mrs. Lloyd gazed around the room, as though mere mention of her mother and the sight of her possessions triggered deep emotions. "I did live here once, of course," she said, more to herself. "I slept in the upstairs nursery, where my mother lives now. It's been converted to a lovely large studio, of course."

"Of course," Maddie said, echoing Mrs. Lloyd with laughing eyes and a serious expression. Faye cast her a stern glance.

"My two daughters often visited with their grand-mother Wendy as well." Mrs. Lloyd's eyes turned misty. "I wanted them to sleep in the old nursery, as I once had. Ah, the nursery," she sighed wistfully. "Such a magical place it was while growing up. The dreams I had. Won-derful dreams!" She sighed again. "My mother could tell the most wonderful stories, you know."

Tom tugged hard at Faye's skirt, his eyes entreating. Faye stroked his head and nodded.

"Perhaps your mother would like to tell my children stories? Maddie and Tom adore them. They could visit each other. It might be nice for them all."

"Oh no," replied Mrs. Lloyd, drawing herself up with indignation. "That wouldn't do at all."

"Well, of course if you'd rather not. . . ."

"Mrs. Forrester is a very old woman now. I doubt she's up to telling anyone any more stories. No . . . no more stories." A crease of worry crossed her forehead. "You most likely won't see much of Mrs. Forrester, you see. She isn't well and keeps to herself. Children upset her."

Maddie frowned and stuck out her chin.

Mrs. Lloyd sent off sparks of discomfort, and Faye attributed it to the concern of a daughter for her ailing, elderly mother. She also heard in Mrs. Lloyd's tone the clear message that the children were not to bother old Mrs. Forrester.

"We'll be sure your mother is left undisturbed," she assured her.

Mrs. Lloyd turned, smoothing her suit jacket with trembling fingers. "Yes, good. Very good. Well, let's see the rest of the flat, shall we?"

She led a path to the small but well-appointed red-and-gold dining room with cove ceilings and deliciously elaborate molding. Faye's exclamation of delight was squelched in her throat when she saw the minuscule kitchen beyond it—more a couple of round electric burners atop a cramped metal box stuck in a large closet. She loved to cook and in the sorry space of the kitchen, boiling water would be a challenge. A narrow, spindled staircase, which was once probably employed by the servants, led the way to the second floor of the flat. The two bedrooms were spacious with tall, open windows that fluttered with lace, faded blue and white hydrangea wallpaper, and narrow beds draped in crisp linen and topped with fluffy goose-down pillows. The single, Spartan bathroom, however, had ancient fixtures that dripped water through a choke hold of lime. As she stood in the hall, she thought the house whispered to her of a lifestyle, of values, of dreams long past, and in her wanderings, Faye closed her eyes a moment to listen.

"The kitchen is so small . . ." Maddie blurted.

Faye, hungry for charm in her life, tapped Maddie's shoulder. "But the sun pours in," she pointed out. And looking through the window, she saw a charming, if rundown, garden enclosed by a brick wall. "Look, Maddie and Tom. A garden! Go have a look-see,'' she said, making the British lingo her own. The children scurried down the stairs with a clatter that had Mrs. Lloyd cringing.

"These two floors were once the main rooms of the house," Mrs. Lloyd explained as they followed the children down the staircase at a more adult pace. "The nursery was upstairs, and the house's original kitchen, now in the garden flat, is very large indeed. This one is, of course, an add-on."

"Oh?" said Faye, eyes and ears alert.

"That flat is taken, I'm afraid," she replied, hearing the hope in Faye's voice and hastening to dispel it. "A visiting professor from America. Dr. Graham."

"Oh, an American?"

"Yes, we have a very nice relationship with American companies looking for temporary lodging. The downstairs flat should be available in the fall when he returns to America, but I fear it would be unsuitable for you, Mrs. O'Neill. Though the kitchen is spacious, the rest of the rooms at one time housed the servants and are quite cramped. It isn't nearly as large or homey as this one."

Maddie rushed in through the back door. "I like it, Mom! The garden out back is awesome. It's like that book you read us, you know?"

"*The Secret Garden*?"

"Yeah." She hitched up her skirt and brushed the bangs from her eyes. "I guess it'll be okay here."

Faye was quick to notice that the sullen shadow that had clouded Maddie's face of late had dissipated. She was almost smiling, and there was even a sparkle of excitement in her bright blue eyes. Faye's heart expanded, and she said a quick prayer that her little girl would be happy here.

"What about you, Tom?" Her thin son was scratching his head, looking at the large cabbage roses on the foyer wallpaper with skepticism. He shrugged his shoulders without comment.

Faye took a final look around the narrow flat furnished with old Mrs. Forrester's personal collection of furniture and bric-a-brac. Each stuffed chair, each piece of Staffordshire porcelain, each pair of heavy blue-and-cream floral curtains suited Faye perfectly. She'd rented this flat without having seen it. That was an enormous act of faith on her part, she who laid her clothes out each night and filled out forms in triplicate. Perhaps this was a good omen. A signal of change. Perhaps, she thought with a shiver of trepidation, a change for the better.

"Thank you, Mrs. Lloyd. The apart . . . flat should be fine."

"Good! Very good." Mrs. Lloyd was all smiles. "Then it's all complete, except for your signature." She hurried forward with her clipboard. "Just sign this lease, and we'll be done with it. Your references were excellent, of course."

Faye refrained from another round of "of course" and quietly checked the papers fastened to Mrs. Lloyd's clipboard. Everything seemed in order. The advertising agency had done a fine job finding a suitable place at an affordable rent. In fact, the flat seemed a relative bargain for the price. She would have expected to pay top dollar to live in a building like this in such a lovely neighborhood. Was there something about the place she hadn't noticed that kept the price down? She shooed away the suspicions from her mind. Wasn't it her turn to have a little good luck for once?

Mrs. Lloyd smiled when she held the signed lease and

tucked it neatly back onto her clipboard. "Very good then," she said, handing Faye an envelope. "In here you will find two sets of keys and various papers explaining features of the flat. If you have any questions, my number is included in your packet. Well then," she extended her hand. "Very nice to meet you, Mrs. O'Neill. And your children. I hope you will be happy here."

Unconsciously her gaze darted upward toward the ceiling. "Oh, and if you should hear any rumors or such about Mrs. Forrester, please remember that they are just that. Rumors. She's perfectly harmless."

"Harmless?" Faye swung her head around, alarmed.

"A bit eccentric, that's all. Ta, now!"

Harmless? Eccentric? Suddenly Faye wondered if this flat was such a bargain after all.

"Mrs. Lloyd! Oh, Mrs. Lloyd," she called after her.

"Got to run, dear. I have another appointment!" She clutched the clipboard and the lease to her breast, and, with a brief turn of her hand as regal as the Queen Mum's, she hurried away down the winding lane.

Faye stood on the front stoop and watched the older woman disappear around the corner. A shiver of suspicion trickled down her spine. She could have sworn that was relief she caught in Mrs. Lloyd's eyes when she signed the lease.

Before reentering the building, Faye cast a curious glance up at the third-floor window. With a start, she saw a small hand dart away and the lace curtain fall back.

The evening wind whistled eerily outside the children's bedroom window. Faye's lips were pressed as tightly as her hand around the curtains while she scanned the outside shadows for any movement. Crabapple branches, laden with spring blossoms, swung pendulously in the breeze of an oncoming storm, scattering the white petals like snow.

This was her first night in London. Everything she knew seemed as far away as the stars twinkling in the purple sky. Everything felt so . . . *foreign.* She had nothing left but the clothes in the luggage and a meager bank account, enough to barely scrape by. Faye felt the weight of her responsibilities keenly tonight, the two most important ones lying tucked in their beds beside her. She'd do anything for her babies. Sometimes, you had to give up everything to be free.

Faye sighed deeply, then shut the window and locked it.

"Don't shut it, Mommy," complained Maddie from her bed. "You always close the window. We like it open."

Faye looked at her daughter lying on her side in her twin iron bed. Her chin was propped in her palm, and she was eyeing her with a critical expression more suitable for a forty-year-old woman than an eight-year-old child.

"It looks like rain," Faye replied quickly.

"Does not."

"Let's play it safe," Faye responded.

"It's because of Dad, isn't it?" Her pale skin and sunken eyes attested to the fact that Maddie wouldn't be fooled any longer.

Faye let the blinds drop with a snap. Sometimes, a perceptive child could be annoying. "Of course not," she lied. "I just don't like to keep the windows open anymore. We don't really know what this neighborhood is like. God knows what's out there."

"You mean Dad's out there." Maddie's lips pushed out.

Faye took a deep breath. *Yes*, she thought. *Dad's out there. Somewhere.* She didn't know how long an ocean would keep him away.

She saw her own fear reflected in her daughter's eyes. She'd seen that fear too often in the past years. She walked to Maddie's bed and settled on the mattress, then reached out to stroke a few gold strands from Maddie's forehead. *Such downy hair she has*, she thought, feathering away with her fingertips the worry line from her little girl's brow.

"Yes, Dad's out there somewhere, but he's so far away he won't be able to take you away ever again. No one will." Faye hugged her and spoke softly in her ear. "Your mama will take care of you."

Maddie's eyes flashed with doubt, then she frowned and pushed her mother away, turning her back. Faye felt like crumbling inside, but held firm by force of will. Still, she could almost hear the chink in her armor.

"Tom hates him," Maddie ground out.

Faye swung her head around to look at her son. He was lying with his arms tucked under his head gazing at the artificial stars glowing on the ceiling. Tom was small for his age, a wisp of a child, pale and silent. She knew that though he chose not to speak, Tom heard every word and understood every nuance. His tiny chin protruded angrily, like a sharp blade. Anger like that was too hard for a child to bear.

"Tom, dear," she said, "it's not good to hate. Especially not your father."

Maddie snorted, and Tom's scowl deepened.

She couldn't blame them. Rob had been a horrible father, self-centered, mean, and cheap. And brutal. How could she admonish her son not to hate when she hated Rob O'Neill herself? She wasn't a child. At thirty-five, she had no qualms admitting it. Yet the children's therapist had said it wasn't healthy for them to hate their father, so she bit her tongue and was careful not to bad-mouth her ex in front of them.

"If he tries to take us again, I'll run away," vowed Maddie, turning to face her mother again. The circles under her blue eyes deepened against her pale cheeks. "I know how to do it, too."

"He won't take you away."

"But supposing he does. If I just took a cab to the police station, I could call you, right?"

"You won't have to."

"I'll call you," she continued forcefully, her fingers agitated against her pink coverlet. "The police will pay for it all. They've got special money for that, don't they? Sure," she answered herself primly. "I've got it all straight in my mind. I'll take care of Tom, too." Her pitch was rising and Faye ached, listening to her daughter's young mind work out what-if-it-happened scenarios.

Suddenly Maddie sat up sharply. "They call the police here the Police, don't they? Is there some special word for that, too? Like telly or petrol?"

"Hush, Maddie," crooned Faye, placing her finger over Maddie's tight lips. She looked at her daughter's fierce expression and wondered for the hundredth time how much she'd seen over the years. Damn Rob! It wasn't enough that he'd made her own life miserable, but now he'd succeeded in making the lives of his children unhappy as well.

Maddie impulsively hugged her mother tightly, and

Faye, caught by surprise, wondered which of them needed the hug more. Tears threatened. How could she have allowed her precious children to feel so afraid? From Tom's bed she heard a whimper.

"Hush, hush," she said, now hurrying over to Tom and kissing his tense cheeks. He wrapped thin arms around her neck. She could feel his little rib cage pressed against her and the bone of his jaw hard against her own. Her poor, quiet boy.

"You've got this all wrong," she said, forcing lightness into her voice, releasing him with a teasing shake. "It's *my* job to worry!" The tension in the room eased as she tickled and tucked Tom back under his blanket. "I'll make you a pact. I won't worry if you won't worry. Deal?"

"Deal," replied Maddie for both of them. Faye was rewarded with smiles of relief on their faces. Smiles that didn't reach their eyes.

Faye knew that telling herself not to worry was like telling the sun not to rise and set. As a single parent, she worried over every detail that concerned them. She worried if they were late coming home from a friend's, then worried whether she'd checked out the friend carefully enough. At school she was the first in line to pick up the children, then studied the faces of all the adults who lingered in the school halls or yard. Each morning she warned them not to talk to strangers, and each night she checked that every window was locked and that all the dead bolts were secured.

Then, just when she'd begun to listen to the people who told her to loosen up, her worst fear was realized. Rob had tried to snatch the children. She was determined never to lower her guard again.

She patted a pair of rumps and gave final kisses, then double-checked that the windows were locked tight. Fay stood at the door an extra moment and watched as her children settled, yawned noisily, then mumbled good nights. They were just children, she thought. Life for them should be carefree. It wasn't right that they should be so wary and afraid.

"Good night. Sleep tight," she sang out, turning off the light. In the corner, the night-light instantly turned on, glowing green. Viewing her children nestled in their beds, Faye quietly vowed, "I promise you, my darlings. I'll never let anything harm you. Not ever."

Chapter 2

"EXCUSE ME, DR. Graham?"

Jack Graham blinked several times, vaguely aware that someone was calling his name. A frisson of irritation coursed through him. *Not now*, he thought to himself. *Just go away.*

"Dr. Graham?"

Sighing in resignation, Jack tossed the pencil down on his desk, mopped his face with his palm, and looked at the young, eager research assistant standing at his side. Damn, the train of thought was lost. He'd felt he was getting close to answering that elusive equation but . . .

"Yes, Robert, what is it?" His voice was as thin and taut as steel wire.

The graduate assistant cleared his throat, shifted his weight, and offered the large, white envelope to Jack in the manner of a peace offering. It was common knowledge in the lab that if Dr. Graham was working at his desk, he didn't like to be disturbed. He took no prisoners.

"This just came for you, sir. Oh," he added in a rush, as though to further quench the fire in Dr. Graham's eyes, "and you wanted to be told when the liquid nitrogen was being poured to cool the magnet. I believe they're about ready. In the chamber.'' He swallowed. ''Sir.''

''Say there, Jack!'' called out Dr. Irwin Falk, the lab's director, as he approached from across the lab. ''Did you check those connections for the counters? We're about ready to go.''

The research assistant's shoulders dropped in relief at this confirmation.

''Yeah, thanks, Irwin,'' Jack replied, the old wood-and-cane chair squeaking as he leaned back. ''And thanks to you, too, Robert.''

Robert nodded then rushed away to the viewing window of the large stainless-steel vacuum chamber used for testing spacecraft. It glistened in the artificial lights of the lab like the proverbial silver bullet. And in this lab, Dr. Jack Graham was the Lone Ranger. He was the maverick, the ringer, the hired gun brought in to solve the problem.

''Do my eyes deceive me, old boy, or does that return address say CERN?'' asked Irwin. Falk was Jack's colleague at the Institute. He was casually dressed in jeans and a polo shirt underneath his white lab coat, but his mannerisms were strictly old British upper crust. He was a baron or a lord or some such title which Jack could never get straight in his mind.

''Yep,'' Jack replied, tearing open the envelope with his finger. He pulled out the letter and scanned the contents.

''Well? Is this top secret or can the rest of us common blokes get in on it?''

Jack handed over the letter and watched curiosity then pleasure then another emotion which he figured was normal human envy flicker across Irwin's features as he read the letter.

"So they want you at CERN . . . Wow. This is first-rate, don't you know. Things are happening so fast now. Your future is assured. Bad luck for us, though. Shouldn't think there's much hope for us now to try and convince you to stay here at the Institute."

Jack felt the satisfaction deep in his gut. Not because of the prestige, but because he wanted to be there when they found the top quark, the only one of the six quarks still a mystery. He'd spent years at Fermi Lab in Illinois when the race between CERN and Fermi Lab was hot. But since the funding was cut for Fermi, all the action was in Geneva, Switzerland. And now Jack was invited to participate. Jack could feel his competitive juices flowing. He loved solving puzzles, and the top quark was the main piece of the biggest puzzle in science today: the Theories of Everything.

He looked up to smile at Irwin when from the corner of his eye he caught a commotion at the viewing window. Robert was sprinting into the chamber while others pressed at the hatch. He darted his glance to the chamber where he saw the technician in a white apron, thick gloves, and a face mask with his hands raised askew in the air. He was stepping out of the way in awkward, woozy steps.

Instinct caused Jack to spring to his feet. "Damn, the liquid nitrogen must have spilled. Irwin, call the paramedics! And get those fans blowing!" he called out as he ran into the chamber.

Robert had run in ahead to help but was already confused and tangled in the heavy black cable. Jack ran to his side, grabbed his arm, and dragged him out of the chamber. A small coterie of assistants gathered at the hatch door, wide-eyed with fear. Jack shoved Robert into their extended arms.

"You there. Close this door after me. Then make sure you open it quick when I come back. Got it? Nobody else goes in there, understand? No matter what."

"Jack, you can't go in there!" cried Irwin, holding back his arm. "There's no oxygen in there. You'll be asphyxiated."

"So will that guy," he shouted back. "Now get out of my way. We're wasting time. Just get those damn fans blowing!"

"Oh, bugger the fans! They're not responding!" cried Irwin, red-faced and flustered.

Jack took a quick look at the room strewn with scientific equipment, but there wasn't a piece of rope in sight. So he grabbed a handful of computer cables, ripped them off the machines with a fierce yank, then, taking a deep breath, signaled for the hatch to be opened and leaped in after the technician, who'd already collapsed to the floor. Jack wrapped the computer cable around the man's feet, grateful for years of Boy Scouts and knots, then ran back out, bursting through the hatch just as his breath gave way. The assistant closed the hatch behind him.

"Okay, you, you, and you," he panted out, pointing to the men, "get over here and pull on the cue. Ready? One, two, three—open the door. Pull!"

Four men pulled the cable hard, and, in several heaves, they dragged the technician across the floor to the chamber hatch, where Jack lifted him out over the rim into the arms of assistants. The fans clicked on at last as the hatch was sealed again.

The technician wasn't breathing, but he had a shallow pulse. "Get the medics here!" Jack called out, ripping off his tie. Then, positioning himself over the technician, he began CPR. *Nobody's gonna die on my shift,* he thought to himself as he counted out the fifteen/two ratio of breaths. *Come on, whatever your name is,* he thought, wishing he'd taken the time to learn it. Come on . . .

Moments later the paramedics arrived and, with practiced efficiency, administered the much-needed oxygen. Jack stood limply aside and only breathed normally again once the medic gave the thumbs-up sign. People milled about in silence, watching, as the team carted the technician off to the hospital.

Jack lowered his head and blew out a deep breath with a prayer that the young technician's brain cells were all intact. Then he slipped his tweed jacket off his slumped shoulders and threw it over the nearest chair. He only wore the darn jacket on days he had to lecture.

"How are you?" Irwin asked, worry shining in his eyes.

He felt wiped out, but waved away the solicitous inquiries. Sweat soaked his white oxford shirt, and he tried unbuttoning the top button, but his damn fingers were shaking too much to get the job done.

"Here, let me help," said Rebecca Fowler, a tall, leggy graduate research assistant. Her long, nimble fingers completed the job with calm, expert precision.

"Thanks," he said, clearing his throat and taking a step back. "Thanks, everyone," he said in a louder voice, addressing the nervous clusters of technicians and assistants in the room. "It'll be okay once those fans get some air blowing in there. But you all did a real good job of working together. I'm proud of you."

His words had a soothing effect and, in a short while,

the lab was humming along normally as the scientists got caught up in their work.

"That was real Buckeroo Bonzai stuff you did there, Jack. You'd better get that bio written while you're still alive," Irwin quipped in a friendly manner, offering him a cup of cold water. "No one will ever know your history."

"Yeah, well . . ." Jack gulped down the water. "I don't have much history to know. Just my work. That's says it all." He crumpled the paper cup and tossed it in the trash. "That's all that matters."

"Say, old boy," Irwin said with a laugh and a slap on the back, "don't get shy all of a sudden. We all have a history, no matter how dull."

Jack laughed, then turned his head away as his smile slipped. *No, not everyone,* he thought with an unconscious wince of pain.

"Anything the matter, Dr. Graham? You're not hurt, are you?"

Jack looked up to see Rebecca Fowler moving in closer. He was tall, but she could look him in the eye and did so as she raised her hand gently, flirtatiously, to smooth back one of the dark, wayward curls from his brow. He held his breath.

Rebecca was gifted in every area imaginable, brains, beauty, and money. Looking at her statuesque body, her gleaming raven hair, and brilliant blue eyes staring seductively into his own, Jack thought that she was even overblessed. Every red-blooded man in the lab had wondered aloud what it would be like to be stranded on a space station alone with her.

"No, thanks, I'm fine," he replied, breaking eye contact and, no doubt, the best chance he'd ever get with her.

Right now, he just wanted to be alone. To think. Irwin's comments rooted up thoughts about his past he thought he'd buried deep. He took a step back.

"That was quite a scare," Rebecca persisted, patting his arm as though he were a little boy. He found it more annoying than alluring. "Why not come home to my place and let me make you a drink? Maybe some dinner. You can . . . relax."

He doubted that. Relaxing didn't seem to be part of the menu, and he'd had all the excitement he could handle for one day. "Rebecca, that's a great offer, but I can't," he replied. "I've got things I've got to take care of."

He ignored her pout of disappointment and Irwin's look of astonishment and ducked out of the lab early, feeling drained.

That thing he had to take care of was a nagging question. A question that dogged him for most of his thirty-six years: Who was he? Other than a few flashbacks, Jack had no memory of his early years. Life began for him as a six-year-old, shivering and abandoned on the doorstep of a London orphanage with a note looped his neck. No better than some unwanted, discarded mutt.

Before going home, he took a long walk in the park, his head tucked into the collar of his raincoat and his hands deep in his pockets. Why couldn't he remember? What might have happened that left six years in a murky blackness? No matter how hard he tried concentrating, pressing all of his 156 IQ points to the limit, he couldn't pull up images of his early-childhood years. Presumably he'd been born in England. When he'd returned to London about a year ago, he'd considered hiring a private detective to dig up his past. In fact, it was one of the lures of the offer to come to England to do a year of guest teaching and research. But once here, excuses why he couldn't begin the search cropped up; either he couldn't get a decent referral for a detective, or he was too busy to make the call, or he decided the search was pointless after all.

Tonight, however, the uncertainty nagged at him again, with more bite than usual. He realized that if he'd died in that lab accident, he had no next of kin to be notified. No one who cared, really cared, if he lived or died. Walking in the park in this foggy twilight, passing solitary streetlamp after streetlamp, hearing his footsteps sound on the damp pavement, Jack Graham realized how utterly alone he was.

He went to bed early after stuffing down a handful of chips washed down with a scotch for dinner. For hours, he wrestled with his sheets, pounded his pillows, and cursed the mind that wouldn't stop churning. When at last he quieted and drifted toward sleep, one familiar image flashed in his mind. It was his single childhood memory, one that haunted him before he fell asleep most nights, in that strange limbo between wakefulness and sleep. In it someone—a man—was hitting him, hard. He'd see the fist coming for his face before he shook the vision away.

Jack opened his eyes and swore softly under his breath. Enough was enough. He rose from his bed, having made the decision. Walking to his desk in the next room, he flicked on the light, pulled out a stack of Post-it notes and scrap papers from the IN box and sifted through them till he found the one he was looking for. *Ian Farnesworthy, Private Detective*. Well, one was as good as another at this point, he figured, and, without further qualm, neatly punched in the number.

As expected, he got the answering machine, but he left

a brief message and his phone number, then hung up. Jack stared at the phone for a moment, blew out a long stream of air, then, after flicking off the light and climbing back into bed, fell into a welcome deep sleep.

The following morning, in a flat upstairs from where Jack Graham lay sleeping, Maddie and Tom O'Neill slumped over the banister and whined.

"Mom, what can we do now?"

Faye drew her hands from the bucket of hot, soapy water to listen to the umpteenth question from her children in the past hour. Maddie's hair hung in a tangled mass around her shoulders, and Tom was dressed in a mismatched collection of prints and plaids that he'd stubbornly selected himself that morning.

"Did you unpack all of your toys?"

Maddie rolled her eyes, and drawled, "Yes."

"Well, how about helping me wash the kitchen? Each of you can grab a sponge."

This was met with loud groans that caused Faye to tighten her grip on the sponge. She was exhausted from days of unpacking, assembling necessary supplies, and scrubbing the flat to meet her rigid sanitary requirements. And if that wasn't enough, she would begin work at her new job in a few more days, and she still hadn't found a baby-sitter. Faye felt as squeezed dry as the sponge in her hands. The last thing she needed right now was to entertain her children.

"We're bored," Maddie whined in that needling voice that makes mothers everywhere cringe.

It was on Faye's tongue to say something along the lines of how she'd *give* them something to do, but held back. It was, after all, a tough time for the children. They didn't know where to go or what to do in this strange new place filled with funny noises and odd smells. Nothing was familiar, they were adrift, and a long summer loomed ahead before school began in the fall. What they needed were friends.

Right now, however, Faye was busy being the mother and the father. She just didn't have the time to be their friend.

"I have an idea," Faye improvised. "It's a beautiful spring day. Why don't you go outside and play?"

Their faces scrunched up in disappointment. "We don't have anything to do out there."

"Sure you do. How can any child not find something to do on a day like today? Didn't you say you wanted to start a garden? Well, go on! First you have to prepare the soil. You know, dig out all those weeds. I saw some shovels and trowels out in the back shed. I don't think anyone would mind your borrowing them to spruce things up."

She saw the idea take root in their imaginations by the light in their eyes and the stillness of their faces.

"Will you come with us?" Maddie asked, straightening and brushing her bangs out of her eyes with a hasty swipe.

"You two go ahead. I'll join you when I finish the kitchen."

"You promise?"

"Yes, yes, I promise. Now go on with you."

Maddie's face lit up, and she pushed back from the railing. "Come on, Tom!" she ordered, and took off. Tom followed close at her heels.

Faye watched them tear our of the flat with relief. During the past week she'd discovered the hidden defects that she'd overlooked during the initial flush of pleasure at the charm of the house. Some of the lovely plaster walls had been damaged by moisture, presumably from a leaky roof, leaving a musty smell. Paint chipped and flaked in corners, lights flickered when the children ran or jumped upstairs, and the plumbing rattled and spit out miserly bits of water through a thick crust of lime and corrosion. It was a shame that such a lovely building was so neglected.

Still, she thought, her hands resting on the bucket as her gaze swept the rooms, she loved the house. Loved dusting the old mahogany furniture, washing the thick-mullioned windows and scrubbing the creaky wood floors. It had only been a few days but already No. 14 seemed like home. The walls around her embraced her and spoke to her of a security and lifestyle she'd coveted. Indeed, sometimes the old house felt like her first friend in London.

She craned her neck to look out the rear window to check on her children. Maddie was scooping mounds of weeds and dirt from the garden, making a terrible mess, and Tom was whacking at a bush with stick. Faye shook her head, chuckling yet pained for them. They didn't have a clue how to create a garden. What they needed was a friend, a teacher. A mother with time to spare.

For one fanciful moment, Faye felt an overwhelming urge to tug off the yellow rubber gloves and exchange them for cotton gardening ones. To feel the warmth of the sun and her children's smiles on her cheeks.

Then common sense returned and she swept away her idle thoughts like motes of dust and focused once more on her bucket and sponge and that greasy spot in the small box-like oven. Time waited for no man—or woman, she told herself. She had to grab the moment to get these chores done while her children amused themselves. Or lose the moment forever.

*   *   *

Downstairs in the garden flat, Jack pried open an eye to scowl at the shaft of bright morning sun that peeked through a narrow opening between the curtains to shine directly in his eyes. Scratching his head, Jack yawned groggily, hearing in the distance horns beeping in the street, and a few chatters and chirps from noisy spring birds. He'd passed a merciless night of tossing and turning, wrestling with his thoughts. Even sleeping in until eleven this morning didn't shake the drowsiness away.

Working on automatic pilot, he stuck his long legs into sweatpants, pulled a ratty Stanford sweatshirt over his head and padded down the hall to the enormous kitchen. His stomach growled more loudly than any other noise so Jack grabbed a cup, sniffing it first to make sure it was clean, poured yesterday's coffee into it, then stuck the cup into the microwave. Waiting for the beep, he prowled for breakfast, deciding leftover pizza met the four basic food groups. After stuffing it down and gulping a few bitter swallows of coffee, he splashed cold water on his face, ran his hands through his hair, and, considering himself decent, followed the surprising sound of children's voices.

Outside the sky was cerulean. The apple tree had shed its heavy, fragrant spring blossoms and littered the crooked flagstones. In the distance, a light green shadow of buds covered the ancient wisteria vines that clung like snakes along the old brick walls. He stopped abruptly at the door, surprised to find two small children as busy as spring bees cleaning out the old fountain.

The girl was older, by about two years, and she obviously was the one in charge. She was perched high atop a rickety wooden ladder polishing the bronze boy's face while giving orders to the boy, who appeared to be her brother. Despite her thinness and sweet, pale features, she was as efficient a drill sergeant as he'd ever come across.

The boy, in contrast, appeared meek, quietly doing as he was told. A slight, pale child, he had eyes too big for his face and hair that stuck out in all the wrong places, making his face seem even smaller. Looking around the garden, Jack saw with amusement that they'd been working darn hard. Sprays of dirt littered the flagstones, remnants of a great war between tenacious weeds and stubborn, stubby fingers. They'd made enormous progress. *But man oh man,* he thought, looking over the thick, overgrown ivy, crumbling bricks, and legions of weeds. *There is a war to be won to bring this ruined garden back into shape.*

Smiling, he realized that these must be the two American children that Mrs. Lloyd was so worried would scuff the good furniture. He liked kids himself. Usually preferred talking to them than to adults. There weren't many little ones in this neighborhood, and he missed the excited shouts and laughter they always brought to the streets, not to mention a few pickup games of ball. These two were more quiet than most, however. He had to listen hard to catch their conversation.

"He seems nice," the young girl was saying as she polished the statue's face. "I wonder who he is?"

Jack stepped forward into the sunlight. "That's Peter Pan," he replied.

The girl sucked in her breath and swiftly turned her head his way, on guard. Immediately, she checked on the whereabouts of her brother. He stood beside the fountain as frozen as the boy of bronze, his eyes round with fear.

"Who are you?" the girl rasped.

Jack moved slowly, not wishing to frighten them any further. "I'm your neighbor," he replied with an easy tone. "My name's Jack. Jack Graham." He was met with silence. "What's yours?"

The girl cocked her head, studying him with suspicion.

He smiled, hoping to break the ice.

She wasn't convinced. "I'm not supposed to talk to strangers."

"I'm not a stranger," he argued back. "I live downstairs. This is my garden, too, you know."

Now her eyes narrowed. "My mom said we could clean the fountain." Her tone dared him to argue the point.

"And a very nice job you're doing, too." He began walking leisurely toward the fountain, whistling softly as he looked around. "You know," he said, pointing to the small pile of wet, rotting leaves lying on the stones, "there are probably dozens of nice fat worms in there. Unless you plan to go fishing, I'd toss them back into the dirt. Worms are good for the garden."

"They are?" She twisted around toward her brother, gripping the ladder tighter so as not to fall. "Tom," she ordered. "Go pick through those leaves and pull out the worms and throw 'em in the dirt."

Tom scowled and shook his head.

She rubbed her forehead. "Oh yeah. He hates bugs."

"Worms are our friends," Jack said amiably, strolling across the garden to pluck out a few choice earthworms and toss them into the dirt. Wiping his hands nonchalantly on his pants, he thought again how charming the old circular brick wall was. Here and there, bright yellow and purple crocus defied the weeds to sit cheerily in the sun, remnants of a great garden gone by.

"I've always meant to fix this place up, but I've just

never found the time. I always seem to be too busy. It's great that you're taking it on. So, what do you plan to plant? Some tomatoes I hope?''

"Nope. Flowers. Lots of flowers.''

"I should've guessed," he groaned. "I was hankering for a good, juicy Midwestern Big Boy tomato. Well, I suppose flowers will look pretty beside this fountain. I wonder,'' he added, reaching out to touch the elaborately carved basin of the fountain, then stooping over to inspect the hardware. "Maybe I could get this thing working again. I'm pretty good with my hands.''

The cloud of doubt passed from the girl's eyes, replaced by a sunny smile. "Really? You could do that? That would be so great. Wouldn't that be great, Tom?''

Tom, in contrast, narrowed his eyes into tiny, doubtful slits, then scuttled behind an overgrown boxwood shrub. Only a pair of muddy tennis shoes and bony knees were visible under the glossy leaves.

"I don't think he likes me," Jack said with a shrug.

"Oh don't mind him. He doesn't talk to strangers.''

"Well, we'll have to find a way to fix that, won't we?'' He placed his hands on his hips and thought a moment. "What does it take for me not to be a stranger anymore? After all, we'll be running into each other quite a bit I imagine, sharing the garden. Summer's just around the corner.''

The girl chewed her lip. "My mom has to say it's okay. She doesn't want us talking to anyone she doesn't know. ''

"Ah, I see. She's the careful type.''

"Yeah. But she has to be.''

"Has to?''

The girl shut her mouth tightly.

Jack didn't press. "How about I meet your mother?"

She nodded, then threw back her head and, holding tight to the ladder, yelled at the top of her lungs, "Mooooom!"

"That ought'a do it," Jack muttered. He glanced at Tom, who was peeking out from the shrubs. The minute he made eye contact, however, Tom darted back behind the shrubs. It might have been annoying if it wasn't so comical.

Within a minute, a woman came running out the back door, her face white with panic and soapy bubbles dripping down her forearm from a sponge. She was small, like her children, and with her pale blond hair pulled back into a lopsided ponytail and her jeans rolled up above her ankles, didn't look much older than her daughter. Though she seemed pretty ferocious for such a mousy-looking little thing, he thought.

Mrs. O'Neill was small, but lithe. Her straight nose was lightly freckled and her delicate nostrils flared like a beautiful, graceful lioness defending her cubs. Energy crackled around her. No, he decided, there was nothing mousy about this woman.

"What is it Maddie?" she asked, her blue eyes bright as she searched the garden. "Where's Tom?"

The boy stepped out from behind the boxwood with his eyes lowered.

"We . . . we wanted you to meet our new neighbor," the girl explained sheepishly. It was obvious she hadn't meant to scare her mother this way.

The woman's relief was palpable. She almost smiled with it as her gaze gobbled up the sight of her children. Then she spotted Jack standing by the shed, and her guard shot right back up. From the lethal way she was sizing him up, Jack felt he either looked like an ax murderer or his curly hair was sticking out at odd angles again. He raked his hand through it, just to make sure.

"And you are . . . ?" Her voice was like a deadly purr, velvety but dangerous. She wasn't unfriendly, but then again, she wasn't exactly neighborly either. He thought of the girl's words. *She has to be careful.*

Reaching out his hand in a friendly gesture, he said, "I'm your neighbor. Jack Graham. I live in the garden flat."

"Ah, yes, Dr. Graham," she replied slowly. He could almost hear her mind rifling through the files, finding his and scanning it. He must have passed some first barrier because the wariness dissipated, replaced by cautious curiosity. "The scientist living downstairs."

He was well aware that Mrs. O'Neill was busily summing up his athletic physique under the baggy, gray sweatpants and torn sweatshirt and wondering to herself, *This bloke's a scientist?*

Not that he could blame her. Most people expected a research scientist to be old, bent over, and pale, to wear heavy framed eyeglasses and a pocket protector, and not to know a baseball from a football. A stereotype that didn't fit today's young breed of mavericks. Jack knew that his own tall, lanky build, his soulful brown eyes, his deep-dimpled smile and his head full of unruly chocolate-colored curls, made most folks he met think he was a good-looking, if rumpled, student-teacher on campus. Not a renowned theoretical physicist.

Anyone who paused to look beyond the facade, however, would see that his face was more somber than sweet, his dark eyes were edged with lines that reflected the depth of his thoughts, and his mouth worked with a thousand as yet unanswered questions.

An awkward smile escaped Faye's lips as she slipped the sponge into her other hand, dried her palm quickly on her apron, then, after a second's hesitation, accepted his outstretched hand.

"Nice to meet you. My name is Faye O'Neill, and these are my children, Madeline and Tom. Children, this is Dr. Graham."

"Nice to meet you, Miss O'Neill. Or may I call you Maddie?" His demeanor was far too formal for seriousness. He was rewarded with a half smile from Maddie.

"Sure."

"You can call me Jack," he added with a smile that revealed deep dimples.

Maddie's smile broadened. "Tom, say hi to Jack."

Tom lowered his eyes and turned his shoulder. He didn't say boo.

"Give him time," Faye said, walking to her son's side and wrapping a protective arm around his shoulders. Tom immediately scooted closer to her and buried his face in her belly.

Seeing the interaction, Jack felt a twinge in his own belly. He was left to wonder about, to envy, to covet, that kind of love.

"He's shy, and he doesn't talk much," she said, stroking her boy's hair.

"That's okay, buddy. Take your time. But remember, we're not strangers anymore." Turning to Faye, he added, "You'll be pleased to know that neither one of them divulged name, rank, or serial number."

"Yes, well . . ." Her crisp demeanor returned. "I teach

my children to be cautious. One can't be too careful these days.''

Jack squinted, noting her wan face, her fine blond hair escaping pins and poking out all awry, and that dripping sponge in her small, tightly clenched hand. Faye O'Neill had the strained, hunted look of someone under too much stress. She had a nice smile, though, when she didn't have her back up and deigned to show it. It lit up her eyes, like Maddie's. A brightness so breathtaking yet so elusive it encouraged one to do whatever it took just to see it one more time.

It would take a lot, however. The three of them were as locked and guarded as a chain gang.

''What did you say his name was?'' Maddie called out from the ladder. She was once again busily polishing the face of the bronze boy.

''Peter Pan,'' Jack said, drawing near.

''Oh yeah. I've heard of him. A movie, right?''

''Right. But first it was a book. A wonderful book all about this clever boy, Peter Pan, his magical island called the Neverland, and three children, Wendy, Michael, and John. Have you read it?''

''Nope.''

Tom moved one step closer, pretending not to listen.

Jack noticed, however, and added spice to his story. ''Well you're in luck. The all-time best storyteller in the world lives upstairs from you. Wendy Forrester. And her favorite story is about Peter Pan. She knows more about that character than even Sir James Barrie.''

''Who's he?'' asked Maddie.

''The man who wrote the book.''

Maddie and Tom turned their heads in unison and cast curious glances up toward the third-floor windows.

"Mrs. Lloyd made it clear that we shouldn't bother her mother," said Faye.

"Ah yes, dear Mrs. Lloyd. Don't pay any mind to that old battle-ax. If she was my daughter, I'd hide upstairs, too," he replied with a sorry shake of his head.

"Is she okay?" asked Faye. "I mean, normal?"

"Mrs. Lloyd? Frighteningly normal, I'm afraid."

"No," Faye replied, wondering at that remark. "Mrs. Forrester, on the third floor."

"You mean Crazy Wendy?" he said with affection.

Maddie quickly turned her head away from her scrubbing to stare at Jack. "*Crazy* Wendy?" she asked, curiosity sparking in her eyes.

Faye, however, paled. "Please tell me she's not crazy . . ."

"Not like lunatic crazy. But she's, well, how can I put it?"

"Eccentric," said Faye deadpan.

"Bingo. There's nothing better when you're old than to be eccentric. I plan to be certifiable by the time I'm Wendy's age."

"Great." Faye walked over and sat on an overturned clay pot and wearily wagged the sponge between her knees. "Okay . . . So what do you mean by eccentric? Sit in the park all day and feed the birds kind of eccentric? Or run naked down the streets with a butcher knife kind of eccentric?"

"Hard to say," Jack replied, stroking his jaw. He was enjoying himself, knowing full well it was shameless to tease a cautious type like Faye O'Neill. He could hear his adoptive mother now, standing broad-shouldered and upright, shaking her head and saying with a stern frown,

"Naughty!" He put his hands in his pockets and leaned back on his heels, as he had as a boy.

"There are a lot of rumors about the old girl," he said in all earnestness. "You'll find people in the neighborhood love to speculate. She doesn't come out during the day, you see. Only at night, when she sits at her window. Some say she talks to the stars. Others say she runs a drug ring."

Faye smirked, and they shared a look of amusement before he turned more serious. "Actually, stargazing is my hobby, too. I guess you could say it's my job, too. I go up to check on her from time to time. At first I did it out of concern; she's alone so much of the time. Now I go because I enjoy my visits. She's quite knowledgeable about stars, and we've had some illuminating conversations."

"That's a nice enough hobby for an old woman," Faye replied with an easy shrug. "It's peaceful and nonstressful. There's nothing unusual about that."

"Oh, to be sure. A nice normal hobby . . . only it isn't Wendy's hobby. The stars are her friends. She converses with them."

Faye blinked heavily, several times. "You mean . . . she talks with stars?"

"Mmm hmmm," he replied, nodding. His eyes were twinkling like the stars they were discussing.

. "Maybe she's just lonely. Lots of old people are."

"Probably. She has family nearby. Her daughter, of course, Jane Lloyd. Grandchildren, great-grandchildren even. Problem is, they steer clear. Only her daughter comes from time to time to check on her. And on the building. I think she has more interest in the latter, frankly."

"I get the feeling our Mrs. Lloyd doesn't enjoy her visits."

"Who knows why? Family problems often run deep. At any rate"—he shrugged and gazed up at the third floor—"Mrs. Forrester sits alone and looks longingly at the sky."

"That's it?" Faye said with relief on her face. "She just sits at her window at night talking to herself? Well, half the women in Chicago would be called crazy if that was all it took."

"And," he added after a moment's pause, "she talks about this boy all the time." He indicated the bronze statue.

"Who?" asked Maddie, bobbing her head. "You mean Peter Pan?"

"None other. She knows every detail about his life in the Neverland. It's her reason for living. Her world, I guess."

"What's crazy about that?" Maddie shrugged and looked again toward the third-floor window.

"She believes the stories," he said, holding back a grin. At Faye's astonished face, he added, "Yes. Poor old Mrs. Forrester thinks she's Peter Pan's Wendy."

Faye dropped her forehead into her palm and nodded in agreement. "Yessiree," she replied with sarcasm. "That's crazy all right."

"What do you mean?" asked Maddie, leaning over the ladder.

"In the book, *Peter Pan*, Wendy Darling is the little girl who flies to a marvelous island in the sky called the Neverland with Peter. At the end of the adventure she returns to the nursery and grows up. Our upstairs neighbor believes she is that same Wendy and sits by the window every night, waiting for Peter Pan to return. She's convinced that he will.''

"That's neat," chimed in Maddie. It was like electricity was flowing from her head to her toes. "What if she is?"

"Don't be silly, Madeline," her mother replied a tad too sharply. Maddie squinted back at Faye. "There is no such thing as Peter Pan. He's just a character in a story."

"How do you know?" Jack asked her.

"What?" she asked sharply, turning her head toward him. Then, shaking her head, "Oh, I get it. Please, don't tease about such things. I want my children to know the difference between reality and fantasy."

"I'm not teasing. I'm serious. I deal with this kind of thing every day. How do you know Peter Pan doesn't exist? Or UFOs? Adult assumptions are based on two things: the physical world and logic. Yet every day in my work I discover that what we considered law is not."

"Look, Jack. I'm well aware of the strange mysteries going on in science today. And I want my children to be aware of them. Yet I respect Maddie and Tom enough not to force-feed them childish notions such as Santa Claus."

"I see. Then I take it they . . ." Jack paused and cast a cautious glance at the children. Seeing that their eyes were fastened on him, he raised his hand, and mouthed to Faye, "They don't believe in Santa."

Faye laughed lightly. "No, they don't believe in Santa Claus," she said loudly. "Or the Easter Bunny, or—for that matter—Peter Pan. Those are false beliefs designed by the media to manipulate the emotions of the weak. I work in advertising and know full well the power of the media. I'm raising my children not to be taken in by advertisements or propaganda—or anything or anyone else for that matter. We try to base all of our decisions firmly in reality.''

Jack straightened with the scent of a challenge. ''What would you say if I told you I could prove to you the existence of an alternate reality? Perhaps even of Peter Pan himself?''

Faye rolled her eyes. ''I'd say my luck was holding out. Not only do I have a crazy old lady living upstairs, but I have a wacky scientist living downstairs.''

Faye turned to the children and scooted low to meet them face-to-face. Then taking their hands, she spoke in a serious tone. ''Children, try to understand. I'm not being critical of Mrs. Forrester. Sometimes, when people get very old, they get a little confused. They mix up what's real with what's in their imaginations.'' She glanced up at Jack with an arched brow. ''Sometimes not only old people.''

''Careful of your words. You'll only have to eat them.''

She turned to her children again, shaking their hands to get their attention back from Jack, whose eyes were dancing as brightly as Maddie's. ''Sometimes, they forget what's happening today and live in the past. That's what happened to Mrs. Forrester. If that poor woman upstairs believes her stories about Peter Pan are real, well, then you just be nice to her. But keep your distance.''

Tom leaned forward, burying his face in her neck and maneuvering so that Jack could not see his face. ''I like stories,'' he whispered fervently.

''I like stories, too,'' snapped Maddie.

''I'll bet she'd love to tell you some, pal,'' said Jack.

Faye shot Jack a warning glance. He was standing with his arms crossed and a mutinous expression on his face not unlike Tom's. "Mrs. Lloyd said that children upset her."

"Bull. She loves children. And it might be nice for the old woman to have some company."

"I said *no*." Her tone was sharp and decisive. She stood up and squared her shoulders in front of him. He might be her neighbor but to her mind, he'd crossed the line. "Dr. Graham, this has gone far enough. When it comes to my children, I don't play games." Then lowering her gaze, she said more softly, but still with an undercurrent of iron, "Children, you are not to bother Mrs. Forrester. Is that clear?"

Maddie and Tom nodded to their mother solemnly.

Jack could feel his temper rising as he viewed the disappointment etched across the children's faces. He loved kids—their optimism and their imagination. It killed him to see it cut off in its time of flowering. If ever children needed saving, these two did. It wouldn't hurt to loosen up their mother a little, too, he decided. She made the Statue of Liberty appear relaxed. Yes, he thought, warming to the task. He might have had a brutal childhood, but he might brighten these two children's a bit. The notion eased the nagging in his heart to call a detective. He chuckled to himself. This might even be fun.

"I've got to go," he said, lifting his hand in a quick wave. "Nice to meet you, Faye. And you, too, Maddie . . . Tom."

The family waved, and he turned to go. Stopping at the door, he couldn't resist turning his head, raising his brows, and throwing in a final shot.

"Oh by the way. Just for the record, I believe in Santa Claus *and* UFOs. And I'm open to the possibility of Peter Pan."

Then he offered the children a quick wink. It was the *It's up to you—if you dare* kind of wink that kids make to each other. Maddie's eyes widened; Tom's narrowed. Looking up, Jack caught Faye's eye as well. She stood erect, with her arms crossed across her chest and a finely arched brow raised as disapprovingly as any schoolteacher about to give a demerit. He couldn't resist—never could. In his mind's ear he could hear his mother say, "Naughty!"

With a one-sided smile, Jack met Faye's gaze with a challenge sparkling in his eye—then winked at her. When he saw her shocked expression, he turned and walked away whistling, sure that he'd just won round one.

Chapter 3

AFTER A FEW long, hard days, Jack felt that he'd at last brought his team and his research project back on schedule; all was in full working order. He'd managed to get home at a decent hour and was just about to sit down to his first hot takeout meal in days when the front doorbell rang. Dropping his tableware with a frustrated clatter, he hurried to open the front door. A short, portly, clever-eyed, middle-aged man in a green raincoat stood at the entry, politely holding his hat in his hands.

"Dr. Graham, I presume?" The man's articulation was a study of precision.

Jack leaned against the doorframe and tried to figure out who the man might be. "If you're selling something, I'm not interested," he replied.

The man twitched his mustache. "If you're Dr. Graham, I believe we have an appointment. I'm Detective Ian Farnesworthy. You did say seven o'clock, didn't you?"

Jack's mouth pursed while he mentally kicked himself. He'd been so busy he'd completely forgotten about the appointment he'd hastily set up with the detective. In his gut he felt a tightening. Did he really want to hire a detective? After all these years? For a fraction of a second he regretted having made that late-night call and beginning the search at all. He was happy enough being the Jack Graham he knew. A sworn bachelor. A loner with no strings attached. He'd long felt he didn't need to know his past to build his future. Not that he felt sorry for himself. Far from it. He had built his own family. His friends were his brothers and sisters, and he had friends from all walks of life.

"Oh yeah, sorry. Of course. Come in," replied Jack, opening wide the door to whatever came next.

Ian Farnesworthy removed his overcoat and stood at the flat's threshold, surveying the clutter with more confusion than disdain. He could date the building's conversion to the 1970s by the well-worn Bauhaus-type furniture in the small front room, what was probably the servants' living quarters once upon a time. The shabby brown-and-gold window treatments and the bold geometric pattern in the carpet brought forth a wince. The carpet was covered with stacks of books, piles of papers, a few empty cups, and assorted bottles of ale. Farnesworthy rocked on his heels, coat in hand.

"Oh, sit here," Jack said easily, grabbing the detective's coat with one hand and scooping up a pile of papers from a chair with the other. He slipped the coat across the back of a nearby chair, then, not finding another clean surface, carelessly set the papers on the floor. He didn't apologize for the mess of his surroundings because he simply didn't notice it. Jack leaned his weight against the curled arm of the sofa and casually observed the detective.

Farnesworthy was surprisingly agile and maneuvered his way over and around the tilting stacks of clutter on the floor as gracefully as any ballerina. Jack watched the performance with awe, for Farnesworthy was a bulky man. His rear split the vent of his cheap navy wool jacket in two and it was anyone's guess whether the detective wore a belt under that belly.

"So you're the man who's going to uncover my past, are you," Jack asked, rubbing his hands together. "I've never done anything like this before. The closest I've come to cloak-and-dagger is games. You know, Miss Scarlet did it with Professor Plum in the library."

Farnesworthy looked up, perplexed.

"Never mind. Where do we start?"

"Well, sir, this is what I like to call a preliminary visit. A sort of starting point for both of us, really. Perhaps if you could tell me what precisely you want me to uncover, I could ask the old who, what, when, where and how."

"It's simple really. I want to know who I am."

"Oh, is that all?" Farnesworthy held back a smile, but his eyes were filled with mirth.

Jack liked a man with a sense of humor. "I'm speaking biologically—but any help on the other is always welcome, too."

Both men chuckled, knowing it was man's fate to go through life wondering who he was. "Well, sir, perhaps you could tell me what you do know."

"Very little. I was born in England, but I have no birth certificate. I also have no memories of the first six years of my life. All I know is that I was brought to some orphanage in London at age six. Spent two years there, though my memories are pretty hazy. Then I was adopted by an ex-British family who'd emigrated to America. Warner and Anne Graham. Spent the rest of my life in the States." Jack spread out his palms and shrugged.

"That's it. No siblings. No relatives. Not much to go on, is it?"

"It is a start."

"Mr. Farnesworthy . . ." Jack paused to rub his palms on his thighs. He didn't realize until this very moment how much this search meant to him. The answer seemed within his grasp; it made his palms tingle. He lowered his voice as all humor fled. "What I really want to know is . . . Who is my mother? Who is my father?"

He looked up to see Farnesworthy watching him with sympathetic eyes. Embarrassed, Jack stood up and put his hands on his hips and shrugged with feigned nonchalance. "Not too tough a case, right?"

Farnesworthy flipped his notebook closed and cleared his throat. Then, standing, he put out his hand. His face was serious. Farnesworthy was not frivolous in manner or with his employer's time. "I'll do my best, sir."

Jack took the detective's hand and shook it hard, feeling for the first time in his life that this time he might just get his answer.

That same evening, in another section of the city, across a long expanse of mahogany, Jane Lloyd stared at her husband as he stabbed at a tough chicken breast. They were the only two people in the spacious, well-appointed dining room, though the table could readily accommodate another ten. Jane had always insisted that all of the table's leaves remain in, even after the children moved out. Most of her friends had moved to the breakfast room for most of their meals, or had sold off their family homes in favor of a more intimate, "easier to care for" flat with nearby medical facilities.

Jane and Hugh Lloyd would never even consider such

a move, despite the enormous expense of their lifestyle. The formalities of a world gone by suited them, and they were far too stuck in their ways to change. Jane had read fairy tales as a child and Regency romances as an adult, so moving into this charming, historical Georgian home in Regent's Park as a young bride was a dream come true. Even if the dream weathered a bit as she, and the house, grew older, Jane still tried to maintain what she considered proper standards.

Also, she did not find it a bother to be seated a distance from her husband during mealtimes. He rarely spoke to her anyway, and when he did, he spoke with a condescension that upset her digestive system. Staring now at her husband, her appetite was put off by how cadaverous he'd become since his last heart attack, a state that his horrid low-fat diet did nothing to improve. Looking at him as he hunched over his plate, she couldn't help but think of a large, mangy bird pecking at seed.

"I've let the first-floor flat in Number 14," she began, picking up her napkin and smoothing the linen upon her lap. When there was no response, she continued. "To an American woman and her two children. I do hope it wasn't a mistake to let children into the flat. Mother has some nice pieces in there that I would hate to see marred. So much as a scratch can bring down the value, you know. Hugh, did you hear me?"

After a pause to swallow and dab at his mouth with his napkin, he nodded with a bored expression on his face. "Much of the furniture was removed when the house was converted to a three flat, if I recall." He sniffed. "What's left isn't good. I shouldn't get worked up about it if I were you."

Jane bristled. Not good indeed. Did he realize how

much relatively modern turn-of-the-century antiques were worth these days? Perhaps they weren't as *good* as the centuries-old pieces that he'd inherited from his family.

"Nonetheless, the furniture in the O'Neill flat is worth thousands of pounds. I shouldn't care to see it ruined by careless children."

"If that is the case, why did you let to them in the first place?" he asked laconically.

"It isn't easy to find short-term tenants, you know. We've been lucky with Americans. They only want to let for a year or so. Of course, it would be different if we let the flat long-term, but"—she sighed—"one never knows how long Mother will remain at Number 14."

Hugh merely grunted in reply and returned to his unembellished dinner.

Jane frowned. He was never much interested in discussing her mother. Or even his own children for that matter. All he seemed interested in were those silly stamps he was so mad about. Still, his brain was as cagey as ever, and even though he'd retired from the bank years ago, he still kept up-to-date on market trends and real estate. It was the latter that took precedence in her thoughts tonight.

"I don't know how much longer I can allow Mother to stay in that flat. She's positively ancient now. It simply isn't decent for her to be living alone."

"It isn't a question of what you will *allow*, is it, my dear? It never is with your mother."

Jane shifted in her seat as though she were sitting on a tack. "She must see reason. For once in her life."

"Ha! That will be the day, when Wendy Forrester sees reason."

Jane frowned, thinking that her mother's infatuation with fairy tales had been a source of embarrassment to her all of her life. Well, perhaps not all of her life. She did recall with great fondness her early years in the nursery, her mother sitting on her bed, telling her wonderful stories of the Neverland. She'd even dreamed she'd traveled to that magic island with Peter. The difference between herself and her mother, however, was that as Jane grew up and realized that the dreams and stories were simply fantasy. As her mother grew older, she lapsed into a second childhood and, sadly, couldn't separate the stories from what was real.

"I don't know what to do, Hugh," she fretted. "I really don't. She is getting so frail. I worry about her."

"She still has that nurse come round? That horsy-looking character?"

"Jerkins. Yes, she comes every day. Quite reliable, I'm glad to say, though private nursing is frightfully costly. And I don't like leaving Mother alone at night."

"She'll never go for anyone staying with her at night," Hugh pointed out.

"That's just the problem, isn't it?" She sighed and, giving up on dinner, reached for her wineglass. "It's all this Peter Pan nonsense. And with those children moving in, I'm worried that she'll get carried away again. You remember the Macmillan incident?"

His face clouded and he, too, reached for the one glass of wine he was allowed each evening. The Macmillan incident involved two neighboring children who came to No. 14 to listen to Wendy's stories. Mrs. Macmillan claimed, though there were no witnesses, that she'd arrived just in time to avert disaster. Wendy was about to allow the children to leap from high atop the mantel in an attempt to fly. It took all of Jane's persuasive ability to convince the woman not to consult her solicitor.

"Must keep an eye on the situation, eh what?" Hugh said.

"But I cannot be there to mind Mother all day and night," she whined. "She needs proper care. Professional care." She paused. "Full-time care."

Hugh swirled the wine in his glass a moment. "Nursing homes are expensive . . . How much has she left from your father?"

"Enough. Barely." No one could miss the bitterness in her voice. "Every time I think of how well-off she could be now, my blood boils."

"Don't beat that old horse again."

"But it's to the point. If she hadn't wasted away my father's fortune on that ridiculous London Home for Boys that she founded, there wouldn't be any concerns at all as to whether she could afford full-time care or a nursing home. As it is, she lives like a pauper. She doesn't spend a farthing on herself."

"No, she doesn't. The woman is an enigma. Your mother could very well afford a nursing home—if she would consent to go to one. Which, of course, she won't. So this entire labored discussion is moot."

"You're missing the point entirely," she said, arching in her chair.

"I doubt it. It's always the same point, isn't it? Your mother's money . . . or lack of it."

Jane's temper was warmed by the wine. "The point is that my mother hasn't made very sound decisions in the past, and her stubbornness persists in her refusal to leave Number 14 for a nursing home. At her advanced age, you have to admit it's crazy."

Hugh offered a slight, sarcastic smile that caused Jane

to gasp slightly at her unfortunate choice of words. Everyone was well aware of Wendy's nickname.

Jane sat in a tense silence while her husband lit up a cigar, one habit he was adamant about keeping. While allowing her temper to cool, she perused the dining room she adored for its lavish architectural features. Yet, like most old houses, it was chilly and damp. She shivered under her shawl when she saw the peeling paint in the corners, the worn edges of the Aubusson carpet and the thinning fibers of the Napoleon Bee silk fabric she had been so mad for when she covered the chairs thirty years earlier. There was no doubt that this was an expensive house to maintain. She supposed she could sell it or convert it to mutiple flats, as her mother had done.

But no, she loved this house too much. It meant everything to her. Her mother might not care about the loss of social standing, not the invincible Wendy Forrester. Everybody adored Wendy. *Very well for her,* indeed, Jane thought, feeling the age-old resentment flare up. They loved Wendy for giving away her father's fortune to that boys' home. Money that should have gone to Jane!

Pouring herself another glass of wine, she thought again of how her mother was always dedicated to her boys. Working tirelessly on charity balls and fund-raising. Wendy had never cared that things such as public school, social registers, and important addresses mattered to Jane—and to Jane's children. Didn't she know this bred resentment?

Well, she thought, raising her glass to her lips, *it's up to me, as always, to find the practical solution. Thank God someone in this family was born with common sense.*

"Hugh," she asked, diverting his wandering attention

back from his cigar. "How much would you guess Number 14 would bring on today's market?"

There was a long pause as Hugh exhaled a long stream of smoke and considered. "The neighborhood is turning around, being gentrified again," he began in a slow, deliberate voice.

Jane leaned forward, the better to capture every word. "Yes, quite true. Young people with loads of money are paying outrageous sums for houses that can't compare to Mother's."

"It's close to shops, to parks, to museums."

"The shops are becoming exclusive, which is always a good sign."

"Yes," he murmured, watching the smoke from his cigar curl high into the air. "A lovely spot once, and on its way to being lovely once again."

Jane's fingers danced upon her wineglass. Perhaps she should raise the rent? As it was, the rent was reasonable, but with all that Hugh was saying, she was wondering if it wasn't a bargain. Still, to sell would be the thing to do.

He stroked his chin, calculating. "I should imagine upwards of five hundred thousand pounds."

Jane leaned back in her chair. "That much?" she said with astonishment.

"Give or take a farthing. It doesn't matter, you know. This is all speculative. Your mother will never sell."

She gazed at the peeling paint and the faded fabric on the chairs. "I'm just concerned about Mother, of course. She is much too old to be living alone with her childish fantasies. Someone must be responsible and see that the right thing is done." She took a final sip of her wine, then licked her lips.

"For her own good."

*   *   *

The entrance to Jack's garden flat was through a small, black, wrought-iron gate, then down a deep stairwell to below street level. It was a lovely entry, not at all the gloomy basement Faye had expected. Large terra-cotta pots overflowing with more red geraniums filled the corner, and the front door was painted an equally bright cherry red. She raised her hand and knocked on it three times.

After a moment the door swung open, and Jack's face reflected his surprise at finding her there.

"Mrs. O'Neill," he said with the devil sparkling in his eyes. "A bit late for borrowing a cup of sugar, isn't it?"

He filled the doorway and she realized he was much taller than she'd first perceived. His smile, however, was just as she'd remembered: deep-dimpled and slow to blossom. But once it did, it was an utterly charming one that made her feel he had all the time in the world for her.

"I've come to borrow a bit of compassion, Dr. Graham."

His smile slipped from his face, replaced by curiosity and, she was relieved to see, concern.

"I see. Well, won't you come in?"

"No, that won't be necessary. This won't take long." That sounded rather abrupt, she knew, and she watched something akin to amusement ripple across his face, but he smoothly adjusted the expression to reflect utmost seriousness. He crossed his arms and leaned against the doorframe, his attention riveted.

"Dr. Graham," she began slowly, feeling the power of this man's focus and choosing her words carefully.

"Jack."

She hesitated and frowned. "You see," she said with

exasperation, "that's exactly what I want to talk about. My children have been raised to be cautious with strangers. Not to be too friendly. There are reasons for this I don't wish to go into, but suffice to say I prefer that they remain on their guard."

She looked at him beseechingly, hoping that he would catch her drift, but he only raised one eyebrow, indicating she should continue.

"It's not that I don't appreciate your neighborliness, but frankly, well, you come on rather strong. Within one day's meeting the children call you by your first name, they're asking if they can come down to your flat for a visit, and, worst of all, all they can talk about is poor old Mrs. Forrester and whether or not she's Peter Pan's Wendy and how they might see Peter themselves! You see how it is!" She spread her palms out as if to say, "Aren't children unbelievable?"

Instead of a nod of understanding, to her dismay Jack Graham's face broke into a triumphant grin.

"Great!" he said with enthusiasm. "God, I love kids."

She stared at him. The man was incorrigible. "Dr. Graham, I really must insist that you don't encourage them in this fantasy about old Mrs. Forrester and Peter Pan. It isn't . . . Well . . ." She fumbled for the word.

"It isn't grown-up?"

She looked up, nettled. "No. It isn't realistic."

"How old are the children?"

"Maddie is eight and Tom is six."

"What do they do for fun? I mean, they're new to the area, to the country. They can't have many friends. I see them in the garden quite a bit, but I doubt pulling weeds will hold them for the summer. What do they do all day?"

Faye had worried about that herself, but she didn't

think that it was Dr. Jack Graham's concern, and she could feel her temper sizzle beneath her calm facade.

"I'm still working on that. It's not your worry, I assure you. Why? Are they bothering you?"

"Not at all," he answered easily. "I was just wondering. They must be lonely, and there aren't many children in the neighborhood. It's no wonder that they've latched on to Wendy. She's a mystery. Someone who holds magic. A great big question mark that lives on the third floor. For kids, that's a powerful magnet." He chuckled and shook his head. "Their imaginations must be going wild."

Faye felt her anger fizzle and couldn't help but chuckle herself. "They are. Full blast. I can hear them whispering in their beds when the lights are off." She raked her hand through her hair and sighed. Looking up, she noticed that Jack was watching her. She could feel his gaze roam her hair, her face, then settle on her eyes with new interest.

"Are you sure you won't come in for a drink?" he asked.

"No, I can't. The children are waiting for me. I just came to ask . . ." Her voice trailed away. In light of what Jack had just said, it suddenly seemed cruel of her to take away her children's game of fascination with Crazy Wendy. She shook her head in defeat. "I don't know what I came to ask anymore."

"Faye," he said straightening, tucking his fingertips into his rear pockets. She felt him loom over her. "Tell you what. I won't encourage their interest in Wendy, but I won't discourage it either. Because you asked it of me. In exchange, I'd like to ask something of you."

This caught her by surprise, and her face expressed it. What could he possibly want from her?

"Summer is looming large on my horizon, too. And it looks pretty bleak. I've worked pretty much around the clock since I arrived last fall, and, frankly, I hate to leave this city without exploring it a bit. And"—he shrugged— "I'm kinda lonely, too. How about we join forces and have some fun? We can take the children to the parks, museums, see Big Ben and Buckingham Palace."

She pursed her lips, considering. She was sure the children would love the excursions and he was amiable and it certainly would be easier to tour with a companion.

"I don't know much about you," she said, hedging.

"Nor I about you. Let's have a drink in the garden this week, and I'll tell you more than you'll ever want to know."

He must have seen the hesitation in her face because he pushed on.

"We're neighbors. Countrymen. Come on, Mrs. Faye O'Neill of flat 1A." He lifted his right hand from his pocket and extended it out toward her in an age-old gesture of peace. "Let's be friends, too."

Faye worried her lower lip. He seemed so sincere, and his brown eyes were the very picture of trustworthiness. A friend in London would be a nice thing to have, she thought with yearning, acknowledging her own loneliness.

"Friends," she replied, deciding.

She took his extended hand, felt his long fingers dwarf her own, felt her nerve endings tingle as palm met palm. She almost jumped; it was like she'd touched a live wire. His eyes searched hers, leaving little doubt in her mind that he felt it, too. She cursed the heat of a blush she felt scorching her cheeks, a blush that no doubt was giving her feelings away. To counteract, she gave his hand a firm shake—strictly neighborly—then slipped her hand free.

"Got to run," she called, and turned away to hasten up the stairs. She knew without looking that his eyes were on her like searchlights, and, turning the corner, she felt as though she'd just made good her escape.

The rain came down in torrents all the following day, trapping the children in the house. They stared out the window like mice at a peephole. By bedtime, they'd already played with all their toys, watched television till they saw spots before their eyes, and exhausted their mother's voice reading stories. So when Faye turned off the lights and closed the door softly behind her, the children perched on their elbows and began chattering in heated whispers, bubbling with mischievous energy.

"Okay now," said Maddie, giving Tom her most serious look. "Remember what we planned. We're just going to sneak up the stairs, right? Just to see what's up there. We aren't really disobeying. We just want to see, right? Right," she replied, answering her own question aloud while Tom nodded across the room.

The two children slipped out from their beds and, after checking to make sure the coast was clear, tiptoed past their mother's bedroom, where Faye was working at her desk with her back to them, down the stairs, through the living room, and out the front door, careful to leave the door wide-open for a hasty retreat. Just in case.

Only a small, single-bulb lamp on the Hepplewhite table lit the foyer, and it seemed to the children a mighty long way up to the first landing, where a wall sconce dimly lit the steps. In the quiet darkness their shadows stretched long and eerily upon the hall walls.

"Okay, you go first," Maddie ordered Tom with a small shove toward the staircase.

Tom backpedaled against her.

"Aw go on, don't be a wuss."

Tom's face was mutinous but he straightened his narrow shoulders till they stood like sharp arrow points through his thin cotton T-shirt and with his chin stuck out and his arms spread-eagled, ready for a quick flight from danger, he began his slow trek up the stairs to the first landing.

Maddie's heart pounded in her chest as her gaze followed her brother's trek up one creaky step after the other. When he reached the landing he turned and offered her a tremulous smile. Maddie quickly followed him up to the landing and patted his shoulder like a good general.

"That was great, Tom. Real great. You're so brave. Now, go on up to the next landing."

Tom's smile slipped as he focused on the next long stretch of stairs to the third-floor landing. This was no-man's-land. The haven of Crazy Wendy. At the top was the dim, dismal cave of uncertainty. Once again, Tom balked, shaking his head and moving into the corner.

"Oh, okay. We'll go together," Maddie conceded, her own knees knocking. They'd had plenty of conversations about the mysterious Crazy Wendy. Was she really Peter Pan's Wendy, or was she some ugly, wart-nosed, bad-breathed, haggard old witch who ate small children, or at the very least, captured them if they were skinny like they were and put them in a cage till they fattened up and *then* ate them. They'd heard a great many stories of witches and had many conversations at night after the lights were turned off and the door was closed about the mysterious Crazy Wendy who was only seen at night. And all of these conversations were flitting through both of their minds as they took step after step to the third-floor landing. By the time they reached the top they were crouched and panting, partly from fear, partly from excitement.

"We've done it!" Maddie whispered, standing straight with feverish color flooding her cheeks.

Tom wasn't paying attention to her. He was still crouched with a look of deep concentration. He cocked his head to listen. Maddie immediately did the same. After a moment she heard what Tom had heard: a faint tinkling sound of bells. They stepped closer to the door of the third-floor flat, ears almost wagging, they were listening so hard. Again, they heard the tinkling of bells. Then, in a flash, they saw a flicker of light shine from underneath the door, perhaps the beam of a flashlight passing the threshold. There it was again, fast. And again! Maddie took a step back.

"Let's get out of here."

Tom, however, was curious and bent at the waist to peer under the door.

Suddenly a ball of light shot from under the door. Maddie gasped and fell back against the wall as the ball of light bounced from the banister to the ceiling then around Tom's head. His eyes crossed as he followed it, and he smiled brightly. Then the crazy ball of light went straight toward her. Maddie yelped when she felt a sharp pinch on her cheek.

That was enough for Maddie. With a spin on her heels she pounded down the stairs, Tom right behind her, while a bright ball of light chased after them, swirling around their heads like an angry bee. Maddie and Tom ran through the front door, slamming it behind them, tore up the stairs straight into their bedroom, slamming that door shut as well, then dived into their beds, pulling the blankets over their heads.

"What's going on here!" Faye demanded, stepping into the room and turning on the overhead light.

"Nothing." Maddie kept her head under the blankets. "We were just playing."

"Well, enough playing," Faye snapped. "Go to sleep. I mean business now." With that, Faye turned the light back off and closed the door with a firm swing.

Maddie remained shuddering under the blankets. Tom, however, peeped out from under, crawled to his knees on the mattress, and stared out the bedroom window, craning his neck to get a good view of the third-floor window.

He touched his cheek, remembered the kiss, and smiled.

Chapter 4

BEFORE THE SUN even rose Faye was already leaning far forward in front of her vanity mirror applying a dark line of gray eyeliner to her lid. Despite her resolve, her hand would not stop quivering. When she sat back to view her work, the line looked more like a series of dots and slashes.

Cursing under her breath she pulled out a tissue and began wiping away the evidence of her nervousness. Heavens, she was spooked. It was only her first day at work. She knew how to handle this, right? Her hand stilled, then fell to her lap as her expression altered to reflect her despair. Wrong. She *was* terrified. She could count on two hands the number of years since she'd left the ad agency.

"My God," she whispered, reaching up to gently smooth the ragged line of makeup. "Nine years . . . Where did the time go?" Her fingertips moved from her lid to smooth other lines etched by nature at the corners of her eyes. Leaning back, she focused on her reflection. Who was this woman who stared back at her? She barely knew her. The difference was in the eyes. She had aged, not so much in years, but in experience. By that count she was very old indeed.

Would Bernard Robbins notice the change, she wondered? Bernard had been her former boss at Leo Burnett in Chicago. Applying foundation, she thought back on how, as a fresh sprout out of college, she had been given her first chance at pitching a big account by Bernard. She'd nearly killed herself in gratitude, not only proving him correct in his faith by landing a hot client, but earning herself a promotion to account executive after only two years at the firm. Faye had a reputation as a sharp, productive worker. She pushed her team hard, too, but never harder than she pushed herself. In the end, the whole team reaped the rewards of her productivity, several rising in the ranks alongside her.

One had been her ex-husband, Rob O'Neill. He was a handsome, sharp-witted copywriter pinpointed for stardom in his field. He had more than talent. He had style. He knew it, she knew it, everyone knew it. When he turned his formidable charm on her she was as completely bowled over as any client when targeted by one of his campaigns.

Young, foolish, and in love, she childishly gave everything up for Rob, including her common sense. She closed her eyes tightly, wincing at the memory of how she'd practically forced Rob to marry her. He didn't want to be tied down. Yet when determined, Faye could be a formidable force herself. She'd pushed. She'd persevered and, in rapid-fire order, they married, Faye quit her job at Leo Burnett, and Maddie was born. At first, Rob got caught up in the whole idea of having babies. It was novel, as exciting and emotional as any ad campaign. Babies were cute, they smelled good, and with Faye home to take care of them, they were fun. He joked that at last he understood why so many advertisers wanted babies in their ads.

Soon after Tom was born, however, Rob got bored. Two babies were a lot of work, and they tied him down. Eventually, he felt trapped. Then, like so many other cornered animals, he began to snarl and fight.

Faye leaned toward the mirror and, bringing up her hand, gently moved her fingertip along the delicate skin surrounding her eye. How many times had she applied makeup here to try and hide the swelling and bruising? Her first mistake was not to leave him after that first, resounding hit. Her second mistake was to let him hit her again.

In the well-appointed living room of the charming North Shore home that she'd moved into as a young, dewy bride, he'd shouted foul obscenities at her, screamed how he was sorry that he'd married her. How she'd trapped him. That he'd never wanted to be saddled with a wife and kids. Plagued with guilt, she tried all the harder not to make him angry, to do things the way he liked them. To keep the peace. She even turned a deaf ear to the gossips who told her she had a right to know about that account exec he met with so often.

Yet no matter how hard she'd tried to please him, he was never satisfied. He sought ways to berate her: snide remarks about her appearance, mockery of her opinions, a cold shoulder in bed, a smack with the back of his hand. In time, she grew too numb to care one way or the other. Like gold under the pounding mallet, her softness crumpled into a tight, compressed, hard ball.

Faye sighed and stared at the tight and drawn face in the mirror. What had happened to the enthusiastic, eager-eyed girl who had once entered the doors of Leo Burnett with such confidence? Had the divorce robbed her of that as well as her savings account?

What a sobering experience it was, getting back into the job market. She was a has-been at thirty-five. No one was hiring an account exec who'd been out of the business for a decade. No one was hiring, period. Just when she was desperate enough to plead for the receptionist job at the agency, Bernard Robbins called her from London. He'd recently been appointed agency president of Leo Burnett's London office. This was a big move for Bernard. He was a man on the way up and wanted people loyal to him at his side. When he offered Faye a job on his London team they both knew this was more than a job offer. It was her opportunity to reenter the game as a key player. If she won the new account he was bringing her in for, the job was hers. If she lost it, he couldn't promise her she could stay. It was the best he could do.

Now it was her turn to do her best. For Bernard, for herself, for Maddie and Tom. The stakes were never so high.

Her hand tightened around the small tube of lipstick in her palm as she felt the stirrings of determination shake up the dust of doubt within. Whatever else, she must not let Bernard or anyone else know how far she'd fallen from the pedestal she once stood on. She didn't want their pity. She couldn't afford to lose their respect. The Faye O'Neill that Bernard Robbins remembered was a flash of red in a world of gray print. Nothing stood in her way.

With that determination shining in her blue eyes, Faye applied a coat of bright red upon her lips, a steady line of liner to her lids, and smoothed out the muted colors of her eye shadow and blush. Last, she pulled her hair back into a severe chignon at the nape of her neck. Surveying herself in the mirror, she was satisfied with the immaculately groomed, sensibly dressed, no-nonsense woman she saw reflected. Perhaps not so young and enthusiastic, but also not as naive. She would wear this mask of confidence, she swore, even if it was only painted on. In time, success would breed confidence inside as well. She would make this work. Whatever it took.

Faye stepped out into a glorious London morning, took a deep breath, threw back her shoulders, and marched down the front steps. Looking over her shoulder to make certain the front door clicked tight, she collided with Jack Graham as he stepped from his garden flat stairwell. They both shuffled back muttering apologies, but it was Jack who recovered first. When she looked up again she saw him standing with his arms crossed over his chest surveying her with a wry grin and eyes crinkling in the corners.

"Mrs. O'Neill, I presume?" he said, mimicking the upper-crust British accent. "I hardly recognized you without a sponge in your hand."

Faye twisted her lips to hide her smile and smoothed her skirt. She allowed her gaze to travel lazily over Jack's gray flannel suit, the starched white shirt, and black-and-red tie.

"Surely this gentleman before me can't be my neighbor, Dr. Jack Graham? Where are the jeans, the sweatshirt? My goodness, he's not only wearing shoes, he's wearing wing tips!"

"Uniform," Jack quipped, eyes lively. "Required for all lectures, meetings with VIPs, and whenever I need to impress my new neighbors. So, how am I doing?"

She tapped her lips teasingly, but inside her heart flut-

tered. His long, lean body fit his business suit with the
sleek, sexy polish of a Fleet Street model. Even his dark
curls, which up till then she'd only seen in a lazy mass
about the head, were slicked back from his forehead with
obvious care.

"You definitely had me fooled, neighbor. You look,
well, quite dapper. Yes, I think that's the best word for
it."

"God forbid. Dapper . . ." Then, openly surveying her
own apparel, he said, "Let me return the compliment.
You look quite dapper yourself this morning, Mrs.
O'Neill."

"Thank you," she replied with a neat nod, trying desperately to defuse the flirtatious turn of this conversation.

"Is today your first day at your new job?"

She nodded, and her lips tightened with her stomach.
"Yes, but I'm not off to a very good start. The baby-sitter
arrived late, and I still have to find my way to the subway.
I'm a bundle of nerves."

"They call it *the tube* over here. If you're in a hurry,
the thing to do is to grab a cab. Follow me."

She didn't have the spare money to pay for the luxury
of a cab ride, but, checking her watch, she realized she
had no choice but to take his advice.

He took hold of her elbow and guided her down the
block. She felt the strength of his fingers on her arm and
when he deftly commandeered her away from a hole in
the pavement, she realized that someone had taught Jack
Graham manners. At the next corner traffic whizzed by
on a main thoroughfare. Jack raised his hand, placed his
teeth on his lower lip, and let out a piercing whistle that
any New Yorker would have been proud of. In a flash, a
cab swerved over and stopped at the curb.

"Your chariot awaits you, madam."

"Aren't you coming, too?"

"No, I have to go all the way out to Oxford today. Guest lecture stuff." He leaned inside and handed the driver a few bills. "Take the lady where she wants to go."

"You don't have to do that," she said, opening her purse.

"I know I don't. But I'd like to. Consider it a first-day-on-the-job gift. We're friends, remember?"

Friends. This time when he said it, she believed him, even though she couldn't quite grasp the concept. Still, it seemed to settle the butterflies in her stomach a bit. And he did have the nicest, most contagious smile.

"I remember," she replied as a hesitant half smile eased onto her own face. "Thanks, Dr. Graham."

He leaned forward and his dark eyes sparked. "Jack."

Now the butterflies began flapping in her stomach again. "Jack," she conceded.

"Good luck today. Faye," he added with an appreciative grin, then closed the door and waved. The cab lurched and sped off.

Not, however, as hard nor as fast as her own heart.

At eight-fifty that morning, Faye strode through the carpeted halls of Leo Burnett's London office, listening to the familiar buzz of voices, the ringing of phones, and the click of word processors. Everything was so alive. Fast. She felt sure if she blinked she'd miss something. Faye took the elevator up to the inner sanctum, where the carpet was upgraded and the artwork was original. Bernard's secretary checked her name on his calendar, announced her with indifference, then indicated the direction with a languid turn of her hand.

"Come in," boomed the familiar baritone. It was a loud, I-don't-care-who-hears-me voice that could shake the rafters. There was a time years back when Faye heard that bellow as a rallying call. Today, however, her breath caught in her throat.

Opening the door, she stepped into an immense office of glass and steel. In a business where the size of the office indicated position and power, Bernard's office made a clear statement of his success. The building was one of the few skyscrapers on the block and as if to shout out that fact, the interior design conveyed a high-tech, cutting-edge impression. It suited an advertising agency that prided itself on its clean, creative, energetic campaigns.

Bernard looked powerful and svelte sitting behind a desk the size of a small car. He was leaning far back in his high, black-leather chair and chatting on the phone in a staccato voice. He looked up when he saw her and waved her in with a free hand. Faye attempted to appear nonchalant and returned a brief smile, then turned to stroll and stand before his windows. His office offered a spectacular view of London. In contrast to the cold steel of the skyscraper, the history and romance of the historic city were welcoming. Staring out at the vista, she marveled that this magnificent city was her new home.

"Faye! Long time no see."

She turned and saw Bernard rise from his seat and walk, arms extended, across the carpet. It was more a swagger than a walk, with movements strong and self-assured. When he reached her, he surrounded her with his powerful bulk and delivered a warm, affectionate hug.

"Bernard," she said softly, stepping back and smiling into his face. He hadn't changed much at all in the last ten years. A little more gray in his dark hair, perhaps. It suited him. He had piercing black eyes and a bulb-tipped nose, a combination most people found intimidating. She was glad he was on her side.

"God it's great to see you again," he said, his gaze roaming her face intently. "You look great. Just great."

Faye tried to remain relaxed, but she sensed he was picking up all the signs of wear and tear she'd noticed in her mirror earlier that morning. "Thanks," she murmured.

"How are the kids?"

"Fine, thank you. Just fine," she replied, skirting over the question. She wondered how much he knew about Tom. "You know I appreciate your offering me this opportunity. Especially now. I . . ."

"Hell, Faye. I don't want your gratitude. You're my ace in the hole on this project. I need you. I've been angling for the Hampton Tea account since I got to England. They want to move into the American market, and who better to help them do just that than an international ad agency headquartered in the Midwest? I just happened to be looking for a first-rate American account executive when I heard you were available." He shrugged his wide shoulders. "I made the call. No big deal."

She knew he was being modest, and she was filled with just the kind of gratitude and loyalty that he wanted from her. Well, he had them, she concluded.

"You know I'll do my best."

"Know it? I'm counting on it. I want this account, Faye. But I gotta tell you, it'll be a challenge. There's a lot of competition on the street for this one."

Her lips curved slightly. "My biggest challenge right now is trying to find a good baby-sitter," she said, not entirely joking. "It has to be easier than that."

He gave off a short laugh, then, skewering her with his gaze, said, "No. Your biggest problem is trying to find a pitch that will snag the Hampton Tea account."

Zing. Faye's toes curled inside her navy pumps. "Of course," she blurted.

"You're not a housefrau any longer, Faye. I'm counting on your best here."

"Of course," she repeated, mentally cursing herself for sounding as inane as Jane Lloyd. She was mistaken to think this would be a nostalgic homecoming. Bernard Robbins might be friendly, but he was not her friend. Time was money, and she'd better be careful not to waste either.

"The Hampton Tea account could be important." He hesitated. "For all of us. I'm putting my best people on it."

A deliberate compliment. Faye stood straighter but said nothing.

"Right now they're just sticking their toes into the American waters," he continued. "But I believe we can convince them to dive in. They should. It's a damn good product. Ever try it?"

Faye said a quick prayer of thanks for her perspicacity. The first item she bought upon reaching the English shore was a tin of Hampton English Breakfast Tea. She knew that Bernard was a stickler for his people trying and believing in the product they represented.

"Yes, sir. I've tried a number of their teas. Frankly, I'm surprised how much I like them," she replied, exaggerating the truth. "So rich and full of body. I'm usually a coffee drinker."

"Not anymore you're not." He laughed loudly at her expression. "Well, maybe we can allow coffee once in a while. We also represent a Colombian coffee company.''

"It's tea for me until I land this account."

"That's the spirit. Have you reviewed the material I sent you on Hampton Tea?"

"Yes, thoroughly. I've a few questions."

"Good . . . good. I'll introduce you to Research later today."

He moved over to his desk and rummaged through the papers littering the polished surface. Faye waited quietly beside the desk. From both his demeanor and his expression, she knew the cordiality was over. He was all business now. It was as if she'd never stopped working for him. He tucked a slender silver pen in his vest pocket, then picked up a few manila file folders.

"Here are some additional copies of the research our team has come up with," he said, walking toward her. He handed her the folders. "They focused on the quality of the tea. Better go over them before you meet with the Hampton boys. Set you up with a meeting next week. Your secretary will review your calendar with you later."

"Yes, sir."

He fixed her with a smile. "Well then. Let's go meet the troops. They're assembled in the conference room. I want to get started on this campaign."

Faye's mouth went dry and her palms grew damp. "Now?"

He raised his brows. "Of course now. Everyone's waiting. Why not?"

Faye wanted to say because she'd only just stepped in the building. Because she hadn't seen her office yet, met her secretary, or had the time to get a feel for the place. Damn, because she needed a cup of coffee. Knowing Bernard, at the meeting there would only be tea. Looking into his eyes, however, flashing with impatience, Faye knew that it was out of the question to refuse. What could she do but hoist a loyal smile, and reply, "Why not, indeed?"

Bernard seemed pleased. "Remember the routine? Okay. Let's go snap the whip."

Snap the whip? Sitting on the edge of her seat in the conference room, she felt more like she was being flogged by one.

When she first walked in the room, she'd felt the heat of a dozen pair of eyes boring into her. She smiled a cool greeting, not too friendly, not too hostile, well aware that her conservative, beautifully cut, navy suit would stand the scrutiny. Her shoes, too, were well worth the weeks of eating peanut butter it took to purchase them. After she sat down, Bernard introduced her as his protégé from Chicago. Instantly the pairs of eyes surrounding the attractive, petite woman narrowed in suspicious regard.

Bernard was right, everyone was there. He first introduced the account supervisor, Susan Perkins. She was a dramatically attractive type with a hard smile and piercing blue eyes that peeled away layers like a laser. Patrick and Harry, the copywriters, and Pascal, the art director, made up Bernard's "Creatives." From production and media she met George and Jaishree.

Smiling and committing their names to memory, she thought to herself that though individual features varied and accents differed, ambition was the common thread. How accurate indeed was Bernard's analogy of being a lion tamer in the circus ring surrounded by hungry cats ready to pounce and devour her when she wasn't paying attention. Bernard liked his people hungry. He felt it kept the creative juices boiling. There was a time, ten years earlier, when Faye thrilled at the crack of new ideas as they whipped the air. She relished the growls of frustrations when opposition was crushed.

Today, however, sitting at the edge of the conference table, facing the circle of gleaming eyes and teeth shining through hard smiles, Faye shuddered. A lion tamer who lost her edge was a lion tamer in danger. For the first time in all her years in the advertising business, Faye Armstrong O'Neill felt fear.

And the lions surrounding her could smell it.

Chapter 5

SUMMER BECKONED. THE days grew longer, birds sat on eggs in the nest, and there was a lazy lushness in the brilliant green trees and in the way dandelion seeds floated on a scant breeze. Maddie patrolled the small patch of flowers she'd planted around the fountain as fearlessly as the mother birds did their nearby nests. Jack chuckled as he lay on the cold, hard flagstone tinkering with the fountain, listening to Maddie croon to the frail green seedlings that struggled through the finely cultivated earth. He'd spent every rare, spare moment from his work in the past weeks trying to get the old fountain to work again and had discovered in the process that he enjoyed being in the fresh air and sunlight again after months of an around-the-clock routine of teaching and poring over theories in stuffy labs and libraries.

"Would you like some water, Jack?" Maddie asked, bending low to catch a glimpse of his face beneath the overhang of fountain.

Jack wiped the grease from his cheek and smiled back at the gamine face that stared at him with adoration. He had to admit that he was enjoying his stature as hero in

Maddie's eyes ever since he began his repairs of the fountain. She still bullied Tom around, keeping the poor boy running from one errand to another, but with Jack, her words were sugar-coated. *Little minx,* he thought to himself, chuckling. She'd be a heartbreaker someday. He was no fool, though. He knew this preferential treatment would last only until he got her beloved Peter Pan fountain to spring to life.

"Some water would be great, thanks."

"Um, Jack, how's it going?"

"Don't know yet. This old thing's rusted solid down here." Then, seeing the disappointment on her face, he wiggled his brows and added, "But I'm hopeful."

Maddie's face broke into a wide grin before she nodded and sped off into her flat for the water.

From the corner of his eye, Jack spied Tom watching him intently from his usual hiding place in the overgrown boxwood. They'd been playing this game of cat and mouse for several weeks now, and Tom had yet to make a squeak. What a timid little guy he was, all wide eyes and twitches. When he wasn't staring at him, he was gazing up at Crazy Wendy's window. Maybe, Jack thought, it was time to add a little bait.

Jack grabbed his pliers and made a big show of trying to budge one of the rusted bolts, grunting loudly, pretending to push with all his might. Discreetly, he noticed that Tom had emerged from the shrubs, cautiously watching.

"Whew, that's a tough nut to crack," he said aloud. "I wish I had some help."

Tom stood as quiet as a mouse, eyeing him suspiciously.

Jack couldn't help but wonder what had happened to

make that boy so skittish. He knew if he so much as spoke his name right now, Tom would tuck tail and scurry off into the boxwoods, or to his bedroom, where, as Maddie reported with childish disgust, he crouched under the bed reading a book. That he could read chapter books alone at age six indicated the boy was certainly bright enough. And he wasn't deaf or mute. Maddie told him that. So what was it that kept that scowl on his face and his lips silent?

Trying another strategy, Jack moved his foot, accidentally-on-purpose kicking the screwdriver closer toward Tom. Then he made an excellent show of reaching for it.

"Now how am I going to get that screwdriver while holding on to this bolt?"

Tom stood staring at the screwdriver, wringing his hands with a worried look on his face. Jack held his breath, careful not to look directly at the boy, not daring to utter another sound.

"Come on, boy, come on . . ." he whispered.

Then, with a look of intense concentration on his small, round face, Tom bent at the waist to pick up the long, heavy tool. He held it in his child's hands for a moment, weighing its heaviness, measuring his courage. Jack saw the boy's brow wrinkle with worry, as any old man's, and he felt an impulsive longing to hold Tom in his arms, to tell him, "there, there," then to tickle him and make him laugh. Anything to take away that wizened expression that violated his childish features.

He felt as though his heart broke for the kid, and in the fissure, suddenly, he saw the faces of other boys he'd seen wearing that same hangdog expression. The faces of boys he'd known at the boys' home. A first memory . . .

He squeezed his eyes tight, capturing it. Through the dark mists he saw shapes, heads: red hair, black hair, blond hair. Faces, all bearing the same knowing sadness as Tom. Yes, he remembered them now: Eddy . . . Bobby . . . Mac . . . Eddy was deaf in one ear where his dad had cuffed him. Bobby never talked about it, but he limped a little to the left. And Mac . . . he never knew what happened to Mac. Like Tom, he never spoke a word. None of the boys ever talked details among themselves, but everyone knew they'd been abused in one way or another. Himself, too.

When Jack opened his eyes he spied the screwdriver lying close to his hand. But the little boy, like the brief memory, had quickly vanished.

Later that afternoon, long after the children had returned indoors, Jack tossed down his tools and gave up his combat with the ornery fountain. He stretched his cramped muscles, then collapsed in one of the four green wrought-iron chairs that wobbled on the crooked flagstones. Sighing with contentment, he picked up his feet and sipped a long, cool gin and tonic. On the table sat a thermos filled with the ambrosia and an empty glass. He was on his second sip when the back door opened and Faye O'Neill stepped out onto the patio. Perfect timing, he thought.

"Come to take me up on that drink, I hope?" he asked with one brow raised, watching her approach.

She startled and quickly tucked a tendril in her hair. "Oh. Hello, Dr.—" She stopped herself. "Jack," she amended. "Actually, I've come to pick up my children's mess. Look." She tsked and shook her head. "Shovels and gloves and sprays of dirt everywhere. One of these days they'll have to learn to clean up after themselves."

"If you find a way to teach kids *that* lesson, you should write a book. You'll make a fortune."

"Well, we have to try." She bent over to pick up a muddy pair of gardening gloves that looked to Jack like they'd fit a leprechaun.

"Come on, Faye. Put your feet up and have a drink. It won't kill you to take a break, you know. I've been watching you around here, and from what I can tell, slaves have better hours. You work round the clock. I've done that, and I'm here to tell you there's no percentage in it for the long haul. Besides, I seem to remember a promise you made to have a drink in the garden."

"I don't remember giving a promise," she said with a wry smile, slapping the gloves against her thigh to shake off the dirt.

"Semantics," he replied, lifting his feet off the chair and motioning for her to sit down.

"This mess . . ."

"I'll help you pick up if you'll sit down and have one small drink. Whaddya say?" He swirled the thermos and the sound of liquid and ice rolling around inside was a symphony of temptation. "Gin and tonic. Ice-cold. The perfect summer drink."

"God, that's tempting. Oh, all right. We are neighbors."

"Friends."

"Agreed. But just one. To get to know each other better."

"One will be more than enough to hear my whole life's story."

"You'd need a pitcher to get through mine," she said with a short laugh, slipping into the chair. "Ow, what's that?" She turned her shoulder to find flakes of green paint and rust clinging to her white-cotton blouse and arms. Brushing the flakes away she said, "These chairs are beautiful. Heirlooms. It's a shame they're in such bad shape."

"Poor Wendy doesn't get out much, and Mrs. Lloyd isn't likely to take care of things."

"Funny how you call the old woman Wendy and her daughter Mrs. Lloyd. It speaks a lot about the women, don't you think? Still, it's a shame about this place. It's so beautiful, but it's so neglected. They just don't build 'em like this anymore. I mean, the craftsmanship. The style."

"Now that you mention it, these chairs *could* use a coat of paint. The table too."

"I'd do it myself but between my work and my kids, I swear I don't have a moment to catch my breath."

"What do you do?"

"I'm an account exec for Leo Burnett. I'm here to snag a hot account."

"Ah, so they brought in a ringer. Which account?"

"The Hampton Tea account. Ever heard of it?"

"Yeah, sure. Who hasn't? But frankly, I'm a coffee man myself."

"Really?" she replied, eyes narrowing. "That makes you my target market. I've got to find a way to sway you over to tea."

"You've got your work cut out for you." He raised his glass to her.

Faye groaned and took a long swallow from her drink. "Tell me about it," she replied, resting her forehead in her palm. "I've been wracking my brain going over the research and trying to figure out an angle."

"But . . ."

She looked up at him and found him leaning forward, his attention riveted.

"But it's not easy. Americans are coffee lovers."

"And . . ."

She smirked and shook her head. "Isn't that enough?"

"I sense something else."

Her smile slipped, and she stirred her ice with her finger. "I'm nervous," she said, surprising herself that she'd admit something like that to someone who was a relative stranger.

"What are you nervous about?"

"That the idea won't be good enough. That my boss won't like it. I don't want to let him down. I haven't worked for him in years, and he has such faith in me."

"Well, maybe the faith is grounded. Besides, the one you have to worry most about letting down is yourself."

She rolled her eyes. "Yeah, right."

"No, Faye, I mean it. Ideas are gifts from the gods. When we receive one we have to bow to them and offer thanks. Humbly. And believe in the idea. Passionately. If *you* don't have faith in your idea, then how can you expect others to?"

Faye sat up in her chair. His words rang true. "But . . ." she began, furrowing her brow, "how do you know if it *is* a good idea?"

He shrugged. "Trust your instincts."

Her enthusiasm wavered in her breast. "My instincts," she said in a tone that implied she'd long ago lost faith in those.

"I have this theory," he said with a trace of a smile. "We all have instincts, but some of us have them more finely honed than others. We have to learn to listen to them. I believe that you have to spend time alone with your thoughts. To nurture your creativity. Oh I dunno, do things that bring you close to nature. Things that bring you pleasure. Take walks in the park, see, smell the change of seasons. Feel the wind on your face. Squish your toes in the mud. Or just pick up your feet and enjoy a gin and tonic on a balmy summer night with a good friend.''

''Sounds great,'' she said softly. ''But I have this problem. It's that time thing.''

He looked her in the eyes, and when he spoke his gaze reflected a seriousness that underscored the gentle tone of his voice. ''Make time for yourself, Faye. Make time for play in your life.''

She didn't reply but kept her gaze steady while a lump formed in her throat.

''You have an idea in that head of yours, don't you?'' he asked, turning crafty and tilting his head. ''I can tell. See? There's a smile. I'm right, aren't I?''

She nodded and released the reluctant smile.

''I knew it!''

''Oh stop being so smug,'' she said with a laugh. ''It's just something I've been mulling over.''

''Go with it, friend. Trust your instincts. My money's on you.''

She glowed inside, even as the afternoon's light dimmed. A hush settled in the twilight. The birds sang their farewell songs, and the trees grew purple against a pink sky.

''Look, Jack,'' she said, pointing to the setting sun. It appeared in the sky as a large red ball balanced atop the crumbling brick garden wall. ''It looks like it might roll right along the wall and topple into the trash can.''

She relished the sound of Jack's hearty laugh in the

quiet night and laughed out loud along with him. Leaning back in her chair, she remembered back to when she was a young girl who loved to laugh, laugh without fear of being unladylike or overheard. Laughed for the pure joy of it. Something in Jack's words kindled that youthful enthusiasm, that unerring belief that the world was her oyster. She was filled with a sweet gladness she hadn't felt in years.

"Thanks, Jack, for a wonderful evening," she said, setting down her drink. "It's getting late, and I'd best go in." Then, looking up, she smiled at him, hoping her gratitude shone through. "And suddenly, I have this strange compulsion to work."

That night Faye worked late on her idea. When she finally crawled into bed hours later, her thoughts drifted sleepily away from tea and marketing figures and wandered back to Jack and his insights and how he always made her feel good about herself. So unlike Rob, who'd never lost an opportunity to criticize her and to chip away at her self-esteem. Closing her eyes, she brought to mind the image of Jack's deep-dimpled smile and the way his pupils quivered when he spoke with fervor about something he believed in strongly. He was a man of many convictions. Faye counted his qualities instead of sheep and when she finally fell asleep, it was with a smile curling her lips.

The next morning she awoke full of energy and eager to stay on top of her idea. She worked straight through lunch and, at quitting time, called the baby-sitter and informed her she'd be working late. She hated to do that, but she needed to plow through before she lost the idea's spark.

When she finally tossed down the pencil it was nine o'clock in the evening. She felt as though her brain had been drained of all gray matter. Rubbing her temples, she looked around her sterile ten-by-ten office high up on the twenty-third floor of the steel-and-glass building. Her metal desk and chair were the only pieces of furniture in the small, square office; the walls were barren of any pictures or plaques. Her windows didn't even open. It was a cold, impersonal space, void of charm, crammed with boxes not yet opened, reams of paper waiting to be loaded into her printer, and stacks of reference books that needed to be shelved.

She couldn't be bothered with decorating or organizing when there was a deadline on the horizon. She yawned, stood up, and stretched her arms and fingers far over her head, then walked to the window to gaze out at the park across the street. Lovers strolled hand in hand, a vendor sold flowers from his cart, an old man walked his little dog on a long leash.

Her heart softened at the sight, and she leaned forward, resting her forehead against the glass. She loved nights like these. Early-summer nights when the warm breezes smelled of honeysuckle and melted the bones to a heap of lassitude. On nights like these she felt her loneliness intensely, longed for a man to hold her hand and buy her posies and take her for a long walk in the park. What would it be like, she wondered, to squish her toes in the mud?

Nonsense, she scolded herself, standing upright and rubbing her eyes. She was just getting slaphappy. She had to concentrate on her work, finish up, and hurry home to her children. They were safe with the sitter, she knew. She called them on the phone several times to make sure they'd finished their dinners and brushed their teeth. And to tell them that she loved them before they fell asleep. No child should go to sleep not knowing that they were loved.

She returned to her desk and picked up her pencil, but her weary mind wandered. Leaning back in her chair, she opened a drawer and pulled out a blue-plastic thermos. What she needed now was a cup of coffee to get her going. Yes, one good solid jolt of caffeine. Unscrewing the top her nose twitched with the heady aroma of the steaming hot Java. "Mmmmm," she sighed aloud, eyes closed, almost slumping forward with anticipation.

"Caught you."

Faye jerked back and snapped open her eyes. Bernard was standing at the door, his dark eyes peering with judgment over his imperious nose. She quickly popped the top back onto the thermos and tried to stuff it back into the open drawer.

"Not so fast," Bernard said, stepping into the office. "What's that I smell?" He raised his nose and sniffed the air like a great bloodhound. He looked ready to bellow out the howl after catching the scent. "That's not tea, I'll wager."

"Well, it's late and . . ." Faye stammered.

"No, no, no, definitely not tea. Only one thing I know of has that deep, dark, deliciously tempting aroma."

Faye raised her brow and pulled the thermos back out of the drawer. "Okay, I confess. Guilty as charged. It's coffee."

Bernard crossed his arms and smirked.

"Look, Bernard," she began, feeling the hours of work coiling in her like a cobra about to strike. "I know more about tea at this very moment than I'd ever hoped to learn in a lifetime. Starting back from the legend of some ancient scholarly Chinese emperor with a thin mustache that reached his knees who accidentally discovered tea when a leaf from a nearby tree dropped into his boiled water, to Anna, seventh Duchess of Bedford, who one day idly declared that the best way to stave off her midday hunger pangs was with a brisk cup of tea, say about four o'clock each afternoon.'' She picked up a pile of papers and let them sift through her fingers.

"I've studied the history of tea, the drinking customs, the tea market, British and American tea-drinking habits, and the health advantages of tea.'' She raised her hand and began counting off fingers. "I've had black tea, green tea, and herbal tea. Tea from India, Sri Lanka, Kenya, Malawi, Indonesia, and China. I've had it bright, brownish and burnt. I've tried it straight black, with cream, with skim milk, and teaspoons full of sugar, honey, and sometimes late at night, when I need a jolt, both.'' Her voice began to rise. "Morning, noon, and night I've had tea, tea, tea. And no matter what blend or what variety of leaf or what I've put into the brew, I just can't get used to that astringent, mouth-drying, puckering bitter taste in my mouth!'' She reached over, grabbed the thermos, and opened it with a fierce twist. "I don't know about you, but I'm desperate for a good cup of coffee!''

Bernard sneaked a look over his shoulder and quickly closed the door behind him. He eyed her pouring out the black liquid with wide-eyed adoration. "God, that smells great. What kind do you have? French Roast? Kenya?''

She looked up, curious. "Colombian.''

"Damn.'' He rushed toward her desk. "Do you have enough for two?''

Faye reached into the drawer to pull out another mug

that had the Hampton Tea crest printed on the green glass and poured the traitorous coffee into it. They huddled over the desk like two conspirators. Bernard practically groaned as he sipped.

"Nectar of the gods," he murmured.

"Me mother's milk to me," she replied in a purr, drinking greedily.

"Look at us, huddled in secrecy. We're like a couple of addicts getting our fix."

"I'm a good girl. I work hard, keep my nose clean, don't have many vices. I figure I should be forgiven this one addiction."

"Yeah," he agreed, sipping loudly. "Me too." After pouring himself a second cup, he sat on the edge of her desk and poked around the papers that covered every inch of the surface. "So, O'Neill, how's the campaign coming along? We still have to come up with something that sells the swill."

"It's coming along," she said cautiously. "In fact, I think I know how to get the job done." She leaned back in her chair and sipped. Her eyes met his over the rim, and they shared a jolt of excitement, same as from the old days when she had a bang-up idea. He leaned forward slightly. She did the same.

"Talk to me, Faye."

She took a breath and dived in. "The way I see it, Hampton Tea wants to enter the American market," she began. "A land of diehard coffee drinkers. Folks who once dumped bales of British tea into Boston Harbor, an action I'm totally sympathetic with, by the way. Bottom line, we don't want to switch to tea. We like our coffee. Take me. I've tried a gozillian different blends and varieties and I still don't want to give up the Java. So what's to get folks like you and me to switch to tea?''

"Job pressure?"

She chuckled. "Well, that works for me . . . But for the million other coffee drinkers from California to New York?"

He shrugged, eyes flashing with anticipation.

"Health."

"Health?" The light in his eyes dimmed a bit.

"Yes," she replied, sitting up and placing her mug on the table. Tapping the papers, she continued, ''There is an increasing body of evidence that tells us that not only is tea not harmful to the body like some folks claim coffee is, but that tea is actually good for you."

She wagged her brows and smiled like a carnival barker reeling one in. "And it helps fight heart disease."

Bernard brought his coffee to his mouth, looked at it, then thought differently and set the mug down on her desk.

"Fights heart disease?"

"And lowers cholesterol and blood pressure. Look at who is out there buying the coffee, Bernard. The Baby Boomers are aging. They want to take care of their bodies, their teeth, their hearts. I say the health advantages of tea drinking is what's going to bring them over from the coffee camps to the tea camps. Health. Fitness. Long life. That's where we should focus our campaign."

Bernard stood up and tucked his hands into his suit pockets as he paced her office floor, considering. She held her breath, praying. This wasn't how she'd meant to tell him. She wanted the charts and the graphs, the punchy lines, the bells and whistles when she presented the idea. Her first campaign idea for him in a decade. But the moment seemed right tonight. The sparkle was there. She went with her hunch.

When he stopped in front of her desk and met her gaze, her breath slipped out in a wheeze. There was no sparkle in Bernard's eyes.

"So you really think that a factual-based campaign is the way to go?"

She nodded, feeling the excitement in her veins freeze and the coiling in her stomach tighten. "Yes," she replied, clearing her throat and appearing as businesslike as possible. "We'll hit them with solid medical claims. The research studies are there, Bernard. The statistics are there. We'll be clever, of course. The Creatives can work out all the details. But I really believe that a well-thought-out, rational approach will appeal to a nation of health-conscious, aging adults. No one wants to believe in fairy tales anymore. We're too educated. Too smart to be fooled by romantic images of high tea with white-lace doilies, high-fat buttery crumpets, and women sharing secrets. Women today don't want secrets. They want the hard facts."

He stroked his jaw and narrowed his eyes, looking long and hard at her. Finally, he dropped his hand with decision.

"Okay, O'Neill. I'll go along with your idea."

Her heart skipped a beat and she half rose to thank him.

"Hold on there," he said, his palm out in an arresting pose. "I've got to be honest with you. It doesn't send me. The juices aren't flowing. I'm used to your zinger ideas. Slogans that zig and zag right to the heart. This is, I dunno. Sensible, practical, maybe even convincing. But kinda flat. Safe."

"But if you consider . . ."

"You've got some good ideas, and I said I'd give you a shot. I'll back you on this." He shrugged. "I don't know how the Creatives will react. That's between you and them."

She nodded, feeling suddenly subdued. "They're champing at the bit to go all out for some wacky out-there idea. They want a rallying call. Something along the line of *Just Do It*."

"I know. I know. But it's not them I'm worried about. The one you have to convince is Susan Perkins. She's the account supervisor. If she says no, it's no."

"But Bernard, you just said you'd support the idea."

"I will. But I won't go to bat for it. It's more that I won't pitch against you. I'll let it be known I'm on your team."

Now she really slumped in the chair. Bernard was definitely dim on the idea. "If you think it's not good . . ."

"I didn't say that. I said I'm not swept up by it. I have to admit, though, that heart disease stuff caught my attention. Look, Faye, it's up to you. This is your campaign. You just have to be absolutely, drop-dead-on sure that this is the best way to present the campaign, that Hampton Tea will go for the idea, and that their product will sell like the proverbial hotcakes in the States." He speared her with one of his piercing, cut-to-the-chase glances. "Are you sure?"

She swallowed hard, eyes wide, and nodded.

"Then go for it." He set down the mug and strolled toward the door, opening it to the hall. Before leaving, he paused, then turned to look at her over his broad shoulder.

"One last question. You mentioned that women don't want romance. That they just want the hard facts. Do you think you're typical of women today?"

She paused and thought of how she was getting up early each day, packing her children off to school, toiling for eight hours for low pay, traveling home in rush hour to rush again to put dinner on the table, check homework, then catch up on laundry and housework. Then maybe she could do the work she brought home in her briefcase before collapsing into bed. She thought of how gullible she'd once been, of how many times she'd been burned. She thought of the dreams she'd believed in as a child and the nightmare of a marriage gone bad. Life was hard for women, young and old, but especially for single mothers. They had to scrape at the day to dig up one moment of joy.

"Yes," she replied, meeting his searing gaze. "I think I'm typical."

He nodded thoughtfully. "Then why are you still drinking coffee?"

Chapter 6

THE MOON ROSE full and heavy in the night sky, and in the soft, bluish light Jack saw a small boy tiptoe across the flagstones, coming to a stop in the center of the garden. Jack sat quietly in the darkness, unobserved. The boy's knobby knees protruded under the hem of his boxer shorts, his long, thin arms hung at his sides, and his shaggy blond head was tilted back as he stared at a fixed point in the sky.

What an odd child that Tom O'Neill is, Jack thought, crossing his arms across his chest and observing him. It was very late, near midnight. What was it that brought a six-year-old boy outside at this time of night? Maybe it was the stars? Certainly by the age of six he himself was already hooked by the night sky. In fact, he could recall being chased off the orphanage's roof many a night by horrified attendants. Jack stretched his neck to follow Tom's line of sight.

Ah, so that's it, he thought with a smile twitching at his lips. No Big Dipper or Milky Way captured this boy's imagination. Tom's gaze was fixed on the third-floor window of Crazy Wendy.

"Look higher, boy," he said quietly with a sad smile and a sorry shake of his head. "There is more than enough mystery to greet a boy's imagination in the heavens."

Boy and man quietly gazed upward for a long while, neither moving a muscle. Time enough for Jack to come up with a scheme of his own. The stars had been his ticket to excitement and fulfillment, as it had to a history full of boys. He smiled broadly at the prospect of introducing another boy to that wonderful world. Space was a great adventure: the greatest.

"Ah Tom," he said softly, watching as the knobby-kneed, wispy haired boy lowered his head, then sneaked barefoot across the flagstones back indoors, no doubt to his room and the comfort of his blankets. "Tomorrow I'll teach you to set your sights a little higher."

The following night, filled with excitement, Jack carefully waited by his window until Maddie and Tom had finished their supper and were back at work in the garden. He knew they'd come out; it seemed that they were always there, digging or tugging weeds, or scrubbing the fountain. He found their cheery intensity fascinating. When he stepped into the garden, the children immediately ceased their chatter and looked at him with reproachful, suspicious eyes. Jack merely nodded, smiled politely, then carried his telescope to an open spot on the flagstones and began setting up.

From the corner of his eye he saw the children cast questioning glances at each other. Neither of them seemed pleased to see him invade *their* garden. Maddie eventually shrugged and went back to her project, not, however, without casting several part-curious, part-begrudging glances his way. Tom scurried like a frightened mouse to the boxwood and hid.

Pulling up a chair, Jack made himself comfortable and began scouring the night sky, occasionally adjusting his sights, from time to time whistling or mumbling, "Wow," or "Look at that!" when he spotted a satellite or a fascinating constellation.

Perhaps the little girl wasn't so contrary as she appeared, or maybe her curiosity simply overwhelmed her, but after thirty minutes of stubborn silence, she wandered over to his side and peered over his shoulder.

"What're you looking at?" she asked.

Jack felt a thrill of success but was careful to keep his eye on the lens and his voice noncommittal.

"The stars," he answered.

"Can you see them good?"

"Mmm hmmm."

"Can I take a look?"

At first he made no response. Then he leaned back and motioned her over. "Sure."

She huddled over the eyepiece, then let out a gasp of delight. "Oh, look! They're so pretty!"

Jack smiled and cast a glance from the corner of his eye at the bushes. Tom, who was peeking out, poked his head back in, more like a turtle than a mouse. Jack chuckled and brought his attention back to Maddie. She was dancing on her toes with excitement.

"I thought all stars looked alike, but now I can tell they're different. Some look kinda blue and some kinda red. What's that I'm looking at?"

"Oh, just some stars and planets."

"There are so many of them."

"More than we can count. Tonight's not a bad night,

for the city. You can see lots more in the deep dark, away from the city lights.''

''Wow,'' she breathed. ''Do you think we'll ever go out there? I mean, in a spaceship or something?'' She turned her head, and when she gazed at him he saw an excitement and wonder unique to children and those few adults who kept the dreams of youth beating in their breasts. ''I've always dreamed that someday I'd fly to the stars,'' she said in a gush.

''Me too,'' he confessed, thinking again how her face was transformed when she gave up the frown and smiled. Behind the bright blue there was a keen intelligence, and he chided himself for falling into the trap of thinking the boy would be interested in his telescope rather than the girl. Then he recalled that it was Maddie, not Tom, who liked bugs.

''There are galaxies just waiting for folks like us to discover them,'' he told her.

Her smile stretched from ear to ear at being included in the ''us,'' and she arched up on her toes in excitement and whispered in his ear a big secret. ''I want to be an astronaut when I grow up.''

''Good for you!''

She nodded, her pointed chin stuck at a jaunty angle. ''Can I look some more, Jack? Please?''

''Sure, kid, all you want. Here,'' he added, moving his chair to give her more space. ''You look, and I'll point out some neat stuff.''

Jack enjoyed himself immensely teaching his favorite constellations to such a rapt pupil. Maddie was quick to learn the names and asked a thousand questions, firing one after the other in staccato. When he was careful not to look directly at the bushes, he spied Tom peeking out from time to time. After a while, the boy got bored enough to step out and wander around the garden, poking bushes and the dirt with his stick, always with his ear cocked toward their discussion. By the end of an hour, Tom worked up the courage to stand an arm's length from the telescope, but no closer. Jack was careful not to direct any questions his way or establish eye contact.

"Maddie! Tom!" Faye's voice sang out and she poked her head out the kitchen window. "Oh," she said, spotting Jack. She lowered her lids while color bloomed in her cheeks. Jack could tell instantly from whom the children inherited their beguiling charm.

"Hello, Jack. It's very nice of you to share your telescope with the children," she said, making an effort to be neighborly. "I hope they haven't been bothering you. They've been a bit bored lately, I'm afraid."

"They're no bother at all. They're welcome to use my telescope anytime." He glanced at the Maddie and winked. "We're pals."

Faye's expression swept from wonder to open gratitude. When she smiled as she did now, he thought again how she resembled her daughter in the brightness of her eyes and the sweetness in her expression. He sensed in Faye the same loneliness that he'd sensed in Maddie. After all, it took one to know one.

"That welcome includes you, Faye." He didn't know what made him offer the invitation, but now that he did, he was glad.

"Oh . . . uh, thanks," she stammered, the color deepening on her cheeks. "But I haven't time to look at the stars, I'm afraid. Not that I didn't take your words to heart," she hurried to add. "But right now I'm under a deadline."

He didn't reply, but wondered at the longing he caught in her eye.

"But *we* can, can't we? Maybe tomorrow night?" Maddie asked, turning pleading eyes Jack's way. "Will you bring the telescope back out, Jack? Tomorrow night?"

"If the sky's clear, absolutely. Maybe Tom would like a look." Then with a quick grin toward the window, "And maybe your mom, too. It's play, remember?"

Faye returned a genuine smile this time. "Maybe."

Jack's chest expanded, victorious.

Maddie looked at her brother, then shrugged. "It's hard to tell with Tom, though. He has to like you first. Besides, he's much more interested in the lights."

"Lights? You mean satellites?"

"I dunno. I mean those funny little lights that we see."

"Children, come in. Now!" Faye called out with a bit more firmness before the window rattled shut.

"Well, gotta go," Maddie said, pushing the bangs from her eyes. "See you later. Sure hope it doesn't rain. Come on, Tom," she said, wrapping her arm around her brother's shoulders and escorting him inside. "Maybe tomorrow night we'll catch one of those lights."

"Catch them?" asked Jack, confused now. "You mean fireflies?"

"No," Maddie called over her shoulder as she went in the door. "I mean the little lights that fly down our hall."

Jack sprang to his feet with a thousand questions of his own ready to burst from his lips, but the door had already closed behind them.

Later that same night, when the Andromeda Galaxy was shining in the northern hemisphere and the Large and

Small Magellanic Clouds were visible in the southern hemisphere, Jack stood at the kitchen window watching one lone boy standing alone in the garden, staring up not at the heavenly wonders, but again at Crazy Wendy's third-floor window. He watched as Tom walked over to the fountain, then bent over to pick up something that he found on the ground beside it. It appeared to be a book. Holding the treasure close to his breast, he scurried back inside.

Something about the boy, perhaps his intensity, perhaps his loneliness, or perhaps his stubborn curiosity, tugged at Jack's heartstrings. Maddie, he thought with chagrin, might have a thousand questions to ask.

But Tom had only one.

Detective Farnesworthy rocked on his heels, his hat in his hand. "I didn't find much, I'm afraid, sir."

Jack felt a searing flash of disappointment and slumped against the sofa's cushions. Damn, he liked answers to his questions.

Farnesworthy shifted his weight, seemingly uncomfortable with this admission. "Of course, there wasn't much to go on . . ."

"Well, what *did* you find?"

The detective cleared his throat as he set down his hat and pulled out a pad of paper. Sitting on a free chair, he flipped through his copious notes. "I've traced your adoption to an orphanage called the London Home for Boys. Your adoptive parents, Mr. and Mrs. Warner Graham, adopted you from that institution in 1970, then brought you to America."

"When I was eight. I know that much. What about my

biological parents? Didn't you find out anything about them at all?''

"Well, sir"—he scratched behind his ear and scrunched his face as though in pain—"you seem to have come from nowhere. There's no record of your birth.''

"There *has* to be.''

The detective sniffed. "There *should* be. The London Home for Boys was rather short in organization, but I gather long in good care.''

Jack scowled. "That's it? Not a shred of genetic background?''

"There was absolutely no record of your birth or your biological parents. Nothing at all. Except for this." He pulled out a yellowed copy of a medical record. "This dates back to the routine physical you received when you entered the home. It—" He paused. "It states that you had a spiral fracture and numerous contusions when you arrived.''

Jack closed his eyes and the old, familiar image of a fist pounding into his face flashed in his mind. "May I see that please?'' Taking hold of the medical record, he read it carefully. "Those injuries," Jack said softly. "They indicate child abuse.''

"Quite right, sir," replied the detective, looking away while his fingers drummed his report.

"Interesting," he muttered. He felt like he'd just been hit again.

Farnesworthy cleared his throat. "I, well, I found something else interesting as well." He leaned forward in his seat. "Not finding much to go on with you, I sniffed around the London Home for Boys for anything at all that might lead to you.''

Jack raised his eyes to meet Farnesworthy's with a

spark of interest. That was smart, he thought. Very good. Just the kind of thing he'd have done in a laboratory if one lead didn't pan out. "So, what'd you turn up?"

"Well, sir." The Inspector moved forward in his seat. "The Boys Home was founded by a Mrs. Theodore Forrester." He wriggled his brows, pausing for dramatic effect.

Jack cocked his head, considering a moment.

"Wendy Forrester?" the detective continued, with emphasis. "Your current landlady . . ."

Jack slumped down from the sofa's arm into the worn cushions and ran his hand through his curls, stunned.

Farnesworthy leaned back against the chair with a satisfied nod.

The London Home for Boys—his Boy's Home—had been founded by Crazy Wendy? After the initial shock, Jack felt a stirring of possibilities. A telltale excitement coursed through his veins, causing his lips to twitch upward.

"Are you sure?"

"Oh yes. Quite. Her husband, Theodore, Teddy he was called, was a squadron leader in World War II. Died leaving her a daughter, Jane Forrester Lloyd, and a considerable estate. Mrs. Forrester used a significant portion of it to establish a home for boys. Presumably war orphans at first. She was extraordinarily generous and over the years very active in soliciting support to keep the place going. Charity balls, donations, that sort of thing. Her name was in the social papers regularly. Even so, for many years Mrs. Forrester was virtually the sole support. I daresay it cost her the fortune." He cast an assessing gaze around the flat. "This was once a posh neighborhood. Pity."

Jack snorted. He didn't think it was a pity. What meaning had poshness or social standing? A life of dedication and service like Crazy Wendy's was to be admired. Yet, perhaps he better understood now the animosity between mother and daughter. A fortune spent by parents too often brought the ire of their idle children.

"Who takes care of the boys' home now?"

"Oh, it doesn't exist anymore. Couldn't keep up. When it finally closed its doors, Mrs. Forrester just sort of disappeared. Hasn't been seen in society for many years."

"No," Jack replied, glancing briefly upward. "She's a recluse."

"According to the newspapers, Mrs. Forrester was once what you Americans like to call a mover and a shaker. All for her boys. Got to respect that, eh what? Don't see enough of that nowadays."

"No, we don't," agreed Jack with a distant air. His mind was galaxies away.

"Well, sir," Farnesworthy said at length, stuffing his papers into his briefcase and rising. "Sorry I couldn't be of more assistance to you. The records, such as they were, unfortunately were not well preserved after the Boys' Home closed. I've exhausted all my leads. Other than the medical record and a date of your arrival at the Boys' Home, there was nothing else I could scrape up on you. Do you want me to discontinue the search?"

"Not at all," Jack replied, sliding with athletic grace to his feet. "We're on to something. I can feel it. Tell you what," he said, slipping his arm around Farnesworthy's stiff shoulders.

Jack had a hunch about Crazy Wendy. The same kind of hunch he often played out in the laboratory. It was a

combination of instinct, acquired knowledge, and luck—
and it usually paid off.

"Keep sniffing around Wendy Forrester. Find out all
you can about her and report back to me. And don't leave
out any details that might seem, well . . ." He thought of
shadows and dancing balls of light. "That might seem
frivolous or even bizarre. There are rumors . . . I want to
hear them all."

"Of course, sir." Farnesworthy looked at his hat with
a worried frown while smoothing its rim between his fingers. "However," he added with deference, looking up,
"I feel bound to tell you, I already know about the rumors. Impossible, incredible stories. Her claims are, to be
sure . . ."

"Yes, Farnesworthy?"

He whistled. "Well, sir," he stammered, "they're plain
unconventional."

Jack's eyes danced under raised brows. "Unconventional?" He was amused by the detective's obvious discomfort at calling a decent old woman crazy.

"Frankly, sir, I don't recommend wasting time on this
impossible lead. Not to mention," he coughed politely,
"the expense."

Jack smiled broadly. He liked Ian Farnesworthy. He
was honest and forthright. And Farnesworthy didn't know
it, but he had just spurred Jack's resolve. The more incredible, unproved and so-called unscientific the theory,
the more he felt compelled to prove it. It was no mere
coincidence that he and Wendy Forrester landed in the
same space and time. There was a quantum connection,
and he was determined to find it. As for the cost, he had
plenty of money from the sale of his family's farm after
the death of his adoptive parents. It was just sitting in

some banks, bonds, and investments, increasing in value. What good was it anyway if he couldn't spend it on what he wanted?

"Bear with me, Mr. Farnesworthy," he said, shaking his hand and handing him his coat. "I'm a scientist, and we're a bunch of curious souls. Keep on it, and let me worry about the expense."

After dispatching Farnesworthy to his duties, Jack paced a tred in the carpet, lost in thought. He didn't know his biological parents; nor did he have any memory of them. Yet it was painful all the same to think that they, that someone, had beaten him as a child. Jack slowly walked into the garden, slumped into a chair, and sat with his chin in his palm for a very long time.

Sometime later, after the stars came out and the crickets began their serenade, a light came on in the O'Neill flat. He looked up and saw the silhouette of a small, delicate woman on the lowered window shade. The shadow sat down, then picked up a brush from a table out of his view and began to brush her hair in smooth, rhythmic strokes.

Faye. A small smile played on his lips as he remembered how those same hands gently stroked Tom's head and how he'd ached with the yearning to feel her long, slender fingers tenderly stroking his own head. In the few weeks that he'd known her, watched her with her children, he'd come to realize that though Faye O'Neill was wary and guarded on the outside, inside she was a warm-hearted, gentle woman.

Jack sighed and pinched the bridge of his nose with his fingers. He'd never known the gentleness of a mother's caress. Anne Graham, his adoptive mother, was a kind woman, meticulous and thorough in her care. Growing up, a morning never passed without a plate full of sausages and potatoes laid out on the table before him, bangers and mash, his mother called them. His clothes were clean and ironed, his homework corrected, his birthdays marked by a cake and a practical gift, usually a book and new clothes. She was a good mother, but she wasn't affectionate in a tactile way.

Jack had never burrowed his face in his mother's belly the way he saw Tom hug Faye. His mother never scooped him up in her arms to plant juicy, wet kisses over his face the way Faye embraced her children. He never felt that he was the center of her universe, and there was no doubt that Maddie and Tom were Faye's moon and stars.

Jack leaned back in the hard, cool, iron chair, crossed his arms, and lowered his chin into his palm, never for a moment taking his eyes off Faye O'Neill's marvelous hands as she brushed her hair. With each stroke, Jack imagined that he could feel her hands in his own hair. He almost winced with longing. He watched, transfixed, until Faye finished her task, laid her brush down, then reached out and turned off the light.

Jack sat in a deep, somber darkness, alone except for a boy of bronze for company. Peter Pan. Another orphan, like himself, he thought ruefully. Always on the outside of the window, looking in on what he could never possess.

While he sat he thought again of Farnesworthy's medical report and wondered again why it was that when he was a very young boy he could not remember the sweet touch of hands tenderly stroking his head. Instead, hands had beaten him. Was he so bad a kid? What could he have done to deserve such punishment?

In the following few weeks, whenever Jack turned around, the two O'Neill children were there beside him.

When he put his feet up at night in the garden, Maddie would suddenly appear, slink into a chair beside the telescope, and begin asking a zillion questions while Tom wandered within earshot. Eventually even Tom sidled up to peer through the lens. Hearing the kids coo with wonder at the majesty of a star or a distant planet thrilled Jack more than any response he drew from his brilliant graduate students when he lectured on mind-twisting concepts. Working in the garden on weekends and stargazing at night became their kind of play, and in time the three of them became real friends.

It was his other new friend, their mother Faye O'Neill, who remained an enigma. He chided himself that he had no time for involvements now. His experiments were coming to an end, and he would be leaving by September. Yet he couldn't deny a strong attraction for her—though he didn't know why. There was something about Faye O'Neill that made him a little nervous. Like a teenager with a crush on the pretty girl next door. At first he'd written it off as a simple matter of proximity. He saw her most every day so, like Henry Higgins, he was growing accustomed to her face.

It was, after all, such a nice face.

The only conclusion he arrived at was an old scientific law by Coulomb: *Like charges repel each other; unlike charges attract.* He couldn't think of anyone more unlike himself than Faye O'Neill. Or anyone he found more drawn to.

Chapter 7

FAYE KNEW SOMETHING was up. Maddie and Tom had been whispering heatedly and hustling back and forth from their rooms to the garden ever since she'd returned home from work that evening.

"Don't look!" they shouted as they passed through the kitchen with their secret treasures.

"I won't," she called back while chopping carrots and celery into small pieces for dinner and hoping that in her fatigue she wouldn't nip off a finger in the process. It had been a long, high-pressure week, and she had a long weekend's worth of work in her briefcase. A squeal of giggles erupted from the garden. Faye smiled. What were they up to?

Three knocks sounded on the back door. Drying her hands on a towel, she hurried to open it, expecting to see a child's face. She was close. It was Jack Graham wearing a boyish, conspiratorial grin on his face.

"I've come to invite you out to the garden for an enchanting evening of drinks and firefly catching."

She heard a giggle and looked over his shoulder into the garden. It was a warm night, and the garden was inviting. Maddie and Tom's red, yellow, and blue flowers were a profusion of color.

"Jack, that's sweet but I'm far too busy making dinner, and right after I get the sweeties to bed I have tons of work on my ad campaign. Thanks anyway."

He was amused by her superior tone that implied behind the smile that *some people* had more important things to do with their time than to drink gin and tonics and watch the fireflies come out. And he loved that cute little manner of hers when she put her hands on her slim hips and arched her brow over those baby blue eyes.

Jack felt he knew better about what was important. So after regrouping, he sent in his secret weapon.

Tom took his mission to heart. The boy marched straight-backed into the kitchen, all serious in the face, tugged at his mother's skirt, and whispered fervently into her lowered ear, "Please, Mom, come out to the garden with us."

To Faye, it was a gold-engraved invitation no mother could refuse. When Tom made a rare request, she followed through. Faye set down her pot, forgot all about dinner, and followed Tom to the garden, where Jack and Maddie were waiting. Jack's knowing grin did not escape her.

The table was set with freshly cut flowers that Maddie proudly announced she'd arranged all by herself. Beside them was the sweeter, brightly colored paper place mats and cards that her children had painstakingly made, fashioning the names in childish script. Her heart blossomed.

She let out a gasp when she noticed that the table and chairs had been freshly painted and searched out Jack's gaze to transmit her appreciation.

"Ah, look who's finally come out to try this thing

called relaxation,'' he said, grinning smugly as he leaned far back in his chair.

''I guess some people just have a gift for relaxation,'' she quipped, her eyes dancing.

''Some of us are lucky enough to be born with it. But don't despair, Mrs. O'Neill. I believe it can be learned.''

''And you plan to teach me?''

''Absolutely. I'm a teacher—it's what I do. And Maddie and Tom have agreed to be my assistants, haven't you kids?''

Two small heads nodded.

''The first thing you have to do is sit down.''

Maddie took her mother's hand and led her to a chair. Faye laughed and surrendered to the game. Tom came to her side and leaned against her. She absently stroked the fine hairs from his brow, and for an instant, Jack could almost feel those delicate fingers stroking his own hair.

''Lesson one,'' Jack said, clearing his throat and swooping his legs down from where they were perched on a chair. ''A gin and tonic, expertly mixed. Add a little ice, some freshly cut lime, and here you go.'' He handed her a glass. ''Call it a refresher course.''

''Thank you, teacher. Don't mind if I do.'' Faye took the icy glass from his hand thinking that with his collar unbuttoned, his striped tie looped around his shoulder and his white shirttail hanging out, Dr. Jack Graham looked more like a boy excused from school than a professor of physics. She found it rather endearing, especially when his wild curls sprang at awkward angles from his head like coiled bedsprings gone awry, as they did now. The mother in her made her want to lick her palm and tamp them down.

''Now for lesson two,'' he pressed on. ''Kick off your

shoes. Go ahead, I won't care if you've got a hole in your stocking.''

''I do *not*.''

''Prove it.''

Maddie giggled as Faye shook her head in disbelief. But she removed her shoes.

''Good. Next, you kids. Socks, too,'' he ordered, tugging off his own. ''Shoes and socks are instruments of torture if you ask me.''

Maddie and Tom instantly scrambled to remove their own shoes and socks, giggling as they wriggled their toes.

Faye's heart felt light seeing her kids act silly once again. She felt a sudden loosening of her heartstrings and an inclination to be a bit nicer to the irrepressible man who made her kids laugh.

After they finished their drinks and crackers and the children their lemonades, and after several under the table kicks from Maddie, Jack rose. In the manner of a master of ceremonies, he delivered the prepared announcement.

''As you know, Faye, the children have worked very, very, hard to create this lovely garden that we're enjoying tonight.''

Maddie sat straighter, and Tom nodded, tightening his grip on his mother in excitement.

''I do know,'' she replied with enthusiasm. ''And a fine garden it is, too.''

''And Jack worked, too,'' chimed in Maddie. ''He worked just as hard on the fountain!''

Faye's gaze met Jack's, and her smile lingered.

''So tonight,'' Jack continued feeling a flush of satisfaction, ''we have the pleasure of welcoming you to the 'Official Turning On of the Fountain' ceremony.''

Faye clapped her hands, more caught up in the animation of her children as they hurried to slip into costume than in the prospect of a mechanical success. They trotted and gamboled like spring lambs. When the stage was set, and the children stood ready, Faye stilled her hands in her lap, more excited than she thought she'd be.

Tom stood up solemnly and began walking toward the fountain.

"No, not yet," whispered Maddie loudly. Tom frowned, embarrassed, and hurried back to his position.

Maddie stepped forward with great flourish wearing a lacy shawl, her mother's lipstick, and a flower tucked behind one ear. When she reached the fountain she stood with her heels together and her shoulders straight.

"Tonight I'm going to read from the book, *Peter Pan*, in honor of the fountain because Jack fixed it and because we think Peter's the one who left the book here for us to find." She dropped her pose and added quickly as an aside, "Or maybe the fairies. I mean, the book was just lying there and it's all about *him* you know," she said, indicating the bronze boy to her mother.

Faye's expression was doubtful.

Maddie raised the book in her hands, cleared her throat and with the look of utmost seriousness, she read Sir James Barrie's words clearly.

" *You see, Wendy, when the first baby laughed for the first time, its laugh broke into a thousand pieces, and they all went skipping about, and that was the beginning of fairies.*"

Tedious talk this, but being a stay-at-home she liked it.

"*And so,*" he went on good naturedly, "*there ought to be one fairy for every boy and girl.*"

"Ought to be? Isn't there?"

"No. You see children know such a lot now, they soon don't believe in fairies, and every time a child says, 'I don't believe in fairies,' there is a fairy somewhere that falls down dead."

Maddie finished her reading and closed the book with the solemnity of a convert. Faye shifted uncomfortably in her seat and shot off an arch look at Jack. He shrugged his shoulders and lifted his palms innocently.

"Thank you, Maddie," he said, clapping his hands. "And now, ladies and gentlemen, the moment we've been waiting for." He turned and nodded with meaning at Tom. The boy's cheeks were rosy, and he wore a look of fervent intent under his paper hat. He marched over to the fountain, reached out, and flicked the switch. Then he ran back beside his mother, eyes round.

They all leaned forward in anticipation.

The seconds ticked by in agonizing slowness.

A cricket creaked.

A bird called, *peent, peent, peent,* overhead.

The wind rustled the leaves.

The old fountain sat quiet and still.

Maddie looked forlornly at Jack. He hurried forward, scratched his head, then gave the fountain a hard kick. Suddenly, the night's peace was rent with a high screeching and grinding noise that took them all a few steps back. This was followed by a slow, seeping hiss which culminated with a tremendous belch and sputter. The children gasped, then held their breaths.

A loud metal clank sounded. Then abruptly, silence. Not one drop of water was squeezed from the pipes.

The collective sigh of disappointment was audible.

"Well, kids," Jack said with a sorry shake of his head. "It's back to the drawing board, as they say in the trade."

This was met with a great deal more heavy sighing and moaning.

"Hey, failure is part of the job. We just have to keep on trying. No point in getting down in the dumps."

"I'll go in and finish dinner," Faye said, rising from her chair.

He clasped his hand firmly on her shoulder. "Faye, let me buy you dinner."

"No, that's not necessary. I can perfectly well go in and . . ."

"Faye," he said, interrupting her. His gaze was steady, and in his voice she heard an undercurrent of iron that his assistants in the lab would have instantly recognized. "You've worked hard this week. The children are disappointed. Why not let me offer you all something special? Something a little fun? Tell you what. I'll order us some fish and chips from the corner. It'll be a real party."

Faye blinked, registering the offer to make her life a little easier. That someone would even try flustered her. She didn't know how to respond. Beside her, Maddie was hopping on the balls of her feet and clapping her hands, silently mouthing, "please, please, please." Tom stood erect and wide-eyed with appeal. How excited they were over a little carryout dinner. And how sad that it took a stranger to point out that even something small and seemingly inconsequential could be a party.

"That would be lovely," she replied, relinquishing her rigid control, at least for an evening. "Thank you."

He tilted his head to study her, then lifted his lips to a genuine smile, and said, "My pleasure, Mrs. O'Neill."

"Faye," she replied with a shy smile which he promptly returned.

A short while later the children were sitting in front of the TV munching fish and chips. Faye and Jack remained outdoors, eating their dinner at the wrought-iron table. They were both aware of being alone with each other in the moonlight, and they were both making efforts to pretend they weren't.

"It's a shame about the fountain," Faye remarked. Then, wagging a chip in his direction, she added, "But that's what you get for making the children feel like murderers if they don't believe in fairies. Shame on you."

"Hey, that wasn't me!" he replied, his chocolate-colored eyes as innocent as a babe's. "Blame it all on James Barrie. Besides, you don't fool me. I'll bet you're a closet clapper."

"A what?" she said with a light laugh.

"You know, one of those folks who lift their noses and claim they don't believe in anything, but whenever they're told a fairy is dying they look over their shoulders to make sure no one is looking, then clap their hands to save the sprite—just in case. Yes, I can tell you're a first-class closet clapper."

"Just how much have you been drinking, anyhow?" she asked, lifting her own glass to her lips to chill the burn of being pegged.

Jack reached out and poured himself another drink. Under his rolled-up sleeves, she noticed his arms were trim and tanned and covered with soft brown hairs. She took another long swallow of the cool drink.

"Not enough," he replied with a frown. "That fountain is driving me crazy. There's no reason that I can figure out why that stubborn contraption didn't work tonight. I'll be damned if I'll let a bit of metal and rust get the best of me. This was just a temporary setback. I made those kids a promise. You'll see water come out of that fountain or . . .''

"Or what?'' Faye's eyes teased. "Seems to me you have a habit of making grand pronouncements. I seem to remember you claiming, what was it? Oh yes, you could prove the existence of Peter Pan.''

"Oh yeah, that. . . .'' He scratched his jaw and cast a wary glance over at the fountain. "I think what I really meant was that I could prove the existence of an alternate reality.''

"Sure, sure. Wheedling out already.''

"Oh really?'' he said, grinning, staring her down. "So you're pretty sure that I can't prove the existence of Peter Pan?''

"Don't take it personally . . .''

"Well, okay then. We'll just wait and see.'' He leaned back and propped his bare feet up on a nearby chair.

She couldn't help but notice he had attractive, narrow feet with curved arches, long toes, and smooth, tanned ankles. Her own toes curled.

"And come to think of it, what do I collect when I do prove it?''

"Don't you think you're carrying this a bit far?''

"Not at all. Things considered a lot more crazy than this have been proven. Take Copernicus, for example, claiming that the earth revolved around the sun. Nuts! Or Gandhi, that fasting and prayer could change the course of government. Insane! Seems to me you're just afraid I'll win.''

Faye smirked, feeling like a gambler holding a pair of aces. "Okay, Dr. Know-It-All. You're on. But if you can't prove the existence of Peter Pan, then you have to admit, to my children, that there are no such things as Peter Pan, Santa Claus—or fairy tales."

"And if you lose, you have to admit to your children that you believe."

Faye felt a shudder and sat ramrod straight in her chair. "No, I won't do that. I can't. I do not believe in fairy tales."

"Who's talking about fairy tales?" He leaned across the table and tapped her hand gently. "Faye," he said in a lower, sincere tone that drew her in, "I'm talking about believing in what can only be imagined. About things like infinity, about alternate realities. About reaching the stars."

"Stars," she said with a heartfelt sigh. "I don't know much about them. I guess you could say I've been pretty grounded most of my life."

Jack leaned back and lifted his eyes to the sky. "Ah, Faye, I've studied stars all my life, and I don't know the first thing about them either. I'm agog at the flood of knowledge pouring in from the Hubble Space Telescope and the Keck Telescope in Hawaii. I can only sit and wonder and speculate in awe. That's why I say we can't limit our thinking to traditional lines of thought and theory. It's time to loosen up, time for a little nontraditional thinking. Look out there, Faye," he said, extending his hand in a wide arc.

She looked at him instead, seeing the brilliance of his intelligence lurking behind long, curled lashes, and a sense of wonder that shone more bright, more enticingly than any constellation.

"The universe is a vast, interrelated system that is revealing new life and new laws," he continued, speaking earnestly. "Though admittedly I can't explain with certainty how it all works or how it all began. We just can't take it all in. There's so much to learn and to understand." He turned his eyes from the stars to meet hers, and they sparkled with enthusiasm. "Don't you see, Faye? Anything is possible!"

For one moment in time, she felt that she could believe him, believe anything at all. Faye found herself leaning forward, getting sucked into his theoretical world. It was entirely too seductive. It made her nervous to think that her own well-constructed world could be shaken at such fundamental levels. She wanted—*needed*—immutable facts and order in her life. Schedules and routines. Low-risk ventures. Expected results. Absolutism.

"You make it all sound so charming. So utterly beguiling," she replied, looking away from the light in his eyes. "Frankly, I believe it's just childish whimsy. Anything is possible . . . Just listen to a baby laugh and think of fairies . . . Really."

"Is that so bad?"

She nodded. "Yes. When reality hits you over the head like a sledgehammer. Then the only stars you see are from being knocked down and out."

He sobered, and asked, "Did that happen to you, Faye?"

She rebuffed him with a wave of her hand. "Tell me someone it hasn't happened to. Listen, let's change the subject, all right? I'll agree that if you can prove the existence of Peter Pan, I'll admit that I believe in all that stuff." She snorted with satisfaction. "I'd say that was a pretty safe bet."

"I would, too. And so would Wendy."

"Very funny. Speaking of whom . . ." Faye moved her

chair closer, and said in a low voice, "I never see her. Are you sure she's all right up there?"

Jack leaned closer and with mock gravity, eyed the third-floor window. "Do you think she's watching us now?"

Faye glanced quickly up at the window. It was empty. When she turned to face Jack he was leaning back in his chair, his eyes dancing and his mouth smirking. Faye flushed with embarrassment. "Well, she might have been," she muttered.

"She was. Earlier. Wendy was watching the show tonight from her window. You didn't see her?"

"No! Darn, I always miss her. Maddie and Tom have seen her several times. They're fascinated with her. Especially Tom. He knows he's under strict orders not to bother her, so naturally, every time I see him he's got his eye glued to her window. At bedtime, he leans out of the bedroom window to check if her window is open."

"And is it?"

"Of course."

While they chuckled at the predictability of a child's curiosity, Jack poured Faye another gin and tonic, then refreshed his own. Faye watched him leisurely stretch across the table while he served. His long, lanky body had a natural grace that was self-assured. If she wasn't careful, she'd find him too attractive for a friendly neighbor.

"How's the sitter situation coming along?" he asked.

She puffed out her cheeks and exhaled a long, weary sigh. "That brings us right back down to earth. It's been hellish, I can tell you. I spent my first week here interviewing candidates sent over from an agency. The 'dream nannies,' I like to call them. Sweet-smelling, plump, middle-aged women who look like Mrs. Doubtfire and speak like Mary Poppins. Unfortunately, they all wanted much more money than I could afford to pay. I'm sure they were worth it—and can get it—just not from me.''

She took a long sip from her drink. ''My job was about to begin, and I had no one. Trust me, this isn't the kind of job where I can ask for a week's extension for baby-sitter problems. As far as my boss is concerned, children only exist as a sales motivation. So as a last resort, I hired an eighteen-year-old local girl, referred to me by the friendly chemist down the block.''

''She must have been the one with the tattoos,'' Jack wryly observed.

''I figured she had one for every year of her life. As luck would have it, Maddie was fascinated . . . Especially with the nose ring. Then there was Angela. A graduate of the Thud School of Baby-sitting. I came home one night to find Maddie serving *her* cookies while she watched television.''

''And where was Tom?''

''Under the bed.''

She waved away another refill, even though she was enjoying the light feeling in her head and the tingling in her toes. It had been a long time since she'd felt her spine soften.

''So I ended up asking Mrs. Lloyd, of all people, and she recommended Mrs. Jerkins. Her mother's visiting nurse. It seems this way she can do double duty. Mrs. Jerkins is happy because at fiftysome years, she earns more with less wear and tear. Mrs. Lloyd has someone in house for her mother without spending more.''

''And that makes Mrs. Lloyd happy.''

''Correct. And I have someone competent. The kids

aren't fond of her, but they tolerate her. It's a compromise, like most things.''

Jack tilted his chair back on its rear legs and skewed his mouth. It was on the tip of Faye's tongue to reprimand him and tell him not to tilt. Maybe it was the gin, but she didn't feel at the moment like being Jack's mother. . . .

''So,'' Jack drawled, circling his thumbs, ''how does Tom like Ol' Horseface?'' He smiled when he saw Faye's surprised expression. ''That's her nickname, you know.''

''Why am I not surprised that you know her nickname? And no, I didn't know. I have to admit Mrs. Jerkins is a nag of an old woman, but damn. Now I'll never be able to look at her without thinking, Ol' Horseface. Jack, please don't tell the children. I don't like them using . . .''

''I didn't. They told me.''

''Oh.''

He shrugged and rolled his tongue in his cheek. ''I'll discourage it of course.''

''Of course you will.'' She shook her head, then took a long sip from her drink. He was irascible, yet she detected in him an open honesty that inspired trust. So unlike her ex-husband who could chat, make jokes, and backslap readily, yet never made a woman feel comfortable.

''Faye, I don't mean to pry, and you can shut me up if you want to,'' Jack said, drawing himself into an upright position. His face grew more serious, and his gaze deepened.

''What's the story with Tom?'' he asked quietly. ''I've spent a lot of time with him, but he never utters a word. Not a sound. I know it's not just me. He doesn't speak to anybody. I only ask because I care about him. I don't want to expect him to be able to do something that he can't.''

Faye pursed her lips and swirled the ice in her glass as the mood for banter fell flat. The evening air suddenly felt degrees warmer, too close. The buzzing of the cicadas pressed, and she felt the familiar pressure of her guilt weigh heavily down on her, making it difficult to breathe.

"If you'd rather not talk about it."

"No," she said with a sigh. "It seems only fair, considering how much time you're spending with the Maddie and Tom."

She shifted her weight and stared down into her drink. The sound of ice cubes clinking in her glass triggered the memory of other nights, horrible nights when Rob had had too much to drink. Those nights their suburban home was a war zone, and she was the main target. She didn't want the children frightened or to feel threatened by Rob and told them to stay in their rooms. But of course they heard. One night, Tom came running into the room, his face red with fury, his fist bunched. She'd called out for Tom to stay away, to go back to his room. But he ran to her defense.

Faye swallowed and closed her eyes, seeing again the man's fist connect to the child's head, wishing she could go back in time and stop it, change it. Instead she was cursed to relive it. It was very, very hard to speak of it.

"Tom's father hit him. Once, very hard."

She glanced furtively up at Jack's face to gauge his reaction. Jack's lips had tightened into a grim line, and there was no disguising the fury in his eyes.

"Rob meant to hit me. I know that. The next thing I knew, Tom was lying on the floor. I took him to the hospital."

"It's neurological?"

She shook her head. "No. The doctors said he suffered no neurological or brain damage. But he never spoke in public again. The child psychiatrist calls it elective mutism. Apparently, Tom chooses not to speak. He can, but won't. Except to Maddie—and sometimes to me. I used to think he was punishing me, you know, for letting it happen." She paused. "Hitting me was one thing, but hitting my child . . . That was my line in the sand. I threw Rob out, filed for divorce, and never looked back."

"I don't think Tom is punishing you. He adores you. It's obvious."

She shrugged. "He depends on me. He's so shy, so afraid. The doctors say he needs a tincture of time. And to feel safe and secure."

"So do you."

Surprised, she looked into his eyes and wondered if he really understood after all. No one had ever thought that she, too, might need a shoulder to lean on. She took a deep, shuddering breath and looked into Jack's face.

"Yeah, so do I," she conceded. She took another deep breath, then sat back again in her chair, returning to the safety of distance. "But it doesn't matter about me. I have to focus solely on my kids."

"Is there any chance he'll come after them?"

"There's always a chance. He did once. I'm always on guard." Her crooked smile said she didn't want any pity. Nor did she want to go into more history. "No big deal. I'm just a single mom raising two children."

He admired her strength and determination, and wondered at the toll it took. She seemed so small and fragile to be so strong. Looks could be deceiving, he knew. Like the new metal composites he worked with in the lab. Thin, delicate woven strands strong enough to go to the moon and back.

"Will Tom get better?"

"You mean, will he talk in public again? I hope so. I'm counting on it." A small smile escaped. "I guess there is one thing I definitely have to believe in. If I could just find some way to get him to open up a little."

"We will."

She looked away, moved close to tears that he'd used the word "we." Not that she entertained romantic notions. Not at all. She felt buoyed simply because maybe she had a friend who cared in this big, scary world.

They sat in a companionable silence while the moon rose high in the sky, bathing the objects below with a soft, almost magical glow. The white flowers were especially luminescent in the twilight. This was their hour, she thought. When the bright, brassy colors of the day receded into the shadows and the luminous, contrasting whiteness reigned. Night insects, too, awakened to the moonlight. Moths buzzed noisily near the light of the windows, and crickets serenaded with the toads near the fountain. In the twilight, the garden did seem otherworldly. She felt her guard slip a little more and propped her feet on the opposite chair, leaning full back.

The moonlight cast a strange glow on the patina of the bronze fountain, too. Faye found herself staring at the boy's face. It was a nice face, sweet yet cocky—a boy destined to find adventures. Maybe it was the gin and tonic, maybe it was the summer's balmy breezes, but she cupped her chin in her hand and smiled affectionately back at the bronze boy, enamored. With a start, she could have sworn she saw the statue smile back.

"The fairies are out," Maddie exclaimed, running outdoors. "Look, Mom!" she cried, pointing to the tiny lights flitting through the garden.

"Those are fireflies, Maddie," she corrected. "Not fairies. See what you've started, Jack? The next thing you know she'll be saying the moon is made out of cheese."

"Swiss cheese." He laughed and waved Maddie over, smiling reassuringly at Faye, who sat in the moonlight looking as delicate and lovely as a fairy. A fairy who didn't believe in fairy tales. "Your mom's right, kiddo. These are fireflies. And do you know what they're doing?"

Maddie leaned against Jack and wrapped her thin arm around his shoulders. "Flying."

"Yes, but not just flying. They're flashing their lights in a dance of courtship. Each beetle has its own light organ that holds over five thousand cells. These are packed with minuscule granules of chemicals and a catalyst called luciferin. When the granules and luciferin meet oxygen, energy is transmitted and, presto! The courtship lamp is lit."

Faye's mouth opened in wonder to match her daughter's. She never knew that. "You really are a good teacher."

"But," Maddie persisted with a frown. "What about the fairies? They die if you don't believe in them. The book said so. You believe in them, don't you?"

Faye cast Jack a victorious glance.

He mouthed back at her, "Closet clapper," as he reeled Maddie up onto his lap.

"Sure I do," he replied to Maddie. "But that doesn't mean I can't accept that at least most of these lovely lights are due to an energy reaction in flying beetles. Look at them all, Maddie. Isn't nature magical, too? Not being fairies doesn't make the fireflies any less a wonder. By September, you'll see all the twinkling lights fluttering in the grass. That's because all the baby larvae live on the ground for two years and use their lamps to hunt snails and slugs, which helps your garden.''

"Wow," she breathed, transfixed.

Faye, too, felt caught in his spell and felt a quiet comfort watching him with her daughter.

"I can hardly wait to tell Tom." Maddie straightened and looked around the garden. When she turned to face Faye, her small face was troubled.

"Hey, where is Tom?"

Chapter 8

"WASN'T TOM WITH YOU?" Faye felt the old familiar fear clutch at her throat. Her heart began racing, and her eyes were popping out of their sockets.

"No," Maddie blurted out, appearing cornered in the iron chair. "I thought he was with you."

"Well, where is he?" Faye's voice was shrill.

"Take it easy," Jack said, standing up. "He can't be far. We haven't even looked around yet. He's probably hiding in the boxwood." He hurried to the hedge, feeling a tightness of apprehension in his chest, and crawled behind the dense shrubs, ignoring the scratches as he searched every nook and cranny. No one was hiding there. He climbed out to see Faye watching with wide eyes, gripping Maddie's shoulders. When he lifted his hands to indicate no one was there, Faye and Maddie turned on their heels and ran back into the flat. The panic in Faye's voice vibrated as she called out Tom's name, over and over, in room after room.

Jack made a quick but thorough search of the outbuilding, then followed them inside. Faye was walking back and forth across the living-room floor, her hand grasping her forehead, mumbling to herself, "What do I do now? He can't have come for them. Not yet. He couldn't have gotten in."

"Who?" he asked, closing the door behind him.

"Their father. He took them once before. That's why I left Chicago. I . . . I don't think he could be in England yet, but I'm not sure. Where could Tom be? He was right here, a moment ago. I never should have left him. I never should have gone outdoors."

"Slow down, Faye. He's around here somewhere. That rascal might be playing a game."

She stopped, and her pale face was rigid with decision. "No, not Tom. He doesn't play those kinds of games. I've got to call the police," she said, striding toward the phone and grabbing the receiver. Then lowering her head on her hand, she said in a panicked voice, "God, I don't want to call the police. Please God, don't let this be happening again."

"Faye," he said, placing a calm hand on her shoulder. He could feel her trembling beneath his palm. "Are you sure he's not under the bed?"

"Yes, I'm sure. How many places can a little boy hide?"

"Plenty. Maddie, you know his favorite hiding spots. Have you checked them all?"

The little girl nodded. She was white-faced with worry, no doubt blaming herself.

"I'm going to call the police . . ." Faye lifted the receiver. Maddie leaned against her for comfort, moaning softly. Faye only punched in the first digit when she stopped and stared just beyond Jack, her eyes agog and mouth open.

Standing in the doorway was a sweet-faced, delicately

boned, fragile old woman with white hair like spun glass piled on her head, and the brightest, merriest delft blue eyes Faye had ever seen. And holding her hand with a look of pure triumph on his face was Tom.

"Tootles wants me to read him a story," the old woman said in a voice that was high and melodic, like a song. "He was kind enough to return my book, you see."

Faye was dumbstruck. She stood with her hand holding the phone in midair, reconciling in her mind that this was undoubtedly Crazy Wendy, that the elfin old woman was calling her son Tootles, and that her quiet, shy son had actually gone upstairs on his own and told this stranger that he wanted her to read him a story.

"Wendy!" Jack exclaimed warmly, holding his arm out to usher her and the boy into the front room. "You found our runaway. I should've guessed a lost boy would go straight to you. Mrs. Wendy Forrester, meet Mrs. Faye O'Neill, the newest tenant of Number 14."

"Charmed, my dear," the old woman replied with a beguiling smile. "I've been looking forward to meeting you. I do so like meeting new people, don't you?"

Faye quickly replaced the receiver in its cradle and reached out to take Wendy's hand. Her bones were as delicate as a sparrow's and her eyes as animated. She had a curious expression on her face and a way of cocking her head to one side that made one wonder just what the old girl was conjuring up in her undoubtedly clever mind.

"Yes, it's a pleasure indeed," Faye replied haltingly. "And this is my daughter, Madeline."

Instead of slouching and firing off a monosyllabic reply, Maddie stepped forward and shook the hand warmly, her eyes aglow with excitement. Faye might have been proud except Maddie exclaimed, "So you're the one who left the Peter Pan book! You must be Crazy Wendy!''

Faye sputtered out some apology, but there was no need. Wendy wasn't the least bit offended. She laughed brightly and hugged Maddie close.

"Yes, that's me. But I'm not the least bit crazy, my dear. It's sad how some people refer to what they don't believe in as crazy. We shan't let little trivialities like that cloud our way, shall we, child? Of course not. I can see right off that we will all be friends. Great, good friends.''

Faye found herself nodding in agreement.

"Very good then. Well . . .'' Wendy looked at the question in the children's faces. "Sorry to say, I think it might be a bit late tonight for stories. There's a full moon, and one never knows what will happen on the eve of a full moon. Full alert! Tomorrow is Saturday. Why not come up for tea? Everyone! We'll have a wonderful visit. Just between friends.''

She blithely turned to Tom for a reply. "How does that sound to you, Tootles? All right then?''

Tom didn't budge or reply but remained holding her hand, smiling up into Wendy's face with a look that could only be described as adoration. Still, Wendy seemed to have her answer. Her pale, wrinkled face softened as it caught the light of her beguiling smile. She reached out to stroke the soft, downy blond hair from Tom's brow, and cupping his chin in her palm, stared deep into his eyes.

"Oh, yes. You are a special boy. You remind me of another boy I know. He is brave like you, too. And loves nothing more than a new adventure. Oh, I have a great deal of wonderful stories to tell you and the very best games.'' Looking up, she included Maddie in her smile. "You, too, my dear girl. Come up to the nursery at four promptly! Two things one must never serve cold: tea and a good story. Ta for now!''

She turned and slipped through the door, climbing up the flights of stairs with a pace and agility that didn't seem normal for a woman of her advanced years. Then again, thought Faye, watching her at the foot of the stairs with chagrin, nothing at all was normal about Crazy Wendy.

Faye delayed as long as she could. She ironed Maddie's yellow sundress so that there wasn't a wrinkle and endured her daughter's bottom-wriggling and fussing while she braided her pale hair into a tidy French braid.

''Almost done,'' she crooned.

Maddie wriggled and leaped from her chair to frown into the mirror. ''I hate it,'' she said, pulling out the elastic in quick, hasty strokes. Now the elastic was knotted in her hair and her teary cries of anger were a spray of bullets.

Faye took a deep breath and walked to her daughter, briskly whisking away her hands. ''It looked very nice. I don't know why you choose to look so plain.''

''What about you?'' Maddie fired back. ''How come you always look so plain?''

Faye saw the sting of hurt in Maddie's eyes and bit back her retort. Instead, she gently tugged the elastic free, then smoothed out the tangled clump of hair with soft strokes of her palm. While doing so, she took a quick glance down at her conservative tan-linen skirt and her prim, white-cotton blouse closed tight around the neck with her grandmother's brooch.

''Perhaps,'' she said, her voice conciliatory, ''you and I are alike. We prefer to keep our creativity on the inside.''

The fire in Maddie's eyes dimmed, and she visibly softened.

Faye cupped her daughter's face and saw in the gawky features the swan that would someday emerge. "You look beautiful. Now go check on Tom, okay?"

Tom stood at the ready by the door, a silent sentinel with a clutch of posies in his hand. He'd been standing there since four o'clock, sighing heavily.

"She said to be prompt, *Mother*," called Maddie. "Wendy doesn't want to serve the tea cold."

"I hardly think that five minutes will put the tea into the deep freeze. And besides, she's quite old, perhaps she's a bit behind schedule." Faye didn't really believe that. She imagined that Wendy had had the table set for hours. Or she'd forgotten about it completely. Who knew with a woman so old?

Faye didn't want to go upstairs at all. She'd been beguiled yesterday, but today she'd come to her senses. She had no time for such frivolities. This morning she'd been late getting back from the market, there was laundry piling up, and she had hours' more work before she made her presentation on the Hampton Tea account on Monday morning. Not to mention, Mrs. Lloyd had specifically warned them not to bother her mother. But the children so wanted to go . . .

The front doorbell sounded, followed by a scuffling of children's feet.

"Jack!" she heard Maddie exclaim. "You're coming, too!"

Oh great, thought Faye as she hurried to slip earrings in place.

"Of course I'm coming," Jack replied. "Couldn't

abandon my old pal Tom here to an afternoon surrounded by ladies.''

Faye peeked down the hall just as Jack patted the boy on his shoulder. Her stomach clutched tight as Tom predictably took a step back, glowering. Jack instantly caught on and tucked his hand back into his pocket. Tom never tolerated being patted, stroked, or hit in any fashion whatsoever. Faye knew it would take time for Tom to trust a man again. Maddie, however, ran right up to Jack and wrapped her thin arms around his waist. Faye sighed, knowing her daughter was head over heels for him already.

Faye stepped into the hall, offering her hand with the detached deportment of old Lady Ashford herself. ''You're joining us for tea?''

''I wouldn't have missed it for the world. Mrs. Forrester was a grand socialite in the old days. I'm sure she knows how to throw a good old-fashioned tea party. I've even dressed for the occasion. Dress whites.''

Faye's gaze swept over his linen suit, crisp, snowy shirt, and red-striped tie. There was something about a man in a white shirt and tie that pushed all of her buttons.

''My, my, my, Dr. Graham. You could pass for a proper English gentleman.''

''Anything for the ladies,'' he replied.

That Jack would endure the discomfort of starch and collars on a Saturday for an old woman—and a young girl—alike touched Faye in her heart where she hadn't felt a twinge in years.

''You look quite dapper,'' she said with an edge of teasing in her voice.

''There's that word again. It's a good thing I'm a gentleman,'' he said with mock severity. Then with his gaze sweeping over her, he added slowly, "Again, let me return the compliment."

"Mom thinks she's plain," chirped Maddie, eyeing with suspicion the interaction between the two adults. Faye looked down at her daughter's narrowed eyes, and if she didn't know better, she'd swear the little girl was jealous.

"Plain is hardly the word I'd use to describe your mother." He looked at Faye's tiny, slim body wrapped tight in buttons all the way up her long, slim throat and all he could think of right now was how he wanted to undo every one of them.

"Shouldn't we head up?" Faye said, not trusting the appreciative look in Jack's eyes.

"Right," said Jack. "I remember something said about being prompt."

Maddie shot off an arch, "I tried to tell her."

"I'm a little worried that we should have put Mrs. Forrester through the trouble," Faye said in a soft voice behind her palm. "She's so old, and her daughter was quite clear that her mother was not to be disturbed."

"She also said Wendy didn't like children. You saw for yourself how off the mark that was. Come on, Faye. Stop stalling." When she moved a hesitant foot forward, he said reassuringly, "Wendy's a dear heart and not the least bit crazy. We'll all have a good time, your children will experience their first proper British teatime, and who knows? You might even get some ideas for that tea campaign you're working on."

"Well," she said, looking into her children's upturned faces, "then I guess we'd better hurry. We don't want a cold story now, do we?"

The relief on their faces was palpable. Tom's eyes widened, and he tore out the door and up the stairs like a cavalry soldier charging the top of the hill, ignoring Maddie's strident shouts for him to slow down. The great stairs thundered under their feet.

"Wait one minute," she said in a rush. "I just thought of something."

She ran upstairs to her bedroom and rifled through her drawers. She knew they were in there somewhere. Nylons and bras littered the floor, but there in the back of the drawer she found them. White kid gloves—just the thing! She tugged her fingers into the tight slits as she ran down the stairs.

Jack's eyes sparkled in appreciation of her gesture, and he gallantly offered Faye his arm. They were playacting a bit, she knew. He being the gentleman in his suit and tie and she the lady in her kid gloves on their way to formal tea.

"Shall we go?"

Although she felt flustered and stiff, unsure of the game's rules, she accepted his arm and allowed him to escort her up the grand staircase to the third floor.

Wendy's door was slightly ajar, and from within she heard the sudden high peal of laughter. Curious, Faye pushed open the door slowly.

Her breath caught in her throat as she stepped into a blur of soft blues, gauzy whites, and the faint tinkling of crystal. It was as though someone had changed the camera lens from sharp and clear to romantic and hazy. Faye moved away from the door, her head turning from left to right taking it all in, stepping lightly as though there was glass beneath her feet. This wasn't a collection of rooms at all. It was a charming, picturesque, sun-drenched aerie!

Her gaze was immediately drawn to an arched alcove

across the room. It was bordered with an intricate fairylike trellis and had a large, mullioned window that was flung open to the fresh air and the sweet garden below. Nestled beneath the window was a charming window seat with plump velvet cushions and tasseled pillows, littered with books. What a perfect place to cozy up for a read, or, Faye thought with a pang of sympathy, for a chat with the evening stars. Looking out the open window, she felt as though she'd shipped off and was floating somewhere high above the city, up where the air was thin and sweet and smelled of . . . She sniffed. What was that? Cinnamon! Yes, sitting on the table was a three-tiered platter of freshly baked pastries with melting icing.

"We've been expecting you, haven't we, children?" Wendy called out in that melodic voice of hers. "You look quite lovely, my dear. That is such a becoming brooch."

Faye flushed with pleasure, inordinately pleased. "Thank you, Mrs. Forrester."

"Oh, do call me Wendy. Mrs. Forrester always makes me feel so old. I don't feel old . . . And Jack," she said, waving him forward. "My, how handsome you look in your suit. So tall and grown-up." She sighed, almost sadly as she took his hands and contemplated the man.

"Well, do come in and make yourselves comfortable," Wendy exclaimed again, fluttering her little hands. Faye thought she looked all the more like a dainty sparrow, all brown dress and white hair and bright eyes.

Faye strolled through the large, airy room in a wide-eyed daze while the children played with a set of figurines on the carpet. There was so much that was charming and quaint that Faye couldn't take it all in. The antique furniture was beautiful but an odd grouping. Faye supposed that Wendy had selected these pieces from all the others when the house was converted without thought to period or style—they must have simply been her favorites. The chairs were all different, a collection of trumpet-shaped legs, tufted armrests, and tassels in amusing places. An immense overflowing bookcase filled one wall. Another was dominated by a scrolled, white-marble mantel topped by a fanciful hanging cabinet. The trestled, spindled concoction had a layered arrangement of open shelves and glass closets that were as amusing as they were functional. Faye brought her hand to her cheek, sighed with awe, and felt drawn to it.

She carefully examined the small porcelain figurines, similar to the ones in her own flat. Only these were not mere animals. She recognized Peter Rabbit in his blue coat, Puss 'N Boots standing cocksure in his signature boots and rakish hat. Rat, Mole, and Toad clustered together with fishing tackle, dainty Alice, clumsy Pooh, and of course in a place of honor stood Peter Pan fighting Captain Hook. An old black-silk top hat filled the left-corner shelf, and in the right sat a very old and very used teddy bear missing one eye. A lower shelf held a breathtakingly beautiful beaded tomahawk with a long tail of shredded leather straps. Stepping closer, she peered inside the center glass cabinet where the smallest treasures nestled. Faye held her breath, finding a small locket that shone in burnished gold, an etched silver box that held a spool of white thread and a single needle, and an empty square of bright blue velvet.

"I had his thimble resting there for the longest time," Wendy said wistfully at her shoulder.

Faye turned to look at the old woman quizzically.

"But the selfish boy took it back!" she snapped, eyebrows raised in exclamation.

Faye's mouth slipped open, but she couldn't think of a thing to say. She looked helplessly for Jack. She found him bending low, nose almost touching the wall, to peer closely at one of the painted figures on the wall. Faye gasped again. Such murals! Each wall swirled with a hand-painted depiction of some place or event from the adventures of Peter Pan.

"Who painted them?" she sputtered.

Wendy replied matter-of-factly. "I painted them myself. Not all at once," she scoffed. "Couldn't have done that. Oh no, it took me many years. Bit by bit as the whimsy struck me. I painted that one soon after I returned," she said, pointing to the mural across the room that showed an enormous tree and, beneath it, a rabbit's warren of rooms fit for young children.

Faye raised her brows. "Returned from . . ."

"The Neverland. Isn't that what we were talking about? And that one after my second trip," she continued, pointing to the mural of a lagoon swimming in blues and greens where an imposing pirate's ship was docked. Sunning themselves on clustered rocks nearby were several ruby-lipped, pastel-haired mermaids. "I did so love the mermaids. Aren't they the loveliest things?"

Faye rolled her eyes and turned to Jack again. Chin cupped in his hand, he was staring intently at the strange boy's figure. Maddie and Tom clustered near, studying the murals with shining eyes and flushed cheeks.

"Were there really mermaids?" Maddie asked, her voice doubtful.

"Ever so many," Wendy replied. "They were quite

saucy, however. Sad to say it took me the longest time to befriend them, and then only because . . .''

"I think we'll wait to hear about the mermaids," Faye interrupted, alarmed. What had she gotten herself into? She didn't like the gullible expression on Maddie's face, or the serious one on Wendy's. "Uh, Jack?" she called out. "What are you doing over there?"

He straightened and turned to them, his face troubled. "It's this mural. This boy."

"Which boy is that, dear?" Wendy asked, coming directly to his side. "There are so many."

It was true. When Faye looked closely at the murals she noted that hidden in small tree stumps or in leafy branches, floating in clouds, fighting duels with pirates and chasing Indians, were boys. The faces of countless, small boys of every description, peeked out from every nook and cranny.

"Who are they?" she asked.

"Those are my Lost Boys," she replied guilelessly. "There have been so many over the years that I like to paint their faces so I won't forget them. Dear, sweet boys, every one of them."

"Lost Boys? What do you mean, Lost Boys?" Jack asked.

"Why, the boys who came to me to find a home, of course."

"What is it, Jack?" Faye asked.

He looked into Wendy's pale blue eyes, so wise and knowing, and felt a shiver go through him. He was more convinced than ever that Wendy Forrester was the key to unlocking his past.

He felt his heart pound but forced his face to remain passive. Pointing to one gamin-faced boy with a cap of lush curls and large brown eyes peeking out from a tree stump he said, "I never noticed this boy before. Who is he?"

She frowned and shook her head. "Oh I don't remember all their names, dear. I can't say as I love one more than another. Except, perhaps for one . . ."

"I'd really like to know if you remember *this* boy," he said with urgency. "You see, I just found out that I was adopted from your boys' home, Wendy." He paused, watching her closely. "Small world, isn't it?"

"Indeed," she replied, bringing her finger to her cheek. "I've often thought that."

"I don't remember anything about my early years, or who my parents were. I was rather hoping you might remember. And help me. It means a great deal to me, Wendy. This boy," he said, pointing again to the mural. "I know this sounds impossible, but this particular boy looks just like I did at that age. It could be me."

Wendy looked at him, and a soft affection flitted across her face. "It could indeed." Then with a change of expression, she added, "What does it matter? Dear boy, we're all lost at some point in our lives, aren't we?" She paused to pat his cheek with her palm. "In the end, we must all find our own way."

"Wendy . . ."

"I'm sorry, Jack," she said with finality in her tone and shaking her head. "I can't help you. I wish I could."

The tall clock chimed, and a sudden breeze wafted through the room.

"Goodness, it's half past!" she exclaimed, clasping her hands together. "And I smell a summer storm moving in. Come along, let's shut the window and cozy up around the table. We'll see if a good cup of tea can't bring the sunshine back. The table is drawn and ready, and the water is at a mad boil.''

Jack took a final thoughtful look at the mural and traced the boy's face with his fingertip.

"I'm sorry, Jack. I had no idea," Faye whispered, moving close to him. "Don't be upset if she can't help you. She's not all together."

"I'm not so sure," he replied at length, eyes narrowing. "I think Wendy is as sharp as a tack."

"Come along, children!" Wendy called, waving them toward a small round table covered with snowy white linen and a gleaming silver tray filled with an elaborate teapot and serving vessels. Maddie and Tom were already seated on the quaint cushioned chairs, anticipation etched on their smiling faces.

"I don't have servants any longer, but Mrs. Jerkins was helpful in setting up," she said, pouring the aromatic black tea into a porcelain cup. "She doesn't have much style, poor dear, but she does try hard. She's rather like the tea she drinks, unsweetened and stringent. It's all in the preparation of course. I'll bet you like yours with lots of milk and sugar, eh what, children?"

"Yes, please," Maddie replied taking her cup, but her eyes looked longingly at the small side table overflowing with tiny trimmed sandwiches, flaky scones, jam tarts, and assorted creamed pastries.

Faye arched her brow in surprise at Maddie's good manners. Tom, as earlier, only had eyes for Wendy. He sat quietly in his seat looking up at Wendy with moon eyes while she popped several lumps of sugar into his cup. "Perhaps a bit more water for you, Tootles? Won't be so strong. I do like a dainty table, don't you, Faye?" she asked, pouring out.

"Uh, yes," she replied truthfully as she accepted the thin porcelain cup decorated with gold trim and tiny sprigs of lilac. "I . . . I do indeed like a dainty table." This was exactly the kind of tea setting that she'd told Bernard American women wouldn't want any part of. Yet here she was, thoroughly bedazzled by the entire fete.

"Sugar, one lump or two?"

Faye smiled slyly. "Love and scandal are the best sweeteners of tea."

Wendy stopped pouring and looked up astonished. "Henry Fielding. How clever of you, dear girl! I've always enjoyed that quote."

Faye bent her head and sipped her tea, thinking that Jack might very well be right. Wendy was definitely thinking clearly. Then how could she reconcile Wendy's obvious belief in the reality of Peter Pan?

Common sense told her this simply wasn't possible or normal or even sane, yet, there was something magical about the nursery that made time and problems meaningless. Outside the storm gathered force. Thunder rumbled in the distance and lightning heralded the oncoming rain. Yet inside it was warm and cheery; no one was afraid. She looked around the linen-draped table at the cozy group. Her little Tom, usually so afraid of thunder, chortled easily, slurping his tea with his fingers held wide over his cup. Jack was leaning back, laughing at something Maddie had told him, while Wendy looked on properly amused. Even the tea tasted pretty good.

They chatted about all sorts of things, mermaids and pirates to be sure, but mostly about the history of the house and all the funny incidents associated with the many years Wendy had lived in it. When a loud clap of thunder rudely interrupted their party, Wendy set down her cup and exclaimed, "Time for a story!"

"Hooray!" called out the children, scooting from the table.

Wendy dabbed at her mouth with her napkin. "I promised the children we'd begin the book today."

"And what book is that?" Faye asked.

"Why, *Peter Pan,* of course. I simply could not believe my ears when they told me they'd never read it. Imagine, missing out on such adventures."

"Imagine," Jack said, popping a candy mint into his mouth and raising his brows at Faye. She felt like sticking her tongue out at him but only glared.

"Are you sure it won't tire you out, Wendy?" She thought of Mrs. Lloyd and Mrs. Jerkins and how this afternoon's pleasure might be getting out of hand.

"I'm sure these darlings could never wear me out. Come, little man." Jack sat up, but Wendy reached for Tom's hand. "We shall begin the adventure today. Right this very minute. Well, perhaps after a quick wipe of the hands, eh? Teatime does make things sticky."

"Do you mind if I listen in, Wendy?" asked Jack. "I confess I've never read the original, and somehow I think I'd like to hear it read by you."

Wendy's eyes moistened, and she reached out to tamp down Jack's curls in what appeared to be a familiar gesture. "Of course, dear boy," she replied kindly. "It is never too late. His stories have nothing at all to do with age. They're for the young at heart. Come. You must sit in my best chair."

Faye stood by the table, hands tightly clenched, and watched them gather around Wendy as she settled in her plump, doily-laden wing chair. "The original title was *Peter and Wendy,*" she said, opening up a thick, green-

and-gold trimmed edition, the leather of which was dried and peeling at the bindings. Tom dragged a small tufted footstool beside her and leaned against her knee. Jack sat in the cushioned armchair with Maddie curled up like a cat on his lap. Faye could almost hear her purr. In the corner, the yellow canary ceased its incessant *chirp-chirping* and settled on its perch, one leg tucked in. All was ready.

Except for Faye. She stood alone, isolated and out of place. She was torn between wanting to cuddle up and listen to the story, too, and going back downstairs to dutifully begin the mountain of work that lay on her desk

Wendy took a breath and began to read. " *'All children, except one, grow up.'* "

Faye looked at her wristwatch anxiously.

Wendy stopped, looked up, and tilting her head, asked, "Faye, dear. Aren't you going to listen, too?"

With an act of disciplined will, Faye shook her head. "I can't, Wendy. I've much too much work to do. Can't wait. Thank you for a wonderful tea. It was a first, believe me. Maddie, bring your brother back down immediately after the reading. I'll be waiting for you. Now, please, don't let me disturb you. I'll just slip away."

Wendy nodded, but her eyes reflected not so much disappointment as sadness. It made Faye feel that Wendy somehow pitied her. It was ridiculous, of course. Maddie ignored her, but Tom eyed her with worry. Even Jack studied her with deep concern.

"I'll walk you down," he said.

"Don't be silly. It isn't necessary."

"Maybe not, but I want to." Turning to Wendy, he said, "Go on, I'll catch up with you later. Scoot up, princess," he said, lifting Maddie. "Keep the chair warm."

Wendy smiled approvingly and returned to her book.

"Really, Jack," Faye whispered, as they closed the door behind them. "I hardly think I'll be mugged going down a flight of stairs in our own house."

"I hardly think so either. Especially since I noticed you've added another padlock to the front entry. Maybe I just wanted to walk with you."

"As you wish."

Climbing down the grand staircase, Faye felt the lingering effects of the cozy tea and marveled at the craftsmanship and style of the old house. Pale gold-and-cream-striped wallpaper, faded but still elegant, and shiny brass wall sconces hinted at the sumptuous lifestyle this old house must have enjoyed during another era in England's rich history. Over tea Wendy had told them that she grew up in this house. She explained how she'd inherited the house from her father. He had claimed he was too old to want to fuss any longer with multiple rooms and flights of stairs, but Wendy believed he simply couldn't live in the house after her mother died.

Imagine, living an entire lifetime in one house, she thought. It was unheard of in these modern times of corporate moves, changing neighborhoods, globe-trotting, and folks retiring to warmer climates. But back then, the home was a person's world. Within these walls Wendy's history was forged, her special occasions were celebrated, her milestones were marked.

Faye imagined Wendy when she was Maddie's age, cheeks flushed and curls flying as she rushed up these very stairs with her long skirt and petticoat clutched in her tiny hands, late for afternoon tea in the nursery. Or when she was older, a young lady in her first evening gown, perhaps a bit of ankle showing, perhaps a wisp of feather in her hair, certainly her mother's pearls around her neck. She must have glided down the stairs with one hand daintily skimming the railing toward the young man who would escort her to the dance.

Wendy as a young mother would have carried her sleeping child up these stairs. The middle-aged mother would have stood at the foot of these stairs and watched, eyes glistening, as her only daughter, Jane, a vision of white lace and tulle, walked down the stairs for the last time as a Forrester on her way to becoming a Lloyd.

Happy days, and sad ones, too. Wendy would have dashed downstairs with Jane to find shelter during the bombings of World War II. Or paused, frozen with foreboding, at the foot of the stairs when a British military messenger entered with a telegram in his hand. "I'm sorry, Mrs. Forrester. Your husband . . ." Wendy would have slowly made her way up these stairs after closing the doors of the London Home for Boys for the last time, counting with each step the number of boys she'd placed in homes for nearly half a century.

A lifetime on these stairs.

"You're so quiet," Jack said.

"I was just thinking what these stairs have seen. What it must've been like living in one place for all those years. I never lived in one place for more than three or four years. I never had a nursery. My father was a troubleshooter for Sears and moved the family to a new city, a new state, every time he was needed. Our houses were nothing like this. They were all suburban modern. Now tell me if you can why it is that every rental house in the nation has ugly brown carpeting and off-white walls?" She shrugged lightly. "Not that it mattered; we never stayed in one place long enough to care."

"You did care. Obviously."

Faye felt a quick pang, remembering how she carefully packed her collection of Pez candy dispensers herself for each move. She wouldn't let anyone else do it for her. The little brightly colored Warner Brothers cartoon characters, the Santa, the Easter Bunny, all were part of her first "collection" and were her only constant from house to house.

"I can remember going home with friends from college and being amazed to see all their old stuff still crammed in their bedroom closets. Yearbooks of friends, some of whom still lived in the old neighborhood! Trophies of sports I never even played, sweaters, old dried-up corsages, and loads of pictures everywhere. I guess I was kind of jealous of all that. You know, security." She shrugged again. "Silly of course. A house isn't security."

"No, it isn't," he replied, leaning against the doorframe and studying her face.

"I'm sorry," she said, glancing up quickly. "Here I am moaning about not having a nursery, and you didn't even have a family. You were at Wendy's orphanage?"

"So it appears. I was adopted from there at age eight. Can't remember a damn thing before six. I did have a family though. My adopted parents took me to their farm in Nebraska, where I grew up. Lived in a small town until I was old enough to leave it, and when my folks died several years ago, I sold the farm and never went back. I never really fit in there, but I still remember waking up to the smell of my mother's cinnamon buns coming out of her old Viking oven, the lazy ripples on the pond as I fished on a hot summer day, and the sound of cows mooing as my father brought them in from the pasture. I don't think it's the house that makes the home, Faye. Whether it's large or small, fancy or poor, city or country. It's what goes on inside the house that creates the memories.''

"Sure . . ." she said with a tone of doubt. She cast a last lingering glance around the delicate bric-a-brac that bordered the entrance to the third-floor landing. She had never lived in a house with any charm of structure—or spirit. In her heart, Faye coveted that bric-a-brac.

"But I'll bet it'd be a lot easier to create those memories in a house like this."

"And *I'll* bet it was Wendy Forrester herself who made this a happy home."

Her lips tightened, and she stared him down. Why was he always so contrary? And it was especially annoying when he was right to boot.

"How sad then that once Wendy became old she was abandoned as senile and useless. Now this old place is more like a tomb than a treasure." She shook her head free of all her nonsensical wanderings. "No way I want that to happen to me. I say to heck with the nostalgia. That and a dollar will get you a cup of coffee. We've got to take care of ourselves."

He furrowed his brow as he watched how she straightened her slim, narrow shoulders, physically adjusting her body to match her marshaled thoughts. She was such a delicate creature, small-boned and fair. But she had the spunk of a terrier. The type that would grab hold of a bone and never let it go. Not even for long enough to listen to a story. He could tell by the longing in her lovely eyes that she'd wanted to. Eyes the color of a summer storm.

The wind rose up, rattling the windows. Faye's gaze sharpened, alert, as she swung her head around to check if the windows were closed and locked. Jack felt a sudden impulse to quiet her anxiety, to offer a shoulder to lean on. Releasing the molding, he dropped his arms, gathering her up in them.

Faye shrank back.

"Shhh, Faye," he said, lowering his head. "I won't hurt you."

He lowered his head and gently kissed her forehead.

She sighed and lowered her shoulders.

Near, he smelled the scent of roses in her hair, and something else he couldn't define. It was sweet, and sensual. It was intoxicating. His breath quickened.

He forced himself to withdraw slowly, feeling as he pulled back that he was fighting against a current of electrons flowing between them, magnetically charged.

She swayed slightly. For a moment they stared at each other, each tugging against the force that pulled them together, like two helpless kissing dolls that when placed in close proximity are drawn together by magnets.

Faye and Jack surrendered to the pull.

He lowered his lips to hers, heard her sudden intake of breath, felt her lips soften against his, smelled again the faint scent of roses in her hair. He meant to offer a gentle peck, just one small kiss of friendship. Yet the kiss sparked as suddenly and violently as the lightning outdoors, sending a hum singing through his veins. His senses were flash flooding, his desire was swirling, and his heart began pounding and rattling in his chest like thunder. It was happening to her, too, because he could feel her melt against him and heard the soft high whimper in her throat. He stepped closer and pressed his body against hers. She raised her willowy arms around his neck, holding tight as a leaf clinging to the quivering branch.

Outdoors the storm was picking up. Thunder rolled and

stirred the wind, slicking rain hard against the windows. Indoors, he felt the storm building between them. Suddenly thunder clapped violently overhead. The windows shook and the electric lights flickered. Faye jumped, jerking back from his embrace, her cheeks flushed and rosy. She brought her fingertips against them, as though to cool the flesh down. As they stared into each other's eyes, measuring the tense silence between them, he tried to gauge whether she was going to smile or slap him in the face. He hoped for the former, but felt he probably deserved the latter.

"That shouldn't have happened," she said softly.

"I know. But I couldn't help it." He raised his hand to loosen his tie and unbutton his shirt collar. Reaching for the molding over her head, he grinned his one-sided smile that carved a deep dimple all the way to his chin and offered as an excuse, "Lightning struck. It was spontaneous combustion."

"Jack," she said starchily, "I'm not interested in this kind of thing."

"What kind of thing?"

"A fling. It's just not my style." She cleared her throat. "This won't happen again."

"As if we can control it."

"Of course I can control it."

He shook his head. "You're fighting Mother Nature, Faye. Now, now, don't go off in a huff. Let me explain. You see, there's this phenomenon about electricity and magnetism." He leaned closer, catching again the scent of roses in her hair.

Faye closed her eyes, hit by the magnetism he'd just described.

"Both of which I believe are flowing between us at this

very moment,'' he said in a husky voice by her ear.

Her eyes snapped open, and she placed her palms on his chest and gently, firmly, pushed him away. "I don't know what you're talking about."

"I'm talking about natural forces, Faye." He brushed a tendril from her face. When she responded by slapping his hand from her face, he tucked it in his pocket with a sigh of resignation.

"I think," she said, turning around and unlocking her door, "that you should direct your natural forces elsewhere, Dr. Graham." The door opened and she slipped inside, careful to keep the door between them.

"Faye," Jack said, holding the door still. All teasing was gone from his eyes. "I didn't mean for that to happen. It just . . . did. I'm as much surprised by it as you are. I'm sorry if I offended you. But I'm not sorry that it happened. It truly was spontaneous combustion. It was nature at its finest. You're a wonderful kisser, Faye O'Neill. A natural. And I hope to have the chance to try it again sometime. But, I promise I'll ask your permission first." He released the door and stepped back. "I'll leave you alone now, neighbor. Good-bye."

Faye held her breath as she watched him turn and climb the stairs back up to the nursery, his long legs taking the steps two at a time. He soon turned the corner, disappearing from view. After closing the door she slumped against it, blowing out a long stream of air, adrift in confusion. She hadn't felt the wham of a kiss like that since high school. Did she ever feel it so strongly with Rob? She didn't think so.

Spontaneous combustion, he'd called it. Oh God, it was accurate. She'd felt an explosion inside of her the moment his lips touched hers. Faye brought up her fingertips and grazed the tender, swollen skin, closing her eyes. Her insides rocked, and her blood ran like lava once more. Aftershocks.

What was the matter with her? It had been several years since she'd been with a man. Could she be sex-deprived? Man-hungry? Just plain horny? There were plenty of expressions, some very crude, that she'd heard to describe this heat she felt glowing throughout her body. She'd never before felt what she felt kissing Jack. That kiss was magical. It was. . . .

"No, no, you don't," she scolded herself, pushing away from the door. She was not going to indulge in romantic dreaming about that kiss. If she did that, she'd lose perspective and start looking for him every time she crossed the threshold of No. 14. Being horny was a good enough excuse for what had happened out there in the hall. It covered a lot of ground. She had to concentrate on her children, on her job.

Her job. The thought was like a splash of icy cold water. She had the presentation to Susan Perkins and her team on Monday. Nothing like a cold jolt of fear and anxiety to squash the sex drive. Faye neatly compartmentalized her thoughts about Jack into a little box labeled "horny" and stored it into the far nether regions of her mind.

"Focus," she told herself over and over again as she gathered her materials onto her desk in her bedroom, turned on the green banker's light, sharpened two pencils, laid out a clean pad of lined paper. "Focus," she told herself after she caught a faint whiff of Jack's aftershave on her skin. "Focus," she groaned when she rested her head in the crook of her arm and felt rocked by a low Richter-scale tremor all over again.

Hours later she yawned noisily and rubbed the back of her neck, exhausted. The children were asleep in their beds. They'd crawled in dutifully. Not, however, before relentless pleas to return to Wendy's nursery on the following afternoon for another installment of the story. Maddie refused to call Wendy's place a flat or an apartment or anything other than the nursery because that was what Wendy herself called the third-floor aerie. Faye couldn't debate that it seemed rather ridiculous to call a grown woman's home a nursery, because in fact the name seemed to fit.

Faye looked at the Queen Anne desk clock and sighed. The small round face revealed that it was almost midnight. She didn't think she could get anything more done on her presentation. Her ducks, as Bernard liked to say, were in a row. Now if she could just get a good night's sleep. Weary, Faye stood up from her long labors and crossed the room to her window, pushing back the thin slip of Scottish lace to peer out at the street below. Yellow halos of light from the streetlamps pierced the light fog. A breeze was shuffling the leaves of the trees lining the dim, deserted street. She bent to open the window, just a crack, to allow some of the moist night air into her room. Perhaps it would help her relax and drift off to sleep.

The refreshing cool night air smelled sweet, and she lay again in her bed and closed her eyes to try to sleep. The breeze was balmy against her skin, and her thoughts slowly dissipated, becoming as thin and wispy as the clouds outside. Before dozing off she heard, somewhere in the distance, the high, haunting song of a flute. A sweet reedy tune, playful and yet insistent, that seemed to call to her in that hazy, foggy place between wakefulness and dreams. As she fell asleep, the tightly wrapped box in her mind that held all of her memories of Jack's kiss tumbled from the shelf and spilled open into her dreams.

Chapter 9

IT WAS TEN o'clock on a bright, sunny morning but from the bored looks on the faces of her creative team, one would think it was quitting time on a rainy afternoon. Faye was standing in the small conference room of Leo Burnett, having just summed up her proposal for the Hampton Tea campaign. Exhaling a plume of breath and casting a sweeping, questioning glance around the conference room, Faye didn't spot a single spark among her colleagues. Her heart sank to her shoes.

Her team slouched back in their seats and looked at her, then at each other, with blank expressions on their faces. Pascal from the Art Department shifted his weight and slung his arm with a French, sexy insolence over the sleek chair's back. Patrick and Harry, the copywriters, sat side by side in their linen trousers and button-down shirts, both tapping their twin clipboards on their laps.

George from Production was a walrus of a man who appeared years older than the thirty-five he owned up to. He began stroking his thick handlebar mustache, feeding the tips into his mouth in a gesture of futility. She knew laconic George wouldn't say much in the group setting, but he always had a storehouse of pithy comments to share in private. The only other woman on the team, Jaishree, a beautiful, Indian media whiz in her twenties, offered no hint of sisterly support. She crossed her endlessly long, slim legs and returned a glazed gaze.

So much for her team, Faye thought with resignation, folding her hands tightly on the table. As for her bosses, Bernard Robbins dominated the other end of the table with his glaring eyes, his dark, Savile Row suit and slicked-back hair. No one disputed that this man carried the whip, yet he remained unusually silent, deferring to Susan's position as account supervisor. Letting her handle her own bailiwick, as he put it. His thick dark eyebrows, however, formed over his nose like storm clouds darkening the peak of a mountain. Bernard's only outward response to Faye's presentation was to signal abruptly for the maid to serve tea.

In her mid-forties, Susan was a seasoned veteran of ad campaigns in England. She liked to claim that the few lines on her face were battle scars. She'd made it clear to Faye that she resented the fact that Bernard went over her own recommendation of a young Englishman from Oxford and selected an unknown American for account executive. That Faye was pretty—and younger—as well only fueled her bitterness.

"Tea isn't a new product," Susan began in her clipped British accent. She raised her pale eyes under heavy tortoiseshell glasses, twisting her lips into a smirk. "Not even in America."

Mild chuckles rippled through the room. Other than herself and Bernard, everyone on the team was either English or foreign. Faye girded herself, knowing full well that this would be the first of a barrage of arguments after her presentation.

"Americans know what tea is, of course," Faye replied in calm defense, "but they tend to think of it as upscale. Something to be had once in a while. Or perhaps when one is sick. Tea is something you might want. Coffee is something you need."

"Amen to that," muttered Pascal. A Frenchman, he made no attempt to disguise his disgust for tea. The one bond he and Faye shared was their occasional midmorning run to a coffee shop in the lobby.

Susan tapped her pencil irritably against her palm and tilted her head to check Bernard's response.

"Okay, keep going," Susan said.

"We should stick with my idea and present Americans with a new slant. One that supports the good health foundation of this campaign. Tea—something you drink when you're healthy. To stay healthy."

"So is milk," said Patrick dryly.

Harry rolled his eyes.

Faye straightened her shoulders and plowed on. "Tea is *natural,* too."

"Now there's an idea whose time has come—and passed," groaned Patrick. "Everything in the store is natural these days.

"Natural is dead," added Harry.

Bernard gave her a piercing glance, watching her response like a hawk.

Faye rallied. "Research says . . ."

"No, no, no," groaned Patrick, shaking his head. "Spare me. No more research. I don't want to hear what research says. And neither do the consumers. We want some emotion going here. Feelings. A bunch of statistics are going to bore the public, not to mention me.''

"He's right," piped in Jaishree. She was born in India, raised in England, but her love for film and TV was strictly LA. "Toss the health bit. It's so . . . well, dull. Tea is fun. It simply tastes good. Picture this," she said, uncrossing her legs and bending over the table with enthusiasm. "A vignette commercial, kids having all sorts of fun. Energy, energy. Ice tea comes out. Sweetened. We give a sound bite. Message: Kids like it, too.''

"You're going in the opposite direction of the point of the campaign!" Faye replied, trying hard not to slam her palm against her head. "Sugar? Kids like it for the sugar? Now tell me the health connection there, please."

"That's the point," said Patrick with a sneer. "There *isn't* one. Excuse me for having to point it out, but Jaishree's going for emotion. That's motion, with an e. As in— that's what we've got to get this campaign in."

Bernard looked at her questioningly, expecting her to come up with the snappy retort. To snap the whip. Patrick was the aggressor here; he was pawing at the air, snapping his teeth and growling. He needed to be put down properly.

But she couldn't. She'd lost her edge. "I . . ." Faye cleared her throat and licked her lips. "I think we can get some motion into this campaign. That's motion without the emotion. Let the facts carry it along."

"Just the facts, ma'am," quipped Jaishree to the response of chuckles.

Faye kept her chin up. "Precisely. A factual-based, nononsense approach. Doctors, pharmacists. Women in conservative suits."

"Now there's an idea the suits will like." Patrick rolled his eyes with sarcasm, then, catching Susan's glare, he coughed, and amended, "The suits at Hampton Tea, that is."

"All joking aside," Susan said, "I believe the problem here is that this team wants a more, oh, what should I say, Bernard? Inspirational idea? Less concrete and more catchy?"

"Okay," Faye replied, conceding. Inwardly she cringed, afraid now even to look at Bernard, whose displeasure was obvious. "Perhaps we could find clever ways to incorporate a catchy slogan or symbol. But I stand firm that the fundamental thrust of the campaign should be the *research*."

"I've got to be honest," Jaishree said in her university accent, rolling her pencil between perfectly filed and polished nails. "I'm British. I've been drinking tea since I can remember. And this is the first time I've ever heard that it was good for me. Frankly, I don't give a flip. I like the way it tastes. To me, a cup of coffee is a fun thing to do once in a while, but for the everyday, give me my tea."

"Yeah, that's what we've got to appeal to," said Harry.

The banter exploded on the table. Looking around, she saw that the lions were on the loose. The whip was chewed up, swallowed, and spit out again. In only fifteen minutes she'd lost control. They were bouncing ideas off the walls and making jokes, most of them at her expense. They were going for an emotion-based campaign all the way. Faye shrank back in her seat, tucking her hands in her lap. When she looked up at Bernard he merely sat staring at her with a pinched expression.

Susan cleared her throat and brought the meeting back to order. "Faye," she began in a low, cool, highly controlled voice. "You've presented some good ideas, but you simply have not generated any life in the project. There are no breakthroughs here. Perhaps you haven't used your research as well as you could."

Faye felt her world crumble and struggled not to let her shoulders slump.

Bernard stood up abruptly and circled the room like a great winged hawk, his dark eyes missing nothing, his shadow far-reaching. At length he stopped and stood at the opposite end of the table from Faye with his hands behind his back.

"I've got confidence in her," he boomed.

Seven pairs of eyebrows rose.

Faye's breath caught in her throat. She could have wept.

"Maybe the pitch isn't right yet," he continued in his blustery manner, "but that's not her job alone. That's a team effort." Now everyone squirmed under his sharp gaze.

"Come on, Bernard," Susan said in a commiserating tone. "The odds of this pitch getting the client are next to nil."

"I say it's a go."

Silence. The team shifted in their chairs. Patrick speared Faye with an antagonistic glare that promised later repercussions.

"I know you all want emotion," Faye said, almost as an apology. "But I honestly think this idea will speak to the people who care about their health."

"Yes, well," said Susan sharply. She seemed irked by Bernard's grandstanding. "But that's not the point quite yet, is it? The first question is—will the Hampton Tea people care?"

Susan stood up and gathered her papers, seemingly

gathering her temper, too. "I don't need to remind you how big an account this is. Nor how much we want it." She paused. "How much *I* want it." She lifted her chin and shifted her gaze to focus on Bernard. There was a moment's impasse while the president and his supervisor came to terms. Then, Susan's face shifted to reflect submission.

"All right, I'll go along," Susan said. Her back was straight and her lips tight. "But I want you all to come together. Pascal, Jaishree, put in a media plan to give ideas of how it might play out. Patrick and Harry, you know what you have to do. It's Faye's concept, but I want you all to work long and hard until you've pounded out so many campaign slogans you've run dry. Then work some more. I want a winner." She leaned over the desk. "I want *magic*."

Then, without another word, she turned on her heel and left the conference room, with Bernard right behind her.

Faye sat swamped in the murky silence that followed. There were no backslaps of congratulations on her successful idea or rallying calls from her teammates for cooperation and some good old gung ho. Only Pascal met her moist eyes with a hint of sympathy buried in his own dark ones. So, she had one ally on the team, but for all she knew, it was because he wanted her body more than her ideas. As for the rest, they made no secret of their frustration and uptight anger. It was clear that she didn't fit in their team—much less lead them.

She cleared her throat, desperately wishing she could somehow bring the team together. "Why don't we meet again, here, say at two o'clock? We can talk about the client, their needs, and get some initial ideas." She smiled tremulously. "I'll bring the tea."

Jaishree raised her dark eyes, and they were as cold as iced tea. "Teatime in England is at four o'clock. I should have thought all your research would have taught you that much. Or will Bernard support you on that, too?"

Patrick leaned over and behind his palm said loudly enough for everyone to hear, "Whatever his protégé wants."

"You do know he's married, don't you?" Jaishree smiled, adding sugar to the ice.

Faye paled but refused to dignify the rude comment with a reply. She gathered her supplies and walked from the room with her head high. Inside, however, she felt like she'd been mauled. She was eager to be alone and lick her wounds. She'd only traveled a few steps down the hall when she stopped abruptly, halted by the sounds of Susan and Bernard around the corner, arguing hotly.

"Look, Bernard, I know she's special to you, but this is too big an account to risk."

"This has nothing to do with being special. She's good, damn good. And a hard worker. I've seen her knock heads with the best of them. She thinks fast, and I tell you, when she's on a roll, her ideas sing. They jump out at you and make you feel good all over."

"Really? Just how good all over does she make you feel? Rumor has it, old boy, that she's been working late most nights. With you."

"I don't like the insinuation."

"Nor do I."

"Christ, Susan. You think I've got something going on with my account exec?"

"It wouldn't be the first time. She's certainly pretty enough. Young enough. Devoted enough . . . to you."

"As she damned well better be," he shot back, ignoring the first time comment that had caught Faye by surprise. She'd never heard that about Bernard.

"You might take a few lessons from O'Neill," Bernard fired off. "*You* might call it devotion. *I* prefer to call it good old-fashioned loyalty."

"Spare me the American platitudes, Bernard. In there I defer to your authority, but privately, let me be frank. The idea doesn't grab me. It has potential, I'll give you that. I know factual campaigns can be successful, but it's not just the campaign idea I'm concerned about." She paused and Faye leaned forward to better hear Susan's lowered voice.

"When you told me you were bringing in some hot shot protégé from Chicago I didn't like it but I thought okay, we need a firecracker on this one. But Faye O'Neill? What's her problem? They ate her alive in there. We need a fighter when we present this campaign to Hampton. Not some reserved, sweet thing. And I swear, Bernard, if we lose the Hampton account, she's out. Protégé or not, problems or not, she's history." She paused, and when Susan spoke again, her voice was conciliatory, as though she realized that she'd gone too far.

"I'm concerned about you, too, Bernard. You've only been here a year. Your first responsibility here in London is to get new business into the agency. That's what you came here to do. Here's your best shot at it. Don't blow it. Or you could blow your job, too. You want to talk about loyalty? You just wait and see how loyal the head men in Chicago are to you if you lose this account."

Faye heard Susan's heels click down the long hall, followed by a heavy sigh from Bernard before he padded down the hall toward his own office.

Faye leaned against the wall and closed her eyes. Bernard's job on the line, too? What could be worse?

The answer came as a roar from the conference room behind her. Patrick was yelling at the top of his lungs, "What? That Yank wouldn't know a creative idea if it kicked her in the head!"

At six that night, after everyone else had left for the day, Faye softly rapped on Bernard's door. When she opened the door she saw he was on the phone again. He waved her in and impatiently indicated for her to take a seat. Outside his enormous picture windows the lights of the ancient city flickered through the fog like candles.

She walked across the mile of carpeting to perch on the end of a modern chrome-and-leather sofa, as uncomfortable as it was cold. After a tense three minutes counted by the seconds, Bernard hung up the phone and approached. He stood beside the sofa, cupping his chin in his palm and studying her as though she were the *Mona Lisa.* She offered him a crooked little half smile.

"Tough day?" he surprised her by asking. It wasn't like Bernard to be solicitous.

"The worst," she replied, tucking her hands along her thighs. "The two o'clock meeting went exactly as I'd expected. The team was unified all right—against me. They see me as your protégé."

"You are," he replied matter-of-factly. Then, frowning, he sat on the sofa beside her. Faye felt his closeness intensely, sensed the odd air between them and scooted a few inches farther down the sofa. She felt as though her entire body was shrinking inward so as not to graze his thigh or to breathe the same, warm air when she turned her head.

"Are you all right?" he asked.

Something in his voice had her inner alarms ringing. Susan Perkins's comment flashed in her mind. *It wouldn't be the first time.*

"Yes," she replied with a nervous giggle that made her want to slap her own face. She crossed her legs, noticed how much thigh was exposed, then quickly uncrossed them. She could feel Bernard's eyes on her, scorching a trail from her lips, down her neck to her breasts, to the bony kneecap that sneaked from under her skirt.

Then it happened. He placed his large, manicured hand squarely on her leg, blanketing her knee. Then he squeezed. It wasn't so much an action as a statement.

Faye stared at the hand in the awkward aftermath. *Why did you have to ruin it?* she thought to herself in agony. Then she thought of Maddie and Tom, and how she couldn't afford to lose this job. She thought of how she was thirty-five, unemployable, and how she had everything banking on this one job. On this one man. She slowly exhaled, catching the rhythm of her thoughts, and quietly took his hand to gently—firmly—move it back to his own knee.

"Please," she uttered softly.

Bernard jumped to his feet and exploded.

"Please?" he roared. "Please? You let me pull that act with you and all you say is, please? Damn it all, maybe Perkins was right. You've lost the fight. What the hell happened to you? A few years ago the Faye O'Neill I knew would have scratched my eyes out like a she-cat if I tried anything like that. Where is that girl now? That's the girl I need—the one I thought I hired!"

"I'm here Bernard. I . . . I just need some time. To acclimate."

"Look. I know it was tough in there. I despise suck-ups and quarrelsome people—and Patrick is both. I'd boot him out on his skinny ass except that he writes such damn good copy. I try to recruit the highest quality at all levels. To build the hottest staff. That's why I brought you in, Faye.'' He speared her with a dark look. ''No other reason.''

She exhaled, then closed her mouth tightly and nodded. ''Yes, sir.''

''Here it is, cards on the table. We've been invited to show Hampton what kind of advertising we would run if they gave us the account. You've got till the end of summer to come up with a solid campaign with a dozen hot, to-die-for slogans. That's going to take smarts, midnight oil, and something else. Instinct. The Faye O'Neill I once knew was up to that task. The question is, are you that same Faye O'Neill?''

She stood up, mouth open to reply.

''No, no, no,'' he bellowed, striding to the door and swinging it wide. ''Don't tell me. Go out there and show me!''

Chapter 10

SHOW ME. As Faye rode the tube home she felt numb and drained.

Faye got off at an earlier stop to pick up supper. Again, the night was foggy and moist. It was no wonder the English had so many inspired authors, she thought glumly. The weather positively bred introspection. She passed by numerous houses, ablaze in light and music, families clanking about in the kitchen. How lucky they were to be together, helping each other, laughing. Nobody seemed even aware of her as she passed them, a ghostly presence in the fog. She tucked her hands deep in her pockets and kept her eyes on her feet as they moved one after the other along the pavement.

Inside she was fighting off an inexplicable urge simply to turn left at the next corner, chuck it all, and run away. Run, run, run with her hands over her ears, screaming at the top of her lungs. Run away as fast as she could from all her responsibilities, from all the unfair expectations, from someone calling her name. Doing her job well wasn't good enough. She had to do a great job, a magnificent job. Nothing less would do. Perhaps most frightening of all was the certainty that when she arrived home there would be no one there with whom she could share her burden. No one to help pick up the slack. At home she had to be the mother, the caretaker, the supporting wall of her little family.

The moist air felt like an anvil lying on her chest, and she couldn't catch her breath. She hastened her pace, trying to outdistance the pressure, to put some space between her and that faceless, formless burden hounding her heels. The greasy brown bag of fish and chips banged at her thigh. It was now the children's favorite. A special treat for them. The thought of their smiles when she surprised them lightened her heart a bit and she reluctantly smiled too. *Smiling Energy.* A Taoist tenet. Dante put it another way: *Overcoming me with the light of a smile.*

As she approached No. 14, she met Jack walking from the other direction. They spotted each other at the same moment, and she knew by the almost imperceptible pause in his step that he felt the same awkwardness that she did. They had avoided each other since the kiss, each taking special pains not to bump into the other. Faye's heart began pounding anew, and she was furious at herself for feeling so flustered just at the sight of him. She could feel the flame of a blush on her cheeks and kept her eyes averted like a schoolgirl. It was as though the kiss had just happened all over again.

"We have to stop meeting like this," Jack said, striving for levity.

"I . . . I was just going in," Faye murmured, stepping back.

"And I was going out." He seemed equally ill at ease, eager to be off. "Dinner?" he asked, indicating the grease-spotted brown bag in her hands.

"What? Oh yes. I worked late and . . ." She stopped her babble and sheepishly raised the limp, crinkled bag. "Fish and chips."

"Maddie will be pleased." He rocked on his heels. His eyes questioned.

"Mmmm . . . yes . . ."

Small talk. Each word was agonizing. Her tongue felt like it had soaked up all the moisture in her mouth, had swelled double in size, and was lying like a bloated, beached whale on a sandy shore.

"The children are well?"

"Yes, fine. Thank you."

"I see. Good." He paused. "Are you all right?" he asked, bending low to peer at her face. His brows gathered in worry. "You look . . . tired."

Faye turned her head away, aware that he must've noticed her red eyes. "Oh, just a summer cold. I've been sniffing all day."

"Ahh . . ." he replied, nodding, though she didn't think he looked the least bit convinced. A couple passed them walking a small Cairn terrier. For some reason, Jack smiled at the little dog as though he were enjoying some private joke.

"Well, I best be going in," she said.

"Oh. Right. Good night then."

"Good night." She gave as good a wave as she could with a greasy bag in her hand, then turned and unlocked the front door and slipped inside the foyer. Closing the door behind her she slumped against it, exhaling deeply. She didn't think she could handle one more emotional roller coaster today. It must be the full moon. People always seemed to act strangely then. Still, it was too bad that the friendship they'd begun seemed ruined by that one regrettable, unforgettable kiss in the hallway. She really liked Jack. His openness and honesty. It might have been nice to talk to him tonight, free and easily, like they had Friday.

It was simply not meant to be, she thought, pushing herself away from the door. She'd always heard that it was impossible for a woman to have male friends. That in the end, the intellectual attraction always ended with a sexual encounter. Certainly she and Rob had never been friends. All they had between them was sex. It was the weak link of their marriage. Perhaps it was true, after all. Perhaps friendship and sex were mutually exclusive. Like oil and water, they simply did not mix.

She pushed open her front door, wanting nothing more from the world tonight but to hug her children, plop on a chair, kick off the new pumps that were causing a blister, and dive into a nice cool glass of chardonnay. What she found waiting for her was Mrs. Jerkins in a state of extreme agitation, sniffing and snorting like a horse at the starting gate. Faye sighed again, cursing the full moon overhead.

"It's already half past seven!" Mrs. Jerkins exclaimed, raising her nose and eyeing Faye dolefully.

To Faye's ears, it sounded like "hoppusseven." "Yes, I was delayed again. I'm awfully sorry, Mrs. Jerkins, I had the secretary call you. Didn't she reach you?"

"Yes, but no matter. It's still half past seven!"

"I'll try not to let it happen again. These have been extremely difficult days. I . . ."

"Well see that it doesn't because I won't be here past six o'clock from this night forward. I have my own life, don't you know. You can just go and make other arrangements for child care after I leave. For I'll leave promptly at the hour.''

"Mrs. Jerkins, that's impossible. I need more time to find someone!''

"That's not my worry now is it? No, I can't sit and discuss it now. I must be off. The coach will be coming. Oh yes, one last thing,'' she said, doing up the buttons of her sweater that strained at the task. "Mrs. Lloyd asked that you ring her. Says it's most urgent. Something about the children and her mother, old Mrs. Forrester.'' She sniffed again, a tad more loudly as though to say, "Now you're in for it.'' "I told her that I tried my best to keep them away. Especially that quiet one. He pops up there every time I turn my back. He thinks he fools me, but I know where he's off to, yes I do. Those little ones of yours, they can be sneaky you know.''

Faye felt her blood boil. "No, I don't know. Where are my children now?''

She rolled her eyes with feigned weariness. "Where else? It's like bees to honey, I says to Mrs. Lloyd.''

"I should think, Mrs. Jerkins,'' Faye said testily, "that if you were so concerned about Mrs. Forrester, you might have kept the children here. Where they belong.''

Mrs. Jerkins's chest swelled with indignation, and her face pinkened. "If you think that, then I say you don't know Mrs. Forrester very well!'' She gathered her purse in a huff, muttering as she passed outside, "But I'd put a stop to if I was you. Mrs. Lloyd doesn't like it none. Not one little bit!''

"Mrs. Forrester?'' Faye called, rapping at the door softly. "Wendy?''

She heard the shuffle of feet, and the door was opened by Maddie.

"Halloo," Maddie said in a sprightly voice and English accent that was remarkably like Wendy's. She stood taller, too, with her shoulders back, the model of deportment.

"Hi, sweetheart. Gather up your things. It's time to come home. I've brought dinner."

"We've already ate."

"What? Where?"

"Here. Wendy made us itty-bitty sandwiches. Cucumbers and cream cheese and tuna. They were ever so good. And so pretty. They looked like little hearts."

"Really?" Faye disguised her distress. It was no wonder Mrs. Lloyd was worried. The children were mooching meals as well. "Let me speak a moment to Wendy."

Maddie directed her to the window seat where Wendy was seated, tucked under an afghan, a tiny figure bent over a puzzle on the table beside her. The old woman looked up and her face brightened at the sight of Faye. She smiled serenely and removed her spectacles.

"Come in, my dear! You've come back early. What a pleasant surprise. We heard perhaps you'd work a bit late again tonight."

"I hope they haven't been too much trouble. I'm dreadfully sorry for the inconvenience. Mrs. Jerkins should never have . . ." Faye was discreetly peering around the nursery, searching for a sign of Tom.

"Nonsense, dear. I love having them. I have someone to play with."

"Uh, where's Tom?"

"Who dear?"

Faye's heart did a double beat. "Tom? My son?"

"Oh, you mean Tootles! He's here somewhere . . .

fighting off Captain Hook, I believe. Tootles!'' she called out.

A thunder of feet roared from the bedroom, and out ran a bare-chested, bony blond-haired boy wearing an over-size pirate's hat, a patch over one eye, and a dashing scarlet sash around his waist. He came charging forward, brandishing a wooden sword.

"Tom?" Faye asked incredulously.

The pirate lifted the rim of his hat, and shining out from under she saw two sparkling blue eyes, alive with merriment.

"You're a pirate!" She could scarce believe her eyes. Tom had never played dress-up before, much less with a stranger. And he was beaming. Faye's heart melted to butter. "A pirate . . ."

"The scourge of the Spanish Main, he is," Wendy said with a twinkle in her eye.

"Well, matey," Faye said all astonishment. "It's time to haul anchor and head home."

The pirate returned a black scowl, turned on his heel, and sped from the room back into the bedroom.

"Tom!"

"He wants to stay a bit longer, Mummy," explained Maddie sounding so grown-up and proper it sent Faye blinking, wondering if Maddie was in costume as well. "Just a bit. We want to finish building our pirate ship. It's a puzzle, you see, and we've been working at it for hours and hours. Please, pretty please?"

"But I've brought fish and chips."

Maddie licked her lips and looked at the greasy bag with longing but remained firm. "Please?"

"They're no trouble at all," Wendy added. "I hardly

know they're here. They've been working like beavers, the dears.''

"Please, Mom. We want to stay with Wendy."

They wanted to stay with Wendy. Not her. Wendy. Her heart sank to its lowest point. It just wasn't in her to fight with anyone else tonight. She'd no doubt get an earful from Mrs. Lloyd, but what was one more attack after so many?

"Very well," she replied soberly. "But just till eight o'clock. We can't keep Wendy up any later."

"Oh not to worry about that," Wendy chimed in, her face shining. "I'll be up for hours yet. The stars are just coming out. And it's a full moon."

"So I noticed," Faye muttered under her breath. To Maddie she said firmly, "Eight o'clock. Not a minute longer. Got that?"

"Okay, okay. Tom!" Maddie called out imperiously, running into the bedroom. "Mom said we could. You can come out now!"

"She's headstrong, that one is," Wendy said as much to herself as to Faye.

"A handful to be sure. I have to be firm with her."

"She rather reminds me of myself at that age." Looking up, she added, "Maddie tries to always do the right thing, so much so that she is afraid to make mistakes. And Tootles, he worries so about you. Every so often he glances out the window to check if you're coming up the street."

"He does? She is?" Faye felt she should have known this about her little ones rather than being the last to guess. "I try so hard to check on them, to keep close tabs."

"Sometimes the hand that rears a child can hold on too firmly. A gentle nudge encourages the child to fly and to make his or her own discoveries." Wendy's face softened with memory. "Such marvelous discoveries life holds for them . . ." Her gaze traveled out the open window, and for a moment she seemed lost in her own reverie.

Faye looked through the bedroom door at Maddie and Tom, laughing while dueling with swords. They seemed so carefree up in the nursery.

Wendy blinked brightly and drew herself back up. "You look tired, dear. Care for a cup of tea?"

"No, thank you," she replied, mulling over Wendy's words. "I'll just go eat these fish and chips. Are you sure you don't mind, Wendy?"

"Quite sure. Take all the time you want. It would be a shame if they couldn't finish the puzzle. It's always good to let them finish what they start. Gives them a sense of completion and pride that's so important at this tender age. I'll be right here, ears and eyes on the alert. So off you go." She reached over to pat Faye's hand and look deeply into her eyes with a maternal air. "Take a minute to lift your feet in the garden, why don't you? It's ever such a lovely night. The full moon is soft and soothing. You never know what magic might await you. I'll send your little ones down promptly at eight."

"All right then," Faye found herself replying. "Just till eight, though. And Wendy, thank you."

It wasn't until she was halfway down the stairs that Faye realized that Wendy, in her neat and tidy way, had just shuffled her out the door.

The garden, flooded in the light of the full moon, seemed otherworldly. Faye slumped into the coolness of the iron chair, lifted her feet, opened the bag, and began her dinner. When she bit down, the fish tasted cold and

greasy, mush in her mouth. She stuffed the tasteless mor-
sel back into the bag and laid her head on her hands. What
she was really hungry for was something fish and chips
couldn't fill. Her heart cried out for someone to help her.

Please. Someone show me the way out.

Then she heard the music. It was the same, sweet mel-
ody that she'd heard Saturday night from her bedroom. A
flute, or perhaps a reed pipe, and it was coming from
somewhere quite near. It made her feel cozy and safe, like
seeing a light shining from an open window on a dark
night, or coming home from a long journey to find a quart
of milk and a loaf of bread put into your fridge by a
friendly neighbor.

Faye's head darted up, following the sound, but she
could see no one in the shadowed darkness. Only the
bronze boy of the fountain caught the moonlight, he with
that perpetual mischievous grin that both teased her and
promised her escape, if she would only dare. Again, Faye
had the sensation that he was smiling directly at her. As
she stared into the boy's face, the strange, evocative mel-
ody enveloped her. Moved, she reached out toward him,
then, realizing what she was doing, stopped herself
abruptly and dropped her hand.

"Stop looking at me like that, boy," she said aloud,
speaking more to herself. "I can't just pick up and run
away. I'm not a child. I have adult responsibilities. People
who count on me. So just play your music elsewhere."

Suddenly the music stopped. Faye gasped and quickly
looked around the garden, an eerie feeling creeping along
her spine. All was quiet and still. The wind shifted, the
clouds moved, and the brass boy was cloaked in darkness.

I must be losing my mind, she thought to herself. *Or*

someone is playing tricks on me. She heard a faint scuffling noise.

"Who's there?" she called out.

No one answered. The night was as still as death.

"Someone is there! Come out!" Her voice was strident, demanding.

"Hold on there," came a voice from the darkness.

Her hand grabbed the chair as she stumbled back a step.

"It's just me. Jack."

"Jack?" She released a chestful of pent-up air. "What games are you playing now?"

"Games?" He stepped from the darkness. In the moonlight his expression was open and unguarded. "I was in my kitchen, and I heard you call out. I thought something was wrong and came out to check. Is everything okay?"

"You weren't playing music? A flute or something?"

His brows rose with the corners of his mouth. "A flute? Me?"

Faye flushed furiously, embarrassed beyond belief. "I heard some music, and I thought . . . Well, never mind what I thought."

"It's a still night and the music probably came from a neighbor's open window."

"Yes, yes of course. That's the explanation. I guess I'm just feeling a little jumpy."

He frowned and tucked his fingertips into his pockets. "Not because of me, I hope."

"No," she answered quickly. Then, thinking again of another night, "Well, maybe yes. A little."

"I'm sorry about that." He paused. "We've been avoiding each other."

She looked up, relieved to see him looking straight at her once again. "Perhaps we have."

His brows furrowed, and he nodded, accepting her acknowledgment as enough said. Then, turning, he began to walk around the garden, creating a natural transition away from the awkward topic. She was grateful. Often it was easier to leave things unsaid. A kind of truce settled between them.

She breathed easier and sat back down on the iron chair, watching him covertly. Here and there he'd bend over to pick up a fallen twig. A bottle of beer dangled from his long fingertips as he strolled. He was barefoot, of course, and moved with the grace of an athlete. Jack was one of those men who looked sexier dressed in faded jeans and a worn out T-shirt, a good, Midwestern boy with a corn-fed smile that could set a girl at ease and make her blood sizzle all at the same time.

Yet, he was also as full of contrasts as the shadows he walked in. Beneath his sunny exterior, she sensed a dark sorrow and an emptiness as vast and mysterious as the outer space he studied.

"They've been doing a great job," he said. "You should be proud of your children."

She flushed with pleasure. "I am."

"Where are those two wild ones, anyway? I'm surprised that they're not out here with you."

"They are up in the nursery. With Wendy."

Jack broke into a wide grin. "Really? Why that's great. They must be having a ball."

"They are. But Mrs. Lloyd is going to have a fit. No doubt I'll hear from her. Mrs. Jerkins wasted no time sending out the alarm." She frowned. "Ol' Horseface . . ."

"So what if she does? Wendy's capable of making her

own decisions. Believe me. That's one cagey old lady up there.''

"She certainly seems to have some magic over Tom.'' Faye snorted. "Or should I say Tootles. You won't believe it, but when I came home he was running around dressed as a pirate. Bare chest, eye patch, and all.''

Jack's mouth dropped opened. "Tom? The mouse roars?'' He scratched his head in amazement.

"He's not speaking yet, though Wendy does seem to understand him perfectly. It's like they have this special connection.'' She sighed and pursed her lips.

"What's the matter?''

"It's the children. I have a problem. Mrs. Jerkins put her foot down tonight. She won't stay a moment past six. And just today my boss let me know he expected me to burn the midnight oil. I'm stuck between a rock and hard place. I need to find someone to take care of them for the few hours I may be late coming home.'' She sat in the chair and tapped her lips in thought. "If I called the agency, perhaps they could find me someone who only wants to work part-time. I suppose I could afford that. After all, my job is on the line.''

"Faye, you're missing the forest for the trees. The answer is right under your nose. Or should I say above it.'' He pointed upward toward the third-floor window. As though on cue, the trill of children's laughter poured from the window.

"Wendy? Baby-sit? Don't be ridiculous. She's ninetysomething, and I have my doubts about her mental capacity. Besides, Mrs. Lloyd will never allow it.''

"Mrs. Lloyd—or you? Are you sure you're not jealous of her relationship with the kids?''

"I should be. Only . . . I'm not. How could I be jealous

of someone who is doing my son so much good? And Maddie . . . She's positively transformed. She met me at the door as proper and charming as a little princess. No, I'm not jealous. But I can't take any chances where my children are concerned. There's something odd about Wendy. Different. I don't want anything to happen.''

"You have to accept that something might happen. The world is a dangerous place. Bad things happen. That's life. The question is, can Wendy handle it if something does happen?''

"I have to admit, she does seem capable. Responsible.''

"And most nights, I'll be close by.''

"But Mrs. Lloyd said . . .''

"Yeah, yeah, we all know what that old battle-ax said. I get the feeling that Mrs. Lloyd has her own agenda for her mother, and it may not include Wendy's wishes.'' He stepped forward and put his hands on her shoulders. She flinched at his touch, but he held firm. "Faye, in my business, sometimes we have to fly in the face of sense and logic and trust our instincts. I've watched you with your kids. Sure you're persistent and demanding. Moms have to be, I guess. But you've got great instincts, too. What do they tell you to do?''

Faye thought of Wendy's youthful exuberance with the children. Her joy in their company lit up her face, even as it shone in the children's. Faye thought of how lonely the woman must be, all alone in the nursery, without friend or family to visit, with only stern Mrs. Jerkins to check on her. Was it any wonder she befriended the stars, or that she returned to the joys of her childhood to comfort her? She could remember a few nights when she herself spent time gazing out through a cloudy window. No woman should be so isolated.

"But can I trust Wendy with the children's care?"

As though in answer to her question the garden door swung open and the two children clamored out, all smiles and calls of greeting. Tom's face was freshly scrubbed, and he was dressed neatly in his usual shorts and top. Glancing at her wristwatch, Faye noted that it was exactly eight o'clock.

"Here, Mom," Maddie said, handing her a small brown bag. "Wendy said we had to ask you first if we could eat these cookies before bed. And she packed a few sandwiches for you for later, too. In case the fish got too cold."

"Did she now?" Smiling with relief, Faye made her decision. "It seems Wendy is going to take care of all of us," she replied, smoothing the hair on Maddie's face.

Faye suddenly felt a burst of elation, like a burden had been lifted from her back and she was free to run. Looking into Jack's eyes, she felt a bond, as though they were running shoulder to shoulder and had passed one more hurdle. Breathless and giddy, she wanted to run farther. Not run away this time, but onward, fast, with the wind at her feet—toward the finish line.

The following day, at 6:05 P.M., Faye sat back in her cramped office, put her feet up on a box, and sighed with heartfelt relief. Her telephone call to Wendy confirmed that the transfer of command was successful.

"We're learning how to paint!" Maddie exclaimed, breathless. "Wendy said she'd teach us how to paint a mural. Could we, Mom? In our bedroom?"

"It's not up to me, honey. It's up to Mrs. Lloyd."

"No it isn't," Maddie corrected indignantly. "Wendy said it was *her* house. That what happened to the house was up to *her*!"

Interesting, Faye thought, tucking away that bit of information. So, the house was still in Wendy's name. One would never guess, what with the way Jane Lloyd maneuvered Wendy's life decisions.

"How about you paint me a few pictures to frame first, honey. Then we can talk to Wendy about murals."

"Okay," she'd readily agreed, to Faye's continued amazement. In the past few days, Maddie had become less recalcitrant and more ready to compromise. In turn, Faye had felt less rigid with her demands, more inclined to agree. She wondered if the magic ingredient to this sweeter stew wasn't a certain old woman in No. 14.

After she hung up, Faye closed her eyes and imagined Wendy and the children spreading out the paper, lining up the paints, and spouting forth their imagination in bright colors and swirling shapes. Feeling her heart ping, she squeezed her lids tighter. How was she going to manage letting go of that special time with her own children? They were growing up so fast, poised for leaving. Too soon, they would be on their own, painting the world with their own, special colors. These days were, she knew, precious.

She wouldn't always be under such a relentless push, she reconciled in her mind. Tomorrow she'd make time. Or the day after that. As soon as she could. She promised herself that she would pick out a day and mark it on her calendar, in ink.

On the way home she hummed a peculiar little tune that she couldn't get out of her mind lately. It lifted her spirits so much that she didn't panic when she found Mrs.

Lloyd waiting for her in the foyer. Her back was as straight and hard as the wooden chair she sat upon, and when Faye entered, the older woman bolted upright to confront her. Faye could feel the woman's cool waves of anger roll over her as she approached.

"Mrs. Lloyd, how nice to see you again."

Mrs. Lloyd offered a quick, tight smile, but her eyes couldn't conceal her rage.

"I'm sorry for the lateness of the hour, but I felt it imperative that I speak with you. Immediately."

"I see. Well, won't you come in?" Opening the door, she felt a foreboding, knowing full well the reason for Mrs. Lloyd's call. She would have to be very careful how she handled the situation. She needed Wendy, yet she couldn't afford to aggravate her daughter and lose the flat. There was no way she could manage finding another flat, another move, and a new campaign under this pressing deadline.

"Tea?" she asked, hoping to ease the tension.

"No, thank you. I won't be staying long. I've come to speak with you on a subject that, frankly, I'd thought was settled between us."

Faye paused, then lowered her shoulders. "I assume you are referring to Wendy."

Mrs. Lloyd drew her shoulders up. "You mean *Mrs. Forrester.*"

Faye closed her mouth tightly.

"I thought," Mrs. Lloyd continued in her clipped manner, "that I'd made it quite clear that your children were not to bother my mother. Yet I've learned that they are in and out of her flat all day long. Like bees to honey, or so I'm told. This is most inappropriate, Mrs. O'Neill. My mother is very old. She is not well. I should think you'd be more careful than to allow the children free rein." She sniffed and drew her purse close to her chest. "I should have thought you'd have respected my wishes."

Faye could feel her Irish bubbling beneath the surface and struggled to maintain her cool. "Mrs. Lloyd, in the first place, if my children are allowed free rein it is because Mrs. Jerkins cannot manage them. If you recall, you were the person who referred me to her."

"Mrs. Jerkins is quite capable, I'm sure. She's been in my employ for many years. However, her hands are tied when your children are permitted by you to visit Mrs. Forrester."

"The children are permitted to see Mrs. Forrester at six o'clock each evening until I return. This is by arrangement between Wendy and me." Faye heard her voice rising and took a moment to collect herself.

"Precisely!"

"Mrs. Lloyd," she began again in a lower tone of voice, "I believe your mother is capable of much more than you do. She is vibrant, alive. The children bring her pleasure, as she does to them. It is a perfect arrangement all the way round."

"It doesn't go halfway round!" exclaimed Mrs. Lloyd. "You really have no idea."

"Is there something I should know about your mother? You aren't referring to the Peter Pan thing? If I recall, you yourself informed me that was harmless."

Mrs. Lloyd visibly startled. "Silly rumors, is all. It's just that, well, there have been incidents."

A stirring of alarm coursed through Faye. "What kind of incidents?"

"Harmless as I said, but . . . Well, it's hard to explain. You see, when children are near her, they tend to want to try to fly.'' A flush rose up her neck, and she seemed quite exasperated with the explanation.

Faye's lips twitched. ''Fly?''

''It isn't amusing, believe me. We've had near accidents.''

''They don't try to jump from windows or anything like that?''

''Heavens, no. Yet, one wonders what could happen. Children are so unpredictable. It's more likely they'll jump from a high place and bump their heads. Too much trouble.''

''It's working out so well. The children adore her. Why don't you go upstairs and see for yourself?''

''I don't have to,'' she sputtered. ''Children always love Wendy. That's the problem.''

''Why is that a problem? I should think it's a blessing.''

''My mother is . . . well, suffice to say that when she is in the company of children she relapses into this world of make-believe. She loses touch with reality. She becomes like a child herself, playing games, planning new adventures, having much too much fun for a respectable woman of her advanced years. She won't listen to reason and is so stubborn.'' She paused to take a deep breath and settle her rising frustration. ''At this point in her life, Wendy should be dignified, wise. She should allow me to take care of her.''

''Mrs. Lloyd, your mother is the wisest, most dignified woman I have ever met. And she is more than capable enough to take care of herself, and others.''

''I don't believe you are qualified to make that judgment.''

''Are you?''

''I am her daughter.''

"Of course. I don't mean to insult. Mrs. Lloyd, please don't interfere with her visits with the children. Not for my sake, but for theirs. I promise I will monitor the situation closely, and if my children bump their heads, I assure you, I will not sue!"

Mrs. Lloyd drew her shoulders back and met Faye's gaze squarely. Faye saw the resolve ice over the older woman's pale blue eyes, and she realized that Mrs. Lloyd was a woman who liked things to go her way. Defiance flared in Faye, and she stared back, almost daring the other woman to blink first.

Mrs. Lloyd dug in her heels. "I don't like to speak of unpleasantness, but if you persist, I shall be forced to consult my solicitor and ask you to leave."

"I see," Faye replied, coupling her hands before her. She thought of Maddie's comment earlier that evening and suspected that, contrary to all Mrs. Lloyd's machinations, Wendy still held the balance of power in this mother-daughter relationship. "Perhaps I had better discuss this with Wendy."

"My mother?" Jane's voice betrayed her with a hint of alarm. "Why ever would you bother my mother with such business?"

"I don't believe your mother would be happy if we canceled the visits."

"I am asking you, insisting, that you stop the visits."

Faye picked up the gauntlet and stood her ground.

"No."

"What? You will persist? Even over my objections?"

"I will allow Mrs. Forrester to decide and abide by her wishes."

Mrs. Lloyd's mouth silently worked, but her eyes flashed in fury. Faye knew that she had won.

"I warn you, Mrs. O'Neill. Only trouble will come from this arrangement. And when it does, I shall hold you entirely responsible! Good-bye, Mrs. O'Neill. I shall find my own way out."

Chapter 11

FAYE WATCHED THE door close behind Mrs. Lloyd and placed her palm over her forehead wondering what had come over her? She had meant to try to placate her, to meekly smooth things over. Instead she'd stiffened her spine, stood her ground. It had been such a long time since she'd done that. Dropping her palm, her eyes blinked in wonderment, and she took in a deep, gratifying breath. It felt great! Even though she'd only succeeded in alienating Jane Lloyd further. She was probably scurrying home right this minute to phone her lawyer and have him find some loophole in the contract that would permit their eviction. Something like, *No children allowed.*

She slipped her briefcase against the wall, thinking as she did so that it might've been wiser to simply have kept her mouth shut and agreed to Jane's terms. She stopped and bunched her fists. But when she heard Jane Lloyd talk about Wendy like she was some brainless invalid, something snapped. It was cruel to speak of Wendy in those terms. Simply mean-spirited and unfair. Wendy was eccentric, true, but she was also gracious and kind. Wise and generous. A good friend. In Faye's opinion, the world

189

would be a better place with a lot more Wendy Forresters. And in her gut, Faye knew that Wendy was the best tonic for what ailed her Tom. She would fight an army of Jane Lloyds to help her son.

Glancing at her watch, she saw that it was only six-thirty, "hoppassix" as Mrs. Jerkins would say. The house seemed as quiet as Texas after a tornado, and her thoughts wandered to a certain corn-fed boy who would certainly applaud her victorious bout with Jane Lloyd. She imagined how he'd break into an appreciative grin, and suddenly she wanted the satisfaction of seeing it for herself.

"Well, why not?" she said aloud, brimming with a confidence that tingled brand-new. For some inexplicable reason, the approval of Jack Graham meant a lot to her.

She poured herself a short sherry, a bracer as the British liked to say, nipped it back, then marched out her front door before her courage failed her. With a shaky hand, she tapped three times on Jack's door. A moment later, she heard approaching footfall. Faye's hand darted up to smooth her hair, then, fixing a smile on her face, she held her breath.

The door swung open, but it wasn't Jack that stared down at her. A young and exceptionally pretty brunette in dove gray silk stared back at her with the fierce gaze of a predatory eagle. She made Faye feel like a dowdy mouse about to be devoured.

"Halloo," she said in her university accent. "Can I help you?"

Faye's smile faltered. Idiot! Why didn't she think that Jack might be entertaining? She never thought of Jack in that way—with another woman. She blinked as the concept solidified in her mind. Jack with another woman?

Suddenly she was stabbed with an emotion she refused to acknowledge.

"I'm sorry. I didn't mean to interrupt. Excuse me. No, no message." She backed away.

"Faye? Is that you?" It was Jack's voice.

"Never mind," she called, retreating back up the stairs as fast as she could.

"Faye!" Jack called after her. "Wait a minute." He bounded up the stairs after her, catching her elbow as she reached the street. "Why are you running off?"

She couldn't meet his gaze for fear that he'd see her embarrassment and read too much into it. "I didn't mean to interrupt. Go on back to your guest. I'll see you later. Maybe."

"I'm almost done."

Now she did raise her eyes and her gaze was filled with scorn. "Really, Jack. That isn't very nice to the young lady."

"To the . . ." He raised his brows. "Ahh . . . now I understand. You mean the young lady in my flat?" He rubbed his jaw and rocked back on his heels. "Well, you know how it is with us visiting professors. We're just like traveling salesman. We have notches on our calculators, you know. I've only got a few weeks left. Miles to go before I sleep, if you know what I mean."

She blushed and looked at her feet. "I didn't mean . . ."

"Sure you did. I should be complimented, but the truth is, Mrs. O'Neill, I happen to be very fussy about whom I get involved with. The nice young lady, as you called Miss Fowler, happens to be my graduate assistant, and we are working out the final exam."

"Jack, either you're lying, or you haven't a clue what

that lady has in mind for your final exam. From the way she was eyeing me when she opened the door, I'd say she was going to offer you a multiple choice.''

Jack seemed dumbstruck but from the sloping half grin on his face, he didn't appear displeased with the notion.

''Really?''

Faye felt stung again by the sharp prick of jealousy and was mad at Jack for causing it. She told herself that she had no time or patience for this kind of nonsense.

''I really must be going. Have fun with Little Miss College.''

''Little Miss College happens to be a brilliant rocket scientist.''

For some reason, that really irked her. ''I'll just bet she specializes in heat-seeking missiles.'' When Jack barked out a laugh, her blush deepened and she quickly turned away. ''God, did I say that? I can't believe I just said that. It's no concern of mine, I'm sure.''

Jack was grinning openly and moved to block her path. ''Faye, what was it you came to see me about?''

''It was nothing.''

''For Faye O'Neill to stop working long enough to come knocking on my door can only mean one of two things. Either the sky is falling, or . . . well, give me a minute. I can't think of anything else yet, but it'll come to me.''

''Very funny.'' She meant to turn away but the words spilled out. ''It was Mrs. Lloyd. She came by to give me the third degree about allowing Maddie and Tom to visit Wendy. I just wanted to talk.'' She lifted one shoulder casually. ''Never mind. It's nothing I can't handle.''

''Wait, Faye.'' He gently took her arm again to delay her departure, then bent at the waist to peer into her face.

"You look tired. Again." Shaking his head, he said gently, "What am I going to do with you?" He slipped his arm around her shoulder. "No, don't get your back up. I'm not planning on scratching another notch on my calculator. I'm your friend, and it looks like you could use one."

He gave her a little shake, and, without looking up, she knew he was smiling that crooked grin of his that melted her resistance.

"Come on. How about I take you to my favorite pub for a couple of beers?"

She wanted to go, oh so very much. But in her life, there was always some little nail that held her foot down to the ground, some detail that snagged her sweater as she was going out the door.

"I can't. The children will be home soon."

"Wendy will keep them for another few minutes. It's just down the block."

"What about your rocket scientist?"

"I'll blast her off," he said with a lack of concern that shot a rocket of satisfaction through her. "Come on, you're always stalling."

Her lip projected forward as her trigger clicked. "I am not stalling. I can be just as free and decisive as you."

"Can you, now?"

"I can." Then, despite her words, she cast a worried glance at the upstairs window. "But I think I'll run upstairs and check on the children first, just to be sure."

When they walked into the cozy pub with its wood-paneled walls burnished in the glow of old-fashioned lamps that swung from the ceiling, she felt her heart patter with pleasure. She'd not yet been to an English pub, and this one was just like those she'd seen in a hundred movies. Men and women clustered like happy sardines in the small booths, chatting companionably. Jack was greeted as hale and heartily as an old friend. Young and old alike exchanged greetings with him, patted his back, and fondly called him The Professor. It didn't surprise her, though she knew Jack had only been in London a year. A man with Jack's clever wit, friendly swagger, and handsome good looks would easily win the hearts of the locals, men and women alike.

As they made their way through the haze of cigarette smoke in search of an empty spot, she wasn't meant to notice the sly winks or raised brows when a fellow spotted the petite blond at Jack's elbow. Only the tall, lean waitress with the flaming red curls seemed put out to find Faye seated in the booth with him. She offered Jack a saucy smile with the menu and a suggestive remark with the ale. To Faye she served up a glance that could cut steel.

"Another notch?" Faye asked him when the woman stopped hovering over Jack and returned to the other customers.

This time Jack didn't reply but took a gulp of ale instead.

She sipped likewise, surprised that the ale was room temperature. Over the rim of her glass, she watched him exchange jokes with the man at the next table, his eyes dancing and his mouth twitching till the punch line was told and he broke into a loud laugh that made her laugh just to hear it. The force of his personality was palpable, even from across the table. Friends, and even strangers, gravitated toward him, hovering, like planets around the warm sun. She could only wonder why such a man hadn't yet married.

Jack turned toward her, caught her perusal, and arched a brow in good humor. He had the eyes of a microscope, and she knew he'd be able to read her thoughts if she let him. She turned her head and introduced herself to the assembled group as Jack's new neighbor. Instantly, a buzz circulated around the bar, and she was met with a new wave of curious looks and comments.

"So you're the American what's moved into Number 14," the old man at the next table asked with a smile that would have reached his pointed ears were it not for the long, curved pipe that weighed one corner down. He was a caricature of what she'd imagined an English gent from a Wodehouse novel would look like, complete with a rumpled Harris tweed jacket, the long, poet's face, and Barrymore-like hair that curled around the ears. Except the hair was the worst toupee she'd ever seen. It took the willpower of Jeeves not to chuckle, reach out, and kindly straighten the piece.

"I am that same Yank," she replied as soberly as possible.

"It would take a Yank to move into that place." He puffed the pipe and a wispy trail of smoke rose straight into the air, filling the room with the scent of cherries. "It's a queer place. Some say it's haunted."

"In a pig's eye," piped in a plump, sixtyish woman in the booth behind him with gray hair and a gray cardigan, the buttons of which strained at the task. She turned her head and smiled at Faye. "Mary Croft," she offered in way of introduction. "Lived here all my life. Played with Jane Lloyd as a girl, before she got all hoity-toity. Never saw a ghost once, and I've lived right across the street at Number 17 for all of my life." She narrowed her eyes behind thick black glasses. "But there's something queer about the place, no doubt about it. Strange blinking lights at all hours of the night.''

"Lights?" Faye asked, eyes wide.

Jack's smile slipped from his face, and he sat up, alert. "What kind of lights?"

"Hard to say from a distance. Little balls of light, no bigger than my fist. Jane used to tell me matter-of-factly that they were fairies. When we was little." She chuckled in fond memory. "Used to say that when you *believe*, you can see the fairies."

"Here we go again," Faye muttered under her breath.

Jack raised his brows at Mary Croft. "Are you saying you saw fairies?"

Mary's face clouded, and her gaze darted to her beer. "Can't tell you what I saw. It was all so long ago. Now that I'm grown-up, I'm guessing it's UFOs of some sort."

"Now?" Faye asked. "You mean you still see the lights?"

"Sure, from time to time." She looked up, her face quizzical. "You mean you haven't?"

Faye took a quick swallow of her ale and shook her head. She darted a look at Jack, her brows up in query.

"Do you really want me to tell you?" he replied, amused.

"Oh no," she groaned. "Wait, this is another one of your jokes, right?"

"Oh, don't let it worry you none, dear," said Mary Croft, leaning far over the booth now to pat Faye's hand. "Wendy Forrester has been living in that house for years and she's never been bothered by them. Though I'd wager nothing much bothers our Wendy."

"Talking about Crazy Wendy are you?" asked a fellow whose eyes were a tad glazed in his puffy face. He was passing by with mugs of ale in hand. He leaned against the booth, resting the ale on the wood back. "I remember the old girl well. She used to read me stories up in that marvelous nursery of hers, back when I was a little tike. I'd just moved into the neighborhood, and she was my one true friend. I remember murals on the walls. Marvelous things. What was it? Pirates?"

"Peter Pan," replied Mary Croft with certainty.

The man smiled and nodded, the spark of memory lighting up his eyes.

"Everything was Peter Pan," Mary continued, wagging her head sadly. "Still is. It's a pity she's gone on and on about that, isn't it? I think its what drove Jane away in the end. It wasn't so bad a thing to believe in when we was young. Such delightful days of tea and stories and make-believe. There was always a roomful of children in the Forrester nursery or gathered around that fountain in the garden. That was the way Wendy liked it. The more the merrier. Children were always on their best manners with Wendy. She wouldn't tolerate any bad behavior or complaints. Not that she ever was cross. She simply had to give a child a look and"—Mary snapped her fingers—"that was that. No one wanted to displease dear Wendy. Or dared."

"I remember it well," added the old man, nodding, misty-eyed.

"Eventually," Mary went on thoughtfully, "we grew up and Wendy . . . Well, she's not daft, you know. Managed that boys' home and fund-raising and so much more. Poor Jane, though. She just couldn't cope. Status and the good opinion of strangers always meant so much to her."

"Spoiled she was, that's what I always said," the old man muttered.

"She wasn't a bad child," Mary countered. "Just bossy. Once she stopped believing, she couldn't abide the fact that her mother's faith was unshaken. Wendy, of course, won't have nobody tell her which way is up, will she now? They had terrible rows most of their lives. Now it's about selling the house. Jane says that with all the rumors of ghosts and lights and craziness, no one wants to let a flat." She winked and released an easy smile. "Except perhaps an American what don't know better."

"That's a description I hate to own up to." Faye said good-naturedly to the chorus of chuckles.

"It's a beautiful house, anybody would want it, but Jane refuses to live there. The cost of the upkeep of so grand a place is steep, and Wendy, of course, won't move out. Says she needs to stay in the nursery." Mary lowered her voice and leaned forward. "For *himself*, you know."

Jack nodded his head as solemnly as Mary Croft. Catching Faye's puzzled expression he mouthed, "Peter Pan."

Faye rolled her eyes and offered an exaggerated, "Ah."

"Wendy Forrester may be a bit daft in her old age, but she's as true as they come," said the old man, defense flaring in his pale eyes as he sat upright. The sudden movement brought the toupee another quarter inch down the slippery slope. "When anyone needed a bit of cash to make it to next payday, especially after the war, Wendy Forrester was always there to help. Always had a smile on her face, and a kind word of cheer, she had. Never once pressed to have it paid back, neither."

"True, true. Wendy always had cash to lend. I'm not too proud to own it." This came from another middle-aged man who sat in the booth opposite them. The conversation was drawing listeners from across the bar, many nodding their head in agreement, echoing, "Hear, hear."

"Till her daughter took over the finances," piped in another. "It's like water from a stone with that one."

"Has anyone ever seen Peter Pan?" Jack asked. "Besides Wendy, that is?"

For a moment there was a stunned silence and a few furtive glances. Then everyone burst out laughing, pointing at each other and daring each other to admit to it. Another round of ale and lager was served, and they drank with relish. Both the drinks and the good humor loosened a few more tongues.

"Some of us had dreams of seeing the Pan when we was children," confided a woman with a gauzy green scarf tied in a triangle around her head. Drawing near, she reminisced, "Of course, we'd all sat at Wendy's knee. Children have such lovely imaginations," she added with a sentimental sigh. "They're so quick to believe."

"It's part of their charm," commented another dreamily.

Faye's thoughts drifted to her own children. Did Maddie and Tom believe in anything anymore? The divorce was so bitter, and the aftermath seemed to rob them of some of their innocence.

"It's time to go home," she said, suddenly missing them and checking her watch.

"You weren't bothered by all that talk about ghosts and UFOs, were you?" Jack asked when they were walking together down the block, their shoulders nearly touching.

"No," she replied, tucking her hands under her arms. "Of course not. I don't believe in any of that creepy nonsense. A few drinks and people just like to hear themselves talk."

"They didn't mean to scare you. Everyone around here

adores Wendy. She's a favorite topic of conversation.''

"It's simply getting late. Maddie and Tom need to be tucked into their own beds and Wendy should be relieved of her charges.''

"I've been thinking of Tom. I didn't want to mention it in front of all those folks. Friendly as it is, anything said in there is like placing an ad in the paper.'' He took a few more steps. ''I've done some research on elective mutism for you.''

"You did that?'' She turned her head and looked up at him with surprise. She felt a sudden cocoon of warmth envelop her as she studied the length and breadth of the man taking strides beside her, a man who took time out of his busy day to think of her and her children. ''You did that for me?''

"Faye, you know that there's not much I wouldn't do for you.'' He cleared his throat and swung his head to look straight ahead. ''And the kids. We're pals.''

"Yes,'' she answered quickly, dousing the flame that shot through her. ''I like to think so.''

"Most of the time I find that doctors don't know what they're doing. They have such a narrow-minded reference. So I like to do a little digging around myself. I went to the medical library on-line and looked up elective mutism. I learned there are two types, both being rare. The main difference that I can tell is that if you had one kind you had all sorts of behavioral and psychological problems that went on for pages and pages and had a small chance of full recovery. The second type is called traumatic mutism. This one has a sudden onset following a psychological or physical shock. Clearly, that fits Tom's case.''

The image of Tom lying helpless on the floor seared

her mind. She could shake off the specter, but never the guilt.

"What about that one? Is there a cure?" *Or,* she wondered privately, *do they blame it all on bad genes and bad mothering?*

"There isn't a cure exactly, but the outlook is good for cases like these. Tom needs to have some motivation to speak. What got me most excited was the point that play was important, and that make-believe play can be one of the best therapies he can have."

She stopped and turned to face him, astonished.

"Wendy," they both said in unison.

She held her hands tightly together by her heart, breathless with awe. "Sometimes a miracle happens in our midst, and we don't even realize it." Then sticking out her chin, she said, "I defy Mrs. Lloyd to try and stop them from playing together. Oh," she exclaimed, stopping again and tugging at his sleeve. "That reminds me. Why I came to see you in the first place." She quickly told him about her confrontation with Mrs. Lloyd.

"That's my girl," he exclaimed, impulsively reaching out to hug her. Then, remembering in a flash all that had transpired between them and all the promises made, he abruptly dropped his hands in an awkward swing.

Faye blushed and looked downward, appreciating his restraint. Yet in her heart she felt a dangerous, defiant twinge that told her she *wanted* his arms around her, to feel that tight squeeze of affection, one human being to another. People needed touch, men and women, to keep them soft and supple. Without tender stroking humans grow cold and brittle, quick to break. It had been a long, long time since she'd been really and truly hugged.

"Looks like we have another roaring mouse in the house," he said.

"What do you mean, mouse? You don't know anything about me."

"I know that you don't like to rock the boat."

"Wha . . . I live to rock the boat!" She could feel the heat burn her cheeks when he raised one brow and snorted. "Well, is there anything wrong with wanting to know first if the boat has any leaks in it?"

He shook his head. "Hopeless."

"My thought exactly," she quipped. "One doesn't just jump into the water with two children in tow."

"Hey, we're on the same side here. I have an idea. A compromise. Fun"—he cast her a sidelong glance—"but nothing too wild. There's this small amusement park not far away that's called The Neverland. It's based on Barrie's island, which makes sense considering Barrie lived in London. What do you say we take the kids there? Maybe the association with Tootles's hero will encourage him to speak?"

"It's a fine idea, Jack. Let's do it. Soon. Oh, I have such good feelings about this." Her heart felt so full of hope that she felt it would burst. Looking up at Jack she smiled happily, unaware that he watched, transfixed, as a childlike gleam of excitement sprang to life in her eyes.

Chapter 12

THEY SET OFF on their first London adventure the very next weekend. Maddie and Tom and worked themselves up to fever pitch, neither of them quite believing that the trip hadn't been put off because of a deadline or delayed because of bad weather or some other excuse that grown-ups were so good at making. Tom insisted that Wendy be taken along, deaf to Faye's complaint that Mrs. Lloyd would have her sent to the Tower of London. Tom wouldn't budge. He wouldn't go to the Neverland without Wendy.

On Saturday morning all the inhabitants of No. 14, young and old, climbed into a cab, and took off for The Neverland Theme Park. As they bumped along in the backseat, Wendy put her hand to her cheek and exclaimed that this was a much less comfortable way of traveling to the Neverland.

"Flying on the back of the wind is ever so much more fun!"

Tom surprised everyone by laughing out loud at this as the spirit of adventure took the place of sulky shyness in his eyes. Jack squeezed Faye's hand, and she promptly squeezed back.

As they approached the entrance to The Neverland their excitement bubbled, and the children pointed toward the bits of pale pinks, greens, and purples of the rides and carousels peeking through the dark green foliage. Up close, however, it was clear the theme park had seen better days. There was really little more than a sparse collection of out-of-date rides and drooping old confection stands bordered by rickety brown fencing. Stepping out from the cab at the entrance, Faye felt a wave of worry that she tried to keep from her face. Maddie and Tom, however, thought it was all marvelous and hooted with impatience, pawing at the pea-gravel like racehorses at the gate as Jack paid for the entrance tickets.

"Oh look, Wendy!" cried Maddie dancing on tiptoe. "There's the pirate ship. And over there! It's the Mermaids' Lagoon. Just like in the book. And way over there. I think it's a totem pole. It must be where Tiger Lily lives!"

Tom grasped Wendy's hand and peered out with an expression that was part eagerness and part fear.

"It does look a bit like her totem pole," replied Wendy, blinking and looking around at the strange world before her. Her small, wizened face appeared perplexed, and her eyes were sparkling with bewilderment. She shook her head, and, with her fingertip to her cheek, said smartly, "But the lagoon is all wrong! I should hope they don't think that pitiful lump is Marooners' Rock? Tsk. Come, children, let's take a look-see."

Jack issued the tickets, and the children were through the turnstile like a shot.

"Careful, Tom, don't drag Wendy so," Faye called

out, but they were already beyond earshot, a vision of a six-year-old boy tugging at the hand of spry old woman.

"She won't get too tired?" Faye asked Jack, as they stopped to buy peanuts from a vendor.

"I imagine she'll tell us if she does. Wendy's an old hand at this. Come on, Faye. Let's go on the Pirate Ship."

"Oh no, I never go on rides. I get sick."

"Stalling again." He took her hand and raced her to the makeshift pirate ship that swung back and forth, higher and higher, like an enormous pendulum. Faye felt like a child herself, holding hands with her best friend and running. Wendy and the children were already in line, and Maddie danced in excitement as she waved at them to hurry and scoot in line behind them. When they reached them Faye leaned against Jack's chest, catching her breath, feeling a giddy gladness when he looped his arm around her shoulder in camaraderie.

The rest of the morning continued in this happy manner. The children pointed at rides that they recognized from the story of Peter Pan—and others they didn't but had been added on over the years—then took off at a sprint, usually with Jack in tow, sparing not a glance for their mother. She preferred to follow at a more leisurely pace with Wendy, holding sweaters and bottles of water and half-eaten stalks of cotton candy that smelled of pure cane sugar. She rode a few gentler rides and skipped anything that meant she had to go upside down or twirl left to right till her brains rattled.

The children couldn't understand how it was more than thrill enough for her to simply watch them gripping the metal safety bars with ear-to-ear grins plastered on their faces. Maddie's expression lost all of its usual caution, and she jumped and wriggled in her seat like any eight-year-old girl. When she smiled her whole countenance brightened, and Faye was surprised to see that her color was better and she looked not mousy, but pretty. And Tom . . . Faye had to laugh herself when she saw her shy boy throw back his head and laugh out loud. It was his high-pitched squeals that Faye heard over all the other laughter, screaming, and carnival music that pierced the summer's afternoon. The sound of her child's laughter, after so much silence, was the sweetest music she could ever hope to hear.

"Mom, where's Wendy?"

They had just finished a round on the Ferris wheel, and Faye's knees were feeling a bit watery.

"What do you mean?" she exclaimed, quickly searching the faces of her small group: Maddie, Tom, Jack. No Wendy. Her heart leaped to her throat. "She probably just wandered off. You know how she's studying all the park's details."

"Tom," said Jack, stepping up and taking his hand. "Why don't you and I walk to the front gate while your mom and Maddie circle once around? It's not a big park; she can't have gone far."

Tom saw the look in Jack's eyes and quickly took his hand.

"Come on, pardner." The two men walked off while Maddie and Faye headed in the opposite direction. When they met again at the front gate of the park, Wendy was nowhere to be found.

"Where might she have gone?" Faye said, desperately worried now. "She seemed confused. All morning she kept pointing out what looked like the real Neverland and what didn't. It was bittersweet for her to see all this.

Maybe it was too much. What if she, well you know . . ."
She looked at the children and skewed her mouth, unwilling to alarm the children.

"She probably just flew to the real Neverland," Maddie said in a serious tone.

"Don't be silly," Faye snapped, her worry making her
tense.

Jack patted Maddie's shoulder with his large palm, easing away the scowl that had flashed across her face.
"More likely she just took a little stroll. There's a lovely
park just beyond these gates, and you know how Wendy
loves flowers. I'll bet she's right over yonder admiring
the roses."

"You're right." Maddie perked back up. "Wendy especially loves roses."

"She does indeed," added Faye gently, stroking Maddie's hair in a gesture to restore peace between them.

Tom grasped hold of this possibility and began marching with a single-minded purpose toward the exit sign, his
little fists bunched by his thighs. It struck Faye that her
son was an odd, determined little person whom she hardly
knew.

"I guess we'd better hustle before we lose Tootles,
too," Jack said.

"Oh, he'll find her," Maddie chirped, skipping to keep
up. "He always knows where Wendy is."

It turned out that Maddie was right. Like a homing
pigeon, Tom led them past the rose garden straight to a
small patch of trees that created a lovely shaded spot.
Beneath them a few wooden benches clustered, and on
one of the benches sat Wendy. She was busily engaged
in conversation with a young couple while petting, admiring, and lavishing attention on their enormous St. Ber-

nard. On drawing nearer, they could see five roly-poly puppies yapping on the ground beside them.

"Oh, the lovelies!" Maddie cried in pure ecstasy, and ran to join Wendy and Tom in the love fest on the grass.

"Leave it to Wendy to find puppies," Jack said, grinning, daring Faye not to feel the joy. "You realize what's going to happen, don't you?"

"Oh no," Faye said, balking. "No puppy . . ."

"I'm just warning you."

"Faye! Jack!" called Wendy merrily, waving. "Come close, children, and meet Nana! Imagine, after all these years. I scarce could believe my eyes when I saw the Currans walk by the park with their sweet new family in tow. I simply had to dash off to catch them. I hope I didn't alarm you much, running off like that. First The Neverland, and now Nana. Such a day!"

Faye's eyes met Jack's, and she was concerned to see for the first time the flicker of worry in his eyes as well. Even Faye knew that Nana was the name of the dog that acted as nurse to the Darling children in *Peter Pan*. Faye felt so sad for the imaginative old woman, knowing she would have to burst her bubble. She only hoped she wasn't too late and a scene wasn't in the offing. She glanced at the young owners of the dog, expecting to see worry etched on their faces as well. Instead they were beaming, not the least uncomfortable with Wendy's crazy assertions.

"How do you do," she said, stepping forward and extending her hand. "I'm terribly sorry for the bother. Wendy seems to think this dog is . . . well, her own Nana." Her tone implied apology.

"Her name is Lady," replied the young woman breezily.

Faye's heart sank. "Of course . . ."

"But it's the most amazing thing," the young woman continued. "Her mother's name was Nana. And hers before that. It's a tradition. In every litter the pick female must be named Nana, you see, because they're descendants of the very same Nana that James Barrie used as a model in his book, *Peter Pan.*"

"And that Nana was my own dear Nana," said Wendy. "That's how I met Sir James in the first place, so many years ago. I was in Kensington Gardens with my Nana, and he was there with his St. Bernard, Porthos, and I guess you could say the two dogs introduced us." Her face softened with the memory.

Faye's mouth slipped open, but she had no words. Wendy met Sir James Barrie, the literary celebrity? Perhaps, she thought with some relief, that might explain things. Perhaps she was simply mixing up her memories. It still wasn't reality, but it wasn't totally crazy either.

Beside her, Maddie cooed and retrieved one puppy from the pile that was jumping all over Tom, nipping his ears and licking his face.

"It's amazing that Wendy recognized our Lady." The sun reflected from Mrs. Curran's round eyeglasses as she smiled and patted her dog's head affectionately.

"But of course I would," Wendy blithely replied. "There's something in the eyes, and the shape of the head, and, well, so many things. It's a feeling, too, you know. We always know our loved ones. Even in the dark." She looked up as Maddie solemnly, cautiously approached her with one puppy gently cradled in her arms. "And look at that one in particular," she said, reaching out to examine the head of the plump puppy in Maddie's arms. "She's the very image of my Nana."

This was met with another gasp of surprise from Mrs. Curran. "But that's remarkable. That puppy *is* the one we call Nana."

"You see? What did I tell you?"

Jack bent over to whisper in Faye's ear, "Here it comes. . . ."

As though on cue Maddie whined, "Oh, Mom, please may we have her? Please, please? I'll take care of her. You won't have to do a thing."

Faye took a breath, readying the long list of reasons why a puppy would be impossible, excuses she'd made before, excuses many mothers had made through the ages. Not because mothers didn't love puppies, but because they loved their children more. A mother knows, despite the heartfelt promises of her insincere little darlings, that the one who would end up caring for the puppy would be her. The mother knows that the puppy will soon grow into a dog that will chew the furniture and pee on the carpets and bark at the mailman and most likely get them evicted from their apartment. And if that weren't enough, every mother knows that *she* would be the one who falls headfirst in love with the puppy-who-would-grow-into-a-dog, and that *she* would continue to love the dog long after the children lost interest or went off to school.

None of that mattered now, of course. Now, she was simply a Mean Mother.

"We don't even know if the puppy is available," she argued. She lifted her eyes, trying desperately to convey with her eyes the message, "Please say no!" Alas, the couple was young and childless and obviously hadn't learned the signals yet.

"Oh, not to worry. We have a list of people who want the puppies, but it seems only fair that Wendy has an opportunity to have Nana back again. After all, it was she who started it all, wasn't it?''

They were determinedly friendly, unrestrainedly good-natured, and delighted with the unexpected turn of events. Obviously, their dog's heritage meant a great deal to the Currans, and she was their treasured pet. Meeting Wendy Forrester was the highlight of their day, probably even their year.

Faye rolled her eyes. Now she had Tom's pleading looks to deal with, and, beside him, Jack and Wendy plagued her with expectant expressions. She hardened her heart. Someone had to be practical in this crazy bunch.

"No, I'm sorry. No, we simply couldn't. I don't think Mrs. Lloyd will allow it."

"Beans to Jane!" exclaimed Wendy. "It's my house, and I say it's only right that Nana should come back home."

The forces were attacking full strength now. Faye had no choice but to dig deeper into the trench. "Absolutely not. We're scraping by as it is, children. I don't think we could take on a dog, too." She saw Tom turn away in a slump-shouldered sulk that she knew could go on for hours and Maddie's eyes fill with reproachful tears. The flow of guilt was like a tidal wave.

"Really, children, try to understand. I can't. I . . .''

Jack stepped forward and gathered the puppy from Maddie's crushing hold and rested it against his chest. He stroked the floppy ears while the puppy licked his fingers. "She's a pretty thing, isn't she? I love dogs. Have been meaning to get one for a long time and was just waiting for the right one to come along. And since Wendy says it's okay, and I won't get evicted, why don't I take her? That way, you kids and Wendy—and you, too, Faye, can all come and see Nana whenever you want.''

"But she won't be ours. . . ." whined Maddie.

"It'll be just like she is. You two can be in charge of her care. She'll be your responsibility. You can feed her and walk her and make sure she gets a hefty dose of love several times a day. We can open up the back stairwell to my flat so you won't even have to go outdoors. How's that?''

"The locks on the doors are old and difficult," Wendy said. "And I don't have the keys, I'm afraid.''

Jack smirked. "No problem.''

"Excellent, dear boy! Then I'll open my door, too," Wendy exclaimed, hands clasped together and eyes bright. "Why, with Nana back and the children and the doors all open, Number 14 will be a family home once again!''

Chapter 13

ONE OF THE most charming aspects of being proved wrong is that everyone works doubly hard to drive the point home. Once Faye stated that she didn't think the puppy would work out, Maddie and Tom were faultless in their responsibilities to Nana. Jack, too, proved he was as good as his word. With Wendy's approval, he disassembled the lock to the rear stairwell doors that once upon a time servants used to connect the kitchen to the main house. Wendy kept her door unlocked as well so that the children could come and go as they pleased. Lodged between Wendy and her delightful nursery and Jack and the puppy, the children ran up and down the stairs freely all day long, Nana barking at their heels. By the end of another week, No. 14's transition back from a three flat to a single-family home flowed as naturally as three tributaries cascading into one great river.

Faye swept the front stoop of No. 14 and thought she'd never felt such simple joy before in her life. It wasn't just that the walls of No. 14 were as thick and secure as a tank's, or that the garden was charming with its beds of roses and smattering of annuals tended by her children's hands. Nor was it because her children seldom quarreled anymore, or that they were now as brown as berries from hours in the sun, or that the presence of one puppy elicited so many giggles. None of these simple joys could have evolved if she, the mother, hadn't changed. How true it was that a mother's attitude and spirit affected the whole family.

She plucked a few deadheads from the potted geraniums neatly and precisely. It was time to stop blaming Rob for crushing the joy from her soul, she decided. She had no more time for blame. Or the heart for it. The contentment came at last because the anger and fear that had burned in her heart for so many years had been doused by the liberal flow of affection she'd felt within these walls. Her grip of fear had loosened. Faye didn't feel she was alone battling the world. Here she had Wendy. And Jack. Friends who cared about her in ways that mattered. Why did people always think that support meant money or advice? Support is a hand held when you've failed, a smile in the morning when you leave to face the world, a laugh shared till your sides ache and tears flow down your cheeks.

Faye gave the porch a final sweep, then walked down the steps and around back to the garden, passing through the ornate black-iron gate, careful to close it tightly to keep children and puppy in, and strangers out. She relished the scents of Wendy's roses, the soft yellow light pouring out from the tall, charming redbrick house, and the quiet hush of twilight. Skimming her hand along the cool brass of the fountain, she hummed the tune that played in her mind most days, especially on nights like this when she could hear the reedy pipe music clearly in sync with the crickets rubbing their hind legs and the song of her children's laughter pouring out from the nursery windows. The symphony swirled around her, making her so heady and joyous she felt she could almost fly. On a night like this, with her heart dancing in the air in time to her music, Faye simply had to close her eyes and smile to soar.

The following night, there was a crash landing in the children's bedroom.

"Tom," Faye argued, tapping her foot, "you must let me wash your shirt. You've worn that one for three days straight."

Tom's eyes were mutinous and he clung to his hunter green T-shirt as fiercely as any pirate of the Spanish Main would his treasure.

"You've a drawer full of shirts," she argued. "At least let me take it just for tonight. I'll have it clean for you in the morning."

"He won't let you, especially not at night." Maddie explained this to Faye as though she were the adult speaking to the child. "You see, Mom, Peter wears a costume of green leaves held together with sap. Tom wants to be ready should Peter Pan come tonight."

Tom had not only taken to wearing green exclusively. He also dragged a sword from his hip and was forever jumping from high places such as chairs, the third step of the staircase, and, of course, his mattress. His mood had improved dramatically, however, especially since his outing at The Neverland Theme Park and Nana's arrival at No. 14. Faye could hear him laughing and even singing when he was upstairs in the nursery. So she tried to humor him, mumbling to herself about how that wild savage Peter could use a good mother, all right. And a good washing.

"Well, tomorrow is Saturday," she began again. "What if I promise you we'll go to Harrods first thing in the morning, and I'll let you pick out seven new shirts, all green if you like, one for each day of the week. Would you let me have this one to wash tonight? I'm sure Peter wouldn't mind if you wore, say, this yellow one. In the fall, leaves turn to yellow."

Instantly his face softened, and he wiggled out of his dirty shirt and handed it to his mother with an air of triumph. She accepted it gracefully. The shared victory was so much sweeter than if she had chosen to dominate. Faye felt a pang of love when she saw how his arms and belly had filled out in the past weeks. They weren't so much like bean poles, and he had tan lines across his arms, what they called in the Midwest a farmer's tan.

"Then it's only fair I get something, too," said Maddie.

"Yes, that's true. What do you want? A new top? Shoes?"

"I want a thimble," Maddie declared, her arms folded across her chest. "Wendy says that Peter keeps her thimble on a chain close to his heart. He told her it was like keeping Wendy close. I want a thimble so I can give it to Peter, too."

"Very well. Though we'll have to take it to a jeweler to figure out how to get it on a chain." Privately, however, she wished they wouldn't take such a literal translation of Wendy's stories. The lines between reality and fantasy were growing blurred, and it made her uneasy.

She helped Tom into the yellow shirt, supervised the brushing of teeth, tucked them into their beds, then listened while Maddie regaled her with the further adventures of Peter Pan. Tom listened intently, occasionally nodding for emphasis. At the point when the Indians were dancing a tribute to Peter, he grew so excited he had to jump up on the bed and pantomime the dance himself, whooping and hollering like a wild thing till Maddie and Faye were rolling on the bed in laughter.

"Mom, I like it when we laugh like this. I want to laugh all night long," Maddie exclaimed later, after they'd calmed down and were wiping the moisture from their eyes.

"Me too," Faye replied, feeling a twinge on her heart-strings. "But it's already way past our bedtimes. So in you go. Tomorrow we'll laugh some more, okay?"

Maddie and Tom glowed with happiness and scrambled to obey.

Glowing herself, she tucked them in again, gave them sound kisses on their foreheads, and turned out the lights. "Sweet dreams, don't let the bedbugs bite."

"Open the window, Mom!"

Faye pulled back the lace without hesitation this time and opened the double-hung window farthest from the beds. A summer's breeze laden with the scent of Wendy's roses swirled through the room, rippling the lace and bringing a sigh from Maddie. She met her mother's gaze and held it, thanking Faye in a million ways with the heartfelt smile before she yawned and closed her eyes. Tom's eyes were bright in the moonlight as he coupled his hands under his head and stared out through the glass at the stars in the purple sky. *Real stars this time,* she thought with satisfaction. Not fake ones on the ceiling.

Resting her hand on the doorframe and watching her sleeping children, Faye realized that they'd be all right. They had a home, a garden, a puppy. They'd shown responsibility with Nana. Soon school would begin and they would have new friends, activities and experiences that would balance out their preoccupation with fantasy. Her babies were growing up.

With a bittersweet twinge she realized it was time for her to learn not to hold on so tight. She wanted to help them mature into independent adults. Tomorrow, she thought, it would be a good start to let Maddie and Tom choose their own clothes.

Later, Faye fell asleep counting new resolutions, but was awakened from her sleep by high-pitched giggles from Maddie and Tom's bedroom. Prying open an eye she saw the time glowing in green on the alarm clock and let out a puff of exasperation.

"Goofing around till midnight is pushing the envelope much too far," she grumbled, pulling herself out of bed. "Give them an inch, and they'll take a mile," she muttered as she approached their room, ready to lay down the law. Suddenly she stopped, startled to see a small flickering of light shine from under the door followed by another burst of giggles, muffled by palms.

What were they up to, her sleepy mind asked? She pushed open the door and peered inside the darkened room, eyes alert. Maddie and Tom lay motionless in their beds, pretending to be asleep. The flickering light was gone. Her mind raced to recapture the conversation in the pub, something about lights . . . and fairies. *Nonsense,* she told herself, shaking the wild thoughts away. It was all that talking about Peter Pan before bed that got her imagination going.

"No more fooling around! Good night," she said in a stern voice that brooked no further nonsense.

"Good night, Mother."

Satisfied that peace was restored, she closed the door gently behind her. Just before it clicked shut, she could have sworn she heard a faint tinkling of bells.

They had a wonderful time shopping at Harrods. By nature, Faye wasn't a shopper. She never understood the appeal of racing through rack after rack of clothing, trying on a dress or pants in cramped, poorly lit dressing rooms with bad mirrors that made your skin look sallow and your bottom too wide. With children it was far worse, messing about with all those buttons and zippers and the whining and complaining. Usually she'd end up in a bad mood before they even got to the store.

On this day, however, she began by changing her attitude. Instead of considering the day a chore, she viewed it as an outing that her children would direct. She set a budget and let them loose. Maddie and Tom thought it a holiday and though they made a few choices that Faye might not have, she was surprised to discover that her children had their own distinct tastes and preferences.

When they finally returned from Harrods, all smiles despite the overcast skies, they found Jack sitting on the front stoop, tossing a football in his hand. Nana, spotting the children, whined and strained at the leash.

"It's about time you got home," Jack said, looking put out. The day's slight drizzle had seized his curls, molding them into a helmet.

"Aw, what's the matter?" Faye asked, hoisting the parcels from her arms to her hip. "Don't you have anyone to play with?"

He tossed the football to Maddie, who missed it and scrambled to chase after it.

"As a matter of fact, *no*," he replied, standing up and

taking the parcels from her arms. "I thought we'd go to the park this morning and show these Brits that a football is a brown-pointed pigskin, not some black-and-white round ball. Not only were you guys not home, but now the weather's clouded over."

The sight of him in his T-shirt, frayed shorts, and sneakers, worn without socks, of course, sent her heart-strings humming. She couldn't deny she had feelings for the man. Like a brother, she told herself firmly. Sometimes an older brother—kind, patient and mellow. At other times, like these, a younger brother, with as much wide-eyed piquancy as her own Tom. It was part of his relentless charm.

"Well we've had a perfectly splendid time, and it looks like it's going to be rainy all day. You'll catch your death of cold if you play football today. Tell you what. We're all hungry. I'll make us some nice cheese sandwiches and soup."

"And cookies?" asked Maddie, slipping an arm around Jack's waist and handing him his football.

"Sure, why not."

"Great," Jack replied, beaming at the thought of a home-cooked meal, much less fresh-baked cookies. "Let's cook in my kitchen. It's huge, and most of the time it's never used."

Faye's curiosity was piqued. The children had been down in Jack's flat many times to tend Nana; they had no qualms at all about just barging in anywhere. She'd been dying to see it for herself but couldn't bring herself simply to wander in, even if his door was open. Privacy was something she respected too much. So she'd resorted to shamelessly pumping the children for information, but the best she could get from them was that Jack's flat was "big and messy."

"I'll just get the supplies and come on down. Chocolate chip sound good?"

"Is there any other kind? Just give me a minute to pick up a bit."

"Yeah, you mean a lot," Maddie said with a roll of her eyes.

"Come on and help, Miss Priss," he teased. "There are puppy toys everywhere I step."

Of course, she was eager.

"You too, pal," he said to Tom, tossing him the football. Tom caught it and gave it a jaunty flip.

"Nice catch," Jack said with approval. "Keep it."

Faye looked away lest they see the emotion flare up in her own eyes. Did Jack know how much his involvement with her son meant to her? Did he see the boy's growing admiration and confidence with grown-ups?

In her flat, Faye helped Tom into his new sage green shirt, then after he hurried off, she changed into a light cotton sheath dress and freshened her face. She gathered her sundries, cookie sheets and oven mitts then made her way down the back stairs to Jack's flat. The puppy stood at the foot of the stairs and barked when she heard the footfall, then dribbled in excitement at the sight of Faye.

"The story of my life," she quipped, while Tom and Maddie hurried to wipe up.

"Oh my!" was all she could say when she passed through a small entryway and stepped into the marvelous kitchen that dominated Jack's flat. It was as unexpected as finding the bright sun of Provence on a foggy London day. Wendy had explained how once the basement was a warren of rooms making up the kitchen, pantry, and a few servants' quarters. When the building was changed to a triplex, the walls were knocked out to make this one spacious room, painted now a soft, pastel yellow. A delft-tiled fireplace dominated one wall, and before it nestled a long, scrubbed wooden table surrounded by bright-yellow-painted chairs with blue-checked cushions. A narrow hall separated it from the street side of the flat, where she supposed the two cramped bedrooms and a small front room were. French doors opened up and out to the garden, inviting the fresh green and the sweet air in.

It was the old Aga stove, however, that had Faye almost on her knees. After months of cooking on a small metal box with two burners, she almost wept when she imagined cooking on this grande dame of an oven. It was a mighty tool, a proud cobalt blue, six dark black coils and shiny white knobs. Nary a grease spot, a burnt bit, or a crumb littered its surface, because Jack confessed he never touched the thing.

"To think," she said, eyes crinkling with pleasure while running her fingertips over the bright enamel. "When I'm old and dying I can tell my grandchildren that once in my life, I cooked on an Aga." Then rolling up her sleeves, she declared, "It's time to put this warhorse back into action."

"You can use it anytime you like," Jack offered with a hopeful expression.

"I just might," she replied, stroking the blue enamel.

After the late lunch they spilled out into the garden.

While Maddie and Faye dug peat moss into the soil, Tom and Jack played pirates.

"Be careful," called out Faye, frowning at the sight of her son and Jack whacking at each other with wooden swords. Tom wore his treasured pirate's hat, Jack a makeshift hook fashioned from a wire coat hanger stuck into his sleeve. "Someone can get hurt."

"So, my beauty," Jack called back, brandishing his hook. "Do ye dare to give me hook orders? Perhaps ye'd like to walk the plank?"

"You're hopeless," she said, not succeeding in hiding her smile. "Just remember it'll be you who'll walk the plank if anyone gets hurt."

Tom chucked under his enormous tilting pirate's hat.

Jack thrilled at every noise Tom made, whether it was a chuckle, a burp, or an outright laugh like he'd heard at The Neverland Theme Park. Jack's hope was to elicit a word from the boy by summer's end.

"Peter Pan, you codfish," Jack shouted, raising his hook high into the air. "Ye've met your match. Prepare to meet thy doom."

With the gleam of triumph in his eye, Tom had at Jack once again. The wooden swords thudded dully as they met in the air, tap, tap, tap. Jack was jubilant, ducking and swerving, leaping over chairs, escaping from Tom's hot pursuit behind the hedges, having an absolutely wonderful time. In fact, he couldn't remember having such a good time since . . .

Whack. Jack felt Tom's sword hit him squarely in the back of the head. He saw stars and sank to his knees. In the misty, swirling blackness he saw a man in a black pirate's hat approach him, all evil eyes and long, curling mustache. Jack shuddered, drawing back.

"Hook," he muttered.

"Jack, Jack, are you all right?"

Blinking, Jack's vision cleared, and he saw Faye's worried face bent close before him. Sulking right behind her with eyes wide with worry under the pirate's hat was

Tom. Jack rubbed the back of his head and nodded.

"Sure, sure, I'm fine. It was just a tap. Nothing at all."

"See what I mean, Jack Graham?" Faye exclaimed, her relief audible in her voice. "I told you someone would get hurt."

"Naw, I'm not hurt. Just surprised. It was all my fault," he added, reaching out to pat Tom's arm. "Never turn your back in a fight, and never, never, forget to duck."

Tom exhaled mightily, his eyes moist with relief.

"Well, come sit down while I get you some ice," she said, helping him to his feet and clucking with her tongue while checking the back of his head. "That little tap is going to be a big goose egg." She guided him to a chair and, placing her palm on his shoulder, forced him to sit. "Now stay put. I'll be right back."

Before leaving, she gathered the swords and, tucking them under her arm in a righteous sweep, marched into the kitchen.

Jack rose and walked over to Tom, wrapping a consoling arm around his shoulder and giving him a man-to-man shake. "Don't worry, pal. She'll let you have them back after she cools down."

Tom's thin shoulders shrugged with seeming acceptance, no doubt relieved that he didn't get a punishment. He turned to leave, then paused. Suddenly, in a swift, clumsy rush he turned back toward Jack, reached out to hug him fiercely around the waist, then ran off into the house, Maddie at his heels. This time Jack felt the sword directly in his heart.

"I thought I told you to sit down," Faye said, returning to the garden to find Jack standing with one hand on the back of his head, staring off with a bemused expression on his face. "Are you sure you're all right? You look a bit confused."

"Oh, I am," he conceded. "But not from the whack."

"Well come over here and put your feet up."

"Yes, ma'am," he replied with a teasing smile, but in truth he was enjoying the mothering.

He stretched out in the chair, perching his long legs onto an opposite chair, and closed his eyes. He was enjoying the scent of Faye's sweet perfume as she bent over him, the delicate touch of her fingers on his scalp, and the sound of her breathy voice murmuring exclamations of concern. At long last, he had her fingers in his own hair. He was in heaven, loath to feel her move away.

"Don't go," he said, prying open an eye. "Keep me company."

Faye chewed her lip, hearing a new note in his voice, one that spoke of longing and, perhaps, loneliness.

The air was thick and moist with a low-lying fog so heavy that their clothes clung to their bodies and her hair felt like a coil of hemp. Faye pulled her long hair up from her shoulders and gave it a twist, fastening it to her head in a clasp.

"Storm's coming," she said, pulling out a chair.

"It'll break the humidity," Jack replied. "Probably only have a few minutes before the rain comes."

"Let's just sit back and enjoy them then," she said, stretching out her legs on the opposite chair like Jack. She let her head fall back and closed her eyes.

Jack turned his head to gape in surprise. "That's a new attitude . . ." He paused. "For you." His gaze was trapped by the vision of long, smooth leg and taut, shapely thigh that curved beneath the thin dress fabric. Her small, rounded breasts rose and fell with each easy breath.

She sighed lustily, unaware. "Maybe it is."

After another tortuous gaze, Jack turned his head and said, "It suits you." He shifted uncomfortably in his chair then cocked his head, listening to her humming.

"What's that tune you're always humming?"

"I don't know," she replied, wiggling her toes and stifling a yawn. "I hear it at night sometimes. That flute music, remember? I just can't seem to get it out of my mind."

"It sounds so familiar," he said, his eyes taking on a faraway look. "I'm sure I've heard it somewhere before."

"Of course you have. You must have heard it from outside, like me."

"No, that's the strange part of it. I never hear the flute music, and I've been listening for it. But I've heard that tune somewhere before." He didn't tell her that when he heard her humming it, it stirred restless memories that he couldn't quite reach. It was as though they were hidden behind some gauzy veil.

She turned to glance at him, alert again to the longing in his voice. His eyes were closed, and his hand was molded over the icebag on his head, a long, hairless hand with beautifully shaped fingers that looked like they could belong to a concert pianist. She sighed, thinking to herself that those fingers could no doubt play a woman with as much sensitivity and lyricism as any instrument.

Smothering a groan in her throat, she turned away. If only her campaign to keep her desire for Jack Graham at a distance was as successful as her tea campaign was becoming. Not that he was making it any easier for her. She was eminently aware of his presence in the same building, the same garden, the same room. Of his breathing the same air that she did. To his credit, she could never accuse him of being obnoxious or pressing his attention or being anything but the good neighbor. The friend who lived next door.

Yet—there were times when she caught him looking at her with the same desire she no doubt wore in her eyes at this very moment. She'd see it flash in his eyes before he'd quickly turn away. That look never failed to arouse her, to stir her memories of a certain kiss between them, to deepen her longing to feel another such kiss. It was driving her insane. She knew where another such kiss would lead them, and it would ruin the friendship between them, a friendship she'd come to treasure.

What she needed at times such as this when she had feelings such as these was a good whack to her own head, she thought, slumping back in her chair.

"Do you want to go to Kensington Gardens tomorrow?" he asked, unaware of her turn of thoughts. "I bought a toy boat to float in the pond. She's a beauty. Maddie and Tom will love it."

"I suppose. If it's not too much trouble."

"I love spending time with the kids," he replied. He looked straight at her, throwing her a challenge as easily as if it were a pigskin ball. "And you."

She caught the challenge and sat up in her chair. "Jack, you're so good with children. They accept you as one of them. How is it that you never married? Or had children of your own?"

His face clouded, and he rubbed the back of his head gingerly as though being reminded of another, deeper hurt.

"I'm not the marrying kind. I have few possessions and responsibilities, and I like it that way. Though I'm no ivory-tower academician, I'm very good at what I do and

I work very hard at it. My work takes me all over the world. I like flying around at will, meeting new people.''

He looked back at her, his eyes clouded with a brooding intensity she didn't often see. ''The way I see it, making a baby doesn't make a man a father. Being a father means being there every day. Consistent and sure. I'm not ready for that, don't know if I ever want it.'' He reached down to slap a mosquito with a vengeance. ''And I won't be like my biological father. I have no memory of him, other than of a fist slamming into my face. The only thing I know for sure is that I was abandoned by him. And by my mother.''

Naturally, she thought of Tom, and her sympathy redoubled. She leaned closer and placed her hand on his.

''It's never easy for a mother to leave her child. Maybe she thought it was for the best.''

He looked at her hand covering his for a moment.

''I'll never know.'' Then rubbing the top of her knuckles with his thumb he said, ''Sure I like Maddie and Tom, like them a lot. They're wonderful kids. I like going places with them, talking with them, playing with them. But it's just another game. I'm playing make-believe father.''

''Being a free spirit is a kind of play, isn't it?'' she asked gently. ''To avoid real relationships?''

He cast her a sidelong glance. ''It's not me who's been avoiding.''

She comprehended his meaning and slipped her hand out from under his and tucked it safely in her lap. ''Relationships and sex are two different things entirely.''

''You're right about that,'' he said, his sarcasm a ready response to the sudden chill in her voice. ''I imagine it's great when they're combined.''

"I wouldn't know."

That silenced him.

In the distance a faint thunder rumbled, heralding the oncoming storm. Hearing it, Nana whimpered, retreated to the door, and scratched at it. Maddie opened the back door to her rescue, carrying her indoors, clucking her tongue, and crooning, "Poor Nana."

The door slammed behind her, leaving Jack and Faye in a silence as thick and weighted as the air that enveloped them. Not a birdcall, a cricket's song, or the hoot of an owl pierced the pause before nature unleashed her fury. Memories of another storm, and a certain kiss, flashed through their minds like the lightning in the distance. A sigh escaped Faye's lips, and the sound of her soft, high-pitched voice floated like a wisp of wind.

"Faye," Jack said in a rush, dropping the ice, swinging his legs around and inching to the edge of the chair closer to her. The stirred air sent their electrons charging. His knees grazed her legs, and she felt each hair against her tender nerve endings. He took her hand again in his own while his corona of curls fell over his broad forehead, obscuring his lowered lids.

"I wouldn't know either, Faye," he said at last. "And I wonder if it might not be possible. With you."

"A sexual relationship?"

"No. Not just that. A relationship that includes sex." His fingers pressed against her palm as his voice grew more urgent. "We already have a wonderful relationship. Don't we? I can't deny that the times I've spent with you and the children have been some of the happiest in my life."

"Jack, you don't have to say that . . ."

"It's true. My adoptive parents were older than most.

And by nature distant and formal. I always felt well cared for, but I never shared with them the relaxed, loving, cozy atmosphere of family that I share with you. You've included me, brought me into your family." Now he paused, and when he spoke again, his voice was low. "But I still want more. I want *you*, Faye." He tugged her closer till their faces were a breath apart. "Tell me that you don't feel the same for me."

She opened her mouth to deny it.

"Faye, I've watched you, observed every slight movement of your face. It's too late to lie now."

Her mouth went dry, and she closed it without speaking. It was no use lying, to him or to herself. To pretend any longer that her feelings for him were merely those of a friend, a kind neighbor, or a sister. She found Jack Graham every inch a virile, seductive, utterly desirable man.

She confessed all this with her silence.

"I'm a patient man, but it seems to me you take two steps back for every one I take closer to you. Why are you avoiding me? I've tried to give you space and time, but it's been hard, Faye. Very hard."

She closed her eyes, giving herself a moment to let reason overcome her own choking desire.

"I'm not avoiding you. I'm giving you signals that you refuse to accept. Jack, it's not that I don't find you attractive. I do! Very. It's just that . . . I'd rather not." She met his gaze, urging him to understand. "It's a new experience for me, having a male friend. I accept that it is enough. Why can't you just leave things the way they are? Why must you try and ruin it?"

"You think sex would ruin our friendship?"

"I do. Sex was all I had with Rob. We got married and we never should have."

"How about if I promise not to marry you?" His eyes crinkled at the corners, and she couldn't help the laugh that escaped.

"I'll think about it," she conceded.

His gaze dropped to her lips. "I promised I would ask your permission before I kissed you again."

The air thickened again, and her chest felt constricted, her breath scarce. She knew a sexual relationship with Jack would be wonderful. But she also knew that he was unreliable, like Rob. A free spirit. He'd said so himself. And she'd never push a man to marry her again. Nor could she go through a relationship that gradually disintegrated. She didn't think she could handle that particular pain again, and she wouldn't put her children through it.

"Don't," she said.

He dragged his gaze from her lips back to her eyes. He saw a brightness in her eyes, the source of which was not passion or desire. It was a faint glimmer, as uncertain as a small ember in a cold log, yet it shone bravely, determinedly, through a darkness that he knew was put there by pain.

He could not add to that pain, he decided. Who was he to think he could have a real relationship with anyone, much less a woman like Faye O'Neill? Someone like her needed, deserved, a whole man, someone to be there for her and for her children. Not half a man, a man without a history, like himself. She needed someone who could help that glimmer of light to glow, not squelch it.

He backed away, dropping her hand. It was better this way, he told himself. He didn't need anyone to tie him down. It wasn't his style. He liked his life the way it was.

Nearby, thunder cracked, breaking the tension in the sky. The wind picked up and angrily threw at them a few fat, wet drops of rain that plopped loudly, gracelessly, on their heads, the table, and the bricks.

"Come on, pal," Jack drawled, reeling her up from the chair, close to his chest. They both stood for a moment, whipped by the gusting wind, shivering. "I think Mother Nature is frustrated with us." His breath was warm against the top of her head. Then in a sudden move he stepped back and gently pushed her forward. "Better not tempt her too much. She doesn't like to be ignored."

Chapter 14

THE FOLLOWING WEEK Jack returned early to No. 14, his head swimming from the success of his final series of experiments. All they had to do now was write up the paper and send it out. Irwin and the whole team were still celebrating back at the Institute, but he didn't feel like partying with them. He had an overwhelming urge to share the good news with Faye and the kids. He glanced at his wristwatch. They'd probably be gathered in his kitchen about now, Faye at the Aga stove. He smiled, and his stomach growled just thinking about all the meals she'd been cooking there every night lately, and he told himself it was the prospect of a home-cooked dinner that made him so eager to return home.

So he escaped the many slaps on the back, the come-hither looks of Rebecca Fowler, and the glasses of champagne offered and instead took the tube home, thinking that maybe he'd take the gang out for some ice cream after dinner. They could try out that new sweetshop Tom had spotted just a few blocks over. It was a balmy night and wouldn't it be nice to take a walk? He smiled in anticipation as he entered his flat, thinking that maybe he

233

could convince Nana to try taking her first walk on a leash. Tossing his keys, he thought if he was lucky, maybe he could even try holding Faye's hand.

As he passed through the dark halls of his flat to the rear kitchen, a sense of unease coursed through him. Everything was too quiet. Something was missing. Reaching the kitchen he found that it, too, was dimly lit and empty. He stopped at the Aga, turned his head and searched the deserted room, his mouth agape with disappointment.

He was alone. Faye, Maddie, Tom, even Nana, weren't here in the kitchen where he'd expected them.

Expected them. Jack tugged at the Windsor knot of his tie and unbuttoned the top button of his oxford shirt, feeling a bit choked. What was happening? What had happened to him over the past few weeks? He *liked* coming home to find everyone piled around the long scrubbed kitchen table, smelling the scent of rosemary or garlic or thyme from the garden simmering on the stove, hearing his name called out in cheery voices as he was welcomed home.

Home. He pulled the tie from around his neck and tossed it on the empty chair, staring at it for a few moments longer.

What the hell, he thought, bounding up the stairs to the O'Neill flat. He was too tired to think anymore tonight. He only knew what he felt, what he wanted—and that was to see Faye's face at his table. And Maddie and Tom's, and even that crazy puppy, Nana.

At the top of the stairs he came to an abrupt halt, finding instead Mrs. Lloyd and Mrs. Jerkins with their heads bent close, deep in conversation. That pair was as predictable as the law of gravity, he thought irritably. And just as much a downer.

Jane Lloyd was impeccably dressed as usual in a cool silk dress, polished pumps, and hair that didn't budge even when she wagged her head, as she did now. Yet like the Queen, she still managed to look frumpy. And as for Ol' Horseface, well, the less said the better.

He wished he could escape down the back stairs, but it was too late. They'd already spotted him, on the scent like two long-eared, pointy-nosed hunting dogs. He sighed, resigned to his fate.

The two women raised their brows and exchanged a meaningful glance. Mrs. Jerkins took a step backwards into the flat, far enough to be respectful, but not too far that she couldn't hear every word that was spoken.

"Halloo, Dr. Graham," Mrs. Lloyd said in her high-pitched croon. There was no mistaking the disapproval in the undertones.

He smiled in kind, looking longingly at the exit.

"I understand there have been a few changes in the building since I've last been here. Unlocking doors, are we?"

"Indeed we are, Mrs. Lloyd," he replied, the devil rising in him. "I had no problem at all with the locks, actually."

Nettled, she brushed away some invisible lint from the lace doily on the hall table. "I would have appreciated notice. And would it have been too much to ask permission for a pet?"

"But I did. In fact, Wendy insisted."

The nettle was visible now, a red flush creeping up her neck that was now ramrod straight.

"I see." She tucked her hands together, hoisting her

bosom a good couple of inches. "Dr. Graham, it simply won't do that you and others I might mention in Number 14 feel you can go over my head to my mother. I manage this building. The lease is between us, and I must insist that you lock those doors right back up. As for the dog, well, you may keep the dog since you will be leaving in September anyway and it would be a shame to upset my mother any further. You realize that she honestly believes that your dog is her own Nana, a dog she had as a child! Her condition is only getting worse. I was afraid something like this might happen."

Jack didn't feel the need to explain the puppy's remarkable heritage. "Her condition?"

"Quite. She is not entirely in touch with reality, is she?"

Jack's face grew thunderous. "Everything is humming along just fine here. We're all perfectly happy with the arrangement. No one more so than your mother."

"I can understand why you and Mrs. O'Neill might be happy," she said with a loud sniff. "I don't approve of the goings-on in this building, especially not in front of those children!"

"Goings-on?" Jack felt his temper rise and turned to cast a threatening glance toward Mrs. Jerkins, who quickly darted her gaze away.

"If you can't stay away from Mrs. O'Neill," Jane Lloyd continued, "at least have the decency to leave Mrs. Forrester alone. I don't want you encouraging her in her fantasies. You and those children spend far too much time with her."

"Someone should spend time with her," Jack exploded. "You certainly don't! Good day, Mrs. Lloyd. Mrs. Jerkins," he said through tight lips, then turned and walked quickly back to his flat, not trusting that he wouldn't say something he would regret later.

Jane Lloyd was visibly shaken by Jack's accusation. Mrs. Jerkins sidled close, eyes over her shoulder marking Jack's departure down the rear stairs.

"Tsk ... tsk ... tsk. Trouble's coming, that's for sure," she said from the side of her mouth.

"I simply can't allow that. This situation demands action. It's time for Mother to face the facts. She must be sensible, for once in her life. Mrs. Jerkins, I depend upon you as always to keep a close eye on Mrs. Forrester. We must be vigilant! You know she won't go to a nursing home on her own volition, so I shall need something solid, something that will hold up in court, if we must take things into our own hands. She simply cannot stay here on her own any longer. Then I'll sell this place and put an end to those childish fantasies of hers about strange lights and stars and . . ." She shook her head, unwilling to say the boy's name that hovered at her lips.

Mrs. Lloyd and Mrs. Jerkins nodded conspiratorially, then departed, Mrs. Jerkins back into the O'Neill flat and Mrs. Lloyd up the stairs to visit her mother.

Neither woman saw the small, thin boy tucked inside the crawl space under the stairs, quiet as a mouse.

During the final weeks of summer, Faye concentrated all her efforts on the Hampton Tea campaign, no small thanks to the support of Wendy and Jack. She couldn't have pulled it off without them. No one worked harder than she did, arriving early every day and staying late, overseeing every detail of the presentation, driving for better statistics and acting as liaison between the people at Hampton Tea and the team at Leo Burnett. As account exec, she covered every aspect of the campaign, from direct mailing to TV, so that the presentation the following week would provide her client a clear and consistent message.

Bernard admired people who "bit the bullet," and she overheard him comment to Susan Perkins that his "girl had the old edge back." Even her team begrudgingly followed her lead, working long hours to create the best campaign they could by next week's deadline. They might not have been gung ho about her campaign idea, but they respected her competence and went along. Only Susan Perkins kept her comments in reserve, lying in wait. She chose her moment a week before the presentation.

Faye was just finishing up the final review. She sensed a guarded optimism. Susan Perkins entered the room looking cool and professional as usual in a chic plum suit and white-silk blouse with her dark hair sleeked back behind two impressive mabe pearl earrings. She didn't sit but stood by the door, listening, with a little frown of skepticism. Faye didn't have to look down to see that her workhorse of a coffee brown pant suit was creased and tired after a long day's work.

Susan didn't have to say a word. Her stance, her pose, her animosity rippled through the room, ruining the optimism Faye had so carefully built up for the past two hours. When she finished her summation, Faye knew Susan had succeeded in her ambush. Jaishree crossed her legs and arms, frowning. Patrick immediately slouched and rolled his eyes at Susan, who, catching the glance, lifted her lip in a commiserating curl. After they'd left, Faye's shoulders slumped as she stuffed her materials into her leather case.

"Don't be discouraged," Pascal said, hanging back.

"I didn't need that from Susan—from any of them—right before I have to make this presentation. Don't they know that?"

"But of course they do," he retorted in his marvelous French accent. "Patrick and Jaishree, they are toadies that think the only way to get ahead is to suck up to the boss. And Susan, ha! She lives to bully the little people, like us. She is madly jealous of you and wants to bring you down."

"But why? We're on the same side. I've tried so hard to work with her."

"Forget it, *chérie*. You make her look bad. You're good, and she hasn't had a good idea in a long time. People like her, they don't care about the product. Or if other people get hurt. They care only about their own power. Whether or not Hampton Tea sells well in America is not so important to her. What matters to her is whether or not she climbs the ladder." He shrugged and crossed his arms in front of him, openly assessing her figure. "And you are much more beautiful. That, she can never forgive you for." He raised a brow and gave an insolent shrug. "Did you see those earrings?" He leaned closer to her ear. "Fake."

Faye laughed and leaned against him. "Oh Pascal, what would I do without you?"

"I am wondering what you might do *with* me, *chérie*."

"A wonderful campaign is all the magic I hope to create with you, *monsieur*," she replied, tapping his chest.

"Too bad," he responded, his dark eyes flirting.

"Probably." Suddenly the image of Jack Graham flashed through her mind. It startled her, and she blinked it away. She turned to stuff her papers into her briefcase. "I haven't time for anything but work, work, work. And

I'd better get going if I'm going to make that appointment with the Art Department at Hampton Tea. We'll be discussing your work, by the way. I know they'll go crazy for it.''

"Of course. You inspire me." He wagged his brows, and she laughed again, telling him for the hundredth time that he was incorrigible, which was, she knew, exactly what he wanted to hear.

Her appointment at Hampton concluded earlier than expected, and she found herself with an hour to spare. Thinking again of Jack, she recalled him saying he was giving a public lecture, not far away. Acting on impulse, she hailed a cab and made her way to the lecture hall, where she was informed by a small sign that Dr. Jack Graham was lecturing in the main auditorium that afternoon at 4:00 P.M. As her heels clicked down the long hall she smoothed the wrinkles from her suit and tucked her loose tendrils behind her ear, tidying up should Jack glance up and see her. Wouldn't he be surprised?

The heavy auditorium door squeaked as she pushed it open. Faye paused, stunned. There was no chance that Jack would even notice she was here. She'd expected to find most of the seats empty, like the lecture halls she'd attended while in college. After all, she'd thought with typical creative smugness, this was a science lecture.

The place was packed! Students, professors, and guests alike were busily scribbling in their notebooks and leaning forward in their seats to better hear. Other than the sound of Jack's voice, the auditorium was silent, spellbound. Clutching her briefcase to her chest, she ducked her head and tiptoed to the closest unoccupied seat and slipped in. Once settled, she sat like all the others, transfixed by the tall, lanky, handsome professor who leisurely paced across the stage, one hand in his suit pocket and the other gesticulating in the air.

Who was this somber scientist? He was like a star, a brilliant point of light out there on the stage. Gone was the boyish, sexy man in casual clothes and bare feet that knocked on her door on weekends and haunted her dreams in the night. Standing on the stage was, according to the paper hanging on the auditorium door, one of the world's foremost theoretical physicists. An award-winning, visiting professor from Berkeley with several books to his credit. She had no idea he was anything but an isolated scientist working in some lab with high-tech equipment, computers, and test tubes. But here he was, discussing the possible beginnings of the universe with the same ease that he discussed fireflies with Maddie and Tom. Faye felt her own small world rock.

Faye sat back in her seat filled with awe and respect and something else she couldn't define. She was seeing Jack with new eyes. Eyes that were wide-open. His intelligence was intimidating, but it was his charisma that overwhelmed her. His confidence, both in his knowledge and in himself, shone a little too bright. She felt, in comparison, quite dim.

When the lecture was completed a crowd immediately clustered around Jack like planets around the sun, shaking his hand, holding out books to be signed, eager to ask questions. Faye grabbed her briefcase and slipped out of the hall unnoticed. A heavy fog rolled in, and she had a difficult time finding a cab. By the time she caught one, she was soaking wet. As the cab sped past folks hurrying under umbrellas, several postage-stamp-sized parks, and scattered dress shops whose lights pierced the fog, Faye stared out the streaked window and only saw Jack up on that stage. A different Jack. Someone brilliant, clever, good. Someone beyond her grasp. She felt her old insecurities rumble, and in the recesses of her mind she was haunted by the whisper that she was not worthy of such a man.

Yet, she thought as she bounced and swerved in the backseat of the cab, she'd never before felt so attracted to him. It was as though a veil had been lifted and she saw the whole man for the first time.

And loved him at first sight.

She'd felt so enamored of a man only once before. Her ex-husband, Rob. Despite his faults, Rob O'Neill had been a glowing star in his own galaxy.

She groaned, leaning her head back against the scratchy cushion. Perhaps it was a defense mechanism to compare Jack to Rob, a mental ploy to distance her from the chance of another disappointment. But in truth she'd cared for only two men in her life. And Jack Graham and Rob O'Neill were as different as two men could be.

Or were they, she wondered? They both ran from commitment. They both lived for the moment and relished the exotic. Peter Pans, both of them. She brought her fist to her forehead and rubbed it, as though she could rub the image of Jack from her brain.

"Once burned, shame on you. Twice burned, shame on me," she muttered.

What to do, what to do? She didn't need this now. She didn't want to care for Jack. Didn't want to need him or anyone else. Damn, no distractions now. She rested her forehead against the glass, staring out at the rain with a forlorn expression. Could she take the chance and become involved again in a relationship—with an opposite? Her heart said yes, oh yes. But in her mind, the answer was as plain to read as the periodic table of the elements that hung in the lecture hall.

Even a dummy in science like herself knew that mixing baking soda and vinegar resulted in an explosion.

Chapter 15

BACK AT No. 14, Mrs. Lloyd's high-pitched voice entered the building before she did. While the keys rattled in the front door, Maddie and Tom darted into the rear staircase that led to Jack's flat, carefully leaving the door open just enough so that they could spy. A trick they'd learned from Mrs. Jerkins.

"Here we are," crooned Mrs. Lloyd in that sugar-coated manner that the children cringed at hearing.

Peeking through the crack, Maddie and Tom saw Mrs. Lloyd lead a tall, dark man with a funny black mustache and shiny shoes into the foyer. He narrowed his eyes to thin slits as his gaze swept the room, seeming to take in every detail. Maddie closed the door a wee bit more to be on the safe side.

"Now the house hasn't been redone in years, but I believe you'll see that it is in excellent condition," said Mrs. Lloyd. "Just needs a bit of polish, eh?"

The gentleman merely sniffed and offered some polite muttering that the children couldn't make out as a reply.

Mrs. Lloyd appeared flustered, and that alone might have been enough to raise the children's suspicions. But it was her next comment that had them on full alert.

"Of course I shall have to make the necessary legal arrangements, but," she hurried to add, "I should like to sell the house as soon as possible. Shall we begin in the first-floor flat? It is let at the moment to an American family. With *children*." She said the last with the same tone she might have said, *vermin*. "It is only a one-year lease. Shall we have a look-see? The tenant isn't home, but the nanny is expecting us."

She knocked, and Mrs. Jerkins promptly opened the door and led them into the flat.

Maddie and Tom looked at each other, mouths agape and outrage flushing their cheeks. They knew their mother gave no such permission for Mrs. Jerkins to be opening the flat to strangers. And this stranger was obviously someone who wanted to buy the house. They hurried as fast as their legs would carry them up the stairs to the nursery, where in a rush they told Wendy of all they'd overheard.

"So, she thinks to sell the house from under me, does she?" Wendy's eyes lit with fire, and she lifted her chin so that the delicate point resembled the tip of a dagger. "Tell me, children, are you in the mood for a little mischief?"

Two heads nodded enthusiastically.

Wendy tapped her chin with her finger. "I seem to remember your complaining about ants in the garden, isn't that so, Maddie?"

Maddie's eyes sparkled, and she smothered a laugh with her palm as she nodded, the glint of conspiracy in her eye.

*   *   *

Downstairs, Mrs. Lloyd was busily showing her mysterious visitor the second floor of the O'Neill flat. Upstairs in the nursery, the children were poised on the bed. At Wendy's signal, they began leaping from the bed, the chairs, from any high point they could climb to, then landing hard on the floor. The lights were flickering in the nursery, as they knew full well they were also flickering downstairs.

"Excellent, children! Now man your next stations. Ready?"

At the signal, Tom turned the water on full blast at the kitchen sink. Wendy hustled to turn on the water in the bathtub. The pipes groaned and spit out sprays of water, pushing the pressure to the limits. Meanwhile, Maddie ran to the bathroom in their own flat and timed it so that when Mrs. Lloyd passed through the hall, Maddie stepped out from the bathroom, and complained loudly, "Mrs. Lloyd, the water's not coming out again."

Maddie sauntered by the tall gentleman in the hall, smiling politely. But not before slipping a small dog biscuit into his coat pocket while he poked his nose into a closet. In the bathroom, Mrs. Lloyd was fiddling with the faucets, sputtering out excuses that were as pitiful as the few drops of water that squeezed out from the pipes.

Just before she slipped out of the flat, Maddie heard Mrs. Lloyd exclaim in a loud wail, "I really don't know where all those ants came from! I shall call an exterminator immediately, of course!"

For the coup de grâce, Wendy gave Tom a glass of water and dispatched him to the front foyer, then sent Maddie in search of Nana. A few moments later, when a frazzled Mrs. Lloyd and her gentleman visitor emerged from the flat into the foyer, Nana came barking at the stranger's heels, then catching the scent, began leaping up his trousers at his pocket. Maddie put one hand to her cheek and with the other hand pointed to a puddle on the floor, and cried, "Bad Nana! What have you done?"

The tall gentlemen's face puckered like he smelled a foul odor, he shook the puppy from his heel, and muttered something about how dogs did terrible damage to a house and how he'd seen quite enough, thank you very much.

Mrs. Lloyd's face turned crimson as she watched the tall gentleman leave through the front door.

"Halloo, Jane dear," sang Wendy's voice from the upper landing. Her elfin face peeked over the banister, and even from the first floor anyone could see that her bright blue eyes were twinkling like distant stars. "What a pleasant surprise! To think you came for a visit!"

A few days later, Tom once again gave Mrs. Jerkins the slip and scurried up the stairs to find refuge in the nursery. He just couldn't wait till six o'clock to see Wendy. She never scolded him for jumping on the bed like Ol' Horseface did, and she didn't smell of menthol or medicine, and most of all she didn't look at him with that same scary, mean look that he remembered his father had when he talked funny and tripped on furniture and hit his mom. Tom liked it up in the nursery, where the walls were pale blue like the sky and filled with wonderful pictures that made him laugh, where there were fun, curious things to look at, and no one said, "Don't touch." Where the canary chirped and hopped closer to the wire rim of the cage to eat the bits of carrot and apple he fed it, and where Wendy always was so happy to welcome him, to offer him candy and, smelling like roses, to cuddle him beside her on the window seat. She always read to him from her great green book, and sometimes she let him read aloud to her. They'd been working on that skill all summer. It was their greatest secret.

When he tiptoed into the nursery that afternoon, however, it was quiet as a church. He didn't hear Wendy humming or music playing; not even the canary chirped. It hunkered, one legged, on its perch. Tom stepped carefully, slowly, across the great long room, looking from left to right. Then he stopped, his left foot frozen in midair when he heard a soft groan coming from the bedroom. The groan came again, and this time he recognized the voice as Wendy's. If he could have flown, he couldn't have reached her side any faster.

Jack lay on the cold, damp flagstone under the fountain swearing like a sailor. The clanging from his wrenches as he wrestled with nuts and bolts that wouldn't budge echoed in his ears, and he was so mad at the stubborn lump of bronze and brass that sometimes he just banged it for good measure. There was no reason that he could tell for this darn fountain not to work. He'd read dozens of books and it was all pretty straightforward. Water comes in, swirls through the pump and gets pushed out of the boy's pipes. Except that this cocky boy wouldn't play! Well, he'd just see about that, he thought, grinding his teeth and having another go at the mechanics.

Suddenly the door to the O'Neill flat burst open and he saw two small feet in Keds running across the patio toward him. His muscles tightened and his gaze sharpened. Nana had scooted out from the hydrangea bushes barking excitedly.

"Jack!"

Jack pushed out from under the fountain, not sure in

the hustle of motion and the incessant yapping of Nana that he'd actually heard a small boy's voice. He scrambled to his feet, and Tom rushed into his arms, pressing his tear-stained face against his belly and wrapping thin arms tight around his waist. Instantly, Jack closed his arms around the boy.

"What is it, Tom?" His heart was pounding and his mouth was dry.

"It's W...W...Wendy," he stammered. Between the sobs and hiccups he garbled a few more words that Jack couldn't catch. When he tried to loosen his arms, the boy held on tighter.

"Tom, let go now, loosen up. That's right," he crooned, and when Tom did, Jack bent low to look into the boy's face. His eyes were red and puffy and round with worry. "Where is Wendy?"

Tom sniffed loudly and took a deep breath. "In the nursery. In her bedroom. I came in and it was dark and I heard her moan. She's on the floor!" His voice rose. "She must'a falled down." His voice rose higher. "She's lying there, crying. Just like Mom! We gotta help her!"

"We will, Tom. I promise. Now, come on, boy. Show me!"

Tom led Jack to where Wendy lay on the floor beside her bed, just as Tom had told him. She was awake but groggy, alert enough to tell him she had no broken bones.

"Tom, grab hold of Nana," he ordered. The puppy was romping at Wendy's face, licking her cheeks gleefully. Jack lifted Wendy into his arms, thinking as he did so that she was no bigger than a young girl and weighed no more. He settled her gently into her bed. Tom propped a mountain of pillows behind her so she could sit up without effort, then the boy sat on the bed beside her, leaning against the pillows, taking her hand between his two small ones and staring at her face with the devotion of a pup.

"I feel so foolish," Wendy exclaimed, her voice weak. The color was returning to her cheeks, but Jack doubted he would forget the deathly pallor he had seen moments before.

"I'll go get Nurse Jerkins."

"No!" Both Wendy and Tom exclaimed this in unison.

Jack stopped short and looked at them both staring back at him. Then Tom sat up, took a deep breath, and spoke with eyes alive with intent.

"You can't, 'cause I was hiding and I heard Ol' Horseface talking to Mrs. Lloyd and they want to spy on Wendy so they can find a reason to put Wendy into an old lady home for her own good they say but it's so Mrs. Lloyd can sell this house for lotsa money and then you'll hafta move and so will we and then . . . and then Wendy won't be able to talk to Peter because he won't know where she is!"

"Well put, dear boy," Wendy said, leaning back against the pillows with a whisper of a smile.

Tom took a deep breath and exhaled heavily, satisfied that he'd gotten it right.

Jack stood, stunned by the flow of words from Tom's mouth. Wendy didn't seem the least surprised. Of course, he realized. The medical literature was right. Wendy was Tom's best tonic. She'd gradually drawn him out, story by story.

"I see," replied Jack, rubbing his jaw, gathering his wits. "But Wendy, you still must be seen by someone."

"Nonsense, Jack," she replied as though he were a boy who should get his knuckles rapped for such an insinuation. "I know exactly what happened. I simply forgot and took an extra dose of my blood-pressure medicine. I've done it before and it always makes me faint. That's all. It's a blessing Tootles discovered me before that wretched Nurse Jerkins, or I'd have Jane and her doctors and solicitors swarming about me like the bunch of bullies they are.''

"Wendy, I must insist. I'm sorry. Hey, don't the two of you look at me like I'm a Blackbeard. I'm right behind you if you don't want to see Mrs. Jerkins and get involved in that business. How about I take you to your doctor myself? Just for a checkup? No one need know.''

"At my age, there isn't much to check!'' she snapped. "They simply listen to my heart, take my pressure, give me a few more pills, pat me on my head, mutter something ridiculous about how I'll live forever, and send me on my way.''

"Wendy,'' he said, sounding much too much like a stern father for his own liking, "you must go.''

She pouted but nodded. "Very well. But only if you promise not to be a sneaky tell-tale to Mrs. Jerkins.''

He chuckled, raising his hands in the Boy Scouts' honor sign, and said, "I swear.''

Tom was speaking! Faye practically flew home from work, her heart in her throat. By the time she crossed the threshold of No. 14 she was mute with joy, able only to hug her little boy and blubber and thoroughly embarrass him, despite the ear-to-ear grin Tom wore on his face.

She rose to scurry up the stairs to thank Wendy when Jack put an arresting hand on her shoulder.

"Wendy's resting,'' he told her in confidential tones, then led her to a quiet room where he explained the events of the morning.

"Are you sure she's all right?" she asked, fear for Wendy striking deep in her heart.

"The doctor gave her a clean bill of health, but told her to rest. She's not getting any younger."

"To me, she's ageless," Faye whispered, looking out the window. Then, bringing her gaze back to Jack, she saw the worry etched in the lines of his forehead as well. She felt like a dam of emotion was bursting, and she couldn't stop the leaking at the eyes.

"I can't believe my Tom's talking. You don't know, Jack, what this means to me. I can't begin to explain . . ."

"Shhh . . ." he said, wrapping a consoling arm around her shoulder and drawing her close against his chest. "You don't have to explain to me. I have a pretty good idea. I've been choking back tears all day myself."

She leaned against him, relishing his strength wrapped around her. "Of course you do." Then, sniffing, she added, "You're like one of the family."

She heard his breath still and felt his muscles tighten under her cheek. She could've bitten her tongue for the slip. "What I meant," she hedged, "was that we're all such a big, happy family here in Number 14. Me and the kids, you, Wendy. And of course, Nana." She thought if she added the dog that would clearly de-escalate things.

"Sure. Absolutely."

Was that relief she heard? "When I shop at the grocer's for rolls or pieces of beef or even cans of soda, I always count out five now: me, Maddie, Tom, Wendy . . . and you." She didn't look up.

"And when I plan an outing to the park or the movies, I call you. And the kids."

"Right." Why did her throat feel like it was closing up? Looking at her fingers, she was horrified to find that she was twiddling with the buttons of his shirt. She quickly dropped her hands to her sides and backed away, bereft at feeling his arms drop from her shoulders.

"Faye?"

"Yes."

He reached out and lifted her chin to gaze into her eyes. His eyes were emitting messages as fast and powerfully as quasars.

"What does that tell you? About us?" he asked.

She swallowed hard and felt the blood drain from her face. How could she tell him that it told her he'd somehow become part of her everyday? How could she confess that the sun rose and set with his image in her mind? How could she lay herself so bare as to admit that he'd finagled his way deeply into not only her life but the lives of her children? And that when he left in September, as she knew he would, he would create a black hole that they would have to crawl out from?

The answer was she could not.

"It tells me that we are the very best of friends."

He paused, seemingly registering her words. Then with a cocky tilt of his head, he said, "Maybe a bit more than friends?"

She sighed, and her heart took wing. "Just maybe."

For days, Faye's heart seemed to fly from her chest every time she heard Tom utter a word, a sentence, or even a whole bunch of them mumbled together like a brilliant, spectacular bouquet of flowers. Her joy was the glue that held her together during the difficult week of hectic preparations, last-minute changes, and long days and late nights of huddled conferences with her creative team. The big presentation to Hampton Tea was the following Monday and the hysteria levels were building. All had to buffed, polished, and readied for takeoff.

She was at the office with her team most of that Saturday, working straight through the afternoon at a relentless pace. Then just before four o'clock, knowing she couldn't face another pot of Hampton tea that day, Faye threw up her hands, announced that they were as ready as they were gonna be, and told every one to go home and get some rest. Exhausted herself, she limped home, wondering how she even remembered to place one foot before the other.

"I'm home!" she called, popping her head into her flat, but no one answered. A note on the table informed her that the Jack had taken Maddie and Tom to race toy boats at Round Pond in Kensington Garden.

She leaned against the door and closed her eyes, wanting nothing more than to collapse in bed and sleep for twenty-four hours. Yet she knew she should take this quiet time while the children were out of earshot to go the nursery and properly thank dear Wendy, who she was convinced was singularly responsible for Tom's miracle.

She smiled, thinking of all the wonderful changes in their lives since they'd entered No. 14 and Wendy's sphere. Wendy *was* magic. A dose of Wendy was exactly what they all needed every day. Didn't she know that Wendy's optimism and spirit was just what Tom needed? And with all the tension and anxiety of the upcoming tea campaign presentation, she could use a good dose of the tonic herself, Faye thought, beginning her climb up the stairs.

The door to the nursery was open, but on peering in, she found Wendy sitting alone on the window seat, dressed in her best, with a bit of lace at the collar and at her cuffs. She was looking forlornly out the closed window.

"Wendy? Halloo there! It's me, Faye." She sensed immediately that something was wrong and entered slowly.

The table had been set for a formal tea. Drawing near, however, Faye noticed that the tea had gone cold in the cups, untouched. The little cakes and sandwiches sat stale on the three-tiered plate, and not a spoon or a fork had been put to service. Faye frowned with concern to see Wendy sitting dejected with her slight shoulders bent, like old Miss Haversham sitting amid the ruins.

"Wendy? Whatever is the matter? Were you expecting someone? Not us I hope? Oh Wendy, we didn't forget an invitation, did we?"

Wendy blinked as one coming out of a deep reverie, then shook her head slowly and turned to face her. A sad smile flitted across her face. "Oh no, not you. Never you." She sighed and cast a doubtful glance across the tea table. "My great-grandchildren were expected for a visit today."

"They didn't show up?" Faye couldn't believe anyone could be so thoughtless. Not even Jane Lloyd's grandchildren.

Wendy's eyes watered under soft pink lids. "Perhaps they forgot. Or perhaps they don't have time." She sighed. "Perhaps my stories are not so very interesting to teenagers."

Sympathy formed a knot in Faye's throat as she crouched low beside Wendy and took the tiny, delicate hands into her own. She felt the old woman's fragility and noticed that her skin was as pale and translucent as the thin pages of the book in her lap. Faye squeezed Wendy's hand, wanting to lift her spirits as Wendy had lifted hers so many times in the past months.

"Oh no, Wendy, your stories are timeless."

Wendy peered into her face, seemingly surprised. Faye realized with a flush of shame that she herself had never actually sat at Wendy's knee to listen to the stories as the others had. She'd heard them secondhand from Maddie as she sat on her bedside at tuck-in time. Nor had she really paid attention to the words, preferring to watch the emotions that played across her daughter's face. No, she'd always been too busy to linger in the nursery after tea for stories, too sure that they were just fairy tales meant for children. Indeed, she thought with chagrin. Perhaps she'd been rather like Wendy's great-grandchildren, teenagers who thought they were too wise and mature to need advice from someone older.

Slipping down to sit Indian-style on the carpet, Faye said, "Tell me one now, please, Wendy?"

Wendy's countenance brightened with the delight of a fisherman who'd caught the big one. She sat straighter in her chair, mustering her energy, and tapped her cheek with her fingertip as she pondered, "Which one? Which one?" Then she leaned forward and gazed down at Faye's face. It seemed that her unusually bright blue eyes were like lanterns that peered into her mind as she poked around and lifted lids, snooping to discover what troubled Faye. She must have found what she was looking for because she sat back, nodding with satisfaction, and began her story in her rich, melodious voice.

"Peter Pan, as he'd be the first to tell you, can be very clever and very brave. He once employed both these talents to save the Indian Princess, Tiger Lily, from the horrid Captain Hook in Mermaids' Lagoon. You remember that story, don't you? Good, good. Afterwards, you never saw such rejoicing. The Piccaninny warriors dubbed Peter, The Great White Father, which of course he liked a great deal. They presented him with a magnificent headdress, and they all danced around a great, roaring fire. Tiger Lily always had a special feeling for Peter, you know,'' Wendy said archly. ''That night in particular she pranced and preened before him, and that silly boy's eyes were as round and full of dreaminess as the moon.''

Faye held back a smile as Wendy paused to shift in her seat and smooth her skirt, seemingly still vexed by the memory.

''Well,'' she began again, ''despite the happiness of the celebration, as I watched I felt a great isolation. Peter had forgotten all about me. And the boys were too busy hooting and hollering to bother with one prim girl sitting alone beside a distant teepee.'' Wendy looked at her hands while her brows gathered. ''I felt I didn't really fit in on that magical island. I wasn't a boy, that was certain. Nor was I a squaw or a mermaid. Yet I loved the Neverland. I loved . . . Peter.'' She paused and twisted her hands, blushing.

Faye thought, *My goodness, she loves him still!* And her heart felt a pang for the old lady.

''I'm embarrassed to confess,'' Wendy continued, ''that I was a bit weepy that night, feeling terribly sorry for myself and wanting to be home again.'' Wendy looked up and her eyes brightened in the memory. ''Then I felt a fluttering on my shoulder, just touching my cheek. It was feather-soft, and I heard the faint, sweet sound of bells. It was none other than Tinkerbell. Well, you can imagine my surprise, and I winced, fully expecting a hard pinch. Tinkerbell, you see, was not exactly a friend. She was quite jealous of my friendship with Peter. But there she was, plain as day, and in her inimitable fashion, she proceeded to give me what-for. I couldn't translate exactly what she said, not understanding fairy talk, but as I sat back in astonishment and watched and listened to this mad fluttering of wings and bell ringing, it dawned on me.

"Whatever it was inside of me, whatever kernel deep inside that enabled me to believe in fairies, in Peter, in the Neverland itself, *this* was my source of strength. No one could ever take that away from me. As long as I believed, no matter where I was or with whom, I'd always belong. Because I was at home in my own heart."

Wendy reached out to cup Faye's cheek in her palm. "Knowing that I have a fairy on my shoulder, I have nothing to fear."

Chapter 16

THE MORNING OF the Hampton Tea presentation Faye dressed carefully. She didn't care to compete with Susan's dramatic look or Jaishree's leggy, sexy one, and settled instead on her own quietly professional style. Her ideas had to shine through, not her fashion sense.

The navy suit she'd bought on sale at Harrods was still terribly overpriced, but she liked it and it was conservative enough to be another warhorse in her stable. She wound her blond hair into a neat French twist, then nailed it tight with an army of bobby pins and an ocean of hairspray that made her feel like she was wearing a helmet on her head. There would be no loose tendrils today, she vowed! Looking in the mirror, she conceded that her ceremonial armor was in order. Onward to battle!

Her front doorbell rang early, and, opening her door, she was surprised to find Jack at her threshold carrying a small wrapped box.

"I'd kiss you for luck," he teased, "but I don't want to waste it. I have a feeling that with you I'll only get one more."

"A gift? Jack, I . . ."

"Gotta run. Break a leg, Faye," he said, then ducked out the door.

She carried the box to the window where, looking outside, she caught a final glimpse of Jack walking in his long-legged stride down the block. My, he really was handsome . . . and the most thoughtful man she'd ever met. What was she going to do about him, she wondered? She unwrapped the box with shaky fingers. Inside she found a small gold star on a thin gold chain. The note read, *Second star to the right, and straight on till morning!* She slipped the chain around her neck, pressing the star close to her chest, deeply touched.

A crash in the kitchen sent her running. There she found Maddie with one of her aprons tied around her waist, stirring frozen lumps of orange juice in the pitcher and Tom teetering on a chair beside her spreading impossibly huge slabs of butter on toast.

"We made you breakfast," she was informed.

Faye sampled enough to please them, despite the butterflies flapping in her stomach, assuring them with several choruses of "mmmm" and "delicious" that breakfast was utter perfection. At the door Maddie and Tom each kissed her and seriously wished her good luck.

"Hurry home afterward," Maddie ordered, wagging her finger.

Hugging them close, Faye squeezed her eyes and said a quick prayer that she'd not let them down.

When she entered the conference room the tension was palpable. Faye noticed that everyone had taken the same care with their dress. Suits were the order of the day for both men and women. Jaishree had cloaked her long gorgeous body in ivory silk; George had barely managed to gather his stomach into his tan gabardine; and Patrick and Harry were both in black wool. Even Pascal wore a sixties retro number that, though he looked dashing in it, was perhaps a little too high-style for the Savile Row set that marched in from Hampton Tea at precisely ten o'clock.

The mumbling of greetings filled the air as Bernard and Susan welcomed the clients. Faye and her team waited their turn. All were on the alert this morning and plenty of groveling was in order.

Frederick Hampton-Moore, the CEO of the company, surprised everyone by driving in from the country to join the meeting. Over a dozen heads Faye caught Bernard's raised brows, indicating to her that the stakes had been raised. His appearance meant that, so far, the top management liked what they saw. Faye nodded, understanding that Mr. Hampton-Moore's opinion was the only one that mattered. He was the bull's-eye. She'd have one shot at the deal, and it was now.

Faye discreetly stroked her moist palms against her suit as she studied the old man. He was rather short and plump, with a startling white beard that wreathed his face and met up with longish white hair that curled at the collar. Two pink cheeks emerged like ripe peaches nestled in cotton and when he smiled she thought he looked just like Santa. The thought made her shoulders lower and a smile stretch across her face. Mr. Hampton-Moore looked up, caught the smile, and his own face lit up. He came directly toward her, his hand outstretched and his vast stomach well ahead of him.

"You must be Mrs. O'Neill," he said with uncommon friendliness. "Very good to meet you. Heard so much about you." To the cluster of men who pressed close and smiled attentively at his side, he remarked, "Such a little thing to spearhead all this effort, hmmm?"

"Good things come in small packages," Bernard boomed, and everyone laughed.

Faye liked the pleasant man. She smiled broadly and offered a warm response. The room quieted, and she noticed with some embarrassment that she was the center of attention. Glancing sideways, Susan Perkins dutifully smiled but she looked like she wanted to scratch Faye's eyes out.

Susan moved closer and said in loud, saccharine tones, "My, what a charming little star you're wearing. And so appropriate." She leaned close to the vice president of marketing at Hampton Tea in a confidential manner and lightly touched his sleeve. "Our founder, Leo Burnett, created a logo of a hand around a cluster of stars."

"That's right," added Bernard. "He liked to say, 'Reach for the stars'!"

" 'So you don't come up with mud,' " Susan finished, casting a hooded glance at Faye.

Faye reached up and clasped the gold star in her hand as a touchstone.

Bernard shot Susan a warning glance, then smiled broadly, and boomed, "Well, shall we begin?"

As the five important and powerful executives from Hampton took their seats around the long, polished mahogany table, Faye felt suddenly gawky, too thin, too young, a mere girl among men. In contrast, Susan appeared very much at ease, leaning over to chat with Hampton-Moore on her left. Faye envied her panache, her style, and felt her own confidence waver.

Relax, this is it, she told herself as she took deep steadying breaths through her nostrils and forced her hands to

relax in her lap. *You're prepared. Ready. You can do this.*
At Bernard's signal, she stood up and cleared her throat.
The soft buzz of conversation quickly dissipated and, one
by one, all heads turned to face her. Her hands trembled
as she passed around the stack of reports, then, returning
to her seat, remained standing. All eyes were on her. It
was now or never.

A gust of wind blew from the open window, papers
rustled, hands grabbed for them. Outside a wind chime
tinkled its bells.

Then she saw it. It was her imagination, of course, but
there on her shoulder she saw a dainty, saucy fairy, hands
on hips, giving her a wink. Suddenly, Faye knew she
wasn't alone. She had Maddie and Tom. Wendy and Jack.
No matter what happened today, she knew they'd still
believe in her. Most of all, once again she believed in
herself.

She lifted her chin and stood straight. Sweeping the
men and women's faces, she was arrested by Mr.
Hampton-Moore's bright blue eyes. They glimmered with
wit and intelligence and a boyish charm that reminded her
of someone.

"Good morning, ladies and gentlemen," she began
with a megawatt smile. "Let's begin, shall we?"

Faye delivered a clean and powerful pitch. The artwork
was strong, the argument convincing, and everyone felt
buoyed when she ended with a flourish. She was followed
by Bernard, who concluded with a strong summation.

Afterward an awkward silence fell over the table. She
heard several coughs, the clearing of a few throats, and
chairs squeaking.

"Very interesting," said the vice president of marketing, hedging.

"You've certainly done your homework," added the new business director. "What did you think, Miles?"

"Well, I . . ." he turned toward Hampton-Moore, playing to the senior man.

All heads turned as eyes moved to focus on Mr. Hampton-Moore at the opposite end of the table. His round face appeared troubled, and he scratched at his temple with an index finger. The silence grew agonizingly long, but no one dared shift in his or her seat. Finally Mr. Hampton-Moore raised his tufted eyebrows and shook his head sadly.

"I'm sorry," he said, shrugging his rounded shoulders. "I simply don't like it."

He didn't like it. The words echoed in her mind. As each member of the Hampton Tea entourage left she felt her life's blood poured out that much more. She was numb with realization, struck dumb with helplessness for, in fact, there was nothing left to say. It had all been said.

He didn't like it.

She felt the tautness of her chair's leather, the tightness of her jaw as she struggled to maintain a calm facade, staring straight ahead at nothing, thinking to herself through the white haze that it wasn't supposed to be like this. He was supposed to have loved it. There were supposed to have been champagne and slaps on the back. Susan Perkins was supposed to eat her words, not glare at Faye like she had a few choice ones to spew out at this very moment. Most of her team had already quietly left, laying the blame squarely at her feet. Even Pascal slipped away without a word of cheer, carrying his artwork under his arm. Only Susan and Bernard remained with her at the enormous conference table covered with a few scattered reports and dirty teacups.

Faye turned her head to look at Bernard beside her. His huge bulk was slumped back in the chair and he leaned to one side as he rubbed his jaw, a *Titanic* of a man struck a fatal blow to the smooth sailing of his career by this failure. By her failure. The realization left her feeling as cold as any iceberg.

"I'm sorry," she told him, desperately meaning it.

He turned to look at her, his face blank, but before he could reply Susan spoke up.

"You're sorry?" She removed her glasses and leaned forward, no longer attempting to disguise her dislike, speaking through thin lips. "You're sorry? Well, we're all sorry. Damn sorry!"

"Susan, that's enough," Bernard snapped, but his usual bark was gone, indicating to Faye the depth of his defeat.

"No," Susan shot back mutinously. "It's only the beginning, and you know it. You needed this account. I warned you not to leave it in her hands. But you wouldn't listen to me. Even at the end, I told you to let me do the presentation. I have more experience. My British accent would have fallen more comfortably on their ears."

"The campaign was designed for the States. I wanted Faye's Midwestern American accent." He lifted his hand, his index finger out as though to make a point, then lowered it again in resignation, shaking his head. "Damn, Susan, you know it wasn't about accents. Sometimes you win, sometimes you don't. Nobody can explain why an idea sparks or doesn't. In this case, it just didn't. I'm not going to waste time casting blame. Maybe we can come up with another idea."

"Maybe, but not with her," Susan said with such hostility that even Bernard was taken aback. "She's out. You brought her in for the account over my head, and if I'm going to save this account, Bernard—and you know I'm the only one that can—I'm doing it my way."

She looked at Faye with a snooty confidence that was reminiscent of her ex-husband's. Faye knew the type well. The type that would never go second-class, the type that always ordered whatever was desired from the menu without thought to the host's finances. This type couldn't be bothered with that "Do unto others" bit of nonsense if it put her out at all. Most of all, this type couldn't suffer fools. Unfortunately, people like Rob and Susan never thought of themselves as fools. What was most pitiful was that they truly believed in their own greatness. Faye knew from experience that there was no rational dealing with such a person. The choice was to battle or to escape.

"I understand," Faye said, opting for escape. She didn't want to hear Bernard's response, couldn't bear his mumbled condescension to Susan. Faye, however, didn't feel the least beholden to Susan. She knew exactly who and what Susan Perkins was: Captain Hook. Glamorous on the outside, rotten to the core. Bad form all the way.

"That was the deal all along," Faye continued coolly. "No one wanted, or needed, this account more than I did. I gave it my best shot, and I lost. You, Susan, have neither lost nor gained anything. You never offered a single idea to the campaign, not a moment of your time, not an iota of effort. Not for one moment did you do anything to contribute to the good of the team. To you I offer no apology. Yes, I'm sorry. But I'm only sorry that I let my team down. That I let you down," she said, looking at Bernard. His eyes darkened even more over his proud nose. She swallowed hard, thinking of two others that she'd let down. She was on her feet, walking toward the door.

"Now if you'll excuse me, I have important people waiting."

Riding the tube home, Faye smiled at strangers, offered her seat to an old man, and when he kindly asked her what she was smiling about, she told him, "I lost my job!" She knew when she saw his puzzled expression that it was crazy for her to feel so cheery when common sense told her to feel crushed, splattered, a mere mat to be trodden upon. Except she didn't feel any of those things. She felt lighthearted, ready to take wing. Free at last from the constraints of doubt and worry that had plagued her for so many years.

She'd stood up to Susan Perkins, stood up for herself—even if she did lose the account. Well so what? She'd get another job. It might mean packing up and moving back to Chicago or New York, but what were a few miles on a lifelong journey? Her worries and fears about her ex-husband had melted away in the heat of her new confidence. She laughed lightly to herself and clutched the gold star around her neck. Goodness, she was even beginning to think like Wendy!

When she arrived at No. 14 she flung open her front door and found Mrs. Jerkins with her feet up, sipping tea, and reading a paperback novel. The children were nowhere to be seen. Mrs. Jerkins choked and sputtered, lunging forward and spilling tea down her dress.

"Don't trouble yourself," Faye called, backing out of the room, not wanting to wait for her bitter explanation. "I know where to find the children."

Familiar with the entire house now as she was with her own flat, Faye burst into the nursery, flushed and happy, to find her Maddie and her Tom nestled in the window seat, one on either side of Wendy. She craned her neck, but didn't see Jack anywhere. At the sight of her, the children leaped up with a whoop and rushed to her open arms, asking relentlessly, "So how was it? How did it go?"

Faye tried to tell them in an easy way that it didn't go well but that it was all going to be just fine. They had nothing whatsoever to worry about. Her greatest triumph was the shine of faith in Maddie's eyes. Looking over their heads she caught glimpse of Wendy's face, soft with concern.

"I saw a fairy on my shoulder," she said in way of explanation, slowly standing and moving closer to Wendy's side.

Wendy's brows formed question marks as she searched Faye's face. "Yes," she replied, nodding in all seriousness. "I see the fairy on your shoulder now, too."

Maddie and Tom moved closer, squinting at her shoulder.

"What about your position at the agency, dear? What shall you do now?"

"I'll figure something out. I'm not afraid."

"Of course you aren't. Well, this has been an eventful day! Come sit down and have some tea, shall you? Just between friends. Then you can tell me all about it. Children, you will clear away your cups, won't you? And if you wipe your hands after those sticky buns, you can begin the painting I promised."

Later, while the children dabbled at their paints and listened with half-interest, Faye told Wendy all about her morning. How Mr. Hampton-Moore simply didn't like her idea, how disappointed her team was, how responsible she felt for putting Bernard's job in jeopardy. There was no way to tell the details about Susan Perkins without sounding bitter and bitchy. When she was finished Wendy poured her a second cup of tea, oddly quiet. Faye leaned back into the plump cushions and stroked the silky, richly colored tassels, feeling much better for the telling.

"That Earl Grey must have been a wonderful fellow," she said, taking a sip.

"Yes," Wendy replied chuckling. "I've often thought that myself."

"You know it's ironic. I've lost the tea account, but I've found a whole new appreciation for the product. I actually *like* tea now."

"I do, too, dear. It was bound to happen. It *is* a superior drink. The English have always preferred it," she replied in a distracted manner. Then, sitting straighter in her chair, she tilted her head and asked almost coyly, "Tell me, is there always only one idea that you can, how did you put it? Pitch a client?"

"Sometimes, but not usually. In my case, however, Susan Perkins made it clear that I'd not get another chance. I'm out of the picture, out at third, deposed, cast out. I've been given the ax, the sack, the bum's rush, the can. I am finito. She's taking over the account herself."

"Bloody pirate!" Wendy muttered, her back straight and eyes narrowed. She despised pirates, and that sentiment showed in the steely determination of her stance and demeanor. "There's only one way to fight a pirate," she said with contempt, stirring her tea in quick, neat circles. "A surprise attack!"

Faye raised her brow, bemused.

With the glory of battle in her eye Wendy lifted her chin, and asked, "Could you join me for tea tomorrow? Say at four? There's someone I'd like you to meet."

Faye arrived for tea precisely at four, knowing how Wendy liked to pour promptly. Entering the nursery, Faye balked, astonished to find Mr. Frederick Hampton-Moore squeezed like a sausage into a frilly, tasseled chair beside Wendy. The two sat elbow to elbow with their frothy white heads bowed close in deep gossip.

"Come in, dear!" Wendy exclaimed cheerily, looking up and seeing her standing frozen at the door. "Come and join me and my dear old friend Freddy. He arrived early, and we've been catching up, having the best chat. Do sit down and have some tea." She waved her over with her little hands fluttering. "Just between friends."

Faye settled into her chair, clumsily she felt sure, half-wanting to laugh, half-wanting to throw up her hands with an, "Oh what the heck, why not?" and resign herself completely to fate, or Wendy's version of it anyway. After the tea was poured and sandwiches eaten, Faye watched with a tender kind of pleasure as Wendy and Freddy giggled and reminisced like school chums, their cups of joy filled to the brim. From time to time she shared a joke or a memory and laughed right along with them, not feeling for a moment uncomfortable or awed by the powerful CEO of Hampton Tea. Up in Wendy's nursery he was like everyone else, simply there for a cuppa and a good story.

"Just between friends," Faye mouthed.

Then the idea hit her.

It sometimes happened like this, a bolt from the blue when least expected. A clicking of tumblers after two

turns left and one turn right, or the neat fitting together
of a puzzle after lifting a few pieces high into the light,
turning them every which way before placing one down
and having it simply slip right into place. Faye's breath
caught in her throat; she blinked heavily and sat straight
in her chair. It was all there, a new concept for the tea
campaign, in neon in her brain. She could see it all now,
friends—good friends—young and old, women and men,
boys and girls, maybe even dogs and cats for a good
laugh, all sharing stories and secrets, good and bad, happy
and sad, over a steaming, fragrant, pot of Hampton Tea.
Each sip as delicious as the news shared.

Shining with enthusiasm Faye told all this and more in
an excited rush to Freddy, who sat far back in his seat
with his apple cheeks flushed, his blue eyes sparkling behind spectacles, and his expression beaming.

At the conclusion he took Wendy's hand in his own
and, looking into her eyes, told her with a tremor of emotion in his voice, "That's exactly how I feel, you know."
Then reaching for Faye's hand as well, he slowly repeated
the slogan of his new ad campaign, "Just between
friends."

"I got us another chance!" Faye exclaimed proudly to
Bernard after she'd marched into his office the following
morning, placed her hands squarely on his desk, and
leaned far forward. An hour later she repeated the big
news to the entire team, quickly assembled by Bernard in
the conference room, along with pots and pots of
steaming-hot Hampton Tea. With her hands making wide
gestures in the air, she told them in ringing voice how the
new campaign idea had hit her in the middle of a tea party

and how her new pal Freddy had not only *liked* it, but *loved* it!

The team had gathered in a ring around her, standing shoulder to shoulder, each with a look of exultation, and, she sensed, a tremor of excitement. This campaign focused on emotion and nostalgia. At last, an idea they could rally around!

Basking in the afterglow, she watched Patrick and Harry huddle in the corner, whipping copy ideas back and forth. Jaishree and Pascal were leaning over the table, sketching out a media concept, and even George opened his mouth and ventured an opinion in public.

Only Susan stood alone at the farside of the table, saying nothing. They stood separated by a length of polished wood. Faye lifted her chin. Susan clasped her hands, as though to prevent herself from picking up the pot of hot tea from the table and smashing it.

"How did you arrange to meet with Hampton-Moore?" Susan asked accusingly.

"The stars arranged it," Faye blithely replied.

"How would someone like you know someone like him?" Her voice was becoming shrill. "You're . . . you're nobody."

Faye didn't reply.

"Well the whole concept is preposterous. 'Just between friends,' indeed. It will never sell. It's too simple, too gushy warm and sickly-sweet. The market today wants something fast-moving and hip, not emotional and nostalgic." Clicking her fingers, she added to the others, "We have to think, brainstorm, come up with something that zigs and zags." She looked around for support but was met with blank stares.

"What, are you completely mad?" This was from Patrick. Faye had to cover her mouth and cough to disguise her laugh of surprise. "This idea is super. It's really going to fly."

"Absolutely," chimed in Jaishree, sending a commiserating glance toward Faye that warmed her to the marrow. "Take a look at these drawings Pascal has already made. First-rate. I think . . ."

Then, knowing her end was in sight, Susan made a fatal error.

"Listen, all of you," she interrupted, advancing toward Faye and Bernard. "It's *my* account now. I'll be the one to say what goes and what doesn't."

She said it as a direct challenge, not to Faye but to Bernard, and Faye could only wonder as to the extent of their relationship. He frowned and pulled back his shoulders, a great general shriveling his lieutenant with a stare of such imperious command that most would have gone weak in the knees and capitulated. But Susan had come too far to back down now.

"Surely you have to agree with me," she pressed on, her voice conciliatory.

"Surely *not*." Bernard was imperious.

"She's lost one account already. We can't afford to lose our last chance!"

"Lose it? What are you talking about? She's already won it!"

"But it's mine now." She must have heard the childish whine in her own voice, for she stopped short and got very angry and red in the face. "I won't work with her. You'll have to decide, Bernard. It's her or me this time."

"Don't say anything that you'll regret later."

"I'll regret nothing. You will. It's my account, and I

say this idea is a no-go. You're either with me or against me.''

Bernard glared, clearly angry now, while the circle of onlookers tightened around them.

"You're way off base, sister. Remember when we talked about loyalty? My loyalty is always to the client. I'm with Hampton-Moore—and he likes this idea. And he likes Faye O'Neill. It's a go.''

Susan seemed to splinter like broken glass, and Faye saw in an instant how brittle the account supervisor had become. She felt an immediate empathy for the woman, easy to feel this now that she stood on the terra firma of success. She took a step closer, mentally extending the olive branch.

"Susan," she began in earnest. "I know we've had a difficult time in the past but I'm willing to overlook it and try again. If you will. We'd like your input into this campaign. Join us.''

Susan stood tall and straight. Her hair was stylishly groomed, her dove gray silk suit was impeccable, her black patent leather shoes gleamed, the pearls at her neck were impressive. But her face mottled in rage and defeat and the certain knowledge that this one thin woman before her in a modest suit with fly-away hair that couldn't be contained and displaying not a bit of flash save for a thin gold star at the neck and a streak of red on the lips had more style and good form and creativity than Susan would ever possess.

"I wouldn't waste my time," Susan replied, her perfect white teeth flashing. "You haven't heard the last of this,'' she said to Bernard, but they all knew that her words were empty. When she left the room, slamming the door behind her, there was a collective sigh of relief. Followed by a thunderous clap from Bernard.

"Aw, to hell with tea. Where's the champagne!"

Chapter 17

Detective Farnesworthy rocked on his heels while Jack read the slim report of his investigation to date. Scanning the pages, Jack rubbed his jaw, unable to disguise his disappointment.

"So that's it? A few pages that tell me what I already know? Hell, Farnesworthy, this proves nothing more than I'm a mystery."

"I'm sorry, sir. I've turned over every stone I could find, as it were, but there wasn't a shred of information, not the slightest lead I could follow that enabled me to unearth any information about your biological parents." He coughed. "Or the first six years of your life."

Jack weighed the report in his hand. It was light indeed. "Well, I guess that's that. Hey," he said with a levity that belied his hurt, "it couldn't be helped. That's what comes of trying to give a mutt a pedigree."

"Actually, sir, that's not quite *it*, as you put it."

Jack cocked his head and raised a brow.

The detective's brows gathered, and he pinched his lips as though enduring a private struggle. Then he reached into his briefcase and handed Jack another sheet of paper.

"It's just the preliminary list, of course. There were crates and crates of files I haven't even gone through yet. Don't know as I should bother, as these lads aren't any direct relation to you. But there was a connection, and I thought," he paused then stammered out, "well, sir, you told me to follow up on any hunch, no matter how odd."

Jack looked up at Farnesworthy, whose cheeks flushed either from embarrassment or the fact that he was sweltering in his suit, vest, and tie worn despite the summer's heat.

"Right, right," he replied, scanning the list of names on the paper. "But, Mr. Farnesworthy, I'm afraid I don't understand. Who are these boys?"

"That's just the point, sir. I don't know. Nobody does, not really. While going through the files, I pulled out these names on a hunch. What intrigued me about them was how similar their cases were to your own. Young boys and babies, all left at Mrs. Forrester's door, this very door here, sir, then taken to the London Home for Boys for adoption. And not a one of them has records. Strange, it is. Highly strange."

"You say that none of these boys has any background? No parents, no relatives, no history at all?"

"None, sir."

"But there are at least a dozen boys listed here."

"Yes, sir. And who knows how many more are hidden in those crates of files."

"Incredible. I've heard of sloppy record keeping, but this takes the cake."

"But that's what's most curious, sir. You see, in going through these files, I've realized that once the child was taken to the home, the records were quite complete. It was only prior to arriving at the home that the information is missing.''

"What? They came from nowhere?"

"So it would appear. Of course, we know that can't be the case, but the fact remains that for those boys, and for you, sir, there is no history."

Jack was totally nonplussed. He stared at the detective for a moment, then back at the list, then returned his fixed stare to Farnesworthy, who was once again rocking on his heels.

"Oh, sorry, Farnesworthy," he said, pulling out a chair and removing a pile of papers from the seat. "Please sit down. Coffee? Tea? A glass of cold water?"

"No, nothing, sir. Thank you. I can't stay long. I only dropped by to make my report. And to ask if you wish me to continue on in the case. I've found no additional information about your own history, and as for the other, well, as I said, there were crates of files and that would take a great deal of my time to go through."

"Carry on!" Jack exclaimed. "This is too good a mystery to let go of now."

"But it doesn't make sense to follow this lead, sir. It won't lead to any answers about you, and it will undoubtedly raise my bill. Considerably."

"Call it counterintuitive, Farnesworthy, but it's what I'm good at, and it makes perfect sense to me. And while you're digging around in those dusty old files . . ." Jack tilted his head to look upward at the ceiling. "I'm going to have another crack at the memory banks of the cornerstone of the London Home for Boys. Wendy Forrester. And I'm willing to bet those files aren't the least bit dusty."

* * *

Jack found Wendy seated on the floor before a small patch of wall, a paintbrush in her hand and several small tins of paints to her left on the floor.

"May I come in, Wendy? I don't mean to disturb you."

Resting the brush in her palm she looked at him with an expression of delight. "By all means, come in. I'm sure you could never disturb me." Then, narrowing her eyes, she said with a captivating glint, "Yet, perhaps it is you who might be disturbed."

Jack chuckled and shook his head. "I should've known you'd spot a problem at twenty paces."

"Come sit, Jack, and tell me all about it."

In a smooth swoop he slipped to sit beside her, resting his elbows on his crossed knees. The sun flooded the room, warming his back. Behind him he heard the canary twittering and hopping. Looking at the wall, he was heartened to see that Wendy was creating another mural, this one of a pirate ship that swung back and forth like a pendulum and beaming from portholes were two small faces that were unmistakably Maddie and Tom.

"Looks just like them," he said.

"Do you think so? I'm glad. I'd like to put you and Faye in the mural as well but, you see . . ." She struggled for the right words.

"We're grown-up."

"Yes," she replied with a winsome expression. "Speaking of Faye, I haven't seen much of her the past few days. She is always so very busy."

"It's hard to believe she could be even busier. But with the success of her new campaign, which I gather you had something to do with, it's been full steam ahead."

"I see," Wendy murmured, studying his face. "And your ship has already set sail, is that it?"

"What? Oh, you mean my work. Yep, all done. Signed, sealed, and delivered."

"You'll be leaving us soon, then, I suppose." Her voice was quiet and subdued.

Jack's smile fell, and he picked up a paintbrush from the tin and twiddled it in his fingers. "I'll miss you."

"Only me?"

"No, of course not only you. I'll miss the children."

"Only the children?"

He chuckled and popped the brush back into the can. "Okay, you minx. Faye, too. I care a great deal about her. And I think she cares about me."

"Yes, I think she does, too." Wendy tapped her chin with the wooden tip of her paintbrush, then set the brush in a can and rested her hands in her lap. "Forgive me, Jack, but I'm a bit protective of Faye. She's like a lovely, sweet flower that's been trampled under a cruel, heavy boot. She's so afraid to have dreams anymore. To believe in anything that isn't somehow proven. She's responded well to the sun, the warm air, and plenty of what I like to think of as good Number 14 compost. I'd hate to think she might get stepped on again."

"Wendy," replied Jack, feeling a bit crushed himself. "I'd never do anything to hurt her."

"No, of course not. Not intentionally. But a boy like you, so clever, so full of spirit, so . . . well," she said a bit distracted. "You see, its very easy for a girl to fall in love with a boy like you. And once that happens, it's cruel not to love her back. Not the way a woman needs to be loved. The way married people ought to love." She paused and looked wistfully out the window. "I know."

"Whoa there, who said anything about marriage? I care a lot for Faye, but marriage? That's just not for me."

"You remind me of another boy I know," she said wryly, returning to her mural.

He frowned and, looking away, caught a glimpse in a mural across the room of Peter Pan flirting with a mermaid. "Oh, I get it. You're saying I can't grow up."

"No. You are a grown man, chock-full of those male hormones that drive you to distraction. You posture and pose and swagger. But being grown-up is quite a different thing than being an adult. You, Jack Graham, are still very much the little boy I once knew."

Jack swung his gaze away from the mural to focus on Wendy. She was looking up at him with an impish expression on her face, and he homed in on that sparkle that told him that she knew a secret. A very big secret.

"You knew me as a boy?"

"I knew so many boys . . ."

"Uh, uh," he said, sidling closer, gently sliding the brush from her hand. "You're not going to get away with that again. You know something. Come on, Wendy. It's time. I'm leaving soon. I may never have this chance again to find out who I am." He paused, swallowing down the hope rising in his chest. "Please, Wendy. I need to know. Do you remember me? Did you know me as a boy?"

Her gaze roamed his face while affection and memories sparkled in her eyes. Then, with a heavy sigh, she nodded, and a bittersweet smile of resignation settled on her face.

"Yes," she replied at length. "I knew you. And I remember you well. How could I forget you? You were as shiny and bright as a freshly minted coin."

"I was?" His heart ached to know more about himself, the boy before the man.

"Indeed. You were the most curious boy I'd ever met.

You always wanted to figure out how something worked, to see things clearly. Except, the way you looked at the world was different than the way most other people did. It was fresh and new.'' She laughed brightly. ''Oh, you were nothing if not persistent. Could sit and fiddle with one of your experiments for hours. We used to have to come and pull you away to get you to eat. You blew up a few things, started a few fires, that sort of thing. Had the school shaking in its boots, you did. That's what made you so hard to place, my boy. Not many folks wish to adopt a child they perceive as a fire-setter. Then it occurred to me to write Warner Graham about you. He was a dear friend of mine. A brilliant scientist. A physicist, like you are now. Thought he could steer you right—and I believe he did.''

Jack was speechless. He leaned far forward, and asked, ''My father was a physicist?'' He shook his head in disbelief. ''I don't understand . . . He was a farmer. A Nebraska corn farmer.''

''Oh well, that, too, of course; but that was later. When the war began in Europe, he was called up like most able men, but they saw a different use for a man of your father's particular abilities. The government sent him off to America to work on some big secret project.'' She tilted her white-haired head and thought, ''Let's see, it had something to do with the war effort. All the best minds were gathered together. Why am I thinking New York?''

''The Manhattan Project,'' Jack said through dry lips.

''Hmmm, yes, that's right. Only it wasn't in Manhattan.''

''No, it was out west in New Mexico. Los Alamos.'' He scratched his head and exhaled heavily, trying to take it all in, to equate the quiet farmer he knew with the kind of brilliant physicist his father must have been to be called to Los Alamos. "You do know what they were building, don't you Wendy?"

"Yes, surely," she replied solemnly. "Though not at the time. It was all hush-hush back then. Now of course we all know it was the atomic bomb."

"My father worked on the Manhattan Project . . ."

"He did," she said, nodding thoughtfully. "And it changed him. He never reconciled his part in it. He abandoned science completely and became a farmer, and when he married, he never had children. He wrote me once not long after he settled in Nebraska. In the letter he enclosed a check donating all the money he'd saved during the project to my boys' home. His letter was a sad treatise on what a terrible thing he believed he'd helped create and how meaningless life had become for him. He wrote that he didn't want to bring children into a dangerous world. A world that could end, in the space of time of a breath. He had a long spell of melancholia after the project's successful completion. It was most serious, poor, poor man. Your mother was a saint." She sighed heavily. "I wept for my dear friend. He was such an optimist when I knew him. So sure he could make a mark on the world. I daresay he did, though not the one he wished.

"When you arrived at my door, Jack, I saw that you were every bit as bright and inquisitive as he was. Perhaps more so. I immediately thought of my childless friends, Warner and Anne Graham. Well, not immediately actually. You'd picked all the locks at the home and the teachers and administrators were at their wits' end."

"I didn't mean anything by it," he said with a shrug. "I was just curious how they worked. And it was so easy. I love puzzles."

"I was sure that was it," she replied, patting his hand. "I knew Warner could teach you so many things and keep your mind busy in the right way."

"But he never taught me science!" he exclaimed, flabbergasted by all that he'd just heard.

"He must have in some way, for here you are. A scientist, just like him."

Jack thought back at what it was like growing up with Warner Graham. His father was aloof. He'd seemed ancient to an eight-year-old boy. Yet, in his quiet way he did encourage him to observe the world and to accept things as they were without any preconceived prejudice.

"I remember how all the other kids in the area could zip off the names of all the different plants or trees or animals. 'Hey, Graham,' they'd call. 'What do you call this?' Most of the time I didn't know, and they laughed at me, made fun of the 'genius' who didn't even know a maple from an elm." He shrugged and snorted, "I still make mistakes with proper names. But when Warner and I walked through the woodlot that bordered the farm, he didn't teach me those kinds of things. He'd hold my hand as we walked and talk to me about how trees are the most beautiful and useful products of nature. He'd make me take deep breaths of fresh air and explain how the oxygen we breathe is released by trees. He'd take me to slopes where trees prevented soil erosion, or stoop and point to burrows in the base of trees that were shelter for animals. And right before a storm blew in, when the air smelled like sweet rain and the birds were quiet in their nests and the trees began to rustle, he had me close my eyes and listen to them talk. That's what trees were."

"Sounds to me as though he taught you a great deal."

"All this time I thought he just loved nature. What a

fool I was not to realize that he was teaching me that true science *is* nature.'' He rubbed his forehead and closed his eyes feeling a deep, personal hurt. ''Why didn't he tell me?'' He opened his eyes and caught Wendy's gaze and said defiantly, ''Why didn't *you* tell me until now?''

''Adoption is a very private matter,'' she replied looking at him levelly. ''I didn't want to interfere.'' Then, furrowing her brow, she added, ''But you seemed so hungry for knowledge about yourself. And you're quite right about time running out. You're leaving soon and at my age, well, one never knows when I'll go on a journey of my own. It didn't seem right to withhold the truth any longer. Warner was wrong not to tell you.''

''Such a waste!'' he exclaimed bitterly. ''My father and I . . . We could have talked about so many things. We could have been friends. And who knows? Maybe I could have taught him something.''

''Dear boy, don't you realize? You did! Warner Graham was a broken man when you came to him. As a boy you were always so curious, so eager, snooping around looking for Lord knows what. You had this unshakable faith that a miracle was just beyond your grasp if you just kept your eyes and ears open. This was exactly what Warner needed. Faith. You were his miracle. You taught him to believe again.''

It was like a cloud dispersed, and he saw his father for the first time. He always remembered Warner as he was the day he met him when he was a boy of eight come from England to live with his new parents. Warner Graham was a tall, gentle-faced man in his late forties with a shock of white hair and soft, pink skin that seemed to belong more in a library than in an open field. Now Jack understood his father's long, brooding silences, the binges of time spent behind his closed study doors followed days later by a bonfire in the backyard when his father and mother would stand and toss papers filled with his feathery script, what must have been his father's theories, into the flame. He understood, too, the strange gleam in his father's eyes when he talked of the secrets of the galaxy, of myths, of religion, of a million things he comprehended at some deep level but never concretely. His father's quixotic fight to teach his only son his love for science and his desire to keep his boy down on the farm, away from the evils he knew his genius could lead him toward, was the war that had, tragically, separated them in the end.

"Thank you for the truth, Wendy," he said hoarsely, rising to a stand and walking to view the painting on the wall of the little boy peering out from the mural. "So, this *is* me after all?"

"Yes . . ."

He sighed and was silent for a long time. "Okay," he said at length. "I understand about that part now, but I still want to know about my biological parents. What can you tell me about them?"

"Nothing at all. Truly. I simply don't know."

"Wendy, I know you know something more. I can feel it."

She pursed her lips and turned her head away, averting her gaze.

"I see. Well, I've always thought of myself as some unwanted, beaten up, crazy kid who didn't know who he was. A boy without a name. I guess I still am."

"Jack dear," Wendy said patiently, "think of what you just told me! A bird doesn't know whether we call it a thrush or a robin or a warbler. It simply *is* a bird. It doesn't doubt that it can spread its wings and fly. Peter once said, *The reason birds can fly and we can't is simply because they have perfect faith, for to have faith is to have wings.* Have faith, Jack. In yourself. Let go of the past and embrace your future. Fly!''

Jack felt uplifted by the message, yet a nagging question kept him earthbound. ''Wendy, I still feel there's something you aren't telling me. What about all those other boys. The ones without histories.''

''Whatever do you mean?''

''Wendy, I know about the files. About the other boys. Boys like me.''

She shook her head, her fingers at her temples. ''I swore I'd never tell anyone this part.''

He reached her side quickly, bending low to hold her hand. ''Please, Wendy, tell me.''

''You won't believe me.''

''I'll try. At least let me try.''

She looked deep into his troubled eyes, tilted her head, then sighed and said, ''Very well. But please don't tell anyone else. It so upsets Jane when she hears anything about the boys' home. She resented it deeply, you know. Felt for whatever reason that she had to compete with my boys for my affection. And I daresay, my fortune.''

He helped her to a comfortable seat, then sat by her side while she gathered her thoughts. ''It was all because of the Lost Boys,'' she began. ''I really had little choice in the matter. My father took care of the first lot of Lost Boys. They came home with me, and he raised them as his own, dear man. Curly and Nibs, the Twins, and Tootles . . . Mother adored them all.''

''By Lost Boys, you're referring to . . . Peter Pan's Lost Boys? From the Neverland?''

She nodded. ''Years later, when Peter came with the

second lot, however, I didn't know what to do. I couldn't very well say no, but I was a widow at the time. A grown woman with Jane in the nursery. I had no husband to help care for a bunch of wild boys. So I began the boys' home to care for my Lost Boys. It was soon after the war, and there was such a need for other orphaned boys as well. It all happened so quickly. Everything just fell neatly into place. Life can be like that, you know.''

She sighed and gazed off. ''Over the years, Peter always brought me the boys who'd decided to grow up. There were dozens. I've tried to capture their faces here,'' she said, indicating with a wave of her hand her marvelous murals. ''It was my own way of keeping track.''

Jack scratched behind his ear and looked over at the picture of himself peeking out from a tree stump. If those were the paintings of the boys she claimed came from the Neverland. . . . He had no memories of his first six years. . . .

''You're saying that I was a . . .'' He couldn't say it.

''A Lost Boy. Yes, dear.''

Chapter 18

I<small>N THE TENETS</small> of quantum mechanics, until a particle interacts with something, it travels down every possible pathway simultaneously. Only when the particle collides with another does it snap out of its confusion and follow a direct trajectory. After Jack's visit with Wendy, he was swerving left, right, and sideways, throwing shirts, dishes, and books into boxes on a direct path to California.

By the dinner hour, the packed, sealed, and labeled boxes were mounting high against the rear wall. Most of them were filled with his books, and, seeing them, Jack sighed with relief that he at last made enough money that he no longer had to move them himself. Those boxes were as heavy as lead and Lord knew in the past he and a few pals had hoisted them plenty of times. He always swore after a move that he'd dump the books before he'd move them again, but he never could. Those books were his friends; he'd had some of them since boyhood.

Boyhood. His thoughts flashed again to his conversation with Wendy. Hurt Faye? Impossible, he thought, hefting a large box over to the corner. Didn't he do everything

289

humanly possible not to hurt her? It was just as well he was leaving.

Leaving. His arms fell to his sides. Looking at the piles of sealed boxes and those left to be filled, the opened cabinets with contents spilling out as he sorted out what to keep and what to toss, he didn't feel any of the excitement he usually felt at the prospect of moving on. Rather, he felt a bittersweet pang. There was a time when he liked moving and meeting new people. Yet this time the leaving wouldn't be cut-and-dried. This wasn't just some place he'd lived in.

Hell, he'd really *lived* here.

Leaning his weight against the table littered with packing materials, Jack squeezed his eyes tight and realized how much he'd miss Wendy and the infinite flow of optimism from the nursery. He'd miss spending part of every day with Maddie and Tom, hearing them creep down early in the morning to feed Nana, squabbling as children did, careful not to wake him up when, of course, they woke him every time.

Over the summer he had taught them as his father had taught him, asking questions, pointing to natural phenomena, revealing in simple ways how every observer sees the same laws of nature. Teaching them, he had revisited his father in his memory. He recognized that he and his father did have a special bond after all and he no longer felt as driven to discover his biological mother and father.

He'd forged a bond with the O'Neill children, too. Maddie had stolen his heart, there was no doubt about that. She came, she saw, and she conquered, in typical Maddie fashion.

Tom was a part of him. The most tender part. That the boy would break his silence to come to him for help climaxed the campaign that Jack had waged all summer.

And Faye . . .

It struck him hard that he'd miss Faye most of all. He'd miss the crooked little smile that she gave up unwillingly; but when she did, it made her whole face shine like the sun coming out after a cloudy day. He'd miss watching how tender she was with the children, how kind to Wendy, loving her despite her fantasies. He'd miss the way her hair fell into her face, he'd miss the way she blushed when she caught him staring at her, which he did more and more often. He'd miss their chats, their debates, the little wisecracks that only a best friend could catch. His hands fell to his side.

That was it. He'd miss his best friend.

He picked up his football and tossed it in the air, feeling all jumbled and confused inside. Everyone else he could sort into a neat category, but Faye, she was a little bit of this and a little bit of that. She was, simply, everything. He'd never felt this way about anyone before.

"Hello?" He recognized Faye's voice and fumbled the ball. Glancing up at the clock he saw that it was six o'clock. She was home early tonight. My God, he thought with a shudder. *I even know when to expect her home.* It had come to that.

"Anybody home?" she called from the stairs.

"Hi, come on in," he called back nonchalantly, pretending to be hard at work with his packing. "Careful where you step. It's a war zone in here."

She entered the kitchen then stopped short, her hand still resting on the doorframe. He watched as her eyes scanned the opened drawers and cabinets, the piles of newspapers, the rolls of packing tape, and alighted on the large pile of sealed boxes against the wall. Her face could hide nothing from him any longer, and it pained him to watch her smile freeze, then melt away to a frown, the chill moving instead to her eyes.

"You're packing already?"

"Yep," he said, thrusting out his jaw, trying to sound distracted. "Time's almost up."

"I thought . . ."

She paused to clear her throat and cross her arms across her chest, gestures he recognized as those she used to hide distress. He looked away and began tearing tape strips with a vengeance.

"I thought you were leaving in September."

"Faye," he said, resting his hands on the newspaper, "it's September next week."

"Yes, but, only September first. Surely you're not leaving on the first."

"Got to. I'm done with my work here. And there's a major race with my old pals at CERN to be the first laboratory to discover the top quark. I was asked to consult." He saw the stunned expression on her face and hurried on, tossing books into the box. "It's a great opportunity. You should see the accelerator they've got there. Man, it's a huge machine, a mile across, the largest and most powerful in the world. My money's on them. Once we discover that sucker, the puzzle will all fall into place. It's gonna be fun." He sighed, hearing no enthusiasm in his voice.

"So, you'll be leaving soon." She coupled her hands and chewed her lips, a clear sign that she was deeply upset. "I guess I'd better get dinner started then." She rubbed her temple. "Dinner. In all the excitement I hadn't given it a thought."

"Oh yeah, that's right. Big day for you! You signed

the contracts with that tea company, right? We want to
hear all about it.'' He thought, *we*? He and the children?
Listen to him, going on like they were a family.

''I, uh, it went well. Very well. Looks like I'm staying
in London.'' Why didn't it matter anymore, she thought?
All the elation she'd felt rushing into this great, warm
kitchen to share with Jack her day's news slipped away
the moment she saw the obvious signs that he was leaving.

Looking at all the boxes lined up against the wall, Faye
realized that her life was a series of tightly wrapped com-
partments. She packed her feelings into packages, taping
them shut, neatly labeling them and shipping them off
somewhere. Everything had a destination. All her dreams
had been stored for so long she didn't know where to find
them anymore. And for what? She was standing here now,
feeling empty. She'd focused so long on the day-to-day
challenge of raising her children, getting a new account,
keeping her job, that she'd closed the lid and sealed herself off from any bits of joy, love, and spontaneity that
might have slipped in.

Jack tossed a roll of tape in the air like a football.
''Don't fuss tonight,'' he suggested. ''Why don't I go out
and buy us some takeout?''

''No, I'm sure I have some eggs and cheese. Some
bread. I'll just rummage around in my cupboard and see
what I can pull together. I'd love to cook on the old Aga,
seeing as I won't have another chance after next week.''

She saw his brows gather and his mouth twist and felt
a sudden surge of sadness rise up in her throat and
threaten tears. She turned toward the Aga, resting her
hands on the warm metal.

Jack would be leaving Wednesday? That he would be

out of their lives so soon was inconceivable. Jack not be there to rustle them together on a Saturday morning to take them to the park? He would not be there each morning to offer a rushed hello on the front stoop? Or a long, lingering good-bye in the garden at night, their banter laden with innuendo? Did this mean that all their romps in the great, warm kitchen of No. 14 while she cooked dinner and he played with Maddie, Tom, and Nana were coming to an end? That the only happiness she'd ever known as a family would soon be over? Jack gone? She couldn't bear to think of him out of her life.

Faye looked over her shoulder, bereft, and saw that Jack was standing rigid with the same look of disbelief that she was sure she wore herself. His jaw was thrust forward, his nostrils flared above it, and higher, his eyes shone with intensity. His mind was traveling the same path, she knew. They had marched so comfortably, so long, each careful not to step on the other's toes, that neither of them had realized they'd lost their way.

The silence was broken by a loud clumping on the stairs along with short, piercing dog whistles. A moment later Maddie marched in, all business, with Nana hot on her heels. When she spied the stack of boxes and disarray in the kitchen she halted abruptly, her face puzzled.

"Hey, what's going on in here?" she asked with her hands on her hips. A child, and a bossy one at that, she had no trouble voicing what Faye only dared think.

For a second Jack appeared nonplussed. Then he rallied. "Packing, kiddo. I'm heading home."

Maddie's brow knitted over a deep sulk. "Oh."

Faye stepped into the fray. "Well, since dinner won't be for a few minutes, why don't I put on a kettle of water for tea? It's a bit nippy tonight. The weatherman said it might get as low as . . ." She was talking inanely she knew, filling in the sulking silence.

"I don't care what we eat as long as we eat soon," Maddie said peevishly, marching over to the plastic bin that held Nana's food and scooping out a cup. She often hid her tender emotions with anger. "I'm starving. And so is Nana." As she talked, she busily added a bit of water to the dry dog food and stirred it while Nana wriggled her bottom and licked her mouth as she tried to remain obedient to the "sit" command. Both Faye and Jack stood stock-still, hands hanging at their sides, watching her.

"Puppies ought not to wait too long between meals, you know," she continued in that prim voice that she'd learned from Wendy. "They get very hungry and whine, and I have to be very good about feeding right on time. I have been very good, haven't I?" She sniffed and lowered her head as she stirred. "You see, puppies need to be taken very good care of. They're like babies, you know. You can't just learn to love them and have them love you and then just stop taking care of them. It's very cruel to do that to puppies, don't you think? I mean, they don't understand that grown-ups have to move away for jobs. They just know that the person they love is gone, and I wonder if she'll go sniffing and whimpering for Tom and me? And Wendy? Poor Wendy, all alone here with only Mrs. Jerkins and Mrs. Lloyd to look after her. Don't you think that's just too mean?" With that she covered her face and burst into tears and great, heaving sobs.

Faye rushed to her side and held her in her arms. Then for no one reason she cared to give a name to and for a million reasons she could, she started to cry herself, holding her little girl and rocking her, while Jack picked up the puppy in his arms and stood by watching helplessly.

Seeing him standing there through a blur of tears, tenderly stroking a whimpering Nana in his arms, with both their big brown eyes bewildered, Faye cried all the harder, thinking that the big oaf was not the least aware that all the females were crying because they were all head over heels in love with Jack Graham.

When the tears subsided, Jack scooted down, drawing Maddie into one of his long arms so she could rest on his bent leg. While she sniffed and noisily wiped her eyes, Nana eagerly licked her cheeks. Jack thought with a pang that this was the second sobbing O'Neill child he'd held in his arms that week. It felt natural, comfortable, right. And what he felt for their mother ran even deeper. These new feelings were worrisome. Even frightening. He wasn't aware that his hands were shaking. He felt the sudden urge to throw whatever remained into the boxes and leave tonight, while he still could.

''You're right about puppies,'' he said in a husky voice. Maddie's eyes were round with so much trust it made him wince. ''Nana wouldn't be happy without the people she loves most in this world. No one would be.''

He looked over at Faye, brows raised in question. Her breath stopped short, and her heart hammered in anticipation. Could he be . . . ? She didn't dare finish the thought.

''I want you to have Nana,'' he said to Maddie. ''After all, I travel so much, flying to cities all over the world, it wouldn't be fair to leave her all alone, would it? I'm sure she'd be happiest with you and Tom. That is if your mother says yes.'' He raised his eyes again, waiting for her answer.

Faye smiled with numb shock, realizing what she'd hoped he might say, feeling she might burst into tears.

"Yes," she blurted, turning her face to look at Nana, "of course you may keep her." Her voice sounded too high and as brittle as ice.

Maddie jumped up and clapped her hands. Being a child, she would take what she could get. She might be losing Jack, but oh joy! She could keep Nana! She bent to snuggle her face in the puppy's.

Jack was studying Faye's face, his lips pursed. "Maddie, go on up and tell Tom," he said. When she didn't and remained romping on the floor with Nana, Jack lifted her to her feet by the shoulders then bent to lift Nana into her arms. Then with a gentle shove he sent her on her way up the stairs. She ran calling out Tom's name at the top of her lungs.

Jack next extended his hand to Faye easing her up, not releasing her when she rose a breath away. He moved his hand to her chin and gently turned her head, forcing her to face him. Stubbornly, Faye kept her eyes averted.

"Faye," he said.

The magnetism was there again, she couldn't help herself. Sighing in resignation, she followed the sound of his voice.

"You're upset. You didn't want the puppy?"

"Oh Jack," she sighed with exasperation. "The puppy? You asked the wrong question! I would have said yes to so many things tonight. A puppy was the least of it."

His face went very still. He asked, "Are you giving me your permission?"

She laughed lightly. "For a kiss? My one special kiss? Mrs. Darling gave her kiss to Peter. She understood."

"Understood what?"

Faye shook her head. "Jack, what I'm trying to say is

that I know that you'll be flying off soon to who knows where. I don't expect a commitment. I won't hang on to your sleeve. You're like Peter Pan to me. You're adventurous, curious, brave, noble, naughty, incorrigible.'' She smoothed his collar with her fingertips. ''You're as fleeting as youth. Don't you see? I've waited for you for so many years. I want to give you my kiss. Come, take it. And even though you won't be here in the morning when I wake up, I *will* have my moment of bliss. Yes, you have my permission. Kiss the girl, Jack. And take the woman.''

Jack shuddered and swept her in his arms, wrapping her tightly, lowering his head to cover her lips with his. She was small and slight like the girl she had just described. But she kissed like a woman.

The smell of his skin filled her senses, the brusque chafing of his late-afternoon beard pinkened her cheek, awakening her to the passion she'd long denied. The fierce possession of her mouth by his caused her head to swirl, her knees to weaken, and she swayed in his arms. Her head fell back, and she gasped as his tongue traced its way along each sensitive neuron in her neck to return to her open mouth. He dueled with her tongue like an avenging pirate, clever with his thrusts, sure of his win. She wrapped her arms around his neck, stretching on tiptoe to offer more of herself to him. Tiring of the parry, he stepped closer, grasping her rear and pressing her close, leaving no doubt in her mind that he was ready, eager, to continue the duel with other weapons. She felt the heat flow from her body to his, moving fast, while the temperature rose, rose, rose.

On the stove the water was roiling, steam was whistling, and the metal teakettle jiggled with the power of the sizzling hot water.

"Jack, wait," she said, pulling back. She took deep gulping breaths. "The teakettle."

"I don't think I want any tea just now," he said, his lips stretching to a smile.

"Me neither," she replied, smiling too.

His arms drew her in, kissing her again, and still the pesky kettle insisted on being heard. Yet neither one of them broke apart.

"I suppose I should get that," he said, moving his lips against hers.

"I suppose," she replied, punctuating her comment with a nip.

They moved together, lost in the ferocity of this third embrace.

"Doesn't anybody hear the teakettle?" Maddie called out as she pushed through the door.

Faye and Jack clumsily stepped back but not, Faye feared, before Maddie caught them in some semblance of a clutch. She could tell by the way Maddie stood at the entrance with a strange look on her face, as though not sure of what she saw, and if she saw what she thought she saw, whether she should run back up the stairs.

"Let me get that kettle," Faye said, her hands fluttering to smooth her hair, tuck in her shirt, check her skirt. She ducked her head so Maddie wouldn't be able to continue her sharp scrutiny of her cheeks and lips, both of which she felt sure were flushed a telltale red. The kettle gave off a final, angry whistle before peace was restored.

"Would anyone like a cuppa?" she asked, clearing her throat. The invitation was lame, she knew, but her mind was blank. Both Jack and Maddie shook their heads vigorously in the negative.

"Well then," Faye said, clapping her hands together, feeling enormously awkward.

Maddie squinted, then turned heel and ran back up the stairs.

"I sure have a bad sense of timing," Faye said, leaning heavily against the Aga.

Jack came closer, taking hold of her hips and drawing her close. "I'd say your timing was perfect. We almost missed this." He tugged her nearer so their hips joined. His lips hovered over hers so she could feel his warm breath against her cheeks, as hot as steam.

"I want you."

"Yes," she whispered through parched lips. Then, "No. Not here. The children."

"We'll go away. To the seashore. One night, Faye. No ties, no commitments, no history."

No future, she thought. A small bite that stung, then she brushed the thought away.

"Just you and me, Faye. One night before I leave."

She understood what he was saying. One night and no more. He was giving her the chance to back away. To say no. Weeks ago, that would have been her only option. Now, however, she would grab this chance. She'd achieved her goals, hadn't she? She'd provided a secure home for herself and her children. Maddie was smiling, Tom was speaking. Rob hadn't chased them across the ocean. At last, she was an independent woman. Couldn't an independent woman go away with a man she loved for one night? No strings attached?

Yes, of course she could, she answered herself. She would go away for one night. Just for herself. She'd open up, allow the joy and pleasure in. Who or what could it hurt? Just one night.

*   *   *

Maddie and Tom hooted for joy at the prospect of spending an entire night in the nursery. Leaving her children, even for one night, represented a great leap of faith for Faye, and when she confided this to Jack, he assured her that the doctor had given Wendy a clean bill of health and that she was up to the task.

"Nothing will happen," he said. "Faye, no stalling. This is our time together. It's only one night."

Faye had wrapped her arms around him and conceded, her heart breaking that she'd found someone she could love again and she only had one night in which to love him. And he was right, of course. Nothing would happen to the children in one night. But being the worrier she was, she planned for every contingency as though she were leaving for a month.

On Saturday afternoon she stood by the front door with her bags at her heels and papers in her hand, each one filled with lists.

Jack felt no worries or fears. His eyes were dancing with excitement and his mind was already on the road ahead. "We're leaving before dinner, and we'll be home after breakfast. It's only for the time that they sleep," he said, picking up her overnight bag.

Faye nodded, chewing her lip, thinking things through. Faye had left Mrs. Jerkins and Wendy a long list of instructions and phone numbers for her cellular phone, for the hotel where they had reservations, for the children's doctors, the chemist, and God forbid, the police. She'd engaged Mrs. Jerkins as the official sitter, someone to monitor the evening from the command post of their flat. But the children were spending the night with Wendy in a great fort constructed of sheets and mattress and bits of treasures from all three flats. It was to be a great holiday.

"Fly off, now!" Wendy said to them wistfully, gently hustling them out the door. "Ah, I remember the days when I flew away with someone I loved. Be happy, children! Be carefree. And not to worry about Maddie and Tootles." With a twinkle in her eye, she said before closing the door, "I shall give them a night they will never forget!"

Chapter 19

I⊤ WAS A night Faye would never forget. They left on a gray London afternoon and arrived in the deep darkness of a coastal night. Far from the city lights the stars twinkled in a crisp, clear sky. The moist, cold air nipped their cheeks and smelled of sea salt, chimney smoke, fresh fish, and dank wood. She couldn't see much in the darkness save for the lurking shadows of trees thick with leaves and enormous shrubs as dense as a stone wall. She had the sense of green lushness that she'd not felt since her arrival in London. In the rear of the hotel the land dropped sharply, giving the impression that they'd reached the end of the earth. One more step and they might catapult into space. Seeing the wilds of nature again made her realize how much she'd missed it.

Jack had made reservations at one of England's grand hotels. It was a historical place, full of marble floors, crystal chandeliers, elaborate gilt mirrors hung over faded wallpaper, and equal measures of European charm. Jack stepped up to register at the front desk backed by ancient wood mail slots, all intricately carved from thick mahogany with a skill long gone. Faye couldn't bear to stand beside him and pretend that she was Mrs. Graham, so she strolled down the narrow corridor lined with small display windows and feigned a keen interest in the impossibly expensive and chic clothing, bags, and jewelry. She looked up in time to see the clerk reach for a huge brass key from a wall of polished brass hooks and hand it to Jack. As she watched Jack's long fingers enclose the key, she shuddered, wondering what it would be like to feel those fingers upon her body, to lie with a man again, after so long a time.

A uniformed porter hurried up and insisted on carrying her one, small, battered leather bag. Faye blushed to her toes, feeling certain as they rode up two floors in the mirrored elevator that the jockey-sized young man with the averted eyes knew why they had come with so little luggage, to stay but one night. An old scene perhaps, but new enough for her.

Their room was large with high ceilings, yet cozy, recently renovated with bright, floral wallpaper that coordinated with the fabric on the upholstered sofa and the plump bedding. French doors opened to a private balcony obscured now by the cloak of darkness. The bathroom was enormous with shiny, modern plumbing, a marble sink, and a claw-footed tub so large even a man as tall as Jack could stretch his legs. Seeing the real linen towels and sheets, a gracious nod to the past, Faye realized that Jack had chosen a first class hotel, a place with ambience and style, for their night together. A smile flitted across her face and turning, she watched Jack tip the porter and order champagne, chilled, and strawberries, fresh, immediately sent to the room. All with the familiarity of a man who had done this before.

Truth was, she would never know. Jack was a man who

felt comfortable in all surroundings, a five-star restaurant or a pub, at an academic meeting or a sports event and she would not know him long enough to cleverly pry into his past, to ask if he'd been at this very hotel before, with some other woman. Those were not the kinds of questions an independent woman would ask an independent man.

After the porter quietly closed the door behind him Jack prowled the room, opening drawers, checking out the minibar and the bathroom. Faye saw only the bed. The enormous, four-poster, king-size bed that dominated the entire room. It was more than a bed—it was a statement.

Jack yanked open the doors to the balcony and stood, jacket off, his tie loose and hanging around shoulder, staring out at the blackness of sea and sky. He'd thought he was jaded, but tonight he was as nervous as a teenager about to make love for the first time. He wanted everything to be perfect. For her. He wanted tonight to be memorable.

He knew she was nervous too; he'd seen her chew her underlip raw. He'd also caught her expression when she saw the four-poster bed, and almost called it off when he saw her lips tremble. Goodness should be rewarded with goodness and he wanted more than anything else to make her happy, to show her that he loved her in the only way he knew how. Perhaps they should go to the dining room first, he wondered? To give her time to feel comfortable. And if she didn't, well . . . He rubbed his jaw. If it meant securing another room, being satisfied with nothing more than sharing a fine meal and a walk on the beach with her, so be it. He'd settle with being her friend.

Then turning, he saw her smile. The sweetness in her expression shattered his illusions. Liar, he told himself.

He didn't want just to be her friend. He wanted to be her lover. He wanted it all.

The champagne came and they laughed when the cork popped and hit the ceiling. He filled two glasses, amazed that his hands were calm despite the blood throbbing in his veins. Then they raised their glasses and toasted each other.

He wore an amused smile, she a shy one.

"Here's to my best friend," she said.

He swallowed deep, then refilled their glasses and offered, "Here's to a wonderful, unforgettable night together."

She drank her glass quickly, her gaze darting discreetly to the bed.

Electricity vibrated between them like the waves of the ocean crashing on the rocks outside their window. They ranged from ripples to tidal waves, and they both felt adrift in the swells. Faye sighed and swayed against him, resting her head on his shoulder. Jack went rigid, feeling the charge crackling in his veins. For her sake, he controlled the urge to indulge in a quick, sudden explosion. With her, he wanted to experience the full spectrum. He lowered his lips and offered one more toast against the soft hairs of her head.

"Here's to us."

They drank small sips from their glasses, each knowing that the moment was drawing near. They were intensely aware of each other, sitting shoulder to shoulder, knee to knee, sipping wine while conversation failed. Looking around at the pretty room in the soft glow of the filtered light, the enormous four-poster, two champagne glasses partially emptied, Jack felt as though the stage was set for the final act and he and Faye had their roles to perform.

He lowered his brows and stared at her over the rim of his glass. Her small, delicate hands were nervously stroking the crystal stem, her eyes kept averting toward the four-poster, and her cheeks were flushed with high color. Sympathy and desire collided in his heart, and with a sudden move he swooped to his feet. Hell, he never liked performing expected roles.

"Grab the glasses," he said, grasping the champagne bottle with one hand and her hand with the other, dragging her up behind him as he walked quickly toward the bed.

A kind of shock thudded in her chest. So, he would be demanding and impatient, she thought, disappointed.

Approaching the bed he grabbed hold of the heavy down quilt and yanked it off while she watched with widening eyes. Next he gathered more blankets then the pillows into his arms and crossed the room to the French doors and swung them open to the balcony. A brisk, perfumed breeze whistled through the room and she could hear the thundering of the waves upon the rocks below. Curious, she followed Jack out to the balcony, wondering what he was up to, shivering in the cool, fragrant night air. Jack shoved the table and two iron chairs to the side and began spreading out the blankets on the floor, placing the pillows at one end near the bottle of champagne.

"Now turn off the lights and come back out," he ordered over his shoulder, spreading out the down coverlet over the blanket. "It's a clear night and this far out from the city we can really see the stars."

Stargazing, she thought? Her tensioned lightened as a slight giggle of delight escaped.

"Why, Jack," she said, her lips curving. "I haven't lain out and looked at the stars with a boy since I was in high school at Lee Street Beach in Evanston. It was a classic makeout ploy.''

''Who said we weren't going to make out? But I happen to like looking at the stars, too. Don't you?''

''Who doesn't?'' she replied, her heart light. ''And look Jack, it's a full moon!'' Even as she said this, she felt a shiver of foreboding. Didn't Wendy say Peter Pan always came when the moon was full?

''Hurry and turn off the lights,'' he called with excitement, climbing under the coverlet. ''No point in freezing when it's nice and warm under here.''

One flick of the wrist, and it was suddenly pitch-black. Jack called her name, and she followed the sound of his voice through the dark room like a ship follows the horn, guiding her past all dangers of rocky memories to come safely on a straight course to him. He lifted a corner of the coverlet and she slipped into the warm den of down and body. She caught the scent of salt air and sweet skin and heard the sounds of fabric rustling, bodies shifting and soft grunts as they burrowed like animals into the blankets. He reached under and around her, nestling her close, rubbing her arms to warm them, placing her head on his shoulder, his cheek against her hair. Faye closed her eyes for a moment, sighing heavily, relishing the feel of Jack's arms tight around her, her cold nose against his warm neck. Her fingertips splayed against his chest, flexing like a cat's paw against the cotton shirt and playing with the hard plastic buttons.

Eventually they settled, their heads together, their breaths making long plumes of vapor. They stared out at a sky so vast and filled with so many stars that they were struck with awe.

''All my life I loved looking at the stars,'' he said. ''I

suppose that's why I studied them as an adult. Some people feel overwhelmed by their infinity. Not me. I look out there and am inspired.''

''It's all so . . . endless.''

''That's what's so exciting. Researchers have been examining the distant light from stars that exploded before the sun was even born. Think of it,'' he said with his eyes shining and wonder in his voice. ''Our universe is much older than we'd thought it was, and it just keeps on expanding. On and on and on. We're 95% sure that the universe is going to expand forever.''

''That kind of infinity is the kind of thing I usually associate with God.''

''Yeah. Makes you realize your own mortality, doesn't it? We're just blips on the map of time.''

Faye shivered and held on to him tightly as they stared at the sky. Not just the body, but the soul inside. The more insignificant they seemed in the enormity of the cosmos, the more meaningful they were to each other, two souls clinging together as they navigated the sea of stars. He pointed out the constellations: Andromeda, Pisces, Ursa Major, and directly overhead Ursa Minor. They gasped in unison when they caught the fiery descent of a star.

''Stars live and die, like everything else,'' he told her as he looked out, his voice distant. ''Some are hot and dense, burning their fuel at an incredible rate. Others are cool, consuming fuel more slowly, doling out their energy in miserly bits, staving off the inevitable. All struggling against the forces, just as we do. In the end, though, they all collapse, and their light is snuffed out.'' He paused and squeezed her shoulders, and she felt his smile against her cheek. ''Ah, but while they live, they shine.''

His voice was melodic, a baritone that enveloped her. She turned her head and viewed his strong profile with his straight nose and broad forehead, wondering, *Who are you?* He turned too and under his intense gaze she felt he was wondering the same about her.

"Sometimes," she ventured in a tortured whisper, "I don't feel that I shine."

His face turned thoughtful then, and he took her fingers and kissed them, saying between the kisses, "The iron in your blood, the calcium in your bones, the magnesium in your cells, the zinc in your nails . . . Did you know all these ordinary elements are also in stars?" He traced his fingertip from her brow to her chin, capturing her gaze. "You, Faye O'Neill, *are* a star."

She sighed, shining.

One smooth, graceful movement and his lips were on hers. His arms tightened, crushing her close as her arms rose up around his neck, holding fast. Faye closed her eyes, and she was falling inward into a vastness as cosmic as the one overhead. He was the magnetic north pole, she was the south, and between them millions of electrons spiraled into a black hole.

Her fingers fumbled with his buttons, his hands tugged down her skirt. Their hands trembled as their clothes were slipped away, and it seemed so sudden, so sensational, to feel skin against skin, cold here, warm there as they caressed in their cocoon.

She felt a narrow beam focus to that tender point where the heat concentrated and glowed, burning very, very hot. It was pulsing, sending waves of sensations, one after the other, throughout her body. She concentrated on this core, furrowing her brow, tightening her lips, traveling further and further inward. It was as though all of her being was concentrated into that one tight sphere.

Jack moved away to arch over her, wrapping her around him. He said her name, low and firm, calling her back. "Faye."

She opened her eyes, blinking, focusing. His gaze pierced her barrier, uniting them, as his body soon would. Seeing him, she no longer felt alone on this journey. Her senses heightened, she said his name, "Jack," and opened fully to him.

Their heat melted them together, the ashes of each fire serving as fuel for the next, fusing them into one synthesized star. She let go and felt herself spinning, faster and faster, so that bits of her outer shell of doubts and fears were tearing off while her inner core of faith and love was burning brighter and brighter. Suddenly she felt herself splinter and crack. She closed her eyes and shot forward, crying out to the heavens as she imploded in a spectacular cataclysm, a supernova catapulted into the galaxy, dissolving into a million points of light.

It seemed to each of them that it took millions and billions of years for them to speak again. When the dust settled, a new world had been created.

Jack felt as though he were a weary traveler, having spent too many years on the road. A lifetime adrift. Could he finally hang up his hat, settle in, know what it meant to be on the inside looking out for a change?

Looking up, he chose a star and made a wish.

Faye nestled as close to Jack as she could, holding tight to what she'd told herself was only a dream. Here was a man worth holding on to, someone with whom she could join hands and build a life of trust, and honor and mutual respect. Could she really believe that such a life was possible?

Opening her eyes, she found a star and made a wish.

They fell asleep in the open air, wishes on their lips, entwined in each other's arms, mingled in each other's dreams. The sea crashed and thundered on the rocks below. But far above the lovers, high in the heavens, the stars winked.

The morning sun rose in magnificent splendor over the sparkling waters, shining its light on the sleeping pair wrapped in down lying on a small, curved balcony overlooking the cliffs. Faye woke slowly, blinking against the bright, prying light, disoriented. Shielding her eyes with her palm, she heard the sounds of the breakers below, and above, the harsh cries of the seagulls. Beside her she felt the warmth of a man's skin and listened to his gentle snoring. This surely was a bit of heaven, she thought, waking more. She stretched luxuriously with her arms arched above her head and breathed in the fresh scent of sea breeze and the musky perfume of love. As the memory of the previous night dawned she felt a scintillating flush seep through her body all over again, followed by a deep sense of contentment.

"You're awake?" he asked, yawning loudly.

"Mmmm . . ." she replied, feeling inexplicably shy and dropping her palm over her eyes.

He turned to wrap her in his arms, shoo away her palm from her face, and catch her gaze. His eyes were sleepy and his lip curved up on one side, carving a deep dimple that touched his chin.

"I have a confession to make," he said.

"Oh no, don't tell me you're married, you have a dozen children . . ."

"Worse. I'm going to tell you about my dream."

She groaned and pulled the blanket over her head.

"I dreamed of you."

She poked her head out from under the blanket. "You did?"

"Why is that so hard to believe? Don't you ever dream of me?"

"You're fishing. Oh, don't pout. Okay, I confess. I do . . . *Sometimes*."

His smile spread and he seemed enormously pleased. "Well, *sometimes* in the morning when I awake I close my eyes again and try to put together your image. But I can never get it right. So I use my memory for better detail. What had I seen you wear last? How did you wear your hair? I'd want color. I'd want expression." He shrugged, and his dimples deepened. "What I really wanted—was you."

She smiled then too, her heart awakening. She couldn't remember anyone saying anything so lovely to her before. Cuddling beside him, she murmured, "Mmmm, Jack, I wish we could be like this forever."

His brows gathered and his jaw thrust forward. "Faye, I still have to leave on Tuesday."

Faye felt a tremendous stab of disappointment, but it wasn't one she was unprepared for. After all, hadn't she understood his limitations when she came here with him? He'd never lied to her. Despite her hurt, it wouldn't be fair for her to expect more from him now.

"I know," she replied, though her heart was breaking. "Hey," she said, determined to show him how independent she was. "Maybe we can be like Cary Grant and

Deborah Kerr. We'll wait six months and see who shows up on top of the Empire State Building?''

His smile was brief. He took her hand and played with her fingers.

"Jack," she said in a serious tone. "Don't do this. I'm not asking for more than what it is. *An Affair to Remember.* I'm happy we had this time together. I'll always cherish it." She slipped her hand away and tucked it beneath her. "But I'm a big girl. I can take care of myself. And my children."

His face grew thoughtful. "I wish I could offer you more. I'm used to my life being the way it is. It's too late. I'm incapable of change."

"No one is incapable of change, Jack. Like it or not, we *are* grown-ups. But we have to choose to give up our carefree childhood. Adult relationships: marriage, being a good parent, a good neighbor ... Those aren't games, Jack. That's real life and they have their own rewards. But it all takes work."

"All work and no play makes Jack a dull boy."

"No," she said sadly. "You've got it all wrong. All play and no work makes Jack a lonely boy. We are the decisions we make. Isn't that at the crux of quantum mechanics? You tell me. You're the scientist."

"I am," he replied thoughtfully. "And that's part of the problem. It's hard to explain. I'm a scientist of the nonlinear-thinking variety. The logical, slow building on a solid foundation is not for me. That's for engineers like Henry Ford or George Washington Carver. I like to leap beyond the conventional and see things in a new and different way. I'm a dreamer, like Isaac Newton and Albert Einstein."

"Just because you're a born a dreamer doesn't mean you can't live on earth, too. Jack, what is it that you fear so much about compromise? About change? One thing I've learned is that life is all about change, and moving along with it as gracefully as possible." She briefly smiled, and added, "Or as Wendy put it, seeing a fairy on your shoulder."

"I can't be bound by rules and expectations, Faye. I need to roam, physically and in my thoughts. It wouldn't be fair for me to expect anyone to follow, or to put up with me."

Faye looked at his sincere expression and thought how it would be such a pity for a man as kind and good and utterly lovable as Jack to end up a lonely, pitiful old man who clung to the slippery image of youth because he couldn't, or wouldn't, grow up.

Suddenly she'd had enough talking and thinking. Suddenly she missed her children.

Rising and wrapping herself with the blanket against the sudden chill she said, "Jack, I think we've said everything that needs to be said. A storm is blowing in. And it's time to go home."

The closer they drew to the city, the more ominous the clouds overhead became and the further Faye felt from her starry dreams of the night before. By the time they reached London the storm broke and it was raining in earnest. Fallen leaves gathered in wet clumps on the streets and on the steps of No. 14. Pulling up at the curb, all she could think about was seeing Tom and Maddie. Scrambling out of the car, all she could see in her mind's eye was Maddie and Tom. Jack followed her in as she hurried up the stairs to the nursery.

"Halloo! Everyone, we're home!" she called out, opening the door.

"You're back! And so early!" Wendy called back, her smile radiant as she stretched out her arms in greeting. Wendy was sitting on the window seat before the wide-open window, wrapped in her wool throw against the damp chill. The nursery was frigidly cold.

"Wendy, you mustn't sit before that open window. You'll catch your death. Look at you! You're frozen solid. Let's close this window up."

"No!" she exclaimed with some alarm. "We must keep the window open!"

"Just a bit then." She glanced down at Wendy, and though she was as neat and tidy as a pin, as usual, her face appeared fatigued and lackluster, as though she'd been awake all night.

Filled with a sudden uneasiness, Faye's gaze darted around the nursery, past the warm and cheery murals and bric-a-brac, a smile plastered on her cheeks. But she didn't see Maddie and Tom. She felt a twinge which she told herself was disappointment. She'd imagined that they'd fly into her arms at the sound of her voice.

"Maddie! Tom," she called. Only the canary chirped in reply. The nursery was strangely quiet. Instinct flared a warning, and she turned toward Wendy, casting her a questioning glance. The tense expression on the old woman's usually serene face set her own heart pounding. Wendy appeared strangely guarded. Even wary.

"Where are the children?" she asked, trying to keep her alarm from her voice.

Wendy coughed lightly and averted her eyes. "That's what I wanted to tell you. They're gone, dear." She looked up quickly. "But not to worry. They'll be back soon."

"Gone? Where?"

"It's the most wonderful thing."

"Where are they, Wendy?"

"The Neverland!" she replied, her eyes aglow.

Faye blinked, taken aback. Surely she didn't hear right. She cast a consulting glance to Jack.

"Wendy," he said stepping forward, "Faye doesn't like to be teased when it comes to the children. Where are they really?"

"But I told you. The Neverland."

Faye clasped and unclasped her hands. She could not believe her ears. Words couldn't come to her tongue, and her heart pounded loudly in her ears.

"You mean the amusement park?" Jack persevered but she detected a tone of alarm. "Did someone take the children to the park? Who?"

"Why, Peter, of course," Wendy replied. "And no, not The Neverland Theme Park. Not this time." She held her hands together, and her eyes gleamed, challenging them not to share her delight. "He came! Just as I suspected he would. It was a full moon, you know. He especially likes to come when the way is lit. He . . ." She looked down demurely and plucked at her skirt. "He came for me, of course." She looked back up and her eyes flashed. "But Tootles so wanted to go. And Maddie begged. You know how persistent she can be. So I thought, why not? It would be such a wonderful treat for them to see the lagoon, and the treehouse, and to have so many adventures. Peter complained, but he went along eventually. Oh, my dear, I am sorry not to have asked your permission, but there wasn't time. I had to make an instant decision, and I felt sure you would agree once you understood. So you see? There's nothing at all to worry about.''

Faye's hand rose to her throat as she stared at the tiny woman seated by the window with her white hair like spun glass and her inordinately bright blue eyes sparkling and the rapt expression on her sweet face as she clenched her birdlike hands to her breast and she thought to herself, *Oh my God, the woman is crazy!*

''She's delusional,'' she said to Jack, her voice raspy. Then, guilt hit her full force, slapping her head back, shaking her, tearing her heart to shreds. ''What have I done? How could I have left them? Why did I take the chance? My God, where are they?''

Panic clicked in. Rob . . . She ran into the bedroom calling, ''Maddie! Tom!'' Then into the front of the nursery, peering out the window to the street below, then to the back, leaning out the open window, calling their names at the top of her lungs. Jack had already run downstairs to check his flat and she hurried down to her own.

When Faye pushed through her front door Mrs. Jerkins dropped her sewing and clamored to her feet.

''The children, are they here?''

The stunned confusion on Mrs. Jerkins's face sent Faye's hopes spiraling.

''They aren't with Mrs. Forrester?''

''No, they're not. You didn't check on them? Not once all morning?''

''Why, if I thought . . .'' she stammered.

''This is just too negligent!'' Faye cried. With terror racing through her veins, she ran through the rooms, calling out. Her voice echoed in the empty hall. The beds had not been slept in, there wasn't a wrinkle in the pillows, toothbrushes sat dry in the cups, dishes were stacked and clean, jackets hung on the hooks by the back door. Everything was in its place but the children.

Jack raced in, meeting her at the door. His face was grim. "They're not downstairs. Nana's there, but no kids."

Faye blanched, knowing instinctively that the children wouldn't have left Nana alone. She ran back up to the nursery straight to Wendy, who was standing at the window staring out, wringing her hands, her slim shoulders slumped. She was muttering softly, "They'll be back. Not to worry, he'll bring them back."

"I want my children!" Faye screamed, collapsing against the wall, burying her face in her hands. There was only panic now, bordering on hysteria. All her dreams collapsed as she came face-to-face with her worst nightmare.

Her children were missing.

Chapter 20

DETECTIVE INSPECTOR ROSS had the tired, doubt-filled face of someone who, after twenty years in the Criminal Investigation Department, had seen it all. But even Detective Ross was unprepared for the case at No. 14.

"So what you're saying is that you believe the children ran off to the Neverland?" he asked in a heavy Cockney accent. He didn't betray himself with so much as a wry smile.

"Of course I don't believe that!" Faye replied, her voice high with tension. "That is what Wendy told us when we returned."

"The first thing we have to do, Mrs. O'Neill, is stay calm. Have you contacted all the neighbors, friends, anyone who may know where your children may be? Where they may've run off to?"

"Yes, yes, I've done all that," Faye replied impatiently, knowing that each moment that ticked away was precious time not searching. She was sitting in the nursery with Wendy, Jack, Inspector Ross, and two uniformed police. This time, Faye had had no qualms about picking up the phone and notifying the police immediately. Her first thought was that Rob had followed her to England.

"I . . . I know what to do. You see, I've been through this before. My husband kidnapped the children last spring. We were in the United States at the time. I have full custody, but that doesn't mean he didn't fly over and take them. That's why I want to file a missing person's report. Immediately."

"Yes, of course. Well, that does change the picture, doesn't it?"

She handed the inspector an envelope. "In here you'll find an identification kit I had made up, just in case. It includes updated photographs, fingerprints, birth certificates, passports, dental records, birthmarks, and a medical history. I've also included a photo of Rob O'Neill, the father, and some information on him."

Inspector Ross raised his brows. "Very good. Nicely done. This will save us a good bit of time." He signaled to a policeman and handed him the kit. "Looks like we've got a parental abduction here. Notify all the searching agencies. I want an extensive search covering a five-mile radius of the city. Also notify border crossings and ferry-rail-airport services." To the other policeman, he ordered, "Go downstairs to her flat and spin the drum, see if you can find anything at all that looks unusual."

Jack stepped forward. "We've already searched the entire building. Everything is in place. Nothing is missing."

"And who might you be?"

"A friend of the family. I live in the garden flat."

"I see," replied the Inspector, narrowing his eyes in suspicious scrutiny. "And may I ask where you were last night?"

Jack slid a glance to Faye, then, clenching his jaw, he replied tersely, "No."

"It's okay, Jack. We have to cooperate fully," Faye replied.

Jack swung his head back to face the Inspector. "I was with Mrs. O'Neill. In Brighton."

The inspector's brows rose again, then, rolling his tongue in his cheek, he jotted this information in a small notebook. "Mrs. Forrester was the baby-sitter during this . . . this interlude, I presume?"

Faye blushed at the barely concealed criticism and nodded. From under her lashes she looked over at Wendy, sitting slumped by the window, still gazing out forlornly at the incessant rain. She looked decades older, tired and spent with worry. Seeing her like this, Faye berated herself for the hundredth time for ever leaving her children in her care. An old woman everyone called Crazy Wendy. She saw in the inspector's eyes that he questioned her competency as a mother.

"It was just for one night," she tried to explain. "The children love Wendy, and they've spent a great deal of time with her. Nothing bad ever happened before. She was always so loving, so very able. If you had seen them together, before . . ."

"Umm hmmm," he replied noncommittally, scribbling quickly in his book.

"And of course there was Mrs. Jerkins. Their regular baby-sitter."

"Oh? And where was she?"

"Downstairs. She was to supervise. The children wanted to stay with Wendy. It was all supposed to be such a holiday." Her voice broke, and she turned away.

He directed the next few questions to Wendy, politely

drawing her attention away from the outdoors. She leaned heavily against the windowsill, and her face appeared worn and spiritless.

"Mrs. Forrester, did you hear any strange noises last night? See anything unusual?"

Faye held her breath and met Jack's anxious gaze.

"No," she replied softly, still gazing out. "Nothing unusual." Then she turned her head and offered, "There was a full moon."

"Would you have contacted someone if you had?"

"Of course I would have," Wendy snapped back as though speaking to an impertinent child. "Mrs. O'Neill left me a long list of names to call, she's quite responsible. I may be old, but I'm quite capable of dialing a phone, young man."

The inspector frowned and jotted a few more notes in his book. "I assume then that the doors and windows were closed and locked."

"Of course not," Wendy replied, gazing back out the window. "Or how would Peter have gotten in?"

The inspector stopped writing and glanced sharply up. "Peter?"

"Peter Pan, of course. He hates a barred window, so I always leave the window unlocked and open for him to fly in."

The inspector whistled softly through his teeth, then shot a shrewd look at Faye. "I see," he said, frowning, flipping closed the notebook. "Mrs. Forrester, let me understand you. You're saying the children didn't just go to The Neverland as you reported earlier. By that, I mean The Neverland Theme Park. Located in London. You're saying that Peter Pan, the fabled character from a book, flew into your window last night and took the children to

THE Neverland? Second star to the right and all. In the sky?''

She turned her head, met his gaze unflinchingly and replied, ''The very one.''

Faye covered her face with her hands, Jack closed his eyes and shook his head in resignation. Detective Inspector Ross tilted his head and stared in disbelief. After a moment spent collecting his wits, he walked with a composure the British were known for, picked up the phone, and punched out a number.

''Hallo? Detective Ross here. Right, the O'Neill case. I need a psych eval here. On the double.''

A short while later Mrs. Lloyd hurried into the nursery, flush-faced and frantic. She was followed at a slower pace by her husband and her solicitor, a tall, thin-lipped, stately-looking gentleman. Behind him strode a bearish, balding man with a ruddy complexion and round wire-rim glasses too small for his chubby cheeks. The policemen and Detective Ross snapped to attention when they entered.

''I came as quickly as I heard,'' Jane Lloyd announced, hurrying to her mother's side.

Faye watched as Wendy welcomed her daughter with a brief smile that seemed to take an inordinate amount of effort. The lamps were lit against the late afternoon's dusk and a deathly stillness permeated the room, save for the soft murmurs of Wendy's and Jane's voices. Faye thought Wendy appeared even more pale and wan as the hideous day wore on, but she couldn't find it in her heart to worry over her.

The shock she'd felt on finding the children missing had settled into a deep, black anger. She blamed Wendy, blamed Jack, blamed fate, but most of all, she blamed herself. How naive she'd been to let her guard down even for a moment. She should have remained vigilant. Suspected that Rob would try to snatch the children again. It was wrong of her to let down her guard.

She covered her eyes with her palm, unable to look any longer at Jane comforting her mother. Where was her own daughter, her own sweet Maddie?

The large, ruddy-faced man who resembled a four-star general turned out to be the chief inspector, which explained Detective Ross's deferential air. After huddling in consultation with his men, where heated words were exchanged, the chief inspector announced that Rob O'Neill had been located.

"Your ex-husband is still in Detroit, Michigan," he informed Faye with an air of disapproval, as though she were to be blamed for wasting precious time and manpower. "He never left the States."

Faye slumped and sighed with relief, muttering, "Thank God."

"That's not necessarily good news," the chief inspector continued. "At least with your ex we had a target. Most kidnappings of children between ages three and eight are by a spouse after divorce. They're not so much eager to be with their children as they are angry at the spouse and wanting revenge. We've been fortunate to find most of those children. Unfortunately, now we're back to square one. It's a very strange case. There is no sign of forced entry at either the house entry or the individual flats. At the moment we have no suspects."

"Except of course, Mrs. Forrester," chimed in Detective Ross.

"What? My mother is a suspect? George!" exclaimed Jane Lloyd. She was white with outrage.

"I say, Chief Inspector," said the solicitor in a huff, "if you have any notion to charge my client with a crime, you'd best speak plainly. There has been no evidence to support . . ."

"Now, see here. There's no need for agitation," the chief replied with his hand in the air. "No one intends to charge Mrs. Forrester with any crime. We don't even know that a crime has been committed, do we, Inspector Ross?" He turned to glare at Ross who promptly reddened and shook his head.

"However, sir," Ross said in a strained voice, "she *was* the only one at the scene, and her story is, to say the least, quite unbelievable."

"Detective, may I see you a moment?" The Chief jerked his head in a direction, and the two men stepped to the corner to speak privately.

"Do you know who that woman is?" the chief hissed. "That's Wendy Forrester. *The* Wendy. Half the Empire believes that woman is Peter Pan's Wendy. She's a paragon in the eyes of the people. She founded an orphanage. She knows some of the most influential members of our kingdom. Even the Queen is especially fond of the old girl. Bloody hell, everybody is. If we arrest her all havoc will break loose. We've got to have as little publicity as possible." He fixed Ross with a stare. "If you ever dream of collecting a pension."

Ross appeared hunted. "It's a loony assignment. Are you sure it's even our area?"

The chief glared again as though to say, "Nice try, Ross."

"Well, what do we do now? We've got two children

missing, and all fingers point to the old girl, crazy or not. I've ordered a psych eval, but it's a sticky wicket, all way round.''

The chief stroked his jaw, then cleared his throat and joined the group.

''It appears obvious that Mrs. Forrester isn't at all well. What with her advanced age, I think it wise to escort her to the hospital for an evaluation and observation, eh? For her own protection.'' He offered a condescending nod to Jane Lloyd, who lowered her head and agreed, then glanced up at her solicitor for confirmation. Mr. Reese-Jones replied with a loud sniff.

Wendy, however, wished to stay in the nursery. When the police tried to gently escort her out she struggled against them, slapping them away and lurching for the window like a small bird with a broken wing, trying to alight.

''No, take your hands off me. Please. You don't understand! You must let me stay,'' she cried, frantic. ''He said he'd be back for me! I must be here. I must! You can't take me away.''

Near the door she escaped from the policeman's grasp and crossed the room to clutch Faye's hand tightly in her own. Her eyes were brighter than ever, burning with intensity as she bore down into Faye's eyes.

''Faye, child, you must keep the window open!''

Faye couldn't listen any longer and turned her head away, slumping in despair.

Wendy dropped her hand, the last of her energy flowing from her. The police took hold of Wendy's elbow, gently replaced the shawl around her shoulders, and led her, lifeless, out of the nursery.

Jane Lloyd's voice rose to a wail at the sight of her

mother's disgrace. "She's harmless!" she cried to the inspectors, weeping into her handkerchief. "Blameless. The only thing my mother ever wanted was for children to love her. What crime is there in that?" She turned to the chief inspector. "Children are gullible, remember. They believe the stories are real. As I once did, when I was very young. And my children, and my grandchildren. They all came here, to this nursery, to believe for a precious short while in Wendy's stories."

Her husband stepped near to her in a show of support and offered her his handkerchief. Jane Lloyd sniffed loudly, then collected herself into a formidable figure, eyes flashing with scorn and finger pointed at Faye accusingly.

"Mrs. O'Neill encouraged my mother's unhappy delusion. No doubt the O'Neill children believed the stories were real as well. Theirs was an unhappy, confusing home." She glanced with a meaningful air at Faye, then at Jack. "Such goings-on in this house . . . My mother's nurse was the children's nanny, and the stories I heard from her. Shocking! All the doors were open, if you take my meaning. It would not surprise me in the least if those two, poor children ran away from home. Not in the very least!"

"How dare you," cried Faye, leaping to her feet. She felt Jack's grip on her arm tighten. "It wouldn't surprise me if this wasn't what you wanted. Wendy out of the way. Now the house is yours!"

"No! Not this way. Never this way. I warned you!" cried Jane, pointing her finger accusingly at both Faye and Jack. "I told you if you didn't stop this nonsense, something terrible would happen. And now it has. I blame you both. It's all your fault!" She broke down completely and had to be helped from the nursery by her husband and her solicitor.

Jack was livid. He stepped nearer to wrap an arm around Faye's shoulder. "Of course you're not to blame. It's no one's fault. Come on, let's go downstairs. Get some fresh air."

Faye could not be comforted. She felt buffeted by guilt and blame, taking Jane Lloyd's words to heart. It *was* all her fault. She *was* to blame, she thought, placing one foot before the other. We are the decisions we make, she'd told Jack. It was true, and now she had to live with the consequences of her folly.

While the sun set and gloomy shadows began to deepen, Faye walked like a haunted ghost through the sepulchral rooms of her flat, away from the monotonous, low mutterings of the police in the hall. One by one she slammed shut each window. One by one, she locked them.

Chapter 21

JACK DIDN'T LIKE feeling helpless. He was a man of action. Surely there was something he could do to help Faye. There were far too many questions that needed answering. Once back in his own flat he immediately called his private detective and asked him to deliver any and all information he'd dug up on Wendy Forrester and the files. Anything at all. Despite the wackiness of her story, the fact remained that she was the last person seen with the children. Perhaps there was something in her past that could offer a clue to where she might have taken Maddie and Tom.

The following afternoon, Jack opened the door to Detective Farnesworthy. After dispensing with the usual pat greetings they got right down to business.

"I'm not finished going through all the files from the boys' home," Farnesworthy said, "but I've found some pretty remarkable information. Trouble is, I'm not sure what to make of it."

"Let's hear it."

"Yes, sir. I only ask that you listen until I finish, no matter how strange or curious the findings are."

"Yes, yes, get on with it."

Farnesworthy cleared his throat and checked his notes. "To start off, Wendy's maiden name was Darling. Father, George; Mother, Moira. Two brothers . . ."

"Don't tell me. Michael and John."

"True enough. Deceased now, sad to say. They grew up in this same house. Had a big St. Bernard they named Nana. Much like your little pup there."

Jack bent over to pat Nana's head. She rolled on her back, paws up and offered him a soulful look. "Amazing coincidences."

"The coincidences continue," Farnesworthy said, edging up on his chair. "Sir James Barrie, the author of *Peter Pan,* was their neighbor for a while. Used to play with the Darling children and the Davies boys nearby. He took them to Kensington Gardens to sail boats and play at pirate, that sort of thing. George Darling was a barrister. Very influential. Public school, Eton you know," he said, nose in the air as one who had attended British public schools. "Mr. Darling didn't care much for Barrie, a small, boyish Scotsman who could wiggle his ears and seemed bent on playing childish games and indulging in frivolities. There was a terrible row after the incident."

"Incident?"

Farnesworthy's eyes gleamed with meaning. "Indeed. This is where it really gets interesting. There were police reports dating back to the time Wendy would have been about eight years or so. Apparently, one September night, all three of the Darling children, Michael, John and Wendy, were reported missing. It was kept very hush-hush. But"— he leaned forward— "George Darling accused Barrie of kidnapping. He was innocent, of course. Barrie was at the theater rehearsing one of his plays the night the children disappeared. But the bad blood spilled couldn't be forgotten.''

Jack shot to his feet. "Well, what happened?"

"Barrie moved. To Surrey."

"No, no, no, not to Barrie. What happened to the children?"

"Oh, yes." He cleared his throat and leaned closer. "Well, it's reported that they returned home safely. Mrs. Darling's statement was that she walked into the nursery one evening, just to sit and weep, and there were the children, sleeping in their beds as though nothing had happened."

After a stunned pause, Jack said, "I don't believe it."

"It's true. Read for yourself." He handed him a photocopy of the police report.

Jack picked it up and read it. "It says here that the children claimed to have traveled to The Neverland with a boy named Peter Pan? But this is unbelievable! How come this never hit the papers?"

"I can only guess. George Darling most likely didn't want it divulged and took appropriate steps. Who can blame him? Keep in mind that back then there wasn't much sympathy for the horrors that could happen to abducted children. It's a simple case of a father protecting his children. They would have been shunned for life. The little Miss Wendy especially. So it was all very secret. I only found these old reports because I was digging about the records at the London Home for Boys. Mrs. Forrester kept copies in her personal files."

"Barrie pulled the rug out from under Darling when he wrote the whole episode as a play."

"So it would appear. No one ever did find out where the children had disappeared to." Farnesworthy paused to rub his chin in thought. "I'm not a psychologist or such, but I've done a little reading. It makes sense to me that poor Miss Wendy fabricated this Peter Pan story to block out what really happened. I was wondering, sir. Something like this might explain Mrs. Forrester."

Jack rose, no longer able to remain seated. "She had to believe this fantasy or else remember . . . well, whatever."

"Yes, precisely."

"You know," Jack said, pacing the floor and wagging his finger, "there is one other possibility, since we're throwing out theories here. It's possible that the children were abducted by . . . Well." He coughed. "By aliens."

Farnesworthy's eyes widened. "Aliens? You mean little green men, sir?" He swallowed hard and seemed to be considering the theory, if only for politeness' sake. "Well you're the scientist, of course," he said in a stumbling manner. "But that sort of thing is only taken seriously by the tabloids and such, eh what? Science fiction. Not by men of real science."

"Not true. It just depends on who the man of science is. The mind is either open or shut. I mean, just open up a bit and think of it. Wendy talks to the stars. Flew out the window as a child. Did you know, by the way, that many abductees claim they were abducted as children? And now Wendy claims the O'Neill children flew off. Through the window. 'Flew' being the operative word. If your theory clicks, she's blocked out her abduction and, as a defense mechanism, transferred in her mind the alien to something, someone, she could accept. Say, a boy. Say, Peter Pan."

Farnesworthy scratched behind his ear, dislodging his

glasses. "And the spaceship is the Neverland? Hmmmm, interesting. That would be logical."

"You can't use logic here, Farnesworthy. That shuts the mind. Open up a little more. Who is to say that she's suffering from a delusion at all? Who's to say that a superior being of some kind, call him God, might come to us in the guise of a boy? Or an angel? Or anything that would make his wisdom easy for us mere mortals to understand and accept. We create stories around the vision, myths that endure through generations; but through the story, the message is revealed."

Farnesworthy looked over at Jack with an expression of uneasiness. "I'm all confused now, sir. All this Peter Pan stuff, it is just a made-up story, isn't it?"

Jack sat and steepled his hands under his chin. He was a scientist, trained to face the facts without prejudice. What was real and what was imagined? He shook his head, feeling as though the wind was knocked out of him, along with all reason.

"Aw, what the hell, Farnesworthy," he said, slapping his knees then rising to a stand. "Let's go up and tell everyone else what we've found. They'll think we're crazy, but facts are facts and damned if I know what to believe anymore."

Detective Inspector Ross was red-faced after hearing Jack and Detective Farnesworthy's report.

"We can't bloody well tell the Chief that the children were taken by Peter Pan to the Neverland!" he exploded.

"Of course not," Jack replied, sticking his hands in his pockets and pacing the room. "But you're missing the point. Real or imagined, Wendy believes the children have gone off with Peter Pan."

"It's called dissociation," added Farnesworthy. "Its another mental state, you see, where one may not be aware of what the other personality is doing. It would fit. This kind of thing is often a result of trauma."

"Her own disappearance you mean? Hmm, yes, see what you mean," said Ross, nodding and stroking his jaw.

Faye stepped forward, intent. "If this is what's wrong with her, couldn't we try to bring her out of this personality, do something like hypnosis so she could tell us where the children are? Give us some clue?"

"It's possible I would guess," Farnesworthy replied.

"Well how? When?" Faye pressed urgently.

"I don't know, mum. I'm a detective, not a head shrinker. That's when I ask for help."

"It's all a bit far-fetched if you ask me," Detective Ross said, shaking his head.

"There's something else you should know," Jack said. "Actually, Wendy insinuated something to the effect in the past but I, quite naturally, refused to even entertain the possibility." He walked over to the mural that depicted a little boy in a tree stump. "Faye, do you remember how struck I was by this mural? How much it resembled me as a child? I asked Wendy about it, hoping to learn more about my past. You see Detective Ross, I was an orphan. I have no memory of my early years. At age six I was brought to the London Home for Boys. By Wendy Forrester. I was found on her doorstep, apparently. I hired Mr. Farnesworthy to uncover the identity of my biological parents. I didn't know then that the woman upstairs founded the boys' home. It was all more coincidence." He raised his brows. "Except I don't believe in coincidence."

"But Wendy said she didn't know who your parents were," Faye said.

"She said at that time something vague about lost boys. But later," he paused and ran his hand through his hair, squeezing a handful of curls. "Look, I know this sounds crazy, but later she told me that I wasn't just a lost boy, so to speak. She said I was one of Peter's Lost Boys and that Peter had brought me back to Wendy to find a home."

"Stop it, Jack," Faye snapped. "I can't listen to any more of this."

"It has bearing on the case, mum," Farnesworthy interjected. "You see, we're working on the assumption that Mrs. Forrester has been living under a delusion for years. Working on a wild hunch, I looked into the records of other boys at the home. Most of them checked out, broken homes, neglect, the usual. But some of them . . ." He handed Detective Ross a handful of papers. "They had no background. No histories. They seemed to come from nowhere, just like Dr. Graham. They all just showed up on Wendy's doorstep. Odd, wouldn't you say?"

Detective Ross shifted through the papers, then looked up, his face troubled. "Are there more of these records?"

Farnesworthy gave a nod. "Crate loads."

Ross's face sharpened. "We'll have to go through the records first, one by one. If this turns out the way you're hinting it might, it'll be the scandal of the century. Turn the country upside down from the oldest to the youngest. Worldwide ramifications. Scotland Yard will have to be notified." He held the papers up and shook his head. "God's teeth, who'd have thought?"

Jack thrust out his jaw and narrowed his eyes in suspicion. "Thought what, Detective?"

"I should think it's obvious to a man of your intelligence. Isn't this what you were leading up to? We cannot ignore the childhood connection between yourself and Mrs. Wendy Forrester. We don't believe in coincidence either, Dr. Graham. Certainly the fact that other children without a past history all turned up on this doorstep leads one to wonder if you, Dr. Graham, were not a victim of kidnapping yourself. And not just you—dozens of others!"

Faye slammed her hands against her mouth, stifling her cry.

"Now who's crazy!" Jack shouted, furious at where the investigation was heading. "I was talking about dissociation. Something that might explain Wendy's fantasies and help lead us to where the children are. I could better believe that I *was* a Lost Boy before I could believe Wendy was a mass kidnapper!"

Faye listened to Detective Ross with a cold chill, but when she heard Jack's defense of Wendy she felt her blood boil.

"Are you implying that this fairy tale of Peter Pan and you being a Lost Boy, or that she was carried away to some spaceship Neverland, is any more believable than the possibility of a delusional woman's kidnapping scheme?"

"Yes. Absolutely. You know I don't discredit anything until proven false. I believe . . ."

"Frankly, I don't care what you believe," she said sharply, slashing her hand through the air between them. She must have been mad to have played along with his mind games in the first place. Jane Lloyd was right. Things had grown out of hand. She'd created a confusing atmosphere for her children. She should have stayed to the straight and narrow, discouraged fantastical dreaming and kept them rooted in concrete reality. She couldn't allow Jack to confuse her, her children or this investigation any longer.

"I'll thank you to keep your opinions to yourself. These are my children, and what happens to them is of no concern to you."

Jack's mouth slipped open, revealing his hurt. His reaction sneaked right past all of her defenses. Even now, with all his faults, he had a way of penetrating her armor and reaching her heart. She despised the sympathy she felt for him, abhorred the softness in her that still loved him. Hardening her heart she charged on, unleashing her scorn.

"How clever you are to present illogical possibilities. So brilliant. So utterly charming. But I see through you, Jack Graham. We have to deal with the hard facts of life. And they're not always pretty or fun. So just go away. Fly off somewhere and play your games and pretend that Peter Pan exists and my children are off having the time of their lives. But I won't pretend anymore." Her voice broke and she brought her fingers to her tight lips. "I can't play these games anymore."

Jack moved forward, but she pushed him away.

"No! Go away! You're free. You have no responsibility to me, or to my children." She wrapped her arms around herself and turned her back to him. "Please Jack. I don't want you here. Just go. Go today." She glanced over her shoulder. "As you planned."

Jack stood still, absorbing the shock. Then he closed his eyes tightly, nodded, and, without another word, left the nursery.

*   *   *

Down in his flat, Jack threw socks and shirts into his suitcases. Packing was a skill he knew well; he could do it on automatic pilot. As he tossed, he counted the reasons he should go. She didn't want him here. She wanted him to go. He couldn't argue with her. Perhaps she was right. What he suggested was impossible. How could he have been so insensitive? What a fool he was, a damn fool!

Slamming the suitcase shut, he placed his hands on the leather and leaned his weight against it, trying to stop the pain that was stabbing, short and quick, like a sword in his gut. The mark was true. He was reeling. More than ever he didn't know who he was or what he believed. He felt truly lost. What good was he to Faye and the children? he wondered. He was only getting in the way. Making her life more difficult. He had no right to interfere. Yes, he decided, clicking the latches, locking the case tight and hoisting it from the bed to the floor. He should go.

The cab arrived just as he finished making final arrangements with the movers to pick up the rest of his things. He made the trip up the back stairs one last time, seeing in his mind's eyes Maddie and Tom racing up with Nana at their heels. The silence now mocked him. At Faye's door, he delivered Nana and a bag of her things to the policeman with the instructions to take the puppy to Faye with his letter.

"No, don't whine, baby," he told Nana. "You have to stay here. You've got a job to do. Faye needs you right now. More than I do. And you have to be here for the children when they get home." He squeezed his eyes tight and said a prayer that they would return home soon, and safely. Then, with a final look around at the house where he'd spent the happiest few months of his life, he opened the front door, hurried through the rain into the cab, and closed the door tight. He looked back once as the car sped down the street, but in the deep, gray fog, No. 14 was already out of sight.

He got as far as the airport gate. The voice on the overhead speakers was calling for all passengers needing assistance to board the international flight. He looked up and saw a father, harried and fumbling for his tickets, holding tightly on to the hand of his toddler son, who looked up with total trust in his eyes. Beside him a young woman nervously rocked a baby in her arms.

The overhead speaker announced the final boarding call. A long line of people queued at the gate. He checked his boarding pass: one way to Los Angeles. Then later, off again to Switzerland. Then to who knew where to uncover more secrets, to explore new vistas, to meet exciting adventures. A few more steps, and he could fly away.

The boarding light began flashing over the gate door, urging him on. He took one step forward, then stopped. The lights triggered memories: the glow of fireflies in the garden, carnival lights at the park, stars over the ocean. Lights . . .

Suddenly he realized that he'd been more profoundly moved by the lights in Faye's eyes than by mysterious balls of light dancing in the hallway. He knew that the most meaningful relationships he'd ever had in his life were with Faye, Maddie and Tom. He looked at his tickets to freedom in his hand and saw them for what they were: a means of an escape. Escape from responsibility and commitment. Except that he didn't want to escape any longer.

The quantum equation played in his mind: *A particle remains in quantum limbo until forced to make a decision.* Well, he wanted out of limbo. Jack crumpled the tickets in his palm and made his decision. He could live without a past—but not without a future.

He turned on his heel and hurried away from the gate toward the exit, tossing the airplane tickets into the trash on the way. Outside the rain had stopped. The heavy cloud cover was moving out at last, and a ray of sunshine pierced the gray. It was going to clear up. Jack raised his hand and whistled sharply for a cab. His foot tapped the pavement. He had to get back to the city, back to do everything he could to find those children. Because he loved them, and he wanted to take care of them, for real this time.

Poor Wendy might be delusional, who knew what she'd lived through or what was going on in her whimsical brain. But crazy or not, she stuck to one story and, following a hunch, he was going to pursue it.

A cab pulled up, and Jack threw his bag in the back and climbed in.

"Where to, sir?"

"The Neverland."

Chapter 22

AT EIGHT O'CLOCK the following evening Faye answered her door to find an anxious Jane Lloyd standing in the foyer.

"Good evening, Mrs. O'Neill. I've come to ask a personal favor. It's not for me," she added with a tone that made it clear she'd rather have died than to have made this request. "It's for my mother. She is . . ." Her voice hitched, and she paused to regain her composure. "She is dying and calling for you."

"Dying?" Faye said, her hand over her mouth. "How? I mean, so quickly."

"She sat by the open window all night long. The cool air . . . The doctors tell me she has pneumonia. At her age, the slightest thing . . ." She clasped her purse so tightly her knuckles paled. "Well, I hope, under the circumstances, that you can find it in your heart to accompany me to the hospital. She is extremely agitated, you see and . . ." Her voice lowered with emotion, and she dragged out the words reluctantly. "Please, Mrs. O'Neill. She's calling for you and there isn't much time."

"Yes, all right. Just give me a moment to inform the

policeman. We're keeping a constant vigil.''

  "Of course.''

Faye felt the walls of the old city hospital close in on
her as she walked down the dim, hushed halls. Jane Lloyd
informed her in the cranky elevator that her mother was
not in the psychiatric ward, due to her worsening health,
to which Faye felt a flush of relief and replied a hurried,
"I understand.'' In truth, she understood very little at that
point, everything was happening so fast. She prayed she'd
be able to endure this unexpected meeting with some
grace and kindness, to glean some small bit of information
and not resort to pitiful begging to find her babies. After
two days without a clue, she was at her wits' end.

  The elevator doors opened and they passed the nurses'
station, then several rooms occupied by frail old women
in various stages of disease. They lay staring at the blank
ceiling surrounded by tubes, vases of flowers, and blinking machines. A low, keening groan floated through the
hall amid the hum of murmured conversations and prayer.
In the air, mingled with the sour scents of medicine and
antiseptic, was the stench of resignation.

  Faye continued on to the end of the hall to a small,
dimly lit room much like all the others. Wendy lay coiled
on the narrow hospital bed, slightly turned toward the
window with her back to the door. She had always taken
such care with her appearance, took pains to add a bit of
lace or a brooch. Now she was barely recognizable in the
drab hospital gown that exposed her thin arms to the slith-
ering tubes. Her face was deathly pale and crisscrossed
with deep wrinkles. Her breath rattled, and her lovely
white hair lay straggled upon the thin pillow.

  This was the wrong place for Wendy to be, Faye

thought immediately. If she was going to die, she should be in the nursery that she loved, where she had spent her life, surrounded by her cheerful murals and her beloved books and all the curious china figurines that she doted on. Not here in this cold, impersonal space.

Wendy made a whimpering, fretful noise that brought Faye to her bedside.

"She's lucid one moment, then out the next," said Jane from behind. "Mother," she said in a louder voice, bending near. "Mother, Mrs. O'Neill is here. Faye . . . She's come to see you."

Wendy stirred, and her lids fluttered, then turning with aching slowness, she said in a soft, raspy voice, "Faye? Oh, my dear girl. Is that you?"

"Yes, Wendy," she said, taking the tiny outstretched hand. "It's me."

Wendy's thin lips formed a tremulous smile. Was that relief she saw in her eyes?

"You came. I knew you would."

Faye saw the ghost of the woman Wendy once was flicker in the pale blue. She couldn't help but pity her, love her. She didn't have it in her heart to hate Wendy.

Wendy tugged at her hand, drawing her near.

"I'm sorry," she rasped with a heartfelt squeeze of her hand. "I never meant to upset you. So irresponsible of me to let them go."

"It's all right," Faye replied, patting her hand. "Don't tire yourself."

"I only thought . . . How happy they'd be . . . I was wrong . . ."

Faye felt her heart break in two, one-half Maddie, one-half Tom, and her eyes filled as she clasped Wendy's hand and bent nearer. "Please, Wendy, tell me. Where are they? Did they go somewhere? Did someone come by the house? Please, Wendy, try to remember. Anything at all.''

Wendy's elegantly shaped brows furrowed in thought. "Peter said . . ." she began haltingly, then licked parched lips. "Peter said he would bring them back on Tuesday."

"But it *is Tuesday*!" Faye tearfully replied.

Wendy suddenly became fretful and agitated. She shook her head back and forth on the pillow and her small hands fluttered on the bedding. She grasped Faye's arm tightly.

"*You must open the window*!"

Faye drew back. "Please, Wendy," she exclaimed. "No more of this metaphysical nonsense about keeping windows open. I need plain facts now. The truth. Help me, please, Wendy!"

"No, no," Wendy gasped, drawing herself up, alert. "I am speaking literally, my child. You must go to the nursery and open the window. Peter will return with your children. Tonight! If he finds the window barred, he will be angry. I know him. He'll fly back to the Neverland with Maddie and Tom just for spite. You will never see them again."

Faye felt frozen, unable to move or respond.

Wendy took Faye's hand again and looked into her eyes. Her own were bright again, sparkling with fevered intent.

"You *must* believe. I know it is difficult for you. You prefer logic and reason. But just this once, you must let go of your doubts and have faith. Believe because you must. That is why I called you here. What I wanted to tell you." She wearily dropped her hands, sliding back down against the pillow, exhausted.

Closing her eyes, Wendy whispered urgently, "Open ... the ... window."

It was a strange night, eerily quiet, with a multitude of stars. Wisps of silvery clouds drifted like sailing vessels at full mast across the waning moon. Faye paced the garden where her children had toiled so steadfastly in the spring and basked in the golden days of summer. How empty this small, prisonlike yard seemed tonight, she agonized, where once they had spent so many hours of happiness. The heavy silence added to her acute suspense. She stood, her body tense, racked with indecision, desperate to be doing *something*. Everyone was gone: her children, Wendy, Jack. She stood alone at the brink of a fathomless despair.

The last of Maddie's sweet flowers had been nipped by the bitter wind of the storm and lay brittle and wilted, like Faye's own hopes. Leaves, shaken and ripped from the mother tree, littered the flagstones. She couldn't make out the face of the bronze boy in the shadows or hear the reedy flute music she'd come to expect. All was silent as the grave, as though all the magic of the garden had fled with Maddie and Tom.

The clouds shifted, covering the moon, veiling all in darkness. She crossed the uneven flagstones as one blind, her fingertips skimming the crumbling brick of the wall, the cool iron of the chairs. She was determined to confront the bronze boy, this haunting image of her nemesis, Peter Pan. She stared at the cocky face, daring him to speak. The bronze face just stared back with its teasing grin.

She gripped the fountain, stuck out her jaw, and cried out fiercely, full of deep-seated resentment, "Okay, I admit it! I believed in you!"

Her voice lowered to sadness. "Once, long ago, I believed in you. I used to leave my window open for you, every night. I sat in my bed, yawning, shivering in the cold by the window and waited and waited. I even called your name. I was so lonely. I felt sure you heard me and would come."

Her eyes flashed. "But you never came! And when the other kids found out they made fun of me." She sniffed and swiped at her eyes. "Eventually, I closed the window. And after Rob, I locked it. I swore I'd never be so stupid, so naive again."

The Pan still smiled his cocky smile. Resigned, she looked higher up to see countless stars twinkling in the sky. Was it just the other night that Jack had held her in his arms so close she could hear his heart beat, and pointed to this same hazy, glowing trail of stars across the sky? It seemed so very long ago. "We can see over twenty-five hundred stars of the Milky Way," he'd told her, "and these are just a fraction of the billions of stars in the Milky Way galaxy. Who are we to doubt what's out there, somewhere? The possibilities are as countless as the stars. You just gotta believe."

Believe . . . She tucked her arms around her, feeling as helpless as the child she once was, shivering and alone. Powerless. Like a ship without a rudder, a sailor without a compass.

She pressed a balled up fist to her forehead. "I wish I could believe again."

From nowhere came the faint sound of music. She cocked her head, ears alert to catch the familiar reedy pipe tune as it floated in the air. She hummed along, gaining heart as she sang. The music lured her indoors, past her flat where two policeman played gin rummy by the phone, up the stairs to the nursery. The music filled her head, filled her heart, giving her hope. Humming, she walked around the nursery, fingering the many fanciful items scattered throughout, searching for some clue. While she searched she recalled that Wendy had urgently told her to believe.

What did that mean? Believe that her children would come back to her? That Jack would come back to her? In his letter he had said good-bye. If she'd had a heart left, it would have broken. What was this thing called faith? Was it believing in magic or miracles? If so, then surely the sound of children's laughter and reedy pipe music in the night, fragrant tea and tiny sandwiches, luciferin lighting up a firefly's lamp, falling in love, surely these were magic. Faith was a kind of magic. A miracle that had the power to transform. She couldn't see faith, like she couldn't see Peter Pan or the fairy on her shoulder. Or a tiny atom. But she could imagine them. Perhaps faith was the ability to believe in the infinite possibilities of what could only be imagined.

Her heart beat faster as she began to understand. Not fully, no, it was more like seeing something through a haze. Her finger trailed across the old silk top hat, the raggedy teddy bear that was missing one shiny black eye, the small square of crushed blue velvet upon which, Wendy claimed, she'd placed Peter's thimble till he snatched it back again. Detective Farnesworthy's report played again in her mind, teasing her. So many coincidences, she wondered. "There's no such thing as a coincidence," Jack had said.

"What am I looking for?" she said aloud, standing in the middle of the nursery, surrounded by dozens of eyes staring out from the mural, as though they were watching, waiting for her to make the right move.

Then she saw it. Caught in a shard of moonlight, the dusky green leather and burnished gold engraving of Wendy's storybook lay on the window seat where she had left it, beside her mohair throw. Drawn to it, Faye skimmed her fingertips across the deep etchings on the cover that depicted a handsome youth in a cocky pose beside a prim young girl in a nightgown and a ribbon in her hair. *Peter and Wendy*. She opened the first edition book as though it were made of crystal and gasped when she read the inscription written in a swirly, elegant handwriting.

To my dear, Darling, young friend, Wendy Darling,

Thank you for sharing with me the tales of your marvelous adventure with the Pan. You and I shall always know the book is really, Wendy's Story. As you wished, it is our little secret!

Your devoted servant,
James Barrie

Faye felt a tingling awe as she leafed through the tissue-thin, gold-tipped pages to where Wendy had placed a bright red bird's feather as a bookmark. The book was opened to Chapter Sixteen: "The Return Home." Scanning down the page she saw that a passage was underlined. In it, Mrs. Darling was waiting patiently in the nursery for her children, admonishing her husband, *The window must always be left open for them, always, always, always.*

Faye suddenly realized what she had to do.

She rose to stand before the window, closed and shuttered like herself. Wendy had told her to open the window. To do so she would be admitting to herself that she believed. She shivered, afraid to let go of control again, to step beyond reason. To open up meant to risk the possibility of more hurt and pain. Yet it also meant opening to the possibility of great joy and happiness. Wasn't that at the core of Wendy's message? Magic can only come in if you are open for it.

Reaching out, she unshuttered the window, unlocked the hook and with a heartfelt shove pushed open the window. The air gusted in, whistling in the corners, tossing papers onto the floor, playing with her hair and whisking away her doubts and worries like a feather duster at spring cleaning. Faye stood at the precipice and lifted her chin to stare out at the immense, dark blue of the sky, a multitude of stars winking and waiting.

She didn't know how long she stood there gazing at the blue but somewhere inside she felt an unloosening of strings and an opening up of sealed little boxes. She felt sure the magic was pouring in, filling the empty spaces to overflowing. She took a deep breath. A hush seemed to fall upon the heavens while Faye gathered her courage.

"Peter!" she called out, her voice ringing. "I *do* believe! Stars! Shine steadfast and bright tonight. Light the path for my children to find their way home."

Sure that she was heard, Faye curled up on the window seat and wrapped the mohair throw around her shoulders and brought Wendy's book close to her chest. Then opening it, she began to read. While she read she imagined Maddie dancing with Tiger Lily around the campfire, and Tootles at swordplay. And of course Peter, that forever-young boy, flashing his pearly first teeth. Hours passed as she read, keeping vigil, till her eyelids drooped and her head slipped down to lie in her arms. Faye fell asleep dreaming of Peter taking her hand at last and flying with her in the starry night. Except that in her dream, Peter became Jack, and he flew to her side, wrapped his arm around her waist, and took for himself her one special kiss.

Chapter 23

WHEN THE PALE pink sky of the dawn stretched its glory over the tightly clustered, jagged rooftops of London, Faye raised her chin from the crook of her arm and leaned upon the windowsill while she struggled to maintain her faith now that the mystical night had passed and the piercing light of morning broke. The nursery was quiet and still and she was alone. Once more, Peter had not come to her open window. Wendy had been wrong, her children did not return. In her chest she felt a cry ready to explode. Her anger hurt so much tears threatened.

Yet, her mind begged her to hold tight to her belief that all would be well. How easy to believe at night, when the stars twinkled and hours of peace and quiet lay ahead, and how hard to keep the faith when the new day brought to light new problems, hectic schedules, and duties. This was the greatest test: to continue to believe when all seemed hopeless.

She would not give way to her despair, she vowed, rising and wiping the sleep from her face. Yet as she walked with a numbing slowness from the nursery she was unable to dispel the gloom despite the bright, cheery

sunshine that poured in through the windows. "I believe," she muttered under her breath, again and again,
without enthusiasm. When she passed Wendy's bedroom
a movement caught her attention from the corner of her
eye. She startled, instantly alert. Very slowly she pushed
open the bedroom door wider and peered in the room.

There are moments in life, rare and precious, when one
is sure magic exists. For some it is the sight of their
baby's first smile, or a long-awaited letter from a loved
one, or the remission of a terrible illness, or the look of
love in the eyes of a beloved. When it happens, one's
heart swoops up and out into the heavens in a gasp of
joy, then returns again filled with awe and wonder that
tingles as it spreads throughout the body.

That is how Faye felt when she saw her two children
lying like spoons, asleep on Wendy's four-poster bed. She
absorbed every minute detail: Maddie's pale blue nightgown embroidered with pastel flowers, the shock of blond
bangs dangling over her eyelids, her long and delicate
fingers. Tom seemed to have grown in three days. The
green T-shirt that he wore like a uniform was snug and
revealed his round belly and the dimple of his belly
button.

She couldn't move. Like a sponge, she soaked in the
image of her children, her fingertips at her lips as she
shook her head softly. She didn't know that she was crying but it was this sound that woke Maddie from her deep
sleep.

She rubbed her eyes and yawned sleepily. When she
caught sight of her mother at the foot of the bed she
smiled, her face glowing with delight and scrambled to
her knees. "Oh Mother!" she exclaimed. "You won't
believe where we were!"

"I just might," she replied with misty eyes.

Then Tom awoke and he too bubbled over with stories about the adventures they'd shared with Peter and the Lost Boys and all the other inhabitants of the Neverland. His words tumbled over each other in his eagerness to get it all out before his sister who jabbed her elbow and tried to compete.

In all the telling the dears omitted any apologies or phrases of concern for any fretting their mother might have endured during their absence. The children were blissfully unaware that they'd caused the slightest inconvenience. Faye sat on the mattress of the bed with one arm around each child and listened to them chatter on as she would listen to music, or to the gurgling of a brook over stones or the sweet song of birds chirping in the trees. For between the tones and pitch she heard the magic of joy and love and reunion. Her heart missed the low tones of Jack's voice in this sweet medley, but she shooed that sentiment away. She didn't know what to think or say about the children's safe return. She didn't dare make any judgments. If this was all a dream she never wanted to awaken.

"We must tell Wendy!" cried Tom. "She'll be so happy to hear that her tree house is just as she left it."

"And her sewing box," added Maddie. Then, looking over her shoulder she asked, "Where is she?"

Faye's face grew solemn as she told the children of the strange, unhappy circumstances of the past three days. Maddie and Tom listened, astonished, when she told of the kidnapping worries. Faye was irked when she saw the mischievous gleam in Tom's eyes when he heard that Scotland Yard had been notified and that at this very moment a policeman sat in their flat downstairs. When she told them of Wendy's illness, however, their faces paled.

"Wendy can't be in the hospital!" Maddie exclaimed, jumping to her feet. Tom was by her side in a second, stammering and gulping.

"P . . . Peter's coming for her tonight! He . . . he said so. We . . . we're to remind her t . . . to be ready. Mom, if the window isn't open she'll m . . . m . . . iss him forever."

"We've got to bring her home." Maddie stamped her foot, furious.

"It's impossible," Faye replied sadly. "I don't have the authority, and . . ." she paused and took each of their hands. "Children, Wendy may never come back to the nursery. I'm sorry. You must understand. Wendy is dying."

"But she can't be," Maddie cried, tears filling her soft blue eyes. "She's been waiting for such a long time for Peter to take her back to the Neverland. She's been so faithful. She can't die now, just before he comes."

"It won't matter," Tom declared, a strange light gleaming in his eyes.

Maddie turned her head, frowning. She had come to develop a new respect for her younger brother. For she discovered that all the while he was silent and not chatting away like her, he was listening, taking note of everything and everybody. He was very wise for a boy two years younger than her. "What do you mean?"

"It won't matter what happens as long as Peter finds her. He'll make everything okay. I'm sure he'll find her. We've just gotta make sure he can get in the window."

"Well, how can we do that? She's locked up in that stupid hospital with mean old Mrs. Lloyd hanging around all the time."

Two pairs of eyes stared up at her and Faye was struck with the notion that the two children believed implicitly in her ability to solve the dilemma. It was both humbling and inspiring. Just a few months earlier they had looked at her with eyes filled with doubt. *Well*, she thought to herself, *a mother's magic is pretty potent too.* There was no way she would let that doubt creep back into their eyes.

"So we're in this together, eh? Just the three of us? Counting on each other to come through. Same as always?" Again, the painful thought that their group was incomplete without Jack nagged at her heart. The truth was, nothing was the same without him. She saw that realization in her children's eyes as well.

"Same as always," they agreed like troopers.

"Then huddle round," she said, rubbing her palms together. "I've got a plan."

"Oooh," they sighed as they gathered close, their pulses beating faster, quivering with excitement. For they knew that a full-fledged rescue could only succeed with a clever, devious, well-executed plan.

That night, the moon cast its golden light like a warm, soothing blanket over the sleeping city of London. But in Kensington Gardens the night was deep and the first winds of autumn bore the ripe, crisp scent of change. Majestic trees, heavy with leaves, cloaked the manicured lawns and trimmed shrubs in a darkness that revealed shimmering bits of light only when the breeze blew, as it did now.

Jack stood in the shifting shadows, leaning against the elaborate base of a large sculpture of a barefooted boy merrily piping. It was a famous sculpture by George Frampton, created in 1911, the year of the death of Edward VII, in memory of the world's most famous and beloved fictional runaway, Peter Pan. Except that Jack Graham wasn't so sure Peter Pan was fictional.

He'd just spent the whole night and day scouring every inch of The Neverland Theme Park and every other bloody park in London looking for his own very real runaways. He didn't know till now just how many gardens there were in this city. He ended up in Kensington Gardens, of all places. The notorious favorite romping ground of Peter Pan and his consort of fairies. Jack shook his head, wondering what had brought him here? Some perverse, nagging intuition that maybe, just maybe, Peter was real? That magic did exist.

Seeking Maddie and Tom, he'd searched deep within himself and found some dim, distant memories of sword fights with wild-spirited boys, of Indians and pirates, of a world unlike any other. Memories or dreams, who was to say? Either way, he cherished these memories. They replaced the single memory of a fist striking him, a brutal hand without a face. Looking up at the sculpted boy's face, so like the bronze boy's face in Wendy's garden, he fully accepted Wendy's advice to let go of the past and embrace the future.

"Maybe you can fly and I can't, boy, but at least I've got the courage to grow up. Wendy says I made that decision once long ago, but never acted on it. That part's true enough. I kept postponing it, playing the kid, because . . ." He swallowed hard. "Maybe because I don't want to be abandoned again. But that's a risk I'm ready to take now. I'm not a Lost Boy anymore. I'm a man. I want to grow up. And I'm *not* going to abandon Maddie and Tom. Not like I was abandoned. I want to be there for them. For Faye. So if you know where they are, then lead me to them! Help me find them, Peter.''

He ran his hand through his hair and closed his eyes tight. ''Please. Help me.''

The 11:00 P.M. shift had finished, and the nurses had completed their rounds. Maddie thought Peter would most likely come after midnight, so they'd have just enough time to sneak open the window and hustle out before he arrived.

Maddie and Faye entered the hospital lobby with blank expressions and rode the elevator up to the fifth floor without any delays. At this late hour visitors were scarce and the hospital was dimly lit and quiet. Most of the patients on Wendy's floor were asleep, some moaning against a back beat of beeping noises. Faye squeezed Maddie's hand, then gave her a nod. At the signal, Maddie sneaked into one of the rooms at the farthest end of the hall opposite Wendy's. After a moment she came out of the room and called out with fear in her voice.

''Nurse! Nurse! Please come quick. Something is wrong with my grandmother!''

The nurse at the desk leaped to her feet and hurried down the hall to assist. Without waiting a heartbeat, Faye rushed to the nurses' station, grabbed hold of the keys that hung on a hook behind the desk, and ran to Wendy's room, slipping in and quietly closing the door behind her. Not before spying one little girl duck around the corner toward the stairs.

Tom was having a hard time keeping his eyes open. He had taken his mother's place on the window seat beside the window, keeping guard should Peter come and need directions to Wendy. He'd complained loudly at not being able to join them in the fun of creeping around at the hospital, but Faye assured him that his duty was at the nursery and in the end, his devotion to Wendy won him over.

The clock had chimed eleven times, rousing him from near sleep, when he heard a sound at the door. His breath caught and he sat up straight. Then he heard the unmistakable sound of a door sighing open and the creak of footfall on the floor.

"Peter?" Tom called out, fear making his voice crack.

The shadowed figure froze, reached out with his hand, and clicked on the light.

Tom blinked and rubbed his eyes against the blaze of light. Gradually, he recognized the unshaven, droopy-lidded face of the man who stood in shock and surprise at the door.

"Jack!" he cried out, and ran into his arms.

Jack just had time to outstretch his arms and catch the ball of boy that catapulted into his arms and clung tight.

"What? Tom? Is that you?" He whooped out loud and swirled the boy around in a circle, then hugged him tight, afraid to let go. "Aw, boy, let me get a good look at you." His eyes devoured the thin face with the bright blue eyes and the shaggy blond hair that stared back at him with equal measure of happiness. "So where were you? We've been mad with worry and grief."

"I was at the Neverland!" he replied without a bit of conscience. In fact, he was proud and pleased to make the announcement.

"What? But that's impossible," Jack replied with a hint of irritation.

"All grown-ups say that," Tom replied with a knowing nod.

"But I just spent the last twenty-four hours scouring every bit of that park and every other park in London. If you were there, I'd like you to tell me where."

Tom laughed and began another telling of his adventures over the past few days while Jack grew more and more subdued.

"I suppose it's no more strange hearing you tell me that you went off to the Neverland with Peter Pan than to hear you speak the words at all. There were Lost Boys, you say?" he asked, sounding every bit as young as Tom.

"An even dozen, as Peter likes to say," Tom replied emulating a cocky smile that Wendy would have immediately recognized.

"Well you know you broke your mother's heart with worry, don't you? She lay awake at nights crying. I don't suppose you gave that much thought during all your gallivanting."

The cockiness fled instantly. Jack was pleased to see it. "Where is your mother, by the way?"

"She went to the hospital with Maddie. To see Wendy."

"At this hour? And they left you here alone?"

"It's all part of the plan."

"Tom, I'm more confused than ever. Back up and tell me about the plan."

"Mom and Maddie went to the hospital to open Wendy's window. You see, Peter Pan is coming for Wendy tonight," he explained, urgency making his voice high and his pace quicken. "They've got to make sure the window is open!"

Jack's mouth dropped open as he heard this. "Faye? Your mother went along with this plan?"

"Went along with it? It was *her* plan to start with!"

Jack whooped again and clapped his hands together, his eyes sparkling with triumph. Then he brought his one hand to his forehead in a salute, and said, "I'm off to assist in the rescue plan, sir. Steady the course here at the helm." He gave Tom a reassuring pat, then with an ear-to-ear grin on his face, rushed out the door on his way to the hospital.

Faye listened at the hospital door for a moment to make sure that no one was behind her. All was quiet again, except for the complaining of the nurses in the hall wondering where that troublesome little girl went who had called for help. Faye smiled with pride that the little girl who just months before would cower instead of act had executed her daring role in the plan with such finesse.

She turned and saw Wendy on her narrow hospital bed, her dainty hands tucked under her cheek as she slept facing the window. She could hear the raspiness of Wendy's breathing and saw the rapid rise and fall of her chest, like a small bird's caught in a cage. Clearly, her time was drawing near. Lowering her head, Faye placed a soft kiss on her cheek, and whispered, "I'll open the window for you, Wendy. Then you can fly away."

After a few misses she finally found the right key to open up the thick iron window screens. Behind them the old double-hung window was covered with dirt and grime, just the kind that Maddie often wrote "Wash Me" on with her fingertip. Faye climbed up onto the marble sill and unlatched the ancient brass lock. Then, climbing down again, she grabbed hold of the two brass handles and with a mighty "humph," jerked hard. The window didn't budge.

No, this was not part of the plan! She didn't have a

contingency for ancient wooden windows that were stuck from years of swelling and a build up of dirt and grease. She *had* to get the window open. Panic sparked and stubbornness kindled. Taking a deep breath she pulled again with all her might, but the window didn't give. A quick glance at her watch told her she had no time to lose. It was 11:40 and Maddie said Peter would likely come at midnight. Again and again she tried, but to no avail. She slumped her shoulders and gave the window a nasty pound.

"That's a good start," came a whispered voice behind her.

She gasped and swung around. "Jack, what are you doing here?"

"Saving the plan."

She took in the sight of him in his rumpled shirt with the tails hanging out, his unshaven face, his hair a riot of curls. He hadn't deserted her. He'd come back. And he knew about the plan! Smiling, she stretched up on tiptoe and gave him her kiss, the special one from deep in the heart that she'd never given to anyone else before.

Feeling the strength of ten men, he walked over and took hold of the window's brass handles. With a deep breath he gave a great yank, and the ancient, dirty, grimy, stubborn old window gave up the fight and rumbled up the track to open to an unseasonably warm night. Outside, the dogs of London were howling at the moon.

Faye raised her hands to her mouth to smother her cry of delight. Jack reached over to swirl her around in a circle, setting her back on her feet with a grounding kiss.

"Now, let's get out of here," he whispered.

They just reached the door when it swung open, practically nipping Jack in the nose. There stood Jane Lloyd, and she was not pleased.

"What are you two doing here?" she asked, her voice wrathful. "And what is that window doing open? My god, haven't you tried hard enough to kill my mother? Are you trying to finish her off?" She stomped angrily toward the window.

"Don't close it," Faye cried.

"And why shouldn't I?"

"Peter is coming for Wendy tonight, and it must remain open."

"That finishes it." Jane spun around and reached for the phone. "You're all crazy. I'm calling for the guard."

"Please," came a frail voice from the bed.

They all stopped to look over at the bed. Jane hurried to her mother's side and took Wendy's hand in her own.

"I'm here, Mother."

"I asked her to open it," Wendy said in a weak voice. "He's coming for me, Jane. At last." Joy was etched across her small, delicate features. In the dim light, Wendy's thin, frail figure and beautiful, sweet face appeared as a child's once again. "You remember how Peter hates a barred window, don't you Jane?"

Jane's eyes filled with tears and she nodded.

Wendy's face flooded with relief. She cupped her daughter's face with her small hand and gazed at her with a mother's tender love. "You're a good girl. Remember the good times we had together . . . you and I in the nursery. Good-bye, my darling child," she said softly. "My own sweet Jane."

Wendy's hand slid down, and, turning her face toward the open window, she smiled. "See the stars, Jane? How they sparkle tonight! Aren't they the lovelies? And that one . . . It's so very bright. It's light . . . it's reaching out to me. Oh, how warm the light is. Listen! Do you hear? Yes, yes, I hear the music. He'll be coming soon! I've waited ever such a long time . . .'' Wendy closed her eyes with a smile of serenity on her face.

Jane brought her hand to her lips while they trembled, and a long history of surpressed memories flooded the banks and rushed through her mind. Memories of herself in her mother's lap, her head resting against Wendy's soft bosom while her mother's melodic voice enveloped her as warmly as her arms. Jane's face softened as she gazed at her mother; then she bent to kiss her cheek, tuck the blanket under Wendy's chin and tenderly smooth a few hairs from her face. She sniffed loudly and rose to a stand.

"I think you should leave now," she said to Faye and Jack.

Faye's glance consulted Jack's with worry.

Jane saw the exchange. "Oh, be off with you," she said, brusquely wiping the tears from her eyes. "I won't close the silly window. No matter what you might think, I love my mother, and it is her last wish."

Faye took a final glance at Wendy lying peacefully, facing the open window. Her long white hair seemed silvery in the moonlight as it spread like rippling waves upon the pillow. Her lips were turned up in a sweet smile of anticipation. Faye thought she'd never seen her look more beautiful. Jack stooped over Wendy to kiss her forehead and when he spoke, his voice trembled.

"Good-bye, Wendy. Say hello to the Lost Boys for me."

"Jack," said Faye. "It's almost twelve. Wendy must be alone, and Maddie is waiting at the front door." Addressing Jane, she added gently, "We should all go."

"Yes," Jane replied. "I understand. I'll hurry along."

Jack took Faye's hand. "Come on, Faye," he said and led her out from the room, down the hall and to the lobby where they picked up Maddie. Then they all headed home.

Jane followed moments later. Before closing the door she glanced back and with all the love in her heart whispered, "Good-bye, mother."

Jane Lloyd woke in the hospital lounge just as dawn broke across the city. She raced down the halls, past the nurses' station directly into Wendy's room. Sunlight poured in through the open window along with a soft early-morning breeze. It poured onto the empty, stripped bed. Jane saw instantly that her mother had flown away.

From the corner of her eye she caught the flash of something bright and shiny reflecting in the sunlight. Walking to the window, she picked up a small object that lay upon the sill. Recognizing it, her breath caught in her throat as a rush of memories swept away her grief and filled her with a soft glow of a joy. She recalled a certain boy dressed in leaves held together with sap who once taught her how to be free and soar in the sky. At some point in her life she'd forgotten about him, or had chosen to forget. Not Wendy, however. Her mother had steadfastly believed. And from now on, she thought, bringing her closed fist to her heart, so would she.

Looking out the open window to the sky, Jane smiled, feeling the sunlight of a new day warm her face.

Chapter 24

THEY GATHERED IN the great, sunny kitchen of No. 14. Jack lit a small fire in the tiled fireplace to warm the chill of Wendy's passing. They all were putting on a brave face, convinced that Peter had come to claim her in some way and bring her back to the Neverland at last! But still they missed her, especially Maddie and Tom. They missed her voice, her smell, her touch. They missed sitting beside her and hearing her stories. They missed running up the stairs for a cup of sweet tea and a dose of optimism. They missed feeling that anything was possible when they were held in her arms.

Faye came to sit beside them by the fire, gathering them in warm arms close to her bosom where her heart beat heavily with love for them.

"I wish she didn't go," Maddie said softly.

Tom nodded in silence.

"It was her time to go," Faye replied, stroking their heads. "She was ready."

"I wish we could've gone with her," said a forlorn Tom.

Faye held on to her little ones tighter, kissing their foreheads, saying a quick, mother's prayer that this wish would not be answered, at least not in her lifetime. "Let's be happy for Wendy. We'll always have her in our memories. And at night, we can leave messages for her with the stars. Maddie, Tom, I'm sure she's happy now. Can't you feel that too? And wouldn't she give us what-for if she saw us moping about on such a beautiful day?"

The children nodded and wiped their eyes then craned their necks around her shoulder to peer out the garden windows. Outside, the sun was high in the sky and the garden was resplendent with its touch of reds and golds. Tom drew himself straighter, and Maddie bent low to clap her hands and call Nana to her side. The excitement of a brand-new day sparked in their eyes, hope replacing the gloom in a flash. Magic, Faye thought, was indeed everywhere.

Police Inspector Ross arrived midmorning, as did Ian Farnesworthy, to question the children on their disappearance. They sat down at the large wooden table, spreading out their forms, and dutifully filled in all the blanks they could while sipping tea and munching biscuits. Tom was speaking freely now and tried to explain to them that he was fine, that no one had hurt him, and that Wendy did not take him anywhere or leave him anywhere. The latter he said with his fists balled and defiance in his eyes. He wouldn't tolerate anyone speaking ill of his Wendy.

The questions were endless, however, and no matter how Inspector Ross phrased them, regardless of whether he separated the children or questioned them together, their responses were always the same.

"So you went of your own free will?"

Maddie and Tom swung their legs and rolled their eyes, bored. "Uh-huh."

"To the Neverland?"

Maddie searched out her mother. Faye smiled at her from her seat across the table and shrugged.

"Yes."

"Together?"

Tom nodded. "Yes."

Farnesworthy leaned forward and interjected, "He means The Neverland Theme Park. In London. Is that what *you* mean?"

Jack and Faye exchanged amused looks.

Maddie and Tom faced each other, signaling a message between them, then smiled and solemnly returned their gaze to the Inspectors. "Uh-huh," they chimed, nodding complacently.

"We ran away," Maddie said as though in recitation. "And then we came back."

Farnesworthy narrowed his eyes and scratched behind his ear in thought.

Detective Ross leaned back in his chair with a grunt and rubbed his jaw. "I daresay I'm satisfied. Seems open and shut to me, eh what Farnesworthy?"

Farnesworthy looked at Jack, who returned the gaze with an open smile.

"Open and shut."

"Oh by the by, Graham," Ross said, gathering up his forms. He spoke in the tone of afterthought. "We came across a bit of information about you while mucking about in those files."

Jack, who was leaning against the wall, sprang forward, all alert. "Well why didn't you say so? What did you learn?"

"You were abandoned all right. At Mrs. Forrester's doorstep, just as she claimed. By some young, unwed mother. Father unknown." He shrugged and tossed his pens into the bag. "Common enough story. Seems a number of folks were droppin' babies off at Mrs. Forrester's house for years. Probably because she was in the social papers so much. Her and that London Home for Boys. It's obvious that she didn't kidnap you and"—he cleared his throat—"Scotland Yard sees no evidence to support further investigation. Of either Wendy Forrester or the London Home for Boys." He flushed, remembering how he'd been roasted crisp by his superiors for even suggesting it. "Never believed all that kidnapping, multiple personality rubbish."

"Tell me, Inspector Ross," asked Jack, moving closer to Faye and resting his hands on her shoulders. "Did you happen to get the name of my mother?"

Farnesworthy lifted his gaze and rolled his tongue in his cheek.

"Ah, no, no," Ross coughed. "Nothing official. Just some note somewhere."

Jack grinned and leaned over to whisper in Faye's ear, "You see? I still think we were all Wendy's Lost Boys."

Faye reached up to entwine her fingers in his. "Lost, but now found."

"Well I guess we're finished here," Ross said brusquely. "I'm glad it all turned out so well. And you two," he said, turning with a gruff manner to face the children. "Don't let there be a next time, eh? You're very lucky, that you are. I don't want you to worry your mother again with such a harebrained excuse for a lark. God knows what might've happened out there."

"Pirates, wild Indians, who knows?" interjected Farnesworthy, wagging his brows.

The children smirked but kept mum.

A gentle knocking sounded at the door, and, on answering, Jack found Mrs. Lloyd waiting. He ushered her into the room and on seeing her, Faye hurried to her feet and took Jane's hands in her own. Jane Lloyd appeared changed somehow, as though her sorrow had rounded all the sharp edges from her voice and her expressions.

"We're all so sorry that Wendy is gone," Faye said. "We shall all miss her terribly."

"I know," she replied with a small smile of understanding. "I too. I suspect a great many folks will. But I believe she is happy now. She's where she wants to be." She began digging in her deep purse saying, "I came to give you something. If I can only find it. I know it's here. Oh yes, here it is."

She pulled out her hand and opened her palm. In it lay a small gold thimble.

Maddie spotted it and leaped from her chair and ran with coltish speed to their side. "That's Peter's thimble! Wendy gave it to him. He called it a kiss, and he always wore it around his neck on a chain. Close to his heart." Her face was flushed and her words danced from her mouth.

"Yes," Jane surprised everyone by replying. "I recognized it, too."

"Where did you get it?" Tom wanted to know.

Jane smiled wistfully. "I found it on the windowsill this morning in my mother's room. I think . . ." She paused. ". . . I think they left it for us. To tell us that all was well and that Wendy was with him now."

"He wouldn't need it anymore." Maddie sighed.

"No, I didn't think so. And neither do I. Perhaps you would like it?" Jane handed it to Maddie, whose eyes were as round as teacups. She took the thimble in her hand and gazed at it with all the awe and wonder in her soul.

"May I take a look at that?" Jack asked.

Maddie handed the thimble to him with reverence and supervised his handling of the treasure.

"I guess that proves the existence of Peter Pan." He looked directly at Faye. "I win the bet."

She met his gaze squarely. "We all win. And I freely admit that I believe."

Jack's chest swelled. He squinted and stared down at the thimble in his palm with great thought. After a moment he raised his eyes, pursed his lips, then asked, "Tell me, Mrs. Lloyd. Are you still planning to sell this place?"

Faye gasped, stunned by the suddenness of the question. She supposed she always knew, somewhere in the back of her mind, that No. 14 would be sold after Wendy's death. Jane Lloyd had made no secret of her intentions. She'd hoped it wouldn't be so soon.

Her gaze roamed the great warm kitchen of the old house that she'd come to love over the past months, hungrily taking in the charming nooks and bric-a-brac as though seeing them for the last time. She looked at the mullioned windows and smelled the scent of wood burning in the delft tiled fireplace. She brought to mind the blue-hydrangea wallpaper, the plump cushioned sofa, the Staffordshire china, the lemony smell of the foyer and, of course, the magic of Wendy's marvelous nursery. Finally, she let her eyes take in the sight of the wonderful garden where her children's hearts and imagination took seed.

blossomed and now were as brilliant and ripe as the autumn flowers.

Faye had learned that a house was not the glue that bound a family together. As beautiful as a castle, a mansion, a house or a small flat may be, as rich in family heritage, as full of memories as it can hold, no house was a home. Maddie and Tom—and now Jack—they were the mortars of her home. Love was the foundation. Wherever they went in their lifetimes they would furnish their home with treasured memories, old and new. They would plant new seeds in a well-tilled soil.

Still, she thought wistfully, her gaze lingering on the sight of Maddie and Tom rolling and laughing with Nana with all the exuberance of youth, she had been happy here. She would miss No. 14.

Jane Lloyd's eyes widened with surprise at hearing Jack's question. "Well, I don't know. I haven't thought . . ." she stammered.

"You *are* selling it?" he persisted.

"Yes, of course. As soon as possible, I should imagine."

"Good," he replied with finality.

Faye looked up sharply, stunned and a little hurt by his sudden closure.

He looked her way with significance, then, turning back to Mrs. Lloyd, he said in a casual manner, "You can save yourself the real-estate commission. I'll buy the house." Looking at Faye's astonished face, he added, "What? You ̶n't think I'm going to live in this big old place alone ̶̶? This is a package deal. You and the kids are ̶̶̶ and Nana, too." He paused and all bravado ̶̶̶̶ face as open and hopeful as a boy's. ̶̶̶̶ ll say yes."

Faye couldn't speak. This was so unexpected, so spontaneous. So Jack. Her joy welled up in her throat, and she had to keep swallowing or else embarrass herself by crying and muttering all sorts of inane things and oh, she couldn't help herself. The tears began to overflow down her cheeks as she nodded acceptance.

Jack stepped forward to take her hand. The house, a gaping Mrs. Lloyd, the backstepping Inspectors, even the children jumping and clapping their hands all faded from her view, from her world, as she took in his smiling face. It was only the two of them once again, a united force in the cosmos.

Jack placed the thimble on her finger. "There," he said, his eyes kindling with deep emotion. "That seals the deal."

A flurry of action swirled around her as she stood in a daze. The Inspectors gathered their reports and made a hasty exit along with a delighted Mrs. Lloyd, who was muttering something about how Mother would be so pleased. When all was quiet again Jack took Faye's hand and led her out to the garden. Maddie and Tom charged ahead, arguing hotly over which of them would sleep in the nursery while Nana nipped excitedly at their heels. Autumn was everywhere but Faye felt in her heart that it was spring all over again and the fireflies would just be lighting their courtship lanterns and the children would be planting new seeds.

Spring, and she would leave the windows wide-open to allow all that was fresh and wonderful and magical into their home, into their lives. She would keep the windows open, she vowed, every day of her life.

"Look, Mom! Jack, hurry look!" cried Maddie, her voice ringing. "The fountain!"

Faye and Jack joined Maddie and Tom at the temperamental fountain. It rumbled and groaned, clanked and whined. Then, with a great whoosh of air came a spray of water gushing through the boy's pipes. While the children laughed and danced, and Jack hooted with triumph, Faye quietly wrapped her arms around herself and smiled knowingly up at the cocky boy's face. As always, she could have sworn he smiled back at her.

And as always, she heard the music.

Author's Note

Dear Readers,

I've taken liberties with the timing of events in the life of J.M. Barrie, but I trust he would forgive me. There is no greater fan of his writing than I, and I must give the master credit where due. Throughout the story many readers may readily pick up nuances and references to the text, *Peter and Wendy*. Weaving them into the story was part of my pleasure in writing this novel. In particular, Mrs. Darling's kiss and the way she rummaged through her children's minds, the Lost Boys—Slightly, Curly, Nibs, and Tootles—Tinker Bell, Hook and, of course, the thimble. My hope was to add authenticity to the story and to *perhaps* bring a smile of memory to your faces. Where I quoted directly in the text, I used italics.

I was also inspired by the writings of great thinkers, especially Albert Einstein, Richard Feynman, Lee Smolin,

Carl Sagan, Joseph Campbell, and Madeline L'Engle.

As for the little girl who left her window open every night waiting for Peter Pan ... Well, that little girl was me.

Mary Alice Kruesi